The Horror Writers Association

— presents —

BLOOD LITE II: OVERBITE

AN ANTHOLOGY OF HUMOROUS HORROR STORIES

Edited by Kevin J. Anderson

Pocket Books

New York London Toronto Sydney New Delhi

Pocket Books
A Division of Simon & Schuster, Inc.
1230 Avenue of the Americas
New York, NY 10020

This book is a work of fiction. Names, characters, places, and incidents either are products of the authors' imaginations or are used fictitiously. Any resemblance to actual events or locales or persons, living or dead, is entirely coincidental.

Volume copyright © 2010 by The Horror Writers Association, Inc.

First Pocket Books paperback edition October 2011

POCKET and colophon are registered trademarks of Simon & Schuster, Inc.

For information about special discounts for bulk purchases, please contact Simon & Schuster Special Sales at 1-866-506-1949 or business@simonandschuster.com.

The Simon & Schuster Speakers Bureau can bring authors to your live event. For more information or to book an event contact the Simon & Schuster Speakers Bureau at 1-866-248-3049 or visit our website at www.simonspeakers.com.

Cover design by Lisa Litwack

Manufactured in the United States of America

10 9 8 7 6 5 4 3 2 1

ISBN 978-1-4391-8766-1
ISBN 978-1-4391-8770-8 (ebook)

Contents

∽

viii • CONTENTS

Dark Carbuncle

KEVIN J. ANDERSON AND JANIS IAN

A graveyard. Night. Lurid branches scrabble across the blood-red moon. Silence, whispers, then a hush of anticipation. Fifteen boom boxes encircle a grave. Giant woofers (removed just that morning from an unsuspecting car) sit with bass ends flat against the massive gravestone.

> *Here at peace at last lies Thor*
> *Troubled by the Dark no more*

The four aging fans in attendance for the midnight show—the ritual—had polished their studs, mangled their hair, added dye where needed and bleach where not. They wore their finest black leather, but left the jackets open to expose too-small T-shirts from concerts past, fabric memories that paid homage to their hero's

mind-blowing shows, when he'd been alive. *Thor*. The writer of the greatest song in the history of mankind.

"Man, we really should have put a line from 'Dark Carbuncle' on his tombstone instead," Conk said. "I mean, so everybody could see his genius for all eternity." His given name was William, and he went by the handle of "William the Conqueror" from some impressive historical guy, though most of his friends didn't get it. They thought "Conk" just meant he liked to bash things.

"Anybody can hear his *genius* just by playing the song, shithead," said Kutfist, ending with the sharp sneer he'd practiced all week. "Trust me, we didn't want to deal with the rights issues."

"Yeah but, dude, 'Dark Carbuncle' is an awesome song, right?" said Dredd, and though he'd said it many times before, nobody disagreed. Especially not on this night of nights.

The lone girl in the group, swaying to the music of a silent song, twisted a lock of hair around her finger. "Kinda creepy, ya think?" Despite the spiderweb tattooed on her chin, Longshanks was always the first to back away from anything remotely disturbing. "I mean, we're *raising him from the dead.* . . ." Her voice trailed off.

"God, lighten up, 'shanks. You've been this way since grade school. What can he do to us? He'll be in our power." Sneering, Kutfist turned toward the others with a shrug. Women. Jeez.

"Yeah, and 'Dark Carbuncle' is such an awesome song. . . ." Dredd's usual sentence trailed off as a cloud covered the moon.

"It has to be tonight, on the anniversary," said Conk with finality as he connected the last of the speakers. The Wikipedia entry had been very specific on that point.

Kutfist scanned the graveyard in disappointment. "I can't believe we're the only ones here. Elvis gets *tons* of fans on his Death Day every year!"

"Elvis fans don't know that 'Dark Carbuncle' is an awesome song," Dredd assured him. "Or they'd be here."

Longshanks tugged harder on her hair. "And what's he gonna look like with a fractured skull, Kut? I mean, part of his head might be gone. *Ecchhh.*"

Kutfist pushed his trifocals farther up his nose. "Shut up, 'shanks. The man was a *god*. That last show we saw was *unbelievably amazing*. He'd never have killed himself, never. We can finally find out the truth now, so just stop worrying and shut up."

Nodding, Conk stood up. Brushing leaves off his hands, he pulled a few folded sheets from the back pocket of his jeans and handed them each a paper with the lyrics printed backward phonetically. That was the worrisome part. They knew the lyrics forward well enough to sing them the required seven times, but the backward part made Conk nervous. "We've gotta get it right, or we'll end up raising Frank Sinatra or some-

thing. Seriously, you can't be too careful with the Dark Side. Don't screw it up."

With tears in his eyes and excitement in his heart, he reached down to the nearest boom box and pushed PLAY.

Thor opened what was left of his eyes and knew he wasn't in the Ritz. It had been a long time since he'd stayed in high-class hotels on tour, and now suddenly he experienced a flashback rush of the last images he remembered.

A motel room, after the show, his ears still ringing from feedback and amps turned up to eleven. Used to be his ears would ring from the screaming fans . . . used to be all-night parties, used to be groupies and sex—but the groupies were not as attractive now, and Viagra could only do so much. Ditto the gigs, no more backstage excitement when Mick visited, no more telling the roadie to bring the chick from row five back to the luxe hotel. Now, a gig was just a gig, something to get through until he figured out what to do with the rest of his life.

He hadn't slept a full night in months—years—and now somebody was playing that damned song so loud it echoed right through the walls of this fleabag purgatory of a room. Where the hell was this?

Thorton Velbiss—Thorny to his friends (not many of those), Thor to his fans (not many of those either)—

was not having a good day. First, that pounding bass drum was unacceptable. The only noise he wanted to hear with this kind of hangover was the sound of vodka over ice. Second, his fucking hit record from two decades ago was playing, with the bass booming so wide he could swear the damned thing was sitting on his face. The only time Thor would tolerate listening to "Dark Carbuncle" was onstage, during a show, when he lip-synched his way through it for an audience of haphazardly fat metal-heads bent on reliving their youth.

I was ferocious back then, ya know? Really fero. And taller, I think. Maybe just skinny. Now I have to wear a corset. Still, I had a hell of a good run. Just one hit, but it kept me in chicks and booze. . . .

Fuck, no, it's a horrible song. Piece of shit me and Dirk the Drummer whipped up one night while we were wanking off. Farthest wank got to title the song. He won.

I hate that fucking song.

'Sides, I can't hit that high note, never could. Brought a ringer into the studio, never thought it'd be a hit. We had great shit on the album, great shit . . . and all anybody ever wants to hear is "Dark dark dark. Dark dark dark. Dark dark dark, I'm a da-da-da-da-carbuncle."

Makes you want to puke.

Gotta lip-synch it now anyway, can't even hit the low notes. At least I remember the words. Stupid effing words— even I don't know what they mean. Last time I saw the big El, Scotty Moore had to hand him the lyrics to "Love Me Tender." Speaking of hand . . . hand me that vodka, wouldya?

He'd forgotten there wasn't anybody here. What the hell, he'd serve himself.

He'd been an altar boy in his youth, a good little Catholic, though that was part of his secret past. The headbangers would never understand it. He hadn't prayed in . . . what? Thirty years? Not since he'd picked up a Les Paul, plugged it in, and let wail.

Now, as he felt around for the bottle, trying to shake the cobwebs out of his head, he wondered who'd have the nerve to play that scrotum of a song right on top of his room. *Boom boom boom.* Trying to shut out the sound, he drifted back to the last gig.

It was like reliving a nightmare over and over again, singing that song every night. His agent said this tour could maybe revive his career (but then, he always said that)—opening for some fifteen-year-old one-hit wonder. At least if there was any justice in the world, it *should* have been one hit, but the kid was coming off his fourth top ten record. Turned out he was a metal fan, though, and loved "Dark Carbuncle" (and wasn't *that* embarrassing), and demanded Thor as his opener (though what his Top 40 demographic would make of it, only God knew).

Thor had checked into the motel under a fake name, just in case anybody noticed. Grabbed a quick nap (not that the fans needed to know about that either!), packed his crotch, hit the lobby. Out by the kid's tour bus, a few rabid Thor fans began jumping up and down, one paunchy guy with dreadlocks yelling

"Dude! Dude! 'Dark Carbuncle' is an awesome song!" Thor stopped to see if they wanted autographs and noticed that two of them wore pizza delivery uniforms.

"How should I make this out?" he asked a girl with a weird chin tattoo. Glancing at her name tag, he hazarded a guess. "To Tiffany?"

The girl went beet red. "Uh, no, *Longshanks*—just make it to Longshanks."

He smiled inwardly, but outwardly gave her the long, slow *I could change your life, babe!* look. She brightened and giggled at her friends. At least he'd made *somebody's* day.

On to the show, which sucked. Of course. How the hell can anyone play music at two in the afternoon, under a wide open sky, looking out at a bunch of hayseeds whose big weekend excitement was probably going to be the pig race? Real waste of Oreos, that one. He sped through the set, not even bothering with the pyro at the end, sneering when people applauded the opening chords of "Carbuncle." Idiots.

I used to dream about being a Beatle, you know? Back in the day, I played the Garden. Twice. Well, only once as the lead act, but still. Alice Cooper, Ozzie, Rob Zombie, they had nothing on me. Eating a live bat, hell—I used to shove worms up my nose, just to line the coke! Now look at me . . . playing some friggin' rodeo for a hundred bucks. Pathetic, that's what it is.

Why couldn't I have died young, in a private plane crash? At least that would be a respectable ending.

Afterward, back at the motel!—still daylight out!—he drank most of the quart of Stoli that Mr. Four-Hit-Wonderkid had nervously presented him at sound check. Scratching at his empty stomach, Thor decided to surf the vending machines for dinner. Peanut butter cups and a vodka chaser, the perfect road meal.

He barely registered the Muzak droning through the elevator speakers, until he caught himself humming along. Son of a bitch! Bland whiter-than-white harmonies accompanied by easy-listening strings. *Dark dark dark. Dark dark dark. I'm a da-da-da-da-carbuncle, hiding in the dark.* Unbelievable. His song. That frigging publisher had sold him out, turned him into effing elevator music, music for supermarkets and dentist's chairs. Fucking asshole. And his agent was probably in on it, too. Scum, they were all scum.

He'd show them. If he couldn't die young, at least he could die tragic. "Dark Carbuncle" as elevator music—the last straw of all last straws.

Thor stormed back to his room and grabbed the .38 he always carried. Flopping backward on the bed, he spun the cylinder—five bullets, one empty chamber. Go out like a man, yeah, playing Russian roulette. They'd all be sorry then, even those stupid pizza-parlor rejects. Barrel to the head, click click and it's over. Jimi, Kurt, make way for the next dead rock legend.

Thor raised the gun. Winced at the cold feel of metal against skin. Paused. Squeezed.

Click.

Click? A barrel loaded with Super-X 500 hollow points, and all it can do is go *click*? Un-fucking-believable.

He tried again.

Click.

Hell, how could you *lose* at Russian roulette? He hurled the gun across the room, where it skittered to a halt on the bathroom floor. Throwing his legs over the bed, Thor grabbed the vodka, took a long slow drag, and made his way to the bathroom, where he somehow managed to drop the bottle on his toe. Yelling out loud, he jumped—and landed barefooted on the gun, which spun crazily against the tiles while he fell backward.

Sickening crack of his head against the tub. He lay on the cold, hard floor, feeling his life ebb away. Frigging humiliating way to die . . . for both a former altar boy and a former rock star.

On the other hand, maybe God wouldn't consider this a suicide. Good news. His last thought was that he'd finally be able to get some effing sleep. Safe in the arms of the afterlife.

Until some fuckheads called him back for an encore. . . .

Graveyard, night, big speakers booming, a familiar chorus sung again and again with enthusiasm, if not harmony.

Mmm, I ain't no spoonful
Baby I'm a mouth-*full*
and I'm gonna tumble,
rumble crumble tumble
your Dark Carbuncle
Dark Carbuncle

Conk, Kutfist, Longshanks, and Dredd sang the beloved words seven times seven (almost as many times as in the actual song), and three times more backward, until they were hoarse with it. Conk finally signaled the end of the ritual by switching off the boom boxes. They reeled in the sudden hush, breathing heavily.

"How long is it supposed to take?" Longshanks whispered.

"Give him a few minutes." Conk tried not to sound uncertain. The Wikipedia entry had been unclear on that point. "He's coming all the way back from the dead."

Kutfist sneered. "He never started the concerts on time either."

"Yeah, I loved waiting for 'Dark Carbuncle.' What an awesome song," said Dredd. No one disagreed.

Suddenly the earth began to tremble, and something stirred beneath the leaves. The ostentatious tombstone they'd banded together and paid for all those years ago pulled loose and tumbled backward, leaving a gaping hole.

Five grime-encrusted fingers pushed through the

soil, followed by a hand, then another, clawing at the dirt in slow motion. Finally, a body heaved itself out of the grave. Covered in dirt, putrid clothes, and rotting skin, Thor raised himself up and tried to wipe the crust from his eyes.

The four fans cheered, whistled, and applauded as he swayed. "Omigod, it's him, it's really him!" Conk dropped the papers and stared. What a Wiki entry *this* would make!

Longshanks was jumping up and down. "He looks just like he did on the *Avenger's Revenge* tour!"

"He's staggering like he did on that tour, too," Kutfist said, without the sneer this time. He looked nervously around. "C'mon, gotta get him to the van."

The undead rock star lurched and shambled, looking disoriented but not entirely out of character. "Come on, Thor!" Longshanks pleaded. She lifted up her T-shirt to flash her breasts; Thor had never noticed her when she'd done it at concerts, but this time he shuffled toward her, making moaning, sucking sounds from deep in his throat.

"Hurry up, get him into the van!" Conk said in an urgent whisper. "Before some other fans show up. He's ours!"

"Wait! We can't leave the speakers—I borrowed them from my uncle's catering company," Kutfist said. "He's got a bar mitzvah tomorrow; he'll kill me!" Fortunately, since Thor was having a hard time orienting himself toward a vertical life, they had plenty of time

to retrieve the gear and pack it into the pizza van they'd "borrowed" from work.

Conk started the engine while Kutfist and Dredd turned in their seats to stare at Thor, who was crammed into the third-row seat with Longshanks. "Now he's with his true fans!" She sniffed, then frowned. "Is he supposed to smell this bad?"

"I think that's just an old pizza I forgot to deliver last week," Conk said.

As the van careened out of the cemetery, Dredd leaned over the seat and said earnestly, "Dude, 'Dark Carbuncle' is an awesome song!" He extended his hand, then thought better of it and withdrew.

They jabbered excitedly as they headed off to Conk's garage. "I'm gonna have him teach me guitar. We could do some killer riffs together!"

"I want him to sign some autographs—impress my girlfriend for sure," Kutfist said. "Hmm, maybe even sell them online."

Longshanks tentatively nudged one of the scraps dangling off Thor's ruined face. "Hey, we could sell pieces of his skin. Talk about a real collector's item!"

Kutfist returned to the sneer. "What are you thinking? Anybody who bought Thor's skin could clone him—then we won't have the only one."

Longshanks dropped her gaze. "Well, we'd still have the original. A clone is no better than . . . a cover band."

"How about we just sell locks of hair?" Conk sug-

gested. He didn't want them to argue during this ulti-
mate moment of fannish glory.

As the van pulled up to the two-car garage,
the undead legend seemed to be getting his bear-
ings, croaking slightly more comprehensible words.
"What . . . happened? Where am I?"

"You're with us—your real fans!"

Parking in the dark garage, they opened the doors
and helped Thor out of the van. Conk hit the but-
ton and closed the garage door, then triumphantly
switched on the lights to reveal the setup waiting in
the other parking space—a small stage, microphone,
boom box, and guitar.

Herding Thor forward, Kutfist shouted, "We
brought you back from the grave for this, dude!"

Thor automatically stepped onto the stage and into
the light, then stared at them in confusion. Longshanks
sprang onto the stage beside him and shoved the gui-
tar into his hands. "Omigod, Thor—now you can sing
'Dark Carbuncle' for us, night after night after night!"

Thorton Vebliss fell to his knees and screamed.

Surely this was Hell. Surely.

When he'd emerged from the darkness, he'd won-
dered what the fuck was going on. Why was he covered
in dirt? Some superextravagant part of the stage show
he couldn't recall?

Then he remembered, and now he knew exactly

what had happened. This was truly eternal punishment. Every bit of his Catholic upbringing rose in his throat—the priests' lectures, the nuns' scoldings, the fear of damnation. It was too much for any man, let alone a dead one.

Rotting ligaments snapped as he dropped to his knees and began to cry. For the first time in years he prayed, and for the first time in his life he really meant it. He confessed, he repented, he begged forgiveness. He reminded God of his years as an altar boy, how he'd been in the soprano choir until his voice had changed. He also pointed out that, technically— though God seemed to have overlooked the detail— he hadn't committed suicide and didn't deserve damnation. It was merely an unfortunate accident.

"Just please get me out of here! I want to go to Heaven. I'll do whatever you say; you won't regret it! Please!" He put more soul into the request than he'd ever spent on one of his stage performances, but even Thor was surprised when the cluttered garage and tiny group of fans swirled away into mist.

The new place was bright and shining, filled with sunlight and rainbows. He saw smiling beings in white robes with wings gathered on a nearby cloud, and an impressive, bearded man on a gleaming golden throne in front of him.

Holy shit, exactly the pictures the priests had

painted, down to the last cliché! Choking back tears, Thor knelt before Him.

"Welcome Thorton Vebliss, my wayward son." The Almighty smiled with a warmth that made Thor tremble. "I am so glad you are finally among us. We have prepared a heavenly reception for you."

Thor could only stammer, "Thank you, thank you, Lord!" He didn't know what else to say. Everything was so . . . clean. So . . . cheerful.

"Rise, my son. Rise, and greet your Father."

Thor rose and moved toward the throne.

"Later, there will be manna, and angel food cake," God promised, patting him on the shoulder. "But first I have a small request."

God seemed almost shy as he said it, and Thor thought, *I could really like this guy.* "Anything, Your Omnipotence. Um, Your Magnificence. Anything you want, just name it!"

Taking him by both shoulders, the Lord turned him toward the nearby cloud, where the choir of angels suddenly pulled back their wings, revealing the electric guitars they wore. One sat behind a drum kit.

Snapping His fingers, God materialized a 1959 custom Les Paul and held it out to Thor. "Play 'Dark Carbuncle' for us, my son. I have always loved that song."

Thor fell to his knees, screaming.

Death and Taxes

Heather Graham

I am an IRS agent.

But contrary to what you may be prone to believe, or no matter what it might seem, I am not the monster in this story. I swear.

You see most people believe that we IRS agents are horrible individuals—seriously, as if that's a prerequisite when you apply for the job. Not true. We're just working stiffs like everyone else. Everybody needs a job, and I, like the general public with whom I am just another number, needed steady work in order to maintain any kind of lifestyle.

The general public fears an IRS agent—but you can't begin to imagine how IRS agents fear the general public.

Take the case of Mac Keenan. MacDonald Keenan, if you will. I was called in after several agents had tried to deal with the man.

First off, so you can get a general idea, the man is rich. Rich as Midas. He's the kind who tries every loophole known to man while the middle class fellow can't find a slit to slip through. His books are seriously works of art.

It started on a Monday. I was called into my boss's office. "Vlad," he said (my name is Vladimir, my folks are of Russian descent), "we need you."

"Oh?"

"Special case," he told me. He pushed a picture out on his desk. It was a picture of a man of about forty-five, a big fellow, so it appeared. Definitely, a stocky man. "MacDonald Keenan. We believe that he has hidden income in vast amounts, and that his expenses list is a pile of pure bull."

I shrugged. Nothing out of the ordinary.

"So?" It seemed that I was required to say something.

"We sent Josie Valentine about two weeks ago."

"And what happened?"

"Mac got all nice and told her to come to his mango tree; he had great fruit—with no real value—that she was welcome to take. She was trying to stay on good terms with him, so she went."

"What happened?"

"Chimpanzee jumped out of a tree and attacked her—she's still in the hospital."

"Why wasn't this fellow arrested?" I asked indignantly. Josie was a sweet kid. I liked her a lot—so did

most of her clients, even when they wound up paying back the big bucks.

My boss waved his hand in the air. "Big-time attorney, of course. Claimed it wasn't his chimp and he didn't know how the hell the creature got in the yard."

"Okay, so why not meet at Keenan's accountant's office, or downtown in our office?" I asked.

"Keenan doesn't have an accountant, does his own taxes. And he came down once. He saw Ted Larson."

"And?"

"Ted started choking on his coffee. We had to call the paramedics in. Ted's still in the hospital. Choked so hard he nearly suffocated, and then threw his back out. Ted will be laid up for another three weeks. His situation is pretty dire."

"Ah, so was there another attempt made to bring Keenan in or to have an agent out to his place?" I asked.

"Aubrey Dupont went out."

"Aubrey? I don't know her."

"She's out of a different office. Anyway, Mac Keenan came to the door all smiles to greet her. She went in to see him, gave me a call, and said that he was going to try to get some of his bank papers from the bank, said he lost them when a storm came through."

"Okay, that's reasonable."

My boss shook his head. "I was on the phone with her when he walked her out. She tripped on a step on the front porch. Broke her up really bad. Her head caught it, you know?"

"Dear God! I hadn't heard anything about it."

"She's in a coma now. But like I said, she's out of a different office; maybe that's why you haven't heard."

"Haul his ass back downtown," I suggested. I hated house calls. Hated them. You tried to collect, and a woman called in her crying, starving children. She showed you that her washer was broken and she was doing laundry by hand. A man would be in the garage, trying to coax a few more miles out of "old Betsy" because he couldn't afford a new car. He's trying not to lose his house. See, I'm sensitive. That kind of stuff breaks my heart. I'm a softy. I'm willing to stretch when need be, but I sure hate it when I have to do home visits.

My boss hesitated and then said, "Vlad, I'm afraid of bringing him in again. Folks here are now superstitious. If I call him in, every one of my agents will call in sick. I need you for this one; I *really* need you."

I expected a stupendous mansion. What I found had once been a mansion, but the iron gates were rusty, the massive lawn was overgrown, and the little garden ornaments were hairy with growth of lichen and moss. He had huge oaks in the yard that dripped moss.

It would have really made a perfect haunted house.

I parked my car and looked for a call box by the giant, dilapidated, but ornate front gate. There was none. I pushed on the gate, and it creaked open.

I walked up the overgrown tile walk and found the offending porch stairs—those which had sent poor Aubrey to the hospital in a coma. I walked up the steps without incident and thudded the door with the giant lion's head door knockers.

I thought the man might refuse to answer, then we'd have to start proceedings, get cops, all that kind of stuff. And, really, I prided myself on being the "get the job done man" for the government. Hey, the government had taken a chance on me. It was the government, of course—no racial, sexual, religious, or other prejudices allowed. I liked that.

But, despite my misgivings, Mac Keenan came to the door.

He was a big man. Maybe six foot four, two inches above my dignified but fairly customary height.

They had sent Aubrey out to see this giant? I thought. *Poor, poor dear!*

"You the new guy?" he asked.

I handed him my card. "I'm Vladimir Oginsky," I told him.

"Russ-sky, eh?" he asked.

"I was born here in the United States," I told him. "My parents were Russian."

"Aliens," he said. "This country is just full of aliens! Well, sometimes, that pays. So, well, Mr. Oginsky, come on in. Or should I call you Vlad?"

"You may call me anything you like, Mr. Keenan, as long as you justify your taxes."

That made him laugh. "Come on in then, Russ-sky. I have my books set up in the dining room."

I followed him into the house. It was a strange place. It was filled with hunting trophies. Heads lined the walls, and exotic cats, snarls on their feline faces, were displayed full body. The place seemed ancient; there were artifacts from all time periods and a multitude of countries displayed on dusty shelves guarded by a vast nest of spider's webs.

We entered the dining room. A boar's head sat on a silver tray in the center. I felt as if I might have entered a castle deep in the Transylvanian woods run by Dr. Frankenstein. Wrong country, wrong story, I know, but that was the feeling I got.

"Right there," he said proudly, drawing back a chair. "There are some of my receipts—I keep them all; take a look. I don't know why the government has targeted me!"

I looked at the receipts. Most were far too faded now to be legible, but I found one.

"Publix?" I said.

"Where shopping is a pleasure!" he assured, quoting the giant chain's motto.

"Mr. Keenan, you can't deduct your groceries. I'm afraid we'll have to start weeding these out."

"What? A man's gotta eat to live!" he protested.

"I'm sorry, Mr. Keenan. Congress makes the laws; I uphold them," I told him.

I picked up another receipt. "Toothpaste? Oh,

please, Mr. Keenan!" Another receipt for a movie rental; another was for several bottles of red wine.

"I'm afraid that your receipts are worthless, sir," I told him.

"Worthless," he said. He was seated across the table from me. He clasped his hands together and nodded. I thought that he would explode.

"Hermione's Whorehouse, Las Vegas?" I said.

"Entertainment!" he bellowed.

"I'm afraid the government doesn't see it that way. Why, if every man out there tried to deduct personal entertainment like that, the national debt could grow by even more billions. Half of these receipts are from Hermione's Whorehouse. And say that the government made a turn and accepted such expenses—then married men would want exemptions for every present they bought their wives. Then women would want the same equality, and . . . well, Congress will just never pass it. There are still many members on the far right. It'll never fly. I'm sorry—these receipts are worthless."

"You don't understand the Publix?!" he exclaimed, indignant.

"I'm afraid not."

"I'm thirsty," he said suddenly, as if he'd made a quick decision. "Can I get you something? A brandy, bourbon, wine?"

"I'm working, Mr. Keenan," I told him.

"Some food, perhaps? I make a mean spaghetti and clam sauce," he said.

This is it; this is going to be his way of getting rid of me.

"Nothing, thank you," I said.

"Iced tea?"

"Nothing, thank you."

"Coffee?"

"All right, Mr. Keenan. Coffee would be great."

He left the table. I went through the rest of his receipts. He wanted to deduct a new basement, some items for the basement I couldn't read, his taxidermist's bills, and a host of other personal expenses.

He returned with the coffee. I thanked him and sipped it as he watched me like a hawk.

There was something in the coffee, certainly. I had exceptional taste buds—the average Joe might not have noticed. I did. There was an acidic aftertaste. Arsenic? Did he really not care that a coroner would discover the poisoning? Or was it something more subtle that might go undetected during an autopsy?

"Mr. Keenan," I told him. "You can't deduct dog food. Or cat food, for that matter. And, as far as I can see, the only cats you have around here are dead ones."

He smiled. "All right. I understand, I guess, though you might change your mind. I can't deduct dog food, and since you're a stickler, it seems I can't deduct cat food, either. You might change your mind."

I finished my coffee. He watched me, *stared* at me, and seemed baffled.

He was waiting, expectantly.

"And you can't deduct products for personal hygiene, either," I said.

He leaned toward me then. He didn't appear to be quite so affable. "You don't understand, Vlad, Bad, Russ-sky, whatever you are. Yes, you know what? You're wrong. I *can* deduct cat food. It's part of my business. Yes, I'm an investor. But I'm also a show master. I do very special shows for very special people. And I can prove it."

"Oh? You keep great cats around, and the meat bill is for them? Do you have the proper permits?" I asked.

He smiled. "Life, liberty, and the pursuit of happiness!" he said.

"All well and fine, sir, except that those rights come with the unspoken promise that you don't prevent those rights to your fellow man."

He gave me a sneer. "Come to the basement," he told me. "You'll see—every expense is totally legitimate."

"All right," I said.

I stood. He towered above me, that strange, sick, sneering grin upon his face. We passed by the front on the way to the stairs to the basement. He pointed outside. "You're working late, Russ-sky. It's almost dark."

"So it is," I said.

He led me to the stairs. There were few—very few—basements in this area, due to the fact that we were just above sea level. He had built up the ground below his mansion, I thought, in order to have a base-

ment. Interesting. Most people would do so for a billiards table or a home gym.

Not Mac Keenan.

"Stairs are straight out of an old castle from Munich, Germany," he said with pride. "They once led to a dungeon!"

"How fascinating," I told him. "But not deductible. Not until you sell your house, and then, of course, the amount will work against your capital gains."

He was silent as we continued down the stairway. I felt a little dizzy; whatever he had put in the coffee was definitely having some kind of an effect.

"See here!" he exclaimed with pride.

The grand basement room we reached was stone; the walls were lines with various instruments of torture, and I realized slowly that the room had a certain reek to it.

"Sit down, sit down," he encouraged me. "That," he said, leading me to a benchlike seat, "is an authentic garrote from the executioner who worked during the Spanish period in St. Augustine. Many a man met a grisly death with this lovely, historical piece."

"Charming, Mr. Keenan," I assured him. "You say you're a show master. So, who is your audience?"

"My audience should arrive momentarily. Just as soon as true darkness falls and the moon begins to rise in the heavens!" he said dramatically.

"You know, Mr. Keenan, I'm a government worker. Nine to five is my usual."

"But I'm certain your boss wants this problem solved, doesn't he?"

"All right. I'll put in for overtime. It's the government; I may not get it. But you're right, Mr. Keenan, we do want this situation rectified."

He smiled suddenly. "You can run right now, Russ-sky. Run right now. They'll send some other poor schmuck. I like you—I think you should run now."

"I'm feeling a little tired," I told him. "Whatever drug you put in the coffee is getting to me now."

"Well, don't say I didn't give you a chance," he told me.

He'd been at my side; suddenly he was behind me. He took my wrists, and I heard a snap; I'd been handcuffed. I felt the garrote fall around my neck.

I tsked. "Mr. Keenan. The garrote is period. What's with the modern handcuffs? It totally ruins your show, you know."

"Think of it as theater art—*moderne arte*!" he said.

It was then that I heard the baying of the wolves. And the screeches that were made by the great cats. I heard noise above me, and I knew the creatures were coming to life. Mac Keenan was indeed a Doctor Frankenstein.

"What are you, exactly?" I asked him. "Werewolf, demon . . . vampire . . . zombie? Are you controlled by others?"

He laughed, delighted. "Ah, Russ-sky, you have been entertaining. I'm sorry, really. What am I? A show

master, as I told you. My clients are of the wealthiest and most prestigious families. Most are European, though many are South American and Asian these days. Ah, you'd be surprised by my people from India and the Middle East, as well. Show master, Mr. Russsky. All right, a demon, if you will. I have been around a long, long time, as the sayings and songs will tell! I survive off the largesse of my clients, and therefore, you fool, my Publix bill is certainly deductible, and once you see some of my clients, you'll understand that toothpaste is a work expense as well."

"I do understand now," I told him. "And I'd grant you your expenses—if your work was legal."

"What's not legal?"

"Well," I began, but by that time the great cats were making their way down the stairs, snarling and screeching hungrily. There was a jaguar, a lion, a cheetah, and a puma. All stalking into the room, salivating.

No matter what his attempted expense deductions, I was intended as dinner.

"Wait! Wait, my dear pets!" he called out.

There was a thud against the stairway wall, and I looked up to see that a massive wolf was coming down the stairs.

A wolf, and not a wolf. He was going through horrendous and tortuous changes as he made his way. "Russ-sky, meet Max. Maximilian Davenport, werewolf out of Lyons, France. Max—meet . . . Well, let's get honest here, meet your dinner, sir."

Max took on a full transformation and stood on all fours, howling with pleasure. The cats hissed and scratched the air.

Max started a heavy pad towards me.

"No, no, you must wait!" Mac Keenan said. "Wait, the mistress of darkness approaches with the newest love of her life."

With that announcement, I felt a rush of air. There seemed to be a flurry of wings in the room, and then *they* were there. There was a woman—absolutely gorgeous. She was typical of any vampire fantasy ever written, huge dark eyes, dripping lashes, and long dark hair. Oh, and a chest that was brilliantly formed and well displayed in the black velvet dress she wore.

But she wasn't alone. I recognized Ted and Josie from my office immediately. They both looked well enough.

"Vlad!" Josie said with dismay. As I said before, she's a cute kid.

"Dinner is served!" Mac Keenan said angrily. "Shall I shove the chair out a bit for you? Vampires first, werewolf second, and the cats—they will clean up the mess."

"Josie!" I said.

"Mac . . . the chimp destroyed half my face. When Maria-Teresa came to the hospital . . . oh, sorry, Maria-Teresa, Vladimir Oginsky, I had to invite her in, and I had to allow her some blood and . . . then they declared me dead, and, well . . . here I am. Forgive me, Vlad, please?"

She was so pathetic.

"I was dying, too," Ted apologized. "It seemed a good choice."

"Where's Aubrey?" I asked.

"Oh, well, she was really a big girl in excellent shape. I'm afraid that when we brought her out, we weren't paying enough attention. Max was really hungry. He even ate the bones," Mac Keenan explained. "If you all had left my grocery bill alone, things might have been fine. Give all these fellows, native and alien, and—hm, otherworldly?—enough raw meat and pig's blood, and they stay pretty well satisfied. It's your fault—you IRS people, and the government."

"I've traveled some," I told him. "We have our problems, but it's still the best place to live."

"Great. He's a patriot," Mac Keenan groaned. "You've been fun, Vlad, but . . ."

Josie started toward me. She licked her lips and I saw her fangs. She'd been such a cute girl! All brown eyes and long brown hair, she looked like a kid, but she was twenty-six and one of the best math people I had ever met.

The beautiful woman, Maria-Teresa, let out a cry of fury. "I am mistress, and I go first!" she announced. Josie quickly scrambled back; Ted—who hadn't been that close—stepped back as well with a quick leap. He knew his place. I was glad.

Maria-Teresa smiled as she came toward me. She licked her lips and sat on my lap. She was hot, on fire.

She crushed her breasts against me and gave me a soulful look with those nearly black eyes of hers. "I'll try to make it sweet and erotic, sweet and to die for . . . you'll not mind in the least."

I felt her fangs slide into my neck.

I'd have let it go on a little further, but I still wasn't sure just what the arsenic might have done to my system.

Ah, the arsenic. I guess it gave a taste to the blood.

She pulled back, staring at me with confusion and dismay. She started to turn to Mac Keenan, angry. "What is this—" she began.

She might have been beautiful, but I knew—she was pure evil, and there was no negotiating a settlement here.

I burst free from the handcuffs and thrust my neck forward with a tremendous lunge, freeing myself from the garrote, and knocking Maria-Teresa senseless. Not good enough. I caught her head and gave it a massive twist, breaking the neck instantly. Of course, she was a vampire, and that wasn't enough. I twisted harder, until the head came free. It popped with a rather horrendous squishing sound. At least, though, no blood splurged all over the place.

She was old and evil; a pile of dust and ash burst upon us all, clouding the day.

Max, the old werewolf, howled, tucked his tail between his legs, and backed away. It sounded as if he was crying, the way he whimpered.

Josie and Ted just stared at me, openmouthed.

"She made you, so the spell should be broken," I told my two coworkers. "You should no longer be blood-sucking servants of Satan." I shook my head with disgust. "That's horrible behavior for government agents. You should be ashamed! Get upstairs, I'll get you both back to your hospitals. And Ted, if you die, you die, and that's it."

They were in shock, of course. They nodded, and stumbled their way to the stairs. I didn't think Ted was going to die—they would think he'd had some miraculous cure.

I looked at Max, the werewolf. There was something so sad about him. I hate to see any dog with its tail between its legs.

"Snap out of it, Max!" I said. My tone was actually a damned good bark.

In a split second, Max was entirely human.

"I think your ailment might be psychosomatic. Look at you, you don't even have any hair on your chin! Get to a doctor—I'm giving you one chance, and I mean it. Dr. Jimenez, on Main Street, is a wonderful shrink. One chance, Max, you see that doctor tomorrow. I'll be following up on you."

Max was out of the room and up the stairs, nodding as he went, moving faster on two feet than he had ever managed on four.

The cats growled at me. I growled back. They instantly froze back into their taxidermy positions, nothing more than dead meat.

Then I looked at MacDonald Keenan. "Scare tactics, sir, will not keep the IRS away. We all need roads and schools, and like I said, I don't make the laws, I don't decide the taxes."

He stared at me, all tense, looking as if he might explode like a bomb any minute.

I thought he might have a heart attack on the spot. That wouldn't have been good for my career—or the reputation of the IRS.

"What, what . . . what are you?" he asked me.

"An agent of the U.S. government," I told him proudly. "All right, all right, you know why I love my job so much? A lack of prejudice. My parents came from Russia. But their parents came from . . . oh, well, it won't really mean much to you, but they came from a little planet in a far distant solar system known as Aslinovia. It was a great place, until people of different colors started fighting against one another. The beiges, as we were called, were all but massacred. My folks got out. We settled in one place, and then my dad read up on the United States. Not perfect, but trying. So we came here. I served in the military, and I looked for a government job. They hired me at the IRS. Anyway, we weren't so different on Aslinovia. And we're not so different here— just a little stronger, physically, and mentally. So, here's the thing, MacDonald Keenan. You're going to jail, of course. You're going to jail for the injury and death your so-called employment has caused others."

"No one will believe—" he protested.

"Oh, yes. By the time I finish, they will," I assured him. "You're a horrible murderer, Mac."

He shook his head. "You'll never prove it."

"Oh, I believe I will. But that doesn't matter, Mac. I'll get you one way or the other."

"How?"

"Just like they got that other monster, Al Capone. Because you see, if you happen to get out of the murder charges, well, then . . ."

"Then what?" he demanded.

"I'll be just like Elliott Ness," I told him with a broad smile. "All right, so, maybe, in your circumstances, the Publix charges might be justified, but some of those others . . . Mac! What did you take me for, a fool? You'll go down like many a man and monster, for income tax evasion! The Publix bill—now, of course, I'd let that go. But the Hermione's Whorehouse is out, I'm afraid. And God knows, sir, where you've gotten half your income. I will be investigating that next! Damned vampires—the majority of your clientele, I believe. They're the worst. So hard to pin down—and their banking! Disastrous. But I will find your hidden income, MacDonald Keenan. I will. I am a law-abiding man descended from legal aliens, and I will proudly do right for this country! And, of course, there are only two truisms in life for any man," I told him.

"Oh?" he said, still looking shocked and frozen.

"Death and taxes," I assured him. "Death and taxes."

Table for Two

Jeff Ryan

"You know, Bernice," I said, "one of the great things about taking you to a restaurant is we always get a nice parking place out front." Bernice agreed, checking her face one last time in the rearview mirror, then tapping the dangling handicapped parking sign.

Sure enough, we got a spot right out front. I raced to the passenger side to do my gentlemanly thing and open the door for her. With practiced ease, I then grabbed the snow shovel from the car's backseat and eased her out of her bucket seat. I gave the shovel a quick wipe down with a Handi Wipe and tossed it in the backseat. "Italy, here we come!"

Casa Antoni's was the best Italian restaurant in town, and Bernice loved Italian food. She watched the Food Network all day long, and was always pointing out in our talkbook which ingredients I should bring

to her. But as good a cook as she is, we both still love to try new things. We'd hit all the pizza places in town—delivery, of course. But a place as nice as Antoni's was sit-down.

We walked past the tables on the outside terrace. It was Tuesday, so it wasn't that crowded. We chose a Tuesday because Bernice heard that Tuesdays were the best day to go to a fancy restaurant, since the chefs had time to give your meal extra attention.

When they saw Bernice, two of the patrons ran away, yelling what they always yell. One fainted in his (it looked like) penne a la vodka. "Hey, knock it off," I said to them. "How'd you like it if I said something rude about your lady?" I patted Bernice on one of her elbow carbuncles, and we went inside.

I was expecting the maitre d' to be a middle-aged man with a mustache; instead, it was a young, thin, attractive woman. Me and my prejudices! "Can I help you?" she said, looking down at her appointment book. "Table for two, please; uh, keep looking down," I said. She looked up. Why is it that when you ask someone to do something, they always do the opposite? People!

I didn't expect her to try to jump through the window to escape. Luckily for her, the window didn't break. I helped prop her up (no broken bones or bloody nose), and was reaching for my hyperventilation bag (which has smelling salts in it as well: I come prepared!) when she started to revive. Her name tag said "Melani." Pretty name.

"Melani?" I asked, pronouncing it like *Melanie*, hoping I got it right. "Hi. I know, we're not your normal customers. But we tip well, and we're both wearing shirts and shoes." Bernice dangled hers, one at a time, through a slat in her burlap. A little liquid sloshed out of the second one. Technically they were three-gallon Tupperware containers, but Bernice had wide feet and has a hard time finding a good fit. These were her good shoes: the knock-around ones for the house are slitted so the fluids can sluice out.

"Get out," she whispered. "Oh, God, get out of here!"

"I hate to play the lawsuit card here, but you don't have a reason to deny us service. We've been through four suits so far, and we've won them all. We'd really just like a table, please." Sotto voce, I added, "We'll be done in an hour. Bernice eats fast. You'll see."

I suggested a corner table, and Melani mutely agreed. It was set for four, and while Melani was clearing the extra settings I snagged the nicely folded napkins: one to tuck down Bernice's muumuu, one for her lap, and one for cleanup. Bernice put her elbows on the table, and a jet of pus from a boil squirted over the rolls. Time for the cleanup napkin! The rolls were excellent, by the way, crusty and hot, and we used lots of butter.

It was purposeful that I sat myself against the wall looking out, and Bernice looking at the wall. "I'm jealous: you get to look at the beautiful fresco!" I pointed out. Honestly, I also seated us this way because it would

draw less attention. Still, the people at the table next to us finished eating early. They knocked over their chairs while leaving: I righted them. Rude!

"Do you . . . do you know what you want to order?" Melani asked, crying a little but controlling herself rather well, considering. I liked that she was waiting on us herself. Bernice hopefully didn't notice it was because the waitresses were . . . hesitant to approach.

"I've got to try the shrimp scampi," I said. "I love shrimp! And Bernice is going to have . . . hmm . . . the lasagna verdi, how many servings are left?" Melani tearfully said she could check. "Just warm up however many servings are left in the pan, and bring them all. And as a side, two orders of fettuccine Alfredo, please."

"This is a great place, isn't it?" I said. "Such ambiance!" Bernice agreed, whipping out the talkbook to point to "Excellent," the top of the like-dislike scale. Things have been much easier since we put together the talkbook. She doesn't need to try to talk, which is difficult because of the combination of cleft palate, lip keloids, and dental issues.

Bernice then pointed to "notebook," which I dutifully handed over to her. (The pages get too greasy and discharge-y if it stays in her pocket. Good thing we laminated the talkbook!) She gripped a pencil in one flipper and began to write.

I kept my game face on, but I had a bad feeling I knew what she was going to ask. The two of us have an . . . unusual relationship, one where we don't often

get out to restaurants or shows. She knows why, but I just can't bring myself to be cruel enough to remind her. No woman needs to hear that, especially from the man she loves. So, we end up in situations like this, where I just know people are staring at us.

There was a family eating across from us, mom, dad, and a five-year-old boy. *B wAnT ThAT,* she had written, with an arrow aimed at them. (Which confused me at first, because when I held the talkbook the arrow pointed at a picture of a man playing a little accordion!) "Of course, of course," I said. "I want kids, too, with you. But you know our circumstances."

The little boy saw Bernice pointing and scooted off his seat to come over. His parents tried to stop him, but kids are intrepid! "Are you a nice monster?" he asked. She gets this a lot: kids love her. She turned, and the slat in her muumuu opened. It exposed a stripe of her zebra hide, which is the cute nickname we have for the brown and pink intertrigo fungus that lines her torso. Also, Brad's little arm and leg popped out.

"Hey, a baby!" the boy said. "You have a baby monster! Can I see?"

"We're trying to have a private dinner," I began to say to the boy, but Bernice simply pushed her clothing aside to reveal Brad. Brad waved, which was just a trick she could do by rolling her stomach.

"Brad's what's called a parasitic twin," I explained. "He's . . . he's kind of like a decoration. For her belly." Brad opened up his fetal mouth and a thin trickle of

something tan and fecal came out. Doctors don't know what that stuff is, but Brad's been drooling it out for forty years now nonstop.

"Hon," I whispered, "cover yourself up." Bernice gets huffy when she says I treat her like a child, and she made an elaborate show of pulling her dress back down over Brad. But that tugged down the other side of the dress, and her hump popped out.

"Hey, is that a wombat?" the boy asked. He must watch Animal Planet! It was just a kyphosis, of course, with a patch of teratoma that had two fingers, four teeth, and a thick loop of lower intestine. But Bernice's body hair around there was thick enough to make it look like an animal perched on her shoulder. What do you want: her mother's Greek.

"It's time to go back to your table," I said, and the boy reluctantly left. I heard him tell his mom that the monster had an animal and a baby in her: he said the word "blob," which I hoped Bernice didn't hear. She didn't: one good aspect of the eczema skin-sloughing filling up her ear canals.

Each time the kitchen door opened, revealing a tray-bearing waitress, I said, "Is this ours? Is this one for us?" Bernice tolerates my attempts at humor. Finally it was: Melani came out and propped open one of those unfoldable-leg devices they can rest a big serving tray on. What are those called? All nice restaurants have them, so someone must know what they're called. Maybe I·should ask Melani.

Melani dashed back to the kitchen and returned with our drinks (Diet Coke, of course, for Bernice and iced tea for me), two bowls of alfredo, a sizzling shrimp scampi that looked delicious, and plate after plate of lasagna. Really: I asked them to bring the tray out. They needn't have gone to all this trouble.

"We had four servings of the lasagna verdi left," Melani said, doing a good job of being composed. "Enjoy!"

"I really wish you hadn't plated them all," I said, taking out the funnel pot. "It's really not necessary. Just more dishes to wash!" I tilted one of the alfredo bowls, and creamy noodles sprinkled with green flakes exited down into the bag, landing with a loud plop. The second bowl's contents sounded even wetter, since they splashed against even more fettuccini.

"Ready?" I asked Bernice.

She took off her face, then nodded. "Go!" she said, or rather grunted, since her tongue had no upper palate to make a *g* sound against. After her cleft-palate surgery weakened her nose and sinuses so much, the doctors just gave her a prosthetic. But it gets dirty when eating, so she snaps it off for meals. Having no upper teeth also means you can't chew, and the lip fibroid made it easiest to just pour soft foods down her throat. She also popped out her lower bridge: the bottom teeth were cutting into her bare sinuses, so they had to go.

I've gotten used to the sounds of Bernice eating, and the visuals, but it's a little disarming to others. I

hope we can get all the alfredo down before any of it returns. I usually have to climb up onto the table at home to feed Bernice, but we're at a nice restaurant so I make do with standing next to her.

Starting the process, I hold the funnel pot at a tilted angle. (We don't use the term feed bag; that's for horses!) The alfredo begins a mudslide down the pot wall, then hits the funnel and begins to drip out a few at a time. Bernice waits patiently, mouth open wider than most any other human's on the planet can be. (We've applied to the *Guinness Book*: they say it's not a category they recognize.) She looks like Pac-Man, like a cartoon of someone with a mouth so open it would require a broken jaw.

A gleek of saliva from her glands squirts out, then two more. The first noodles hit her mouth, and she slams her jaws closed on them like a bear trap. The sound, I'm a bit chagrined to say, is halfway between gutting a fish and breaking wind. I pour some more down her mouth, and she eagerly swallows it. At home we call it "feeding the baby bird." This way food doesn't lodge in any of the carved-out cavities that line her throat. She can do it by herself, of course, but due to some binocular troubles she can't aim well enough to hit her mouth too often. I don't mind doing this, though, if it gives her some dignity.

Still, sometimes a hank of food will make its way into her sinus cavity, which I can see from this upward angle. Bernice snorts once, twice, then spits out the

chunk of food as best she can into her hand. It's yellowish-green now, from the protective layers that coat the sinus. She pops it back into her mouth two seconds later: five-second rule!

We're halfway through the alfredo when someone across the room vomits. Darn it! This always happens. And, of course, once one person vomits that makes a second person vomit, and then a third. And then Bernice feels bad so she gets up to go over and apologize. But she's got a sensitive stomach, and when she sees people getting sick, she's got the same gag reflex as everyone else. And up comes the alfredo, right onto the floor. And, since she leaned over rather fast to upchuck, her dress hiked itself up over her back, exposing her bottom.

Bernice's bottom is not her best feature. She's a large woman, and large people have certain hygiene issues that people blessed with speedy metabolisms don't have. She just can't reach back there, people! Don't expect every last bit of everything to be scrubbed clean! Plus, she had an asymmetrical cyst that the doctors said was benign but still weighed twenty-three pounds and hung off a delicate part of her. (This also made it impossible for her to wear regular, or any, undergarments.) She turned around to retrieve her dress, and had to turn around two or three times to catch it with her right flipper.

There also was a smell, or rather a series of them. I prefer not to linger on the subject of smells.

"I think we'll just wrap up the rest in a doggie bag, thanks," I told Melani. Two minutes later Bernice and I left, a brisk evening breeze dancing her trail of dandruff around like delicate little white leaves. They didn't charge us for Bernice's chair, which was nice of them. But maybe they didn't notice. Well, it needed upholstering anyway: her spastic colon only helped that process along.

Back in the car, Bernice took out her talkbook, and pointed to the picture of a house. She raised a suggestive eyebrow at me. Well, where the eyebrow would be if not for the ringworm. I shook my head. "You knew the deal, Bernice. I have to drop you back off at your place. We can't go to my house tonight."

She was sulky on the way home, but she has to face facts. I can't be at her beck and call all the time. I'm a married man, and she knew that when she started dating me. I'm not in a position to leave my wife right yet. When the time is right, I am positively dumping her ugly ass for Bernice. Not yet, though. Until then, we'll have our nights on the town, just the two of us.

Treatment

J. A. KONRATH

"It all goes back to the time I was bitten by that were-wolf."

Dr. Booster's pencil paused for a moment on his notepad, having only written a *W*.

"A werewolf?"

Tyler nodded. Booster appraised the teenager: pimples, lanky, hair a bit too long for the current style. The product of a well-to-do suburban couple.

"This is the reason your grades have gone down?"

"Yeah. Instead of studying at night, I roam the neighborhood, eating squirrels."

"I see. And how do squirrels taste, Tyler?"

"They go down dry."

Booster wrote "active imagination" on his pad.

"What makes you say you were bitten by a were-wolf?"

"Because I was."

"When did this happen?"

Tyler scratched at the pubescent hairs on his chin. "Two weeks ago. I was out at night, burying this body . . ."

"Burying a body?"

The boy nodded.

"Tyler, for therapy to work, we have to be honest with each other."

"I'm being honest, Dr. Booster."

Booster made his mouth into a tight line and wrote "uncooperative" on his pad.

"Fine, Tyler. Whose body were you burying?"

"It was Crazy Harold. He was a wino that hung out in the alley behind the liquor store on Kedzie."

"And why were you burying him?"

Tyler furrowed his brow. "I had to get rid of it. I didn't think digging a grave would be necessary. I thought they disintegrated after getting a stake in the heart."

Booster frowned. "Crazy Harold was a vampire?"

Tyler shifted on the couch to look at him. "You knew? Shouldn't they turn into dust when you kill them?"

Booster glanced at the diplomas on his wall and sighed.

"So you're saying you hammered a stake into Crazy Harold—"

"It was actually a broken broom handle."

"—and then buried him."

"In the field behind the house. And just when I finished, that's when the werewolf got me."

Tyler lifted his right leg and hiked up his pants. Above the sock was a raised pink scar, squiggly like an earthworm.

"That's the bite mark?"

Tyler nodded.

"It looks old, Tyler."

"It healed fast."

"Your mother told me you got that scar when you were nine years old. You fell off your bike."

Tyler blinked, then rolled his pants leg back down.

"Mom's full of shit."

Booster wrote "animosity toward mother" on his pad.

"Why do you say that, Tyler? Your mother is the one who recommended therapy, isn't she? It seems as if she wants to help."

"She's not my real mother. Her and Dad were replaced by aliens."

"Aliens?"

"They killed my parents, replaced them with duplicates. They look and sound the same, but they're actually from another planet. I caught them, once, in their bedroom."

Booster raised an eyebrow. "Making love?"

"Contacting the mother ship. They're planning a full-scale invasion of earth. But I thought you wanted to know about the werewolf."

Booster pursed his lips. WWFD? He appealed to the picture of Sigmund hanging above the fireplace. The picture offered no answers.

"Tyler, with your consent, I'd like to try some hypnotherapy. Have you ever been hypnotized?"

Tyler shook his head. Booster dimmed the lights and sat alongside the couch. He held his pencil in front of Tyler's face at eye level.

"Take a deep breath, then let it out. Focus on the pencil . . ."

It took a few minutes to bring Tyler to a state of susceptible relaxation.

"Can you hear me, Tyler?"

"Yes."

The boy's jaw was slack, and a thin line of drool escaped the corner of his mouth. Booster was surprised at the child's halitosis—perhaps he had been eating squirrels after all.

"I'd like you to go back to two weeks ago. When you were burying Crazy Harold."

"Okay."

"Tell me what you see."

"It's cold. There are a lot of rocks in the dirt, and the shovel won't go in very far."

Booster used his penlight to check Tyler's pupils. Slow response. The child was under.

"What were you digging?"

"Grave. For the vampire."

Booster frowned. He'd studied cases of patients

lying under hypnosis, but had never encountered one in person.

"What about the werewolf?"

"Came out of the field. It was big, had red eyes, walked on two legs."

"And it bit you?"

"Yeah. I thought it was going to kill me, but Runs Like Stallion saved me."

"Runs Like Stallion?"

"He's a ghost. He used to be a Sioux brave. The field is an old Indian burial ground."

Booster decided he'd had enough. He wrote "treatment" in his notebook and went over to his desk, unlocking the top drawer. The metallic case practically leaped up at him. He took it over to Tyler.

"Tyler, your parents are tired of these stories."

"My parents are dead."

"No, Tyler. They aren't dead. They care about you. That's why they brought you to me."

Booster opened the case. The gnerlock blinked its three eyes and crawled into Booster's hand. It would enter Tyler's mouth and burrow up into his brain, taking over his body. Tyler was a tad bit young, and the gnerlock would be cramped living in the boy's skull, but psychiatry wasn't a perfect science.

"Soon, it will all be better. You'll have no more worries. You're going to be a host, Tyler, for the new dominant species on this planet. Are you scared?"

"No."

"Open your mouth, Tyler."

Tyler stretched his mouth wide. Wider than humanly possible. And Booster was alarmed to see it was crammed with sharp teeth.

The gnerlock nesting in the doctor's brain popped out through his neck after the wolf decapitated the host body. Its eleven legs beelined for the door, antennae waving hysterically, telepathically cursing that quack, Freud.

Halfway there, a ghostly moccasin came down on the alien's oblong head, smashing it into the carpeting.

Runs Like Stallion gave the wolf a thumbs-up, but Tyler was already leaping out the window, vulpine eyes locked on a juicy squirrel in the grass below.

Dead Clown
Séance

Christopher Welch

Clem's mobile home was strewn with shadows. The sole luminescence came from four candles centered on the table. The flames stretched upward as their amber brightness reflected off the clowns' pasty faces.

Clem, Toodles, Oswald Osgood, and Beeps held hands, forming a circle around the tapers. The poofball at the peak of Clem's conical hat was almost invisible in the surrounding darkness. Toodles tilted her head back so her frizzy green hair would not catch the flames. Oswald's tramp clothing and hobo makeup made him appear more frightened than he felt. Beeps had placed his bicycle horn on the table within easy reach.

Oswald wanted to say *If Lon Chaney had seen us*

by candlelight first, he might have altered his famous comment about clowns in moonlight, but he kept that thought to himself.

Clem was a tad apprehensive about conducting another séance. Last time, his neighbor Andrei filed a noise complaint with the neighborhood association. Clem took a deep breath. He began the séance.

"We call you, spirits of the dead." Clem concentrated his mind's eye. "We call to the departed souls from this mortal world. Come now. Come!"

The flames swayed as a mysterious breeze developed inside the blackened mobile home.

"Are you there, Mr. Flonkers? Come to us. Come to us now!"

The flames lapped as the mystic wind escalated. The house trailer wobbled. Shadows trembled around the four clowns. Loose debris fluttered about as the wind intensified—bits of cellophane, used Post-it notes, Slurpee receipts from 7-Eleven, hamburger wrappers. Clowns love hamburgers. And Slurpees.

"Come, Mr. Flonkers! Come to us!" they shouted in unison over the supernatural gale, except for Beeps, who honked his horn.

Beep-Beep.

The wind died quickly as pale smoke rose from the burning wicks. The smoke twisted into shapes, the shapes curled into a form, and the form became a figure. Above the candles, floating in a vaporous cloak, the ghost they summoned manifested itself.

Mr. Flonkers wore a maroon bowler hat with a daisy in the band and an oversized scarlet ascot. He had pinpricks of white light in otherwise hollow eyes. His countenance was jovial with a red-painted grin and skull-white face.

"Who calls me?" Mr. Flonkers's voice reverberated as if it emanated from the bottom of a well.

"We need your help."

"Toodles, dear, is that you?" Mr. Flonkers asked.

"Yes, it is. Nice to see you again."

Mr. Flonkers removed his hat in greeting. "Likewise."

The spirit assessed her green frizz, her emerald eye shadow that matched her lipstick, and her white face. She wore a jade-and-black checkered unitard over her lithe body. "You're as beautiful as I remember."

Beep–Beep.

Mr. Flonkers moved towards Beeps. The vapor twisted with his movement. "You're here too, my loquacious friend?"

Beep–Beep.

"Oswald as well?"

"Yes, I'm here."

"How did you summon me from the Big Top in the Sky?"

"That's my doing," Clem said.

The spirit turned and the smoke curled once more.

"Clem, my boy!" Mr. Flonkers said with affection. "Four of the finest apprentices of the Mr. Flonkers Clown

Alley, present and accounted for. Again, how did you summon me?"

"My gypsy heritage," Clem said. "My clairvoyant parents were fortune-tellers and psychic readers in the circus. I never turned professional, much to my parents' dismay. After numerous arguments about my career choice, I ran away from home and joined the other part of the circus. My clairvoyance is still active, though."

"I see." The ghost nodded.

"We summoned you, sir, for a specific reason. We need help, and as our mentor—our *departed* mentor—you're uniquely qualified to help."

Beep-Beep.

"What's the situation?"

"Do you recall Otis Oddbody?" Clem asked.

"Of course," Mr. Flonkers said. "I worked with him in the early days, before he formed his own alley."

"Tragedy has struck the Oddbody Alley, and that tragedy has mutated into an unspeakable horror."

"What do you mean?"

"Show him," Oswald said.

"Look into my mind's eye."

Mr. Flonkers's pinprick white pupils gazed into Clem's eyes as Clem opened a wider psychic connection with the spirit. Mr. Flonkers watched everything unfold in Clem's clairvoyant mind as if he were sitting in a cinema.

"This is what I saw two months ago."

• • •

All twelve professional and apprentice members of the Otis Oddbody Clown Alley—Poco, Mooch, Cindy Candy, Big Galoot, Joey Jelly, Smarty Artie, Ms. Pinkyfoot, Choo-Choo, Poundfool, Midge the Dwarf, Benny Buzzy, and Sir Donald Dollarshort, Esq.—saw Otis's neon yellow and purple-polka-dot 1968 Volkswagen Beetle pull up to the tent.

"Road trip!" Otis yelled from the driver's seat.

The twelve clowns loaded themselves in the same rehearsed formation they'd often performed under the Big Top. Their opening bit was to have Otis drive to the Center Ring, and then all thirteen, including Otis, exited the car one at a time—flopping, tripping, somersaulting, and cartwheeling; Poco even came out on stilts, wearing a gray top hat, coattails, and oversized bow tie—to much audience laughter and amazement.

Otis explained their destination on the way.

"We're going to the Circus World Museum in Baraboo, Wisconsin," he said. "That's where the five original Ringling brothers started everything. From there, we're going to Milwaukee and we're marching in the Great Circus Parade."

The pronouncement was met with cheers and applause.

"But we're taking a side trip before the parade," Otis said. "This is a personal pilgrimage. We're going to visit Uncle Uther, who lives in Bark Creek. It's a

small town in rural Jefferson County west of Milwaukee. Uncle Uther performed for eighty years, and now he's in assisted living at an old clowns' home. I first saw him when my father took me to a Shriner's Circus forty years ago and his performance inspired me to become a clown. He had this hysterical bit with a handshake buzzer. I saw him perform many times, and that bit *always* cracked me up. I want to pay my respects in person, clown to clown."

The museum was fun for everyone and surprisingly educational to the younger apprentices. After spending the day in Baraboo, Otis drove them toward Bark Creek.

The July twilight gave way to the silvery darkness of a full Buck Moon. The lunar light cut through the thick leaves of low-hanging maples, burr oaks, willows, and hickories that canopied the back roads of Jefferson County.

At midnight, Benny Buzzy passed around the kazoos. Midge the Dwarf and Ms. Pinkyfoot got high-pitched piccolo kazoos. Big Galoot and Poundfool got deeper-sounding bass kazoos. Poundfool played a mean bass.

"I'm like the Geezer Butler of kazoo players, y'know," Poundfool often said.

They played a remarkably accurate—albeit buzzing—version of "Entrance of the Gladiators" as the VW motored along Riverbank Road next to the Bark River.

Otis was driving too fast and did not have time to swerve from the deadly obstacle left in the narrow lane. He put his hands up and screamed.

The front tire hit the banana peel head-on. The Bug spun wildly, flipped once, twice, bounced off an oak, slid down the embankment, and splashed into the river. The car sank under the surface of moon-glimmering ripples as the kazoo music turned into gurgles.

"How tragic," Mr. Flonkers said, swirling in the smoke.

"Yes, but that's not the worst part," Toodles said.

"What's worse than thirteen dead clowns?"

Beep-Beep.

"Well, yes, *fourteen* would be worse."

"Do you feel their presence, Mr. Flonkers?" Oswald asked.

Mr. Flonkers paused. The ghost swayed in sync with the flames. The mobile home was eerily quiet as the clowns waited.

"No, they're not here in the afterlife," he said after a moment. "How can that be?"

"That's the worst part," Clem said. "Look into my mind's eye again to watch what transpired one month later."

There are no streetlamps on the rural roads of Jefferson County, but the full Sturgeon Moon draped its bright-

ness over the homesteads, farms, orchards, and groves like luminescent silk.

Nobody was near Riverbank Road to witness the Volkswagen Beetle drive out of the river and over the bank. Nobody was close enough to hear the still night disrupted by a macabre kazoo orchestra playing the well-known circus theme. Nobody saw the car patrol the country lanes like a spider on asphalt webs.

At first.

The Lowenbacher family was driving home after an evening game—"cap night"—at Miller Park. Alex wore his Brewers hat backward as he drove the Ford Focus. Beside him, his wife Kristine had taken hers off for the ride home. In the backseat, Timmy and little sister Courtney proudly wore their caps. Timmy still wore his mitt.

"What's that noise?" Kristine asked.

"I know," Courtney chirped. "It's circus bees!"

"There's no such thing as circus bees," Timmy said. His tone carried the annoyed condescension inherent to all big brothers.

"It's coming from the car behind us," Alex said. "Some bozo's tailgating us."

As soon as Alex spoke the tailgating car sped up and passed the Ford on the left. It was a Beetle; it cut back in front and sped ahead. A hand stuck out of the driver's window and waved something.

"Is that a banana peel?" Kristine asked.

The hand dropped the peel onto the road and it

tumbled into the Ford's path. Alex tried to swerve but the front tire hit the banana peel and he lost control of the car. The Focus spun out, flipped onto its passenger side, skidded into the gravel berm, and careened into a tree with a shattering crunch. Miraculously, the impact made the car roll back onto its wheels.

"Is everyone okay? Can you get out?" Alex yelled over the cries of his family. He lumbered out of the car and reached for his wife. She climbed over the gear-shift and out through the driver's door. Timmy assisted Courtney out through his door. She was crying, and so was he, but he tried to be brave for his little sister.

The family huddled in the road, sobbing and hugging, checking for major injuries, praising seat belts and air bags, when the Beetle's headlights landed on them.

The Lowenbachers watched the car stop thirty yards away from their group hug. The buzzing music stopped. The doors opened. The first one out was the driver.

Otis Oddbody wore a black derby over crimpled yellow hair, a horizontally-striped black-and-white shirt, and red suspenders attached to red pantaloons that were tucked into oversized black shoes. On his left suspender was a sunflower blossom. His mimelike face was white except for black lipstick and small black triangles on his cheeks and brows. His eye sockets were hollow except for an eerie red-orange light. He approached the Lowenbachers as the other clowns poured out. The same hellish light pulsed from all their eyes.

The horrified family watched as the horde of ghastly clowns exited the car executing their flopping, tripping, somersaulting, and cartwheeling without missing a step—unless missing a step was required for the bit.

"Stilts," Timmy whispered between sobs. "That one in the gray tuxedo actually got out of the car *wearing stilts*."

Dread slithered down each of their spines as the menacing congregation of clowns closed in around the family.

"You should be laughing," Otis said, his voice sounding as if it originated from a mine shaft. "Why aren't you laughing? Didn't you like our gag?"

The family cried louder.

"I said laugh! We are professionals and we know when something is funny or not. The Oddbody Alley is absolutely hysterical, I tell you! *Hysterical!*"

The clowns hooted and guffawed as their eyes blazed even brighter occult fire. They all laughed, except Otis.

"Go away!" Courtney screamed.

"Are you going to laugh or not?" Otis pointed to the ruined Ford. "Don't you get it? *Don't you get it?*"

"*No!*" Alex and Kristine yelled together, squeezing their shuddering children.

Otis snapped his fingers and the clowns were upon them.

• • •

Clem stopped the vision. "I can't watch that awful moment again."

"What did they do?" Mr. Flonkers asked.

"Cindy Candy, Smarty Artie, Choo-Choo, and Poundfool are experts at twisting balloons into animal shapes," Oswald said.

"So?"

"Imagine what they'd do to arms and legs," Toodles said.

"Oh." Mr. Flonkers lowered his head, trying not to visualize the gruesomeness. He failed. "Odd body, indeed."

"But what are they?" Toodles asked. "Are they ghosts, zombies, or what?"

Mr. Flonkers hovered in thought for a moment.

"They're manifested revenants, spirits made material, echoes of human woe and uncompleted goals," he said. "They're the curse left behind as a by-product of jovial souls taken from the mortal world by stark tragedy. These clowns neither walk among the living nor the dead. They've become un—"

"Unclowns," Clem said.

"As long as they're not vampires," Oswald said. "Stupid vampires are everywhere nowadays. You can't even buy a Slurpee at 7-Eleven without bumping into a brood of vampires."

Beep-Beep.

"Unclowns are malignant creatures," Mr. Flonkers said. "They don't bring fun and cheer into the world.

Rather, they breed fear, horror, and death. The polarity of their funny bones has been reversed. They'll ruin the reputations of clowns everywhere."

"We've barely recovered our public respectability from that Stephen King novel, and that was published over twenty years ago," Toodles said.

"We summoned you for help," Clem said. "I suspect the cursed clown car will prowl during the next full moon, which is tomorrow. We must stop the unclowns before they kill more innocent people."

"What do we need to do so they can rest in peace, sir?" Toodles asked.

Mr. Flonkers scratched his ghostly chin.

"Okay, I got it," he said. "First, buy some kazoos. Then you need to visit a certain nursing home in Bark Creek. Next . . ."

The receptionist behind the desk at the Bark Creek Clown Convalescence Center and Liquor Store saw the Mr. Flonkers Alley enter the facility.

Beep-Beep.

"So you're just here to see Uncle Uther, then?"

"Yes," Clem said.

"Follow me." She led them down a hallway. "There's only one rule in this facility. We have a strict no smoking policy. Uncle Uther begs for cigars every chance he gets. Do not give him any; is that understood?"

"No problem."

The receptionist glanced at her watch. "He may not be too conversant for a while."

"Why not?"

"You'll see. Here's his room. Also, we have a special this week—twenty percent off all tequila. Have a nice day."

They entered the motel-like room. Ninety-seven-year-old Uncle Uther sat in a recliner watching television. He wore bedroom slippers and a gold one-piece suit with a ruffled collar and pom-pom buttons down the front. He sported a hat similar to Clem's conical poof-ball cap, but it was three sizes too small for his bald head and was angled to the left. He had Coke-bottle trifocals on his white face.

The television played the theme from *Days of Our Lives*.

"Uncle Uther, may we have a word with you?" Toodles asked.

"Do you have any cigars, sweetheart?"

"No."

"Then you can't have a word with me until my stories are finished."

"Sir," Clem said. "We have very important—"

"Not now."

They waited quietly for thirty-five minutes until the show was over. Oswald left the room for a moment and returned with a bottle of Jose Cuervo, which made the wait more tolerable.

"I miss John and Marlena," Uncle Uther said to no one in particular after the show ended.

"Sir, can we talk now?" Clem asked.

"Fine." He shifted in his chair.

Clem explained the situation.

"I'll assist you on one condition," Uncle Uther said.

"What's that?"

"I want a box of Romeo y Julieta Short Churchills."

"Come again?"

"Cigars, son. I want a box of Cuban cigars."

"No problem."

Ten hours later Uncle Uther was standing with four other jokers on Riverbank Road under the shine of a full Corn Moon.

Uncle Uther was not exactly sure why he was here, or what he was exactly supposed to do despite what Clem explained, but he was smoking a cigar and had almost a full box on reserve, so he felt *something* was going exactly right.

Clem had scored the cigars from Andrei, his neighbor in the mobile home park. Andrei was a retired midget clown and ex-KGB agent. During the Cold War, Andrei worked as an undercover spy while traveling in Royal Russian Circus tours. He had connections.

The five clowns had driven to Riverbank Road

in Beeps's Smart car. When he wasn't taking care of clown business, Beeps was all about saving the environment. Now they waited.

"I've been thinking, and I believe Lon Chaney was right," Oswald said.

"What about?" Clem asked.

"Here we are," Oswald said. "Two classic Auguste clowns, a hobo, an emerald harlequin, and the lovechild of Harpo Marx and R2-D2 standing on a country road ten minutes before midnight, trying to prevent ghastly fools in a cursed clown car from murdering innocent people."

"Okay?"

"Chaney said, 'There is nothing funny about a clown in the moonlight.' If some yokels drive by us tonight, would they laugh, or would they scream?"

"I'm not sure."

"I think they'd scream. Loudly."

Beep-Beep.

"Yes, shouldn't we get started?" Toodles asked.

Clem distributed the kazoos. "The 7-Eleven was out of piccolo kazoos, so we'll just have to make do. Oswald, you're on bass."

"I'm like the Steve Harris of kazoo players, y'know."

"What do we have to play again?" Uncle Uther asked, blowing a smoke ring.

"'Entrance of the Gladiators,'" Oswald said.

"I don't know that one," Uncle Uther said. "Can we play 'Thunder and Blazes' instead?"

"What's the difference?"

"The one goes *toot-toot-tootle-tootle-toot-TOOT-toot* but the other one is more complex because it goes *toot-toot-tootle-tootle-TOOT-toot-toot.*"

"Mr. Flonkers told us to play kazoos to get the unclowns' attention, then we can help them," Clem said. "I don't think the specific song matters."

They played "Thunder and Blazes"—*zooz-zooz-zoozle-zoozle-ZOOZ-zooz-zooz*—as they stood next to the Smart car on the moonlit road next to the river. They played for five minutes.

The unclowns heard them.

The Beetle drove out of the Bark River five minutes before midnight. The Bug was fifty yards away from them, and it also buzzed with the circus theme. It turned to face those standing in the road, the headlights capturing all five clowns blowing their kazoos. The Bug approached slowly, like a spider unsure what was caught in its web. It finally halted fifteen feet in front of them.

Clem, Toodles, Oswald Osgood, Beeps, and Uncle Uther stopped playing. The music from the Bug stopped as well, but the headlights remained on. After a pause, the driver's door opened.

Otis came out first, then the others followed—Poco, Mooch, Cindy Candy, Big Galoot, Joey Jelly, Smarty Artie, Ms. Pinkyfoot, Choo-Choo, Poundfool, Midge the Dwarf, Benny Buzzy, and Sir Donald Dollarshort, Esq.—except this time they did not do their

normal bit. They approached the still-mortal clowns in silence as their eyes blazed with unhallowed red-orange luminescence.

There was another pause as each clown alley studied the other, neither clown nor unclown sure what the next step should be.

Clem finally came forward. "Otis Oddbody, there's someone here you want to meet." Uncle Uther stepped up and stood next to Clem. "Let me introduce you to Uncle Uther."

Otis cocked his head like a dog who'd just heard a can opener. "Uncle Uther? *The* Uncle Uther?"

Uncle Uther switched his cigar from one side of his mouth to the other. "That's me, son. I understand you want to pay your respects. So come on, pay up." Uncle Uther held out his left palm like he expected cash to exchange hands.

"Yes, I want to pay my respects, clown to clown."

As soon as Otis finished speaking, the sunflower blossom on his suspenders released a stream of water that hit Uncle Uther in the face. It splattered his glasses and almost doused his cigar.

The Oddbody Alley erupted in hoots and guffaws as Uncle Uther let the stream hit him until it dwindled away. Otis remained silent.

Uncle Uther removed his glasses and dried them on the top pom-pom. The Oddbody Alley stopped laugh-

ing as they focused on Uncle Uther's reaction. Uncle Uther replaced the glasses and reignited his cigar with three rapid puffs.

"You know what," Uncle Uther said, blowing smoke as he smiled. "I like your style, son. Put 'er there."

Otis instinctively grabbed Uncle Uther's extended right hand—*ZZZAAAPPP!*—and pulled back, jumped up, and yelped in surprise at the hand buzzer's shock.

Otis's eyes flashed furiously for two seconds . . . then he started laughing.

He laughed hard. It was a genuine, from the gut, true peal of merriment. He looked at his hand and released another burst of hilarity. He slapped his leg a few times as he bent forward in continuous chuckles. Otis turned around and showed his palm to his alley. They too exploded in clamorous jocularity as they pointed at the hand and laughed and laughed and laughed.

Clem noticed the change first, but the others saw it soon enough.

It was in their eyes. The Oddbody Alley no longer had raging light burning in their hollow sockets. The angry glow faded away, and the light which remained became white pinpricks.

Mr. Flonker's Alley and Uncle Uther had succeeded in their mission. They watched as the Oddbody Alley— no longer *unclowns*, but fully restored spirits of buffoonery and foolishness and circus magic—returned to the Beetle. Otis was the last one to enter the car, but before

he did, he turned to Uncle Uther and waved good-bye with his shocked hand.

The VW turned away from the five clowns. The Bug drove along Riverbank Road. An angelic light opened in the sky. The neon yellow and purple-polka-dot Beetle left the physical street and drove skywards along the beam until it reached the Big Top in the Sky. Mr. Flonkers was there to welcome them. The bright ray evaporated.

"Well done," Clem said.

"First round of Slurpees is on Clem," Toodles said. *Beep-Beep.*

They were about to pack themselves into the Smart car when another set of headlights approached. They waited for the vehicle to come close. It was a Chevy convertible with a teenage couple in the front. The girl was driving and she came to a stop.

"Did your car break down? Do you need—"

She froze as she realized to whom she was speaking: five clowns lurking on a lonely road in midnight moonlight. She and her boyfriend stared at the clowns in paralyzed fear.

No one spoke for three heartbeats.

Beep-Beep.

The teenagers shrieked in horror as the girl hit the gas.

"Told you they would scream."

The Day the Devil Swallowed a Heapin' Helpin' of Pride at the Beaulahville Gospel Jubilee

SCOTT NICHOLSON

Tater salad.

That would seem to be a fitting place to start, what with the Reverend Maynard Gray coming through the line. The reverend patted his belly and clutched his Styrofoam plate with determination. He'd even double-stacked the plate in hopes of a heavy load.

The tater salad was in a clay bowl, the pottery

shaped and fired and glazed and painted by Ima Jean Spurgeon herself. The rim was slightly out of round. These God-fearing mortals loved their spiritual metaphors, but no doubt they failed to see the connection between a potter and flawed works. And Ima Jean had used a base of mayonnaise instead of the more common mustard, but this was the South after all, and they were still figuring out how to cook here.

The Devil touched the edge of the bowl. The effect wasn't as dramatic as the parting of the Red Sea—a bit of overblown fiction that the Devil had witnessed as little more than a low tide in a mud puddle—but it did the job. An army of bacteria stormed the crevices between taters, dill, black pepper, and celery, there to wait in ambush for the good folk of Beaulahville, Georgia.

"Hello there," said a woman with frosted hair who was busy cramming serving spoons in various bowls of creamed corn, green beans with fatback, and steamed collards. She smiled at the Devil, who had been staring intently at the tater salad with a distant smile on his face.

The Devil blinked. He'd forgotten his station. "Counting chickens before they were hatched," that's how some put it. He'd already fantasized these godly people over to the dark side and turning on the slow spit, but an overactive imagination had gotten him in trouble before. It was plain old ego and pride, but, hell, he was the Devil, after all.

Except right now, on Sunday, June 24, in the Year of Our Lord 2010, he was Pete Wilhite, a traveling insurance salesman representing the Good Hands people. And he'd do well to remember it, because Armageddon might be another millennium or two away, and patience was a virtue he didn't possess.

"Howdy, ma'am," he said, drawing the words out a little so he didn't sound too intelligent and could fit right in.

"Are you a guest?" She kept her hands busy as she spoke, like the other half-dozen women fussing over the spread and ushering people past the four picnic tables.

"Passing through," he said, plopping a dollop of mashed sweet potatoes on his plate.

"Wonderful," she said. "We're always happy to see a new face around here. I'm Betty."

Yes, I know. Betty Benson, former co-captain of the Beaulahville High Terrapins cheerleading squad, twice divorced, clerk in the county Register of Deeds office. And then there are the deeds you think nobody knows about . . .

"Betty," he said. "I have a cousin named Betty over in Marietta. Marietty Betty, they call her." That sounded like the kind of cousin a traveling insurance salesman would have.

"You want some of this here tater salad?"

"No, thank you," he said. "I prefer mine with a mustard base."

Betty leaned forward and lowered her voice to a conspiratorial whisper. "Ima Jean made that," she said,

sending a shiver of delight up the Devil's spine. "Came from a bad upbringing. You know how that goes."

The Devil indeed did know, but it was always a pleasure to be reminded.

A fourth-grade brat who smirked under his crew cut reached for a fudge-covered brownie, but his mother slapped his hand away and told him dessert came later. The crowd of ninety-three was spreading across the church lawn, sitting on blankets, folding chairs, and benches, talking with their mouths full, sipping red Kool-Aid.

"Which of these delights are yours?" the Devil asked Betty.

"Rice pudding," she said, nodding toward an enamel-plated pot. "Family recipe."

Pride. He could work with that. Of all the weapons in his arsenal, none was as effective as the poison that already saturated each living soul. Preachers liked to rave about lust and greed, because they loved sex and money, but the basic flaw was in the ego. Thank God for that, or he'd have had a hell of a time winning people over to the right side.

"Well, I'll just have to try me some," he said.

He turned the pudding with his spoon, letting a little evil slip down the utensil and into the sweet recipe.

"Jesus Christ!" he exclaimed. Several people glowered at him, and one little old lady's mouth fell open so fast that her gums left her dentures behind. They fell together with a clack a second later.

Betty Benson peered at the rice pudding. It roiled with live maggots.

"I know you're new to these parts, but we don't take the Lord's name in vain around here," she said.

"But flies have bred in your recipe, ma'am," he said, just loudly enough for the closest diners to overhear.

"Oh, that," she said, clamping a lid on the pot and sliding it to the edge of the table. "This Georgia heat, what can you do?"

"Iced tea," said a man whose toupee looked like a possum playing dead on top of his head. He winked. "Of course, you'll want to add a splash of white lightnin' to round out the flavor."

"Don't mind Ray Ray," Betty said. "He's Irish."

The Devil didn't advocate for or against strong liquor. Jesus had turned water into wine, and therefore it bore a certain stamp of moral approval. Yet drunken people often engaged in other activities that weren't exactly sanctioned, some of which had been invented after the King James version of the Holy Bible was concocted. Alcohol dulled the senses and made it more debatable whether intoxicated people were responsible for their actions. God made a big deal out of this "free will" stuff, and what better way to tug that bastard's beard than to have a mortal soberly choose the dark side over the promise of harps and halos.

Pride. It all came down to pride.

"Well, Miss Betty, I'm sorry about your pudding.

But what if you had a shot at a recipe that was guaranteed to take the blue ribbon at the county fair?"

Betty looked skeptical but interested nonetheless. "You don't look like much of a cook."

"Looks aren't everything." *Which is why you've had three husbands.*

"Well, I've been runner-up three times in the casserole category," she said.

"I know." The Devil gave his warmest, most sympathetic smile. "And Ima Jean has that darned secret ingredient that swings the judges over each year."

"It's practically cheating."

"Practically. But I can give you that ingredient, and more."

Betty's mouth parted slightly and she flushed from more than the pudding-spoiling heat. "I'd give anything."

"I know," he repeated. "But I don't ask much. All you have to do is . . ."

He glanced around, making sure people were content with their chicken legs, mashed potatoes, and cole slaw. ". . . eat some of Ima Jean's tater salad and say it was the best you've ever had."

She made a pukey face. "That would be a flat-out lie."

"What's a little white lie if it gets you what you want?"

"That ain't white, it's black as sin, and I'm on church property, right here in the shadow of the house of the Lord."

The Devil glanced at the church, its steeple standing tall and proud, higher than any structure in town, not counting the cellular tower and the water tank that was painted like a giant peach and bore the slogan "Beaulahville: A Peach Of A Place." The Devil had conducted some of his best missionary work inside churches, temples, mosques, and synagogues, and true believers took their faith with them beyond the doors. False witnesses carried their deceptions inside, too, even though God stared right down through the roof and saw them clearly. Only the foolish were easily fooled.

"Ma'am, I have a lot of business here today, and I know you've been taught to never trust a stranger. But to prove my sincerity, I can tell you that you lost three years ago because you gambled with three-quarters of a tablespoon of marjoram when your grandmother's recipe called for cardamom. And last year was the desperate ploy of paprika."

Betty looked shocked. "Nobody knows about that."

"What happens in Vegas," he said.

"Vegas? What does that mean?"

"'What happens in Vegas stays in Vegas,'" the Devil said. "You know, when you go somewhere and—"

"I ain't never been to Vegas."

"The point is that I know and you know, but no one else has to know. Is that so wrong?"

"That's the problem," she said. "I'd know. If I beat Ima Jean by cheating—"

"It's not cheating, it's a redistribution of resources."

"I'd rather go to my grave," she said.

The Devil sighed. This woman's soul was hardly worth the trouble, and her company would get annoying after a few millennia. And, as the country-music songs liked to point out, forever was a long time.

"Fine. Enjoy your next seven years of red ribbons. By the way, her name is Julia and she's currently handling your husband's liquid assets."

"Julia?"

"You'll figure it out." He moved down the line and poked around in a green mishmash that looked like spinach pesto. Slices of French bread were arranged around a decorative plate, the little dish in the center. The display was far too European-looking and had been roundly ignored by the wary folk of Beaulahville.

Ray Ray sidled over to the Devil and gave him a firm handshake. "Ray Ray McEelvy. A pleasure to meet you."

"Likewise. Pete Wilhite, insurance agent."

"An accent like that, you're bound to be from New Hampshire."

The Devil hadn't been there since his humiliation at the hands of Daniel Webster, but the liberals were doing a bang-up job of carrying on his mission in those parts. "I've lived all over," he said. "But I'm thinking of settling down here."

"We've got a strong business community," Ray Ray said. "Beaulahville could always use more insurance.

Sort of like lawyers, the more you have, the more you need."

The Devil consulted his vast mental filing cabinet. McEelvy. Town alderman, real estate salesman, carrying an out-of-state conviction for public intoxication and indecent exposure. McEelvy wasn't the only man ever caught urinating in a Las Vegas fountain. So much for "what happens in Vegas."

"I can see where my services might be needed," the Devil said.

"If you need some property, look me up," Ray Ray said, slipping the Devil a business card. "I have the scoop on a town rezoning that's sure to push up appraised values. Nothing beats artificial equity."

The Devil's hopes rose. "Isn't that illegal?"

Ray Ray gave him a hearty slap on the back. "It's win-win, the right thing to do. Higher values means higher taxes, and that means more services for the poor. Growth for the sake of growth."

"I'll think about it," the Devil said.

"Fine, fine. But I wasn't kidding about that white lightnin'." Ray Ray glanced around to make sure Betty was occupied. The constant demands of napkins and plastic spoons kept her fussing and fidgeting. No idle hands there with which to conduct mischief, but the day was young.

The Devil wondered how many of the fine people of Beaulahville were getting lubricated in anticipation of the coming sermon. A canvas canopy was stretched

over one end of the lawn, and rows of folding chairs were arranged to face the main stage. It reminded the Devil of his adventures in rock stardom, but he'd given up that profession in the digital era. Teenagers these days couldn't receive the Satanic messages that could only be revealed by spinning vinyl records backward. And ever since the advent of Christian heavy metal, the old bait-and-switch techniques had proven a waste of time.

"That's a kindly offer, Mr. McEelvy, but I want to keep my head clear. I'm here on business, after all."

"I understand. I only drink on Sundays myself."

The Devil smiled. On the color wheel of lies, Ray Ray's was neither white nor black. It was a kaleidoscopic rainbow. "What say I offer you some insurance on that backstreet office building?"

"The renovated train depot? How did you know it was mine?"

The property owner was listed in the county deeds office as Railway Enterprises, LLC, with the company principal under the fictitious name of "Lawrence Raymond." "I'm in insurance," the Devil said. "It's what I do."

"The building's already insured and—"

The Devil held up a pumpkin-covered spatula. "Mr. McEelvy, I don't have all day, and I know you need to get to your next drink. So let's get down to business. It's on the books at three-quarter million and you only have forty grand in it, thanks to your buddy at

the lending institution and your inside peek at the local tax foreclosures."

"Those are serious allegations, Mr. Wilhite. I believe you should talk to my attorney."

"Honest men don't need lawyers, Mr. McEelvy. And you have three."

"Are you extorting me?"

"Please." If the Devil kept sighing like this, he was going to sound like a leaking tire. These people didn't appreciate subtlety. "I'm on your side, and you're in good hands. Just let me draw you up a little supplemental policy, so when the building burns down next month—"

Ray Ray's cheeks puffed in alcoholic indignation. "Gunboat Gary. I'll get that bastard."

"Never mind small-time grifters. What happens in Vegas, Mr. McEelvy."

"I'm more concerned about what happens in Beaulahville. This is my town, Mr. Wilhite, and I don't appreciate a stranger waltzing in here and pissing on my turf."

The Devil held his patient smile while an elderly woman hobbled by, her Styrofoam plate balanced on her walker. "This is win-win, growth for growth's sake. A straightforward business proposition. The policy will pay you two million for content damage. It's going to be a shame when those rare William Tecumseh Sherman letters go up in smoke."

"Wasn't he the Union general who said 'War is hell'? I don't got no letters."

"You will. He's a personal friend who happens to owe me a few favors."

"I don't roll that way, Mr. Wilhite." Ray Ray wiped at his mouth. "I believe in stealing fair and square, on my own terms."

"What's the difference? You're going to burn it down anyway."

"Because it was my idea. I don't share the glory and I don't share the wealth."

Pride. The Devil was going to lose this man's soul because of simple human pride.

Ah, what's the use? What good is another arsonist in hell, anyway? I've got bigger fish to fry. Heh. Fish to fry. That's funny.

"Fine, Mr. McEelvy. Good luck with that little endeavor. I'm sorry the Beaulahville Volunteer Fire Department is going to be on the scene within three minutes and your 'total loss' is going to turn into a marshmallow roast. Be proud, my friend. Be proud."

Ray Ray's hands were trembling a little, and it was obviously time for some liver fortification. The Devil left him to his spiked tea and creamed corn and turned his attention to the real reason he'd come.

By now, Betty had swapped out the pot of infested pudding and proffered a foil-covered pie. The Devil grinned. "Just like Mom used to make?"

"She's in the bosom of the Lord, God rest her soul," Betty said.

Actually, the Devil knew otherwise, because Betty's

mother was currently wearing nothing but gasoline while wading through a pit of bubbling tar. But the rules of engagement required the Devil keep such information to himself. All he could do was dig in his usual bag of tricks. "I suppose you're going to lie about your maggot pudding, and that's why you've hidden it away. Because you're so proud."

"Oh, no," she said. "The reverend's coming, and he's a vegetarian, so he can't have maggots."

Maynard Gray was indeed making his way along the buffet, picking over the greens to see if any of them bore the sheen of fatback. He turned up his nose at the fried chicken, skipped over the sliced pork shoulder, and barely even glanced at the bratwurst and sauerkraut. His plate contained only a pile of plain mashed potatoes, a roll, and three pieces of celery.

The Devil reached under the table and pulled out a dish of his own making. Jesus wasn't the only miracle worker to have graced the pages of the New Testament. And the Devil was that book's sole survivor. He'd learned a thing or two along the way.

"Here you go, Reverend," the Devil said.

The preacher lifted the lid and peered down at the plate. "Deviled eggs?" he said, in a sonorous voice befitting his calling.

"Made them myself," the Devil said.

"They look mighty delicious, but I don't eat meat."

"These aren't flesh," the Devil said.

"Well, eggs count as meat," the preacher said.

"Technically, it's not born yet, so it's an embryo and not flesh," the Devil said.

"Are you trying to make a pro-choice argument?"

"I'm all about choice," the Devil said.

The preacher gave a tolerant, patient smile. "Are you a member of the congregation?"

The Devil waved to the sign that stood by the road. "I was just passing through and I saw your sign. It said 'Come 4 bread, stay 4 ever,' so how could I resist?"

The preacher nodded as if he'd never considered the message was an invitation. In the Devil's vast experience, churches loved to recruit, but they didn't really want to strain the resources. The ideal parishioners mailed in tithes and only showed up for services on Christmas. All that talk about leading souls to the Lord was just another type of pride, built on body count but ultimately measured by the bottom line.

"Are your vegetarian principles based on health reasons or moral reasons?" the Devil asked.

"Every decision is based on morality," the reverend said. "Even if it's for your health."

"So your position's supported by verse?"

"The Book of Leviticus. 'Ye shall eat neither blood nor fat.'"

Ah, the Old Testament book, with its restrictive guidelines that people tended to pick and choose among as it befit their various ideologies and sociopolitical needs. Its proscriptions had been used for or

against drinking, homosexuality, working on Sundays, and the eating of meat, depending on the whims of the moment. But its original purpose had been as a cookbook for the priests.

"I know," the Devil said. "But Leviticus also instructs not to cut your hair roundwise or shave your beard, yet you have done both."

The preacher's eyes narrowed, like an animal suspicious of being cornered. "For it is written, the Lord works in mysterious ways."

"That has been written, true; but never in the Holy Bible."

"Let he who is without stones cast the first sin."

"Do yourself a favor, Reverend. Stick to the high spots. For God so loved the world, yadda yadda yadda. Your audience is going to be drowsy from all this food and they might doze off."

"Pardon me?"

"Like what happened in Bible college recitals. You remember."

"The memory of the righteous is pearls before swine."

"That verse you were supposed to memorize. The one written on the back of your hand? That was a good one, the way you clasped your hands like you were praying. Until the instructor caught you."

"You're—"

"Yes. The one your precious Creator said was the master of this world."

The reverend didn't seem surprised. "I figured you'd catch up to me sooner or later. 'Blessed are those who are promiscuous because of righteousness.' You can ruin me now, strip me of the cloth, embarrass me in front of my congregation, but you'll never get back the four-hundred-and-twenty-seven souls I've delivered unto salvation in the meantime."

The Devil winced. "That many, huh?"

"I take pride in the Lord's work. That's why I've studied so hard."

"But you can do better." The Devil held out a deviled egg. "Eat this and I promise you won't misquote a single verse ever again. You'll have your own television ministry, a bestselling set of Bible study guides, a fundraising arm for Christmas charities. And need I bother mentioning that it's all tax-free?"

"Ah, but how much profit does a man make if he inherits the wind but sells his own soul?"

"You misquoted again, but the answer is roughly thirty-seven million and change."

Betty, who was wrapping foil over a few abandoned dishes, hollered, "Fifteen minutes until showtime, Reverend."

The Reverend Maynard Gray glanced at his watch. "No man knows the hour, except the Apostle Rolex."

"It's only an egg. Besides, it's already dead."

"Whosoever shall believeth in Him shall not parishioner, but have ever ready batteries."

"Then perhaps you'd like to try the tater salad?"

"Man does not live by bread alone, but by the biscuits of the Lord."

"Isn't that 'doughnuts'?"

"You need to crack the Good Book now and again, Mr. Devil."

"You're proud of the Lord's work. But wouldn't you be prouder if you got more credit for it?"

"Verily. Pride goeth before a fall."

"Actually, it's 'Pride goeth before destruction, and a haughty spirit goeth before a fall.'"

"For Jesus said, 'Get thee behind me, Satan.' You're cutting in line."

The Devil put the egg back on the tray. Maybe he should have sprinkled the paprika so that it looked like the face of the Virgin Mary. But Maynard was Protestant and would probably think it was Angelina Jolie, Hillary Clinton, or some other sign of the Apocalypse, and that would send him rocketing off in a spastic fervor that would probably win a few more converts.

"We'll meet again," the Devil said to the reverend. But it might take a while. No one knew the hour, except maybe God, and He was keeping it to Himself. For now, he'd had a bellyful of these goodly people.

The Devil walked past the tables where Betty Benson was busy squirreling away Ima Jean's tater salad, perhaps to do an in-depth analysis of its ingredients. He waved to Ray Ray McEelvy, who sat under a tree with his tie loosened, sipping loaded lemonade and playing with his cigarette lighter. The preacher had

taken the stage and was checking the microphone with a booming "Good evening, brothers and sisters! Come and gather around the supper table of God, for man does not live by bread alone, but by the doughnuts of the Lord."

A half dozen "hallelujahs" echoed in unison, while one person belched loudly.

The Devil glanced at the sky. "You win this round, Father."

The Voice boomed in response, cracking across the clouds like thunder, though the Devil was the only one who heard. *"See how wonderful are those I've created in my image? For I give them free will and still they choose the path of righteousness."*

The Devil paused. "Do I detect a little slice of pride, Father?"

No answer, except for the reverend's amplified misquotations in the background and the whisper of traffic on the distant highway.

The Devil grinned as he walked down the dusty dirt road under the Georgia sun. Armageddon wasn't so far off, and if that battle was lost, well, he'd still have the world, only with a lot fewer of these holier-than-thou types around. And not an angel food cake in sight.

That would make him mighty proud. Mighty proud, indeed.

Piecemaker

DON D'AMMASSA

It was supposed to be routine surveillance. The insurance company rep is a friend of mine and she hands me off a job from time to time even though the company refers most of its cases to the bigger investigators. It involved a questionable worker's comp account. You know, some bozo claims to be unable to work so he can collect, and meanwhile he's in his backyard building a patio. That sort of thing. It usually meant sitting in a tree or some other concealed spot with a camera for hours or, more often, days.

This time it was a little different. When I read the case summary, I glanced up at the rep. "Is this some kind of joke, Brenda?"

She looked uncomfortable. "We think there's some kind of hanky-panky going on." Brenda was the kind

of girl who said "hanky-panky." She also described her job as "rinky-dink."

"According to this"—I waved the single sheet of paper at her—"the subject lost an arm in an industrial accident and you tell me the company wants to cut off his benefits if he doesn't come back to work?"

Brenda's eyes skittered away from mine. "There have been some contradictory indications. He might not have lost the arm after all."

I was beginning to think this was a joke. "Color me stupid, Brenda, but couldn't you just send your adjustor by to visit and find out for sure?"

She sighed but still wouldn't look me in the face. "We did that. Mr. Parmenter was very cooperative, even took off his shirt to prove that the arm wasn't just strapped to his chest."

"Then why do you need me? Obviously the poor sod deserves whatever he's getting from you people."

"Ordinarily, I'd agree with you. But there have been reports . . ."

She summarized them. I thought she was crazy and said so, but the company was willing to pay me, so I didn't argue. But I planned to pad my expenses to punish them for wasting my time.

Edgar Parmenter was—or had been—a mechanic at Eblis Manufacturing up north in Managansett. He'd been servicing a rotary polishing machine when the

safety brake on a cart of brass fittings had failed. The cart sideswiped him and his right arm had been pulled into the gearbox and severed just below the shoulder. The arm itself had been crushed to pulp. He had declined to be fitted for a prosthetic arm and naturally he couldn't return to his former profession.

Sounded pretty cut and dried. The spanner in the works was that two deliverymen and three neighbors all insisted that Parmenter had two perfectly functional arms. Two of those neighbors had seen him doing laps in his swimming pool and one of the deliverymen insisted that Parmenter had shaken hands normally. Brenda's boss wasn't sure what was going on, but it sounded fishy to him and he'd suggested that it hadn't been Parmenter who'd been injured at all, but someone taking his place that day.

I drove by Parmenter's house as soon as I left Brenda's office. It was in an attractive, older neighborhood with big yards, lots of trees and shrubs. I spotted a few places where I could probably lurk in the shadows for a while, unless someone went for a walk or looked too closely, and decided I would have to use the van.

The van is specially equipped, of course. Zippy Electrical Contractors doesn't really exist, but it looks real enough. The rear and side windows are one-way glass and there are mountings for still and digital cameras as well as a comfortable seat. I hate using it. It gets stifling in the heat and even when the weather is cooperative, the hours of inaction are boring and demean-

ing. Try pissing into a plastic jug all day and you'll see what I mean.

Parmenter's house wasn't far from a convenience store and I figured I could park there for the better part of a day without attracting too much attention. There'd be a nice clear shot through the rear window. I still wasn't quite sure what I should be looking for. I mean, if Parmenter had a one-armed double, how was I going to be able to tell which was which? I was more than a little irritated with Brenda and her boss as well. After all, someone had lost an arm, so why did they care who cashed the check?

Morning found me in my Zippy uniform, parking as planned. I got a bite almost immediately. Parmenter—I recognized him from the file Brenda had provided—came outside and picked up the morning paper. His body was angled so I couldn't see clearly, but it did not appear that he was symmetrically equipped. I snapped a couple of photos just to be doing something, and to justify the larger than conscionable bill I planned to submit for this job.

He came out again about an hour later, arranged a sprinkler on his lawn, and turned it on. For just a second or two he gave me a great view and I took still pictures and a short digital recording. There was no doubt that his right sleeve was full, but it could have been a prosthesis of some sort, even though he hadn't officially been provided with one.

The morning dragged on into afternoon and eve-

ning with no further sight of my quarry. By the end of the following day, however, I had plenty of proof that the man living at 332 Starfish Lane had two working upper appendages. I had clear pictures of him reeling in a hose, carrying a trash can, even raking leaves. Unfortunately, I also had clear pictures that proved he was an amputee, including one in which he'd answered the door bare chested with a bandaged stump. I was quite sure now that there were two separate but very similar men living there. Parmenter was an orphan with no known relatives, but I supposed he might have run into his long-lost and unknown identical twin. But which of them had lost the arm?

I didn't dare use the van again. A couple of the neighbors had given it odd passing looks already. That was fine with me. I wasn't going to solve this problem from a distance. It seemed to me that the insurance company was going to have to pay someone regardless of whose arm had been torn off, but my own curiosity had been piqued and I planned to satisfy it on Brenda's dollar.

Friday morning I had a Mr. Messenger plaque on my car. I stopped in front of Parmenter's house and walked up to the front door carrying a package addressed to Prudence Tessworthy at 332 Starfish Lane. I rang the bell.

Parmenter showed no sign of recognition when he answered the door. I smiled professionally. "Is Prudence Tessworthy at home today?"

Parmenter, whose right shirtsleeve was rolled up and tied off just beneath his stump, frowned at me. "Never heard of her."

It was my turn to frown. "Are you sure? This is the address on the package."

"Positive." He smiled politely and started to close the door.

"Excuse me," I said hastily. "Do you know if anyone by that name lives in the neighborhood?"

"Sorry, no." He didn't sound sorry.

"Maybe someone else in your household would know. I'd really appreciate it if you'd ask."

"I live alone. Try Mrs. Richardson in the red house at the corner. She knows everyone's business." And the door closed.

Now that Parmenter had seen my face, my options were more circumscribed. What I really wanted was a picture of the two Parmenters together. Then it would be up to the insurance company to sort out which was which, and whether either of them deserved further compensation.

I drove away slowly, as though looking for another address, but I was actually examining Parmenter's property in more detail. The backyard was invisible, surrounded by eight-foot-tall stockade fencing, but I had already noted one vantage point. I drove to the office, changed the signs and plates on the van, and drove back masquerading as Northeastern Telephone Services.

I've climbed telephone poles in the past, and I'll probably do it again in the future, but I've never liked it. With a pouch of tools—including a camera with telescopic lens—slung around my waist, I ascended to just below the wires, where I could hopefully pass for a legitimate serviceman.

As expected, I had a great view of the rear of 332 Starfish Lane. Parmenter had a nice pool—now covered for the season—a small patio, a fancy grill and smoker, and a gazebo. Although it had been warm and calm all week, it suddenly turned frosty and windy and within an hour I was freezing my butt off. There was no sign of life at Parmenter's all morning and I descended stiffly to pee in my jug, eat some junk food, and decide whether I wanted to continue my vigil.

The afternoon was more positive in a negative sort of way. Parmenter decided to grill himself a steak.

He only had one arm when he started up the grill. I surreptitiously snapped pictures with which to impress upon Brenda my devotion to my job. He went back into the house and returned a few minutes later with a nice looking steak on a platter, condiments, and a can of beer. This time he had two arms. Okay, I told myself. They're both there. He's only cooking one steak, but it's big enough for two. If I could catch the pair of them splitting it and toasting each other with Budweisers, I could call it a day.

Parmenter sat and read a magazine while the steak sizzled on the grill. I could almost taste it from my

perch. After a while, he turned it over, then went back into the house, returning almost immediately with another beer. He still had two arms. He was still alone. And he stayed that way. Damned if he didn't eat the entire steak, then shut down the grill, police up his dirty dishes, and take everything inside.

I wondered if maybe his partner was a vegetarian.

He made one more brief appearance a few minutes later, apparently checking to make sure everything had been tidied away. This time he was sporting an empty sleeve and I snapped a picture or two reflexively.

I descended before the sun did, and I was not happy. I would turn in my photographs and the insurance company could refuse to pay the claim, but Parmenter almost certainly would appeal, and when his one-armed version showed up for the hearing, the outcome would be inevitable.

Back at the office, I printed out copies of all the pictures and arranged them neatly to present to Brenda. It was only then that I frowned, noticing an anomaly. In the last two shots, taken from the telephone pole, it was quite obvious that Parmenter's arm was missing. Except that this time it was the left arm.

Sometimes I use bad judgment. This was probably one of those times. I was watching Parmenter's house again from my own car parked just down the street when I saw his Ford back out of the driveway and head off

toward the interstate. Without consciously planning what I was going to do, I found myself walking briskly along the sidewalk. Pretending that I was doing nothing out of the ordinary, I rang the doorbell and waited. There was no answer. It only took a few seconds to circumvent the lock; if I surprised Parmenter's partner I'd have some explaining to do, but curiosity had overwhelmed my good sense.

The house felt empty. "Is anyone home? Your front door was wide open." I waited a few seconds and there was no answer to my lie, so I closed the door behind me. The unwisdom of this was apparent by then, but I was committed.

A quick search of the house—both floors—turned up no sign of Parmenter number two, or anyone else. Only one bedroom was in use, one set of clothes, one toothbrush in the bathroom, one dirty coffee cup in the sink. Every bit of physical evidence suggested this was the home of a rather boring bachelor.

Then I found the arm. It was lying at one end of the couch. I assumed that it was a prosthesis and reached down to pick it up, but recoiled slightly when I touched the wrist. It was much more lifelike than I had expected, even felt humanly warm to the touch. I started to draw my hand back—and the damned thing grabbed me!

I must have looked pretty stupid, dancing back and waving my arm wildly. Its fingers were interlocked with mine and even as my head told me that it was just some

sophisticated piece of metal and plastic, the rest of my
body insisted that this was a living creature. I fell over
an end table and banged my hip, then brought the dis-
embodied arm down against the floor hard enough to
break two of the fingers with audible snaps. It bounced
once and lay on the rug. I had just convinced myself
that it had been an automated electronic reflex when
the arm flipped over and began walking toward me on
the tips of its fingers.

If I had run for the front door, I would almost cer-
tainly have made it, but I was so shocked and revolted
that I retreated into the tiny kitchen at the back of the
house, a strategic error since there was no other exit
except the door to the basement. I grabbed a carving
knife from a rack beside the sink but the ambulant arm
stopped in the doorway. I'd have sworn it was crouch-
ing but how can an arm crouch? I resisted the tempta-
tion to warn it off. No ears, after all.

Then I heard a car drive up. Parmenter was back.

I replaced the carving knife hastily and opened the
basement door. The steps were clean and straight and
barely creaked as I descended. I heard the door from
the garage open just as I reached the bottom. Footsteps
sounded above my head.

It was gloomy down there, lit only by narrow slits of
daylight through windows set in the foundation. There
was a worktable right in front of me and a washer-
dryer combination and furnace. The bulk of the base-
ment was concealed by cheap paneling. I found a door,

not locked, and slipped inside. Fluorescent lights hung from the ceiling, two of them illuminated, enough to give me a good look at my surroundings.

My stomach clenched.

There were four glass-fronted freezer cases, two on my left, two on my right, and a long, narrow table in the center of the room. The freezers were the kind you see in grocery stores except that these didn't contain pizzas and frozen peas and ice cream. One was filled with arms, one with legs, one had four torsos lying flat on racks, and the last contained about a dozen heads. The heads all looked exactly alike and they were all Edgar Parmenter.

I'm not sure how long I stood there, almost as frozen as the contents of the freezers, before the door opened behind me.

"Oh, dear. You shouldn't have come down here, my dear sir."

I turned slowly. Edgar Parmenter stood in the doorway and he was holding a handgun in his left hand. His right arm hung at his side, two of the fingers obviously broken.

"What the hell is all this?" My voice was a quavering croak.

Parmenter seemed perfectly relaxed. "None of your business, actually. You should have picked another house to burglarize." He frowned. "That was you posing as the messenger the other day, wasn't it? I thought there was something odd about you."

I didn't correct him, hoping he'd underestimate me. "You're right. Look, whatever you're doing is no skin off my nose. I'll just get out of your way." I took a step forward and the handgun came up smartly.

"I think not. Please walk to the other end of the room, turn and place both hands on the wall while I think about this."

I did as I was told and for a few minutes we were both lost in thought. Parmenter found himself first. "You've chosen a very awkward time to intrude in my affairs. I have an appointment that I really can't skip. Turn around please."

I thought he might shoot me right there and then, but he had other plans. "Be so kind as to take one of those torsos out and place it on the table for me."

Although I was still convinced that these were artificial body parts, I flinched when I touched the torso. It wasn't as cold as I expected, more like a refrigerator than a freezer, and not particularly heavy. But it did feel like human flesh and I couldn't completely suppress my revulsion.

"Now a pair each of arms and legs. And make sure you get a left and a right for both sets."

Parmenter then directed me to insert each severed limb into the appropriate place on the torso. I gaped at him in astonishment, but when I tried I found that the truncated bones sort of locked into place and when they did so, flaps of skin folded over to conceal the seams.

"And finally a head. Any one will do."

This was the worst part of all. The head was so life-like that I almost dropped it. It also fit into a socket and snapped into place. The result was a perfect imitation of a dead human body. But it wasn't human. And it wasn't dead. The eyes popped open almost as soon as the head was attached.

"Damn, it's cold!" It was Parmenter who spoke, but not the Parmenter who held the gun. The figure I'd assembled on the table sat up abruptly and looked around. "What's going on?"

The first Parmenter gestured toward me with his weapon. "I have a problem."

The second gave me a quick look. "So I do. What am I going to do about it?"

The first sighed. "That's up to me. I have to meet with my case manager this afternoon and I don't have time to deal with this, so I'm going to have to do it for me."

The new Parmenter slid down off the table. "Why do I always have to solve the problems? Why can't I think of something for a change?" There was a cabinet under the table from which the naked Parmenter took out a set of clothes and began dressing.

"I do my part. I all do. Just take him someplace and kill him in an hour or so. I'll have a perfect alibi."

"If I say so."

Once the second Parmenter was dressed, the gun went from one to the other, but remained pointed at me. "If I take the car, how do I take him anywhere?"

"I'll call a cab. But be careful that no one sees the car. They'll trace it back here."

The first Parmenter vanished upstairs and the second eyed me dourly. He was still shaking with the cold, but not as much as before. "Look," I said. "Why not let me go? I won't say anything. No one would believe me and I'd have to admit that I was trying to rob the place."

"I'm afraid I can't take that chance. Upstairs now, and slowly. I'd rather not make a mess down here."

The first Parmenter threw me a set of car keys when we reached the top of the stairs. "I'll see me when I get back. Be careful."

I had to cooperate, play for time, watch for a chance to take him by surprise, so I climbed behind the wheel of Parmenter's station wagon while he took the passenger seat. "Where to?"

"Take Route 13 north."

Neither of us said much for the next twenty minutes. Parmenter turned on the radio and it was Patsy Cline singing "I Fall to Pieces," which I thought appropriate. We headed north out of Providence and then took the exit for Managansett. Parmenter directed me onto a back road that bypassed the town center and looped out toward the reservoir at the far end of town. The road didn't lead to much of anyplace else and we saw no traffic at all toward the end of the trip. Following instructions, I pulled over into a lightly wooded area and stopped.

"Get out."

I let my shoulders slump and dropped my chin, trying to project resignation as I opened the door. Parmenter was already turning to do the same when I slammed my right elbow back hard, taking him right under the chin.

I had hoped to knock him out. The result was not quite that. His head literally popped out of its socket, struck the roof of the car, and bounced into the backseat. I was too relieved to be shocked, or perhaps I was just inured to shock, but I expected that to end the struggle. Unfortunately, now that Parmenter's body—this body—was warm, it apparently no longer needed the head to function. But it did need the eyes to see with. Two bullets smashed through the windshield and a third through the roof.

I opened the door and half fell, half slid out onto the ground. Two more shots sounded and I made my way on all fours into the shelter of a small copse of trees. When I looked back I saw a rather foreshortened version of Parmenter. He had managed to get out of the car and was now groping around in the backseat, presumably searching for his head. I suppressed a hysterical laugh and tried to assess my options.

I could run, of course, but if I tried the road, Parmenter could chase me down in the car. I hadn't had the foresight to take the keys out of the ignition. Assuming he got himself reassembled, that is. The alternative was to hide until he gave up and went away. But Parmenter

seemed to be having a great deal of difficulty reclaiming his head, and I decided to go on the offensive.

I stood up and sprinted toward the car.

Parmenter was bigger than me, even without his head, but an organized minority can always overcome a disorganized majority. I knocked him to the ground with my initial charge and then kept kicking and punching until his body stopped trying to get up. Then I knelt on his back and took one arm in both hands. Since the head had disengaged so easily, I figured, maybe the limbs would as well. I exerted pressure and torque and there was a slight pop. Parmenter was one armed again.

The other three limbs were even easier now that I had the hang of it.

I bundled the body parts into the trunk and drove back to Providence, intending to go to the police until I realized how my story would sound. An examination would certainly prove that Parmenter was not human, but if I drove up to a police station with what appeared to be a disassembled human body, I'd be behind bars really fast. I finally decided to park the car at Parmenter's house and place an anonymous call to the police. They'd conduct a thorough search, find the basement, and what happened after that was anyone's guess.

But it didn't quite work out that way. When I arrived, I decided to take one last look, still not quite convinced that this wasn't all some elaborate hallucination. As soon as I turned the key, the trunk popped

open, forced from within. Two arms tumbled out onto the ground and one snagged my pants cuff and held on until I kicked it with the other foot. I backed away, decided discretion was the better part, and went to retrieve my own car. I never called the cops.

There's not much more to tell. I delivered the photographs to Brenda, along with an invoice, but did not tell her what else I'd discovered. She called me back a few days later to say that Parmenter had vanished, his house had burned to the ground, and the company had no place to send its checks.

That was almost a year ago and no one has seen Parmenter since. But over the course of the last few weeks, I've been feeling increasingly uneasy. Private detectives often develop a kind of sixth sense and I was sure I was being watched. I spent a lot of time looking into my rearview mirror, installed a security camera at my house, and paid attention to my surroundings when I walked on the street, but I never spotted anything out of the ordinary.

Until this morning. In among today's various bills and junk mail was a small package with no return address. Curious, I found a knife and cut through the tape. Inside was a small, rather fancy cardboard box. I opened it and discovered that it contained a single, ordinary looking replica of a human eye.

That was startling enough in itself, but then the most unexpected thing happened.

It winked at me.

Good Breeding

Lucien Soulban

This was the face of Armageddon, the calculated end of the world: Towering piles of human bodies strewn about in enormous, crushing heaps; corpses hung from skeins of veins suspended between gutted skyscrapers; cadavers entombed inside burnt-out husks of vehicles on melted freeways.

Yet for some, the gaiety carried a depressing undertone. And not for the reasons most people expected.

A long, deep sigh—smelling vaguely of rotted fish—escaped from Ka'thulu the Gorger. The ring of tentacles around his puckered, alien mouth fluttered briefly, like so many party favors, before growing still.

"What's the matter?" Shebboth asked. The antennae atop his carapace-covered head twitched, more this way than that.

"They're all gone." Ka'thulu poked the corpses in

the street with an uprooted lamppost for emphasis. Nothing stirred in the way that dead bodies are best at.

"But we won, right?" Shebboth asked. "That's what He-Who-Really-Shouldn't-Be-Named said."

"Who? Hastur?"

A flash and a pop filled the air, and a handful of winged Byakhee appeared; a dash of bird, a dab of insect, and a pinch of bat thrown in as though Hastur made them during a pique of indecision. The creatures searched for whoever dared utter their master's name, then (puzzled) they vanished.

"You shouldn't say *His* name."

"Who, Hastur?"

Byakhee appeared again, this time eyeing the two great giants in displeasure. They disappeared once more.

"Yes!" Shebboth hissed. "He doesn't like it when—"

"You say Hastur?"

Byakhee appeared and promptly vanished.

"Stop it, will you?!"

"Yeah, yeah . . . so old Nameless said that, huh?" Gorger asked. He picked up a blackened SUV between two spikelike fingers and studied the corpses inside. Head shaking, regret, perhaps, he tossed it away. The crash drew up a few faces from the rubble, sharp-toothed beasts studying them with the curiosity of startled groundhogs; then their fish eyes went glassy with disinterest and their heads popped back down. "And what did we win?"

"The war!"

"Some war."

"Wasn't it, though? We set the trap, then bam!"

"Bam? After eons, waiting 'For the Stars to Align'?" he asked.

"That's what I said . . . bam!"

"Meanwhile, there we sat, bored, playing Pin-the-Insanity-on-the-Cultists."

"It's tradition. First we create a mythology. Then, bam!"

"Will you stop saying 'bam!' There was no bam. There wasn't even a mythos until I groomed Lovecraft. And then he gets my name wrong. It's Ka'thulu, not Cthulhu."

"I thought it was Cuthulu," Shebboth said, shrugging.

"So, of course, Cthulhu gets called up to the big office and Cthulhu gets promoted to Elder status while I'm stuck in middle management."

"What about Abdul Alhazred? Didn't he spread your message?"

"The Mad Arab? Sure, lunatics make for fantastic prophets and are great at parties but—I think one of his screams is still lodged in my teeth. No, wait," he said, picking at something among the rows of jagged thorns lining his mouth. "It's just a piece of hope."

"And it wasn't only waiting," Shebboth offered, oblivious in the way of children and car accidents. "We started cults—"

"You mean the idiots who kept invoking us too early. Learn to read an astrolabe! It's 'When the stars are right,' not 'When the stars are right now.' And what in the name of He-Who-Prefers-You-Don't-Name-Him is Cthulhu Fhtagn. It's Ka'thulu Fh'tagn! Fh'tagn!"

"Fh'tagn?"

"Mom's maiden name. Thought she'd appreciate it."

"Oh, very sweet. I wish I knew my mom."

"That's what you get for bursting out of her chest at birth."

"The other broodlings dared me to. Oh . . . didn't we also inspire messiahs—?"

"And who was responsible for that hippie with the two stone tablets?"

"Well, um—"

"Who?"

"That was my fault," Shebboth admitted, raising his claw.

"Right. So instead of drowning all those slaves, you closed the Red Sea late and killed our worshippers. And their screaming chariots of madness. I loved those things. They could babble for hours. And how you missed with the boils and the frogs—"

"I have a fear of success—"

"Which created one religion—"

"—and Mi-Go. They scare me, too. Are they crustaceans or are they fungi?"

"—and then another."

"I mean, make up your collective minds, right? But those humans, we really got 'em good."

"After waiting for the stars to align like a chorus line of the legless. Then it's over in a fortnight. Even the dinosaurs had more fight in them—the way those iguanodons marshaled their forces," he said wistfully. "Pretty savage for a bunch of leaf-eating philosophers."

Shebboth sat down, the building groaning as he pressed his back against it. "Yeah . . . humans were kinda lame. Y'know, I think they actually killed more of each other in the end. I mean, what were those things they kept throwing at us?"

"Cats?"

"No."

"Children?"

"No."

"Nuclear bombs?"

"Them! I barely killed a thousand, but those bombs killed way more. Cthulhu is still brooding over it."

"He should be. All this talk about 'The Great Day' and what does he do? Trips on the shores of Europe and drowns France in a tidal wave. Schmuck."

"My scales are starting to shed from that radiation stuff. Look," he said, opening the mucous flap in his chest. His nostrils stood revealed and wept the salty tears of defiled virgins. "I think I'm bleeding."

"You're wrong."

"I'm not bleeding?"

"You don't think."

"Well. Look at what happened to Shub-Niggurath with all that radiation," he whispered with a knowing nod.

"She always looked like that."

"She?! I've been calling her 'sir' all these eons."

"Yeah. It was good for a laugh. Why do you think she's been trying to kill you since forever?"

"I blamed it on bad hygiene. But when it comes to thinking, I leave that to our great generals."

"And now that we've killed everyone, what's left?" Gorger asked, pushing the rubble of civilization around with his feet. "Ask your generals what're we supposed to do now that no humans are left? We should have saved some for later."

Gorger spent the afternoon skipping cars across the Atlantic. Underfoot, Deep Ones with fish heads ran about on webbed feet, chasing brethren wearing human skins. But the charm died fast, and Gorger stepped on a few to the cheering delight of the others.

Bored again, he wandered away from the city, into the countryside, past fields of humans petrified into still-burning charcoal. Finally, when the others had finished drinking the sun and darkness fell upon the planets, Gorger watched the ruins of a small town. It was a few hours into his contemplation that Shebboth found him.

"What?" Gorger asked, not bothering to look up.

"I; uh. I got you a gift."

"What sort of gift?" he asked, disinterested in the conversation already.

"I wasn't gonna share it with anyone, but seeing how you're my best friend—"

"We're not friends."

"—beat me less often than the others, I thought you should have them."

"Them?"

Shebboth lifted his plated rib. From beneath, he pulled out a city bus covered in black ooze. "Ta-dah!" he said with a chirp that shattered the town's last windows.

"Ta-dah what?" Gorger asked, staring at the mucus-covered bus.

"Oh, sorry," he said. He licked the windows with his massive gray tongue and presented it again.

"Still not getting it."

"Well," Shebboth said, shaking the bus. "They're in there."

"Humans?"

"Found some hiding and caught 'em," Shebboth said, shaking the bus some more.

Gorger snatched the vehicle from Shebboth and peered inside. "They're not moving."

"Maybe they're scared? Or maybe they're playing dead?"

"Or maybe you forgot to punch holes in the lid and they're not playing," Gorger said.

"Oh, no," Shebboth replied. "And I collected them carefully even though I squished a—"

"Squished?"

"—ate a few."

"Yeah," Gorger said, brightening slowly. "But if you found some, maybe we missed more."

"But Cthulhu said we won . . . in his speech."

"Cthulhu wrote a speech?"

"Well, Yog-Sothoth helped. The speech kinda rambled for a bit before the end when a thousand Mi-Go spontaneously burst into flames, but we got the point."

"Right. Well, this makes things easier."

"For what?"

"To find more humans."

"And eat them?"

"Nope. Raise them. And maybe, just maybe, start over."

The sky was black with snow. More buildings fell as the great beasts took to scratching their backs, and more laid about, staring up at the dark heavens and asking, "How crazy do you think *that* cloud is?"

Gorger and Shebboth, however, set about rebuilding humanity. And for that, they needed more humans. They peered inside basements and sent Gorger's tentacles probing, searching through corridors and rooms. After a week, all they had for their efforts were an army

of mannequins that Shebboth called "keepers." Why they earned that distinction, Gorger thought it best not to ask. The only thing that trumped insanity was stupidity, and Shebboth's deck was well stacked in that regard.

As Gorger searched, his arm shoulder deep inside an underground garage, a swath of strange lights fell across him, touching his gray skin like spiderwebs soaked in tar. He looked up. Sometimes a rainbow and sometimes a cloud of indescribable colors shifted and scintillated. Well, indescribable to humans, but to Gorger they were rather kitschy.

"What?" Gorger asked.

"! . ! ?" the Color-from-out-of-Space responded.

"Who says we're looking for humans?" Gorger replied, straightening.

".! . . ."

"He did, did he?" Gorger asked, looking for a strangely absent Shebboth. "And if we are?"

". . ."

"You kept some humans? Why?"

". . . , . . ."

"No, I didn't know they made good hair curlers. But, you don't have— Never mind. You have humans—?"

"!"

"Hair curlers. My mistake. What do you want for them?"

", . . !?"

"Real hair . . . riiiight," Gorger said. "Show me your humans first."

The cloud shivered and stretched, parts of it vanishing from different spectrums. A gap formed, an orifice in the marrow of the universe; a lightless place where colors screamed. From it tumbled a shivering human. He was white-haired despite his youth and well-pruned from the green gel covering his naked body; he shuddered and heaved, before vomiting a stream of green gunk.

And then he began shrieking. Not in any way that suggested sanity, but in that moment of cognitive flight when the near-mad realize that "race car" spelled backward is "race car."

Gorger watched the human for a few seconds, and then glanced at the Color-from-out-of-Space. "Any that aren't lunatics?" he asked.

"! ! !"

"Yes, well, I suppose that would drive someone insane. So all of them? Stark raving?"

" , , . ?"

"Fine," Gorger sighed. "I guess they'll have to do."

If any of the Elder Ones had noticed the Color-from-out-of-Space floating around with a dozen wigs in orbit, none commented.

Gorger, in Shebboth's company, crouched inside a domed stadium . . . their new human colony with a dozen people in all—each of them a chorus of dissonant screams and moans, each very much insane

in ways that went beyond such clever palindromes as "race car" and "pickle."

"I like it," Shebboth said. "Think we could charge for a concert?"

Gorger grunted noncommittally and watched as the humans flailed about on the Astroturf and tore at their hair and faces. Some were still trying to claw out their eyes, but Gorger had anticipated that problem. That's why they all wore giant foam fingers uncovered in the stadium store, duct-taped at the wrists. That, perhaps, was the hardest skill to master, and one Gorger eventually had to entrust to the smaller arms lining his thorax.

"What do we feed them?" Gorger wondered aloud as he watched them.

"The dreams of the slaughtered?" Shebboth suggested.

"No."

"The souls of mountains?"

"No!"

"Other humans?"

Gorger eyed Shebboth. "In all the eons we spent waiting to shatter the veils, you didn't spend much time studying them, did you?"

"I was . . . busy."

"And suddenly Pompeii makes sense."

"I said I'm sorry!"

"And just when we'd gotten them to the brain-insemination stage," Gorger said. "Look, to breed

humans, you need to understand them better. Humans eat meat—"

"Oh! Feed 'em Mi-Go."

"—and plants—"

"Mi-Go are both meat and plants."

"—and fish."

"Mi-Go are also—"

Gorger sighed deliberately loud enough to interrupt him. "Mi-Go are not the universe's answer to the buffet. But we might as well try something. Hastur."

Before Shebboth could protest, five Byakhee appeared, flapping their batlike wings and shrieking their insect heads off. That sent the humans into greater despair, as they pointed their giant foam fingers at the winged servitors of Hastu—He-Who-Should-Probably-Stop-Being-Named. In turn, the Byakhee noticed the humans and tried to sweep down upon them.

Gorger lashed out, grabbing Byakhee and crushing them. The winged creatures fell, pulped, while the humans scampered away.

"Lesson one, Shebboth. Let starvation take its course," Gorger said.

"So, lesson two. Byakhee tartar is a no," Gorger said. The humans had degraded, their diet of profane meat warping their bodies. For some, their spines were twisted 180 degrees so that they stared down the backs

of their legs. For others, they grew webbing between their loins, or their arms and torso, or each other. Flesh flaps covered their eyes and three died when their skin suffocated them. A couple more perished when Shebboth discovered that "mouth-to-mouth resuscitation" and "inhale" were in fact two different sentiments.

"I found more humans for the colony," Shebboth offered.

"Alive?"

"Punched the holes in the bus myself."

"How many?"

"Oh, lots of holes."

"How. Many. Humans."

"Twelve. This time we should feed them the flesh of cooked cows. I found some of those, too."

"Did you," Gorger asked, suspicion lacing his voice. "How convenient."

"Isn't it," Shebboth said, chuckling nervously. "I'll go get 'em."

"Wait," Gorger said. "How'd you suddenly start figuring things out?"

"I don't know," he replied, his chameleon eyes darting left, right, behind . . . anywhere Gorger wasn't. "Evolutionary leap? Maybe I ate someone smarter."

"A retarded lobster says what?"

"What?"

"You didn't eat someone smarter!" Gorger snapped. "Who's helping you?"

"Nobody!"

"Who?"

"Nobody important!"

"Who?"

"Nobody bad . . . okay . . . Nyarlathotep."

"The shape-shifter?!"

"Yeah."

"The Crawling Chaos?"

"I think he's upright these days."

"The Charmer and Deceiver?"

"Well, you can't believe everything his exes say," he replied defensively.

"Shebboth! The colony is a secret!"

"He tricked it out of me," he pleaded.

"Tricked you how?"

"Well he asked if I'd seen any humans around and I said no."

"Shebboth!"

"I said yes. But he was very cunning."

Gorger hesitated and thought about it a moment. "So he has humans and a few cows, does he? What's the exchange?"

At that, Shebboth paused with an expression that suggested he had a thought, and that in coming to it, it was a terribly painful experience. "Y'know, he didn't say. Maybe he did it out of the kindness of his heart."

"He doesn't have a heart."

"Sure he does, I saw it."

"His *own* heart?"

"Oh! I see what you're getting at. Then, no."

"I'm not agreeing to any terms with Nyarlathotep, not without seeing *all* his hands on the table."

"What do I tell him?"

"That you had no right to strike a bargain with him, and certainly not on my behalf. Look, Shebboth, this may be our last chance to find humans. And nobody knows more about them than Nyarlathotep."

"So I say what now?"

Gorger sighed. "Tell him to deal with me."

"Right. And what about the retarded lobster?"

"We'll kill it later. Promise."

Nyarlathotep was a dashing figure—human in appearance, his skin a dark Egyptian bronze. A pinch of a beard, shaven with the precision of a sharp word, black hair greased back and eyes that reflected all gilt of snake. He wore a black suit and sat in the owner's box so that he might stare straight into Gorger's abyssal deep eyes. A scarab pin adorned the lapel of his jacket. It was upside down, because that's how he rolled.

"Something to drink?" Gorger offered. The stadium seats groaned under his bulk as he leaned to speak into the owner's box.

"Please," Nyarlathotep replied, smiling.

"Hastur," Gorger said casually. A squadron of two dozen Byakhee appeared, looking angry. They dive-bombed Gorger, spitting and hissing at him. War had

been declared, but as in all such things, the Byakhee had been partying the night prior and were too drunk to send the declaration in time. Gorger naturally took the ambush in stride, "naturally" being relative here. He snatched one Byakhee from the air and twisted its head off. The black ichor poured out of its neck spout into a plastic cup that Gorger's lower hand carried. Shebboth caught the tossed carcass and devoured it with lip-smacking greed.

The other Byakhee screeched in panic and abandoned the battle; they vanished. Nyarlathotep accepted the cup and sipped the drink graciously before grinning at Gorger.

"They don't seem to like you."

"A misunderstanding," Gorger replied. "They misunderstood their chances."

"Ah. In that case, shall we dispense with the usual verbal parry and thrust and get to business?"

"You have humans."

"Yes."

"And cows."

"And assorted other animals that proved themselves."

"Proved?"

"As lovers. Meals. Both, really."

"How?"

"Well, for starters, approach from the rear least you spook—"

"No, no. *Why* did you hide them?"

Nyarlathotep nodded in sudden understanding. "Forethought." He leaned forward, in confidence. "Just between the two of us?" Nyarlathotep said.

"Uh-huh," Shebboth responded, leaning forward as well. Gorger nudged him back and motioned for his guest to continue.

"I knew this would happen," Nyarlathotep said. "Maybe the other Ancients can get away with an air of otherworldly indifference, but the rest of us defined ourselves by humanity's conquest."

Gorger straightened up in shocked understanding. "Of course. You cannot hate or want something without it characterizing you. And that when humans were gone?"

"Our reason for being vanished with them."

They were quiet a moment, contemplating the significance of this.

"That means—" Gorger whispered.

"One good turn deserves a human?" Shebboth offered.

"No."

"What is the sound of one human clapping?"

"No."

"If a human falls in the forest—"

"No!" Gorger shouted. "It means we're tainted."

"Well, I knew that," Shebboth said. "In fact, that's what Azathoth told me. "Do," he said. "Do, rey, rey fa sol ti ti la."

"And what a wasted initiative that was," Nyarla-

thotep remarked. "Whose bright idea was it to use Julie Andrews to spread Azathoth's musical insanity?"

They both glanced at Shebboth.

"Hey!" he complained. " 'The Hills are Alive,' was a great song until they changed the lyrics."

"So what did Azathoth say?" Gorger asked.

"The higher-ups worry that humanity has influenced us," Nyarlathotep responded. "So, we found a new world, teeming with life. We're going there to—"

"Start over?" Gorger said with a colossal groan that shook the stadium's rafters.

"Well, the first part's not so bad," Shebboth offered. "All the planning was fun. Besides, this time they promised it'd be different."

"They always say that," Nyarlathotep replied. "But when the slaughter comes, we lose control."

"Then it's done," Gorger said, his mouth tentacles slumping. "We've wasted an eternity here and we're looking at the same ahead of us. So much for the human colony."

"Maybe not," Nyarlathotep said. "I have to go because the others no longer trust me. They think I've been among men too long—this is the only way to regain their confidence. But you can stay behind."

"And raise your humans?" Gorger leaned forward with renewed interest.

"Yes! Help my worshippers survive and thrive until the sun shines again."

"Then what?" Gorger asked.

"Then genocide . . . on a small scale," Nyarlathotep replied. "The occasional city, nothing extravagant. But this time, no Cthulhu to flood Europe with his three left feet, or Color-from-out-of-Space trying to dazzle all those blind children at the orphanage."

"They did seem perplexed," Shebboth said.

Gorger exchanged glances with Shebboth and then nodded. "So how many humans we talking about?"

Nyarlathotep smiled deeply.

They could not be seen towering above the human enclave. The ring of glacier-topped peaks and frozen wilderness surrounded the Edenlike jungle below them with its self-contained warmth. Upon closer inspection, the mountains proved to be colossal edifices of staggering height, irregular in proportions and alien in the organic spirals carved into the icy rock. That Nyarlathotep had hidden humans in the Mountains of Madness was, in fact, a credit to his twisted genius. And now that the Great Old Ones had departed with the Lesser-but-Still-Rather-Swell-Ones in tow, Gorger and Shebboth were the remaining greatest of the mythos.

"So," Shebboth said. "What should we do with them?"

"This place should suffice until they become too many. Then," he said, "we cast them to the four corners to populate the—"

A scream followed and Gorger watched as a human went flying over the mountains toward the horizon. He grabbed Shebboth's arm before he could lob another. "Figure of speech," he said quickly.

"Oh," Shebboth said. "My bad."

"We have to be careful now," Gorger replied. "As much as they're Nyarlathotep worshippers, they're still only human. They're still susceptible to insanity and disease and the elements. We leave them to fornicate and grow. And we make sure nothing kills them off."

"So we can't eat 'em."

"No," Gorger said. "That's part of *keeping them alive.*"

"Oh."

"Still, I think this calls for a toast? To our new enterprise?"

"Sure," Shebboth said.

"And I know just the drink . . . Hastur."

The Byakhee appeared, but this time by the thousands. They filled the sky, black against pitch. They rocketed for Gorger and Shebboth, slamming into their faces, their bodies. It didn't hurt so much as surprise the pair.

Gorger swept his arms through the cloud, blindly batting them away by the dozens, but it wasn't until the humans screamed that he realized the ruse. Another panicked sweep of his arms scattered the swarm enough to reveal the carnage below.

The Byakhee, outnumbering them, tore at mortal and animal alike; two or three pulling them apart, slicing through muscle and bone, devouring flesh, carrying them high into the air and dropping them.

"No, no, NO!" Gorger screamed, but that only drove the revenge-starved Byakhee into greater frenzy. Gorger tried stopping them, crushing swarmed humans and Byakhee alike.

"Is this part of the toast?!" Shebboth asked, clapping his claws together.

"No!" shouted Gorger, but it was too late. He killed Byakhee by the score, but the only humans that remained were human remains. The trees dripped with their blood, the ground was littered with their body parts. The Byakhee simply vanished, cackling madly at the mayhem.

Gorger collapsed against the mountain face, unmindful of the bloody litter around him.

"Wow," Shebboth said, examining the surrounding destruction. "This all looks so familiar, huh?"

"Shut up," Gorger said. He sat there a few moments before finally standing and wiping the gore from himself. He could no longer look at the red-glazed jungle.

"What now?" Shebboth asked.

"We join the others at the new world," he said, casting a forlorn last look back at the barren Earth. "This time, we'll do it right," he said to himself, nodding. "This time it'll be different."

"That's the spirit!" Shebboth cheered, patting his friend on the back. Without another word, both of them vanished in a twinkling of the darkness they called home. To face another eon. And dwell on all the might have beens.

Tails

JOHN R. LITTLE

Marie was late getting home from work, but she had a good reason. I could tell as soon as she climbed out of her car.

It's not that I snoop on my wife or anything, but I just happened to be looking out the big bay window in the living room when her tan Honda Civic pulled into the driveway.

She yawned briefly, then clamped her mouth shut as she slammed the door and pushed the button on her keyless remote. I could hear the car's faint beep drift through the window.

She smiled and waved at me, her long blond hair flowing behind her in the wind. For about the millionth time, I thanked the gods that had brought us together a dozen years earlier.

Of course, smiles are deceiving, so although it was

nice to see, that's not what told me she was in a good mood.

It was her tail pointing up to the sky that gave her away. It was doing some serious wagging.

I love Marie's tail. It's a beautiful blond color, exactly matching her hair. She keeps it immaculately groomed, even though that costs her a lunch hour every couple of weeks when she heads to the groomer.

My tail, on the other hand, is pathetic. I can't remember the last time I had the thing trimmed, let alone a complete grooming.

When Marie came through the front door, I smiled and gave her a long hug and kiss. I reached behind her and loosely grasped the base of her tail. The feel of it swishing faster and faster was so damned erotic.

Her tail was average length, about two feet, but wonderfully thick—my fingers barely reached around it. My own tail started to sway slowly as I rubbed hers.

"What's the good news?" I asked when we finally broke apart.

She laughed and glanced behind her. "Can't much hide it, can I?"

My tail was swaying in time with hers now. I was always so happy to have my wife home. She worked in downtown Detroit, twenty miles away, making tons of money investing other people's cash, while I looked for marketing opportunities on the Internet. Most days, my wagger dragged pretty low until I got a good look at her coming through the front door.

"Let's get a glass of wine," she suggested.

I poured as we slid into a couple of old rattan kitchen chairs, carefully guiding ourselves through the wooden slots.

Thwack, thwack, thwack.

I laughed, knowing she was dying to tell me what was up. She wouldn't be able to stop swinging until she told me.

"I got a promotion!" she finally said. It looked like she wanted to leap out of the chair, but she held back at the last minute, not wanting to injure herself. "Vice president of investment banking!"

"That's amazing! I'm so proud of you!"

We clinked glasses while I secretly wondered what investment banking might be. I had absolutely no idea what Marie really did from nine to five, but it was easy to see she was ecstatic.

Thwack, thwack, thwack.

The wine had been sitting in the fridge for a week or more, a bottle partially drunk in front of the latest *Survivor* season premiere. I wondered if we had more wine in the basement. It seemed like we might want to be doing a lot of celebrating.

Thwack, thwack.

I was momentarily surprised that it was *my* tail banging the chair this time. Not as rapidly as Marie's, but at least she could tell I was happy for her. She smiled broadly when she heard the sound, and my heart melted as it always did, which just made my tail swing a bit faster.

We caught up on the rest of the day's news. My side was pretty boring. The letter carrier dropped off a couple of books I had ordered, I picked up a precooked ham to warm up for dinner, and the cat had puked on the living room rug.

I didn't much want to concentrate on the cat mess, so I told Marie about a homeless guy who was wandering the street earlier in the day. "You wouldn't have believed how terrible he looked. Tail just hanging straight down from his tail-hole, and I could see bugs crawling all over it. I thought *I* was bad about getting to the groomer, but maybe it takes somebody like that to really show you how lucky we are." I sipped my wine and added, "No life in him at all. Limp as a dead snake."

Marie nodded. I knew she didn't really care about things like that.

She told me more about the meeting where she got her promotion.

"I hadn't expected anything at all like this," she said. "Robby called me in after lunch, and I'm sure he knew I was worried. I was just swaying back and forth restlessly. He must have enjoyed watching me."

Robby was the president of the investment company. I couldn't remember his last name. I'd only met him once and wasn't impressed.

"He just stretched things out, didn't tell me what we were meeting about for almost ten minutes. Yapping about this and that. He even made me stand the

whole time. I'm sure he was just enjoying watching my reaction. At least I thought so, at first, but . . ."

I looked at her. "But?"

She shook her head. "He was just making a point."

Now I was more puzzled than ever. He sounded like an asshole to me, making her show her emotions in front of him.

"How did you do?"

"Damned tail just wouldn't stay still. Slow circles, but sometimes it tried to hide between my legs. I was worried sick, thinking maybe he was going to fire me or something. There was that series of layoffs a couple months ago. Remember I told you about that?"

My tail drooped and dragged back and forth above the linoleum as I tried to think back. Did she tell me something about that?

"Don't worry," she said, letting me off the hook. "Like I said, he was just trying to make a point."

"I still don't understand," I said.

"My new job . . . so much of it involves talking to *very* senior investors. Chief financial officers of Fortune 500 companies, mostly." She gulped down her wine and went to the fridge to pour some more.

No thwacking anymore.

"What's wrong?"

"Well, it's just that the deals are so much bigger than I'm used to. If I'm talking to a prospective customer, and I know I've got him hooked, I can't have my tail lifting up and pointing up at the ceiling. The

customer would know how excited I was." She shook her head. "The sale would be killed."

I was confused. "But that's just the way the world works."

Marie reached out her hand and touched mine. "I'll have to have it amputated."

I couldn't believe what I was hearing. Her beautiful blond tail cut off? What? How could she even think of that for one second?

"Everyone in a senior position does it these days. When's the last time you saw a press conference by any government official with a tail?"

"But that's different. They're always lying to us, and they don't want us to know."

"Well, yes. I won't be lying to anyone, but the principle is the same. I can't do the job if my tail is always giving my thoughts away."

I never did tell her I approved, and neither did my tail, but of course she did it anyway. I tried to support her as best I could. After all, I loved her more than anything.

We had the stub of her tail cauterized. Now, when I want to see it, I just have to go to the living room; Marie's tail is mounted above the fireplace.

When she comes home now, I can't tell how she feels. She climbs out of her Civic and smiles, but I don't know if it's real or an act for my benefit.

She never mentions that my tail rarely swings for her when she comes through the front door.

I can't help it. She just doesn't look human anymore.

Dog Tired
(of the Drama!)

L. A. BANKS

Generally when Lola came into the bar for a good rare steak and a beer, she tuned out of the human conversation going on around her. But even without supersensitive wolf hearing, the loud table of older women having a divorce party nearby was impossible to ignore.

"Men are such dogs, girl!" a heavily made up woman exclaimed to a thunderous round of agreement from her friends, and then she tipped her Cosmo up to her mouth.

"Chile, don't even get me started," another said, slapping the nearest of the five girlfriends sitting next to her.

Lola kept her eyes on her plate. They didn't know the half of it. Her best friend, Raina, nudged her with her knee under the table.

"So riddle me this," Raina said, leaning in. "If the human males are such dogs, then why have these women spent a mint on nylon hair, false eyelashes, push-up bras, and acrylic nails? Clearly this isn't for each other, right?"

"Because," Lola said, releasing her breath in a rush, "they want to attract a mate, and all of that stuff is what I guess human males like . . . long hair, big boobs, flirty eyes, and manicured hands and feet or whatever."

"But—"

"But they don't want to attract a Neanderthal. They want a mate, but a guy who's sensitive and caring and honest."

Raina frowned and simply stared at her for a moment, the concept not getting through her beautiful skull. "They don't want the strongest in the pack? I don't follow." She glanced at the women. "They want sexy, virile alpha males, yes? But that doesn't come with sensitive and loyal and all of that. That's a beta. A frickin' collie, Lola. Do you get both in one form amongst the humans? What would that be . . . an alpha-beta or a beta-alpha?"

"I'm told they exist, but they're rare."

"Like unicorns, I bet," Raina murmured in awe and then sent her focus back to the table of partying females. "These stories are better than watching those human shows like Jerry Springer. But I still don't understand why they would dress for an alpha when trying to land this elusive alpha-beta or whatever the humans call them?"

"It's complicated. Do you want your vegetables?" Lola asked, swiping Raina's broccoli, already knowing the answer.

Arguing the point was useless to a woman who'd never walked a mile in human shoes. Raina was always hot, and was born into a wolf pack. She'd been bred by old-fashioned natural selection . . . a hot alpha mom, a dad who was the leader of the pack, which meant she had zero-percent body fat, hair that flowed like the river Nile every full moon . . . great nails, long lashes, perfect skin, and a permanent tan, thanks to her Lakota roots. It was depressing. Lola, on the other hand, knew all too well what the women sitting a table away were talking about.

"You seem far away tonight, Lola. What's wrong?"

"Nothing," Lola said quietly. "It's just that . . . I don't fit in."

"Of course you do," Raina said, too cheerfully. "How can you say that?"

"Uh, hello . . . I got left for dead after a rogue beta noshed on my ex-boyfriend during a supposedly romantic let's-see-if-we-can-work-it-out-again camping weekend. So, I got scratched by a criminal you guys were hunting down, which is the only reason I'm allowed in the pack at all. And if I thought dating before was hard . . . sheesh. I'd have to explain really bad mood swings during a full moon to a human guy. Doesn't really play out that well, ya know."

"You make it sound like you've got an STD or something. You're a beta werewolf female. Now get

over it. That's normal. Most are. It's no crime. C'mon."

Lola looked Raina squarely in the eyes. "The only time the pack guys ask me out is when they think I'm in heat, if you haven't noticed."

When Raina looked away, she knew she had.

"Listen," Lola said, sipping her beer. "I know you feel really bad about what happened—"

"It was my fault that your friend got mauled and you got bitten, Lola," her friend said quietly. "The pack knew Jeeter was a little left of center and had planned to send our alpha after him . . . but . . ."

"I know, I know, you went into phase and all anybody could do was howl at the moon."

Lola polished off her beer, also knowing that were it not for guilt, one of the most popular girls in the pack probably would not be spending an ounce of time with her. She owed Raina a lot, too, since it was that friendship that kept the other less tolerant females from messing with her. But Raina was a big ole lovable softy inside, even though she had the capacity to rip your face off.

"I know what," Raina said, raising her apple martini and trying to switch the subject. "We should go for a run."

"Aw, man . . . I don't know," Lola protested. "That means we have to get naked and shape-shift and I'm not that comfortable doing that so close to a full moon."

"Your body is fine," Raina said, clasping one of Lola's hands. "Your coat is a gorgeous ticked brown."

"I look like a gangly German shepherd, let's face it."

"Oh, my God, you do not!"

"It's not sleek and black like yours. My canines are short and my back haunches are fat, plus—"

"Will you stop!"

"No, you go ahead . . . I'm gonna check my email and—"

"Email?" Raina nearly shouted and sputtered on her drink.

"Shush, will you keep your voice down?"

"That's right," one of the ladies from the party table said, leaning way over in her chair. "Tell your girl she's gotta get out and get naked. Gotta drop all inhibitions when they dog you like that."

Both Lola and Raina gaped at the older women who'd clearly been sipping much longer than they had.

"Yeah," another one said, slightly slurring the word. "But she can also get her swerve on through the Internet. She needs to date out, too."

Raina cocked her head to the side for a moment. "Outside the species?"

The women at the table erupted in laughter.

"They are aliens, all men are, so yeah, go outside of your species, girl!"

A rowdy round of high-fives and hoots brought a harried server over to the table for a fresh call for drinks. To Lola's horror, two umbrella drinks got sent to them as a part of the party.

"Thank you so much," Lola said and pasted on a smile.

"Thanks everybody," Raina said, raising her glass.

"Just a little something to get your confidence up," one of the ladies called across the table. "Enjoy, and when you see some women younger than you going through the dog-tired blues, you send them a drink."

"That's right, honey-chile," another said, laughing. "Pay it forward—thank you, Jesus!"

"Ummm . . . I don't really drink," Lola whispered to Raina. "A beer, maybe wine, but this looks really dangerous."

"Aw, live a little and say thank you again once you drain the glass," Raina fussed, and then lifted her glass toward the adjacent table. "Thanks a lot again. Next round is on me!"

"You go, gurl," a heavyset platinum blonde hollered, and then they all lifted their glasses toward Raina and Lola. "We up here in the Poconos for an all-girls' weekend and you are so welcomed to join the festivities. Trust me; we're going primal, hon— so tell your girl to drink up!"

"We'd better finish these drinks and get out of here," Lola said in a nervous whisper.

"Okay, miss party pooper, but let's just play it by ear."

"They have no idea that dating out for us is a whole different experience." Lola shook her head as she watched Raina make short work of her drink.

"Haven't you ever wondered what it would be like to do a vampire?" Raina said in a conspiratorial tone.

"No!" Lola said in a sharp whisper. What she didn't say was that it was hard enough to wrap her brain around the possibility of doing a guy who had four legs.

"Okay, that's fair . . . the whole blood and biting thing could be a little freaky and I'd worry that I could accidentally forget and leave a shade up or something in the morning. Disaster. But you've gotta get out there and try."

"Why?"

Raina finished her drink and ordered another round for both tables, then folded her arms. "When's the last time you've been laid?"

Lola's mouth flew open and her face got hot. "I am so not answering that question!"

"I'm being serious—like before your ex-boyfriend got, er, um, eaten . . ."

"We were broken up and it had been a while. I was healing. On hiatus."

"Which was why when he called with that we-should-get-back-together-and-see-if-we-have-a-chance crap, you went."

"Yeah, I went."

"You know, crazy-ass Jeeter probably did you a great service, even though we had to formally put him down in the pack. Human flesh is such a taboo. Bad for the mind, body, and spirit, especially with

what humans consume today. But from all you told me about him, he was an absolute jerk. And it all worked out—the park rangers said it was a bear attack, so everything was cool. Now all we need to do is get you a real boyfriend—a hot bod."

Lola opened and closed her mouth before any words could come out. "Raina, sometimes I don't even know what to say to you."

"I know," she said, grasping Lola's hand in friendship again as the table beside them erupted when new drinks arrived. "Good, because we're leaving here and gonna go to this cool little vampire blood bar I heard about."

She could *not* believe she was doing this. But how did you tell the pack's she-alpha thanks but no thanks? In a word, you didn't. What had started out as a girls' dinner at Outback Steakhouse was quickly morphing into a hostage-adventure.

A mai tai and Yuengling lager were doing hand-to-hand combat in her stomach, making the steak and potatoes and, of all things, garlic bread and cheese broccoli, repeat on her.

"OMG, I think I'm gonna be ill," Lola groaned.

"It's just adrenaline . . . nerves. The rush of the hunt."

"I ate garlic bread."

The black SUV swerved. "Oh, shit," Raina said.

"Quick, in my purse. Take like five mints and give me a couple."

Lola complied and began rooting around in Raina's purse, bypassing condoms, a couple of joints in a baggie, and her cell phone. "Can I ask you something?"

"Sure," Raina said with a bright smile.

"Uh . . . is Bruno gonna flip if he finds out somehow that you went to a vamp bar—and be mad at me?"

"He won't be mad at you, Lollie-dollie, I promise. Just at little ole me."

Lola sat sideways in her seat, stretching the seat belt around her. "But he is gonna flip, isn't he?"

"Do you know how many women that man has fucked up and down the Eastern seaboard, not to mention throughout all the mountain ranges between here and Kentucky? Screw Bruno! I'm doin' a vampire tonight."

"Okay, that's it. You've had too much to drink and you are so not thinking clearly. Turn the SUV around or let me out on the side of the road," Lola said, holding her head. "I thought you two were doing okay and were a permanently mated pair. I don't want to—"

"We ARE a mated pair!" Raina said, her voice taking on a sudden fractured tone that Lola had never heard. "But he knows there isn't an alpha for miles that would dare dominance challenge him, so, he thinks he can do as he pleases." She glanced at her purse as her cell phone vibrated. "I'm in phase and nowhere to be found. Those older human females

were right. I'm not letting him dog me! Tonight I'll let him twist."

Lola sat back in her seat and just closed her eyes.

She didn't know what she expected. Goth maybe. But the techno-punk beat, neon strobe lights, and naked girls dancing the poles with snakes was not it.

"Welcome to Li'l Hell," the bartender said, flashing fangs. "What'll you fine canine types have tonight?"

"Jack Daniel's, neat," Raina said, scanning the bar, "and give my girlfriend whatever you've got on tap."

The bartender smiled. "Baby, I've got O positive, negative, A, B . . . you're gonna have to be a little more specific."

"Um . . . I'm the designated driver, so a ginger ale will be just fine," Lola replied, leaning in so the entire bar didn't hear her order.

The bartender gave her a thumbs-up and leaned in closer as Raina stalked away from the bar and entered the dance floor solo.

"Your girlfriend looks like she's on the serious hunt tonight—a real alpha . . . is there gonna be a problem in here if her man finds out?"

For a few seconds, Lola simply stared at him, blinking.

"You just answered my question. Thanks, honey. It's my job to know these things so I can telegraph it to my bouncers," he said with a toothy grin. He gave her

a little shrug. "That way we reduce property damage and keep it all in the parking lot. But if she came in here for some action, she came to the right place. Our Barons love this kind of adventure . . . keeps 'em from getting bored."

He handed Lola a ginger ale with a twist of lemon, as well as Raina's drink to hold for her while she was on the dance floor. The only thing Lola could say was "oh," as she watched her girlfriend move with the music.

It was a primal, sultry, sexy dance that drew the attention of several handsome male vampires that had been aloof and monitoring the crowd from the perimeter. Sweat soon stained Raina's shirt and Lola glanced around, watching the males slowly wet their lips and take a slow sip of what looked like merlot but wasn't. Then her girlfriend's head jerked toward a dark-haired suitor's intense gaze. She smiled and gave him her back to consider, seductively gyrating her perfect ass as a temptation.

A blond male in the corner stood at the same time the dark-haired suitor did. Both males locked gazes as Raina closed her eyes and moaned.

From the corner of her eye, Lola watched her girlfriend's small clutch vibrate across the bar. She quickly set down her ginger ale and grabbed it, and then flung it up under her arm.

"Please Bruno, please Bruno, don't come looking for her tonight," Lola said, and then accidentally sipped the drink she was holding and came up sputtering.

"Let me help you with that," a smooth baritone voice murmured so close to her ear that she almost fell off her stool. "The name is Andre."

He rounded her bar stool and blotted the spilled drink with a small square bar napkin. "I've never seen you in here before."

"My first time," Lola said, setting down Raina's drink and taking a huge gulp of her ginger ale. Then she hoisted her purse up higher on her shoulder, awkwardly balancing two purses and her drink.

"So, not being sure how far you wanted to take this adventure," he said in a smooth Caribbean lilt, "you decided to ingest garlic."

Lola covered her mouth and he laughed a deep, rich, belly laugh that warmed her insides.

"I'm sorry," he said, coming to sit beside her. "I didn't mean to tease but couldn't resist. You are simply the most interesting woman I've encountered in a very long time. May I replace the drink that half spilled?"

"It wasn't mine . . . it was for my girlfriend, and like a klutz I accidentally drank it."

"That's all right," he murmured. "Sometimes I drink things that I'm probably not supposed to. What can we do?"

Lola looked up into one of the most handsome faces she'd ever seen and then looked back down at the mess she'd made on the bar. His skin was so dark and even that it made her want to reach out and touch it. Instead, she traced drops of Jack Daniel's with her fin-

ger against the smooth mahogany that reminded her of his skin. Thick, black lashes rimmed his intense, deep-set eyes. Strong African features made him look more like a work of art than a living being; then she quickly reminded herself that, technically, Andre wasn't alive . . . but damn. A stone-cut body sat beside her, openly studying her, and she refused to make a size judgment based on his wonderfully large hands. In that moment she wished that she had on a nicer blouse to go with her jeans and heels, something black and daring and V-neck like Raina wore instead of the scoop-neck purple thing she had on.

Andre leaned on his forearms at the bar but inclined his head toward her. "What you have on is just fine," he murmured. "It is your style and what is within each woman that is different that a man yearns to uncover."

"You read my mind—like, like—"

"It is what we do," he said with a casual shrug. "But some things are written all over a lovely lady's face."

He hailed the bartender. "Please replace Lola's drink for her friend and refresh her ginger ale. Her mouth is going dry."

"Stop that!" Lola replied, sounding testy but couldn't stop smiling.

Andre held his hands up in front of his chest as the bartender removed Raina's drink and knocked back what was left in the glass.

"So, you came here tonight to babysit your girl-friend."

Lola shrugged and took a fresh swig of her pop. "Pretty much."

"I'm a bouncer here and I see this all the time. A beautiful woman comes in, begins tweaking up the testosterone on dangerous males, and voilà . . . the perfect storm."

Lola watched his gaze travel to the dance floor where two interested vampires had Raina between them.

"I think those guys are willing to compromise with a three-way, but I don't think your girlfriend is ready to experiment that deep in the life yet."

Lola choked on her soda. "I've gotta get her out of here!"

Andre nodded. "Yes . . . you do, but the window has passed. So, I'm going to ask you to jump behind the bar with old Matt."

"Jump behind the—"

No sooner had the words passed her lips, than the front door came off its hinges and seven burly werewolf pack males charged the dance floor in full transformation. Vampires took to the rafters and second-floor railings. The dance floor cleared and Raina placed her hands on her hips.

"Excuse me," Andre said, catching a wood-handled baseball bat from the bartender, which had a silver club end. "Now would be a good time to get behind the bar."

Lola scurried over the bar but stood watching in amazement.

"Gentlemen, I'm afraid you're going to have to take this issue outside," Andre called out calmly, advancing on the floor with ten buff bouncers.

Bruno transformed back into his human form, standing before Raina naked and angry with a hard-on. "This is between me and my lady!"

"Then keep it that way and take her home," another bouncer shouted.

"I'm not going home with him, I'm going with them!" Raina shouted, taunting Bruno.

"Lady, you don't have to go home, but you can't stay here," another bouncer yelled.

"Shall we call you a cab?" the rebuffed dark-haired vampire said with a sneer toward Bruno.

"We can see her home before morning," the blond said with a knowing grin.

Andre wiped his free hand down his face. "Come on, dudes. Gimme a break tonight."

The moment Raina stepped back from Bruno, the bar erupted. Chairs went flying, punches were hurled, fangs came out and canines got bared. Pole dancing females screamed and dodged flying beer bottles, carrying off their snakes, as huge bodies took out the stage. A chair hit the bar, followed by a table that shattered bottles above Lola's head. She scrambled to safety just in time as the entire shelf crashed to the floor.

But there wasn't time to dwell on the near miss. Lola kept moving, dodging hurled furniture and hard-landing bodies. Finally, a pump shotgun blast and the

smell of silver shell discharge brought the bar brawl to a screeching halt.

"Enough!" a velvet-suited vampire said, coming down from the executive offices. "Wolves, go home. My vampire staff, reglamour this place and pull it together."

Disgruntled patrons muttered their disappointment. The bartender shook his head. "Damn, just when things were getting good."

"You coming?" Bruno bellowed toward Raina, folding his arms over his massive barrel chest.

"After I get my purse," she said, lifting her chin, unfazed, and going back to the destroyed section of the bar where she and Lola had been sitting.

Lola stood there for a moment gaping as Bruno nodded, and then hunted on the floor and picked up her handbag.

"All right, but hurry up, girl . . . there's still some moon left," Bruno said after a moment when Raina folded her arms.

Stunned, Lola watched Raina collect her bag and then extract her car keys.

"Girl, you don't mind driving yourself home tonight, do you? You know how he gets, all tense and sexy, and I guess I'll have to give his fine ass some." Raina dropped her car keys in Lola's hand and then hugged her, whispering in her ear, "We've gotta do this again soon. Tonight was awesome."

There were no words. Lola stared behind her girl-

friend and the pack alpha, noticing that several of his beta friends were now giving her the appreciative eye. Then a deep baritone voice filled her ear and made her turn away from the group by the door.

"Why don't you stay, boo? Hang out with us tonight. It'll raise your stock in the pack."

She shook her head and found herself chuckling at Andre's hand sign to call him. Yeah, she was dog tired and just wanted to go home. She'd experienced enough drama for one night. But when she looked back, the vampires generally seemed forlorn, as though the mêlée was the most fun they'd had in years.

"I don't have your number," Lola said after a moment and loud enough for the werewolves to hear her.

Andre laughed a deep, rich island laugh as her phone sounded in her purse. "Now you do. I don't mind dating out if you don't. Call me—just not in the morning, and no garlic. Cool, ma?"

A Sweet Girl for Todd

Mark Onspaugh

"Here you go," she said, handing him a brochure for a tanning salon.

It read *Aztec Tan* and featured a tanned and muscular jaguar warrior surrounded by pretty girls in bikinis.

Todd gulped. One of the beauties in the photo was standing before him.

"So, how about a tan?" she asked.

Todd was embarrassed by the attention, especially from a beauty with such large blue eyes. She wore a turquoise silk blouse, open just enough to tempt his gaze. He tried to concentrate on her blond hair, which shimmered in the sun like spun gold.

Like Sif, the wife of Thor, he marveled.

"Mama never let me go out in the sun," he said.

His mother had always made dire predictions about what would happen if he ventured outside, so he had grown up in a world of perpetual dimness. Then, three months ago, she had been installing new blackout curtains and had fallen off the ladder, breaking her neck. After she was gone Todd took his first tentative step outside. Once he discovered that he would not burst into flame or melt like a waxwork figure, he had reveled in the feel of sunshine and open air.

"No wonder you're so pale," she said, shaking her head sadly. Todd felt his heart break to see her unhappy while at the same time his spirit soared because she really seemed to care for him.

"I also had bad skin, but I've been using Skin-Alive and Chum-Scrub," he said.

"I think your skin is beautiful," she said shyly. "My name is Mandy."

"I'm Todd."

"You have family here in L.A., Todd? I can tell you're from out of town by your accent . . . Chicago?"

"Detroit," he said, happy she was interested. "No, it was just Mama and me, and she's dead. I wanted to go someplace . . . sunny."

"So now you're here, seeking your fortune . . . And maybe . . . love?"

Todd blushed a bright crimson and felt it travel all the way from his cheeks to the tips of his toes. It was not an unpleasant sensation.

Mandy took his arm, and her touch sent a shock

wave of electricity through him. He willed himself not to sway, lest she break her grasp.

"So, Todd from Detroit, how about that tan?"

"I'm . . . uh . . . too big for a tanning bed," he said as if imparting a secret.

"Not ours," she said sweetly.

Todd hesitated. He was six foot two and tipped the scales at just shy of four hundred pounds. Todd had come to learn that what might serve most men was either too small or too fragile for him. He was sure it would be that way with her tanning bed and wasn't sure he could take the embarrassment.

"Tell you what," Mandy cooed, "you try a tan and you can join me for dinner."

"You mean, like a date?"

She giggled, and it was not the cruel laughter he had heard as he had waddled down Hollywood Boulevard, or the hateful snickers as he ate lunch at the House of Pies. No, her laughter was melodious and magical. Aphrodite might have made such a sound.

"Of course, silly. You think I'm going to let a handsome, robust man like you get away?"

Handsome! She found him handsome!

Was love beckoning to him? His mother's voice, unbidden, reminded him that sunlight was bad for her little man and that he had a ticket back to cloudy Michigan.

Todd banished her from his thoughts, a first on this day of many firsts.

Mandy led him down the boulevard, and again he was struck by the dizzying array of colors and textures, of people from every country, some pierced and tattooed into tribal fetishes or creatures Conan or John Carter of Mars might have fought.

"First trip to Hollywood?" Mandy asked.

"My first trip *anywhere*," he confessed. "I thought it would be like the Clark Gable days."

Mandy giggled again, the sweet notes making his heart flutter. He suddenly caught her scent, flowery and clean with a hint of something animal underneath, and felt a strange stirring along his spine and down into his pelvis.

Maybe that's love, he thought.

Mandy escorted him all the way to a strip mall down on Sunset near Vine. Even when his hand became sweaty from exertion, she didn't let go, and Todd was sure he had found the sweet girl he had been yearning for since he first read of Dejah Thoris, Princess of Mars.

The shopping center seemed deserted, and weeds had started to sprout in the parking lot. In amongst several failed businesses sat a cheery little storefront with a mural of a Mesoamerican pyramid and a smiling sun with sunglasses. The sign read "Aztec Tan, the Sun Experts!"

Inside it was cool and brightly lit, with posters of Mexico covering the walls. Todd was introduced to the staff, which included Lila the massage therapist and

Derrick the "tan master." This title was delivered by handsome Derrick with a self-deprecating smile. Todd envied Derrick his heroic muscles and dark curly hair. He looked like Apollo.

He might have been jealous, but Mandy introduced him as "my Todd," and he again felt that pleasant heat suffuse his body.

Then Todd filled out a medical history (no illnesses, no next of kin) and a release ("in the unlikely event . . ."), which Mandy assured him was just for "those stuffy lawyers." She shyly gave Todd a kiss on the cheek and that removed any fears he might have had.

After much coaxing, Todd stripped down to his shorts. While he drank a soothing herbal tea, Lila covered him in spicy ointments and buttery creams. By the time she was done, he smelled like Christmas morning.

They helped Todd into their largest tanning bed. Todd chose a recording of ambient forest sounds and they all bid him sweet dreams.

Night birds sang sweetly, but it was the crickets Todd found soothing, restful. He suddenly felt a longing for home and . . . and . . . But the feeling was gone as quickly as it had come, and he thought of sweet Mandy and their date when he emerged bronzed as a jaguar warrior.

As it grew toasty warm, Todd felt a sharp pain in his gut, and then along his spine. As he was about to panic, a warm calm settled over him, and he thought

he remembered his father, lifting him high, high up in arms, long and strong.

Todd drifted off to the sounds of a tropical rainstorm, thinking of his father, his dinner with Mandy, and custard pies, his most favorite dessert. Something large and dark flew across his memory, and then was gone.

Soon Todd was asleep, and they could all hear him snoring, a ratcheting worthy of a frontier logging camp.

Derrick locked the tanning bed securely and turned the temperature up to 350°F. Mandy put out the "Closed" sign and locked the front door, then began setting the table in the employee lounge. Lila called the rest of the clan at various salons in the Valley.

They arrived quickly. Clients like Todd were all too rare, even in a big city like Los Angeles.

Like Mandy, Lila, and Derrick, they were all tanned and dark, with fine physiques and easy smiles. Contrary to popular legend, they weren't bald, or scabrous, or pale. They didn't lurk around cemeteries or avail themselves of raw flesh. Oh, they had certain cousins who practiced this, some even sophisticated enough to act as though theirs was a refined palate, like a Japanese noble dining on sushi.

Disgusting.

They played the old songs and games, and some moved off into other rooms for liaisons with cousins not seen in many months.

Soon Todd's snores stopped, and a delicious aroma filled the salon. Everyone laughed when Mandy drooled on her new blouse, and she was the subject of good-natured ribbing for much of the afternoon.

Then came the ritual "Baring of the Teeth," where they removed their carefully crafted bridgework to reveal strong white teeth filed to points. They played Slash Tag and Bite the Blindman for another hour, then got down to serious drinking and carousing.

Twelve hours later, with hula music playing and all the guests happily drunk, Derrick opened the tanning bed with a flourish.

Everyone stared.

Todd was gone.

In his place was a six-foot lozenge of copper-colored chitin, rounded with hemispherical protrusions at one end, tapered and segmented at the other. It looked like a kind of sarcophagus.

"What the . . ." Derrick exclaimed, but by then the pupa was splitting open, and new Todd emerged. Famished from his change, he devoured every screaming one of them, his stinger paralyzing them, then his razor-sharp forelegs and crushing mandibles more than equal to the task of devouring flesh and bone.

Todd saved pretty Mandy for last, her blue eyes wide with a terror that seemed to his new eyes like love. His venom turned her organs and bones into jellied confections, sweeter than anything he had ever tasted . . .

Even custard pie.

Tastes Like
Chicken

JORDAN SUMMERS

I

I became a detective after I ate Miss Marple.

Nobody tells you when you're a fresh, prepubescent
ghoul that you have to be careful about how much you
eat. When you spend your twelfth birthday scooping
handfuls of brain from the gaping skull of the next-
door neighbor (Miss Mullens, not Marple, but the
effect was much the same) the unpleasant surprise is
that your peculiar biochemistry will do its level best to
amalgamate what you just fed it. In this case, cupfuls
of frontal lobe, corpus callosum and snowflake-unique
collections of synapses that led Miss Mullens to curse
out loud with words like "poot" and "jiminy" and yet
have internal dialogue like a motherfucking stevedore,

as I was to find out to my displeasure when her consciousness exploded into mine as I was lying in the attic, replete, about four hours later. That's the thing about being a ghoul, there aren't any manuals to follow.

She'd dressed me down, up, and sideways, blistering my consciousness with expletives until it felt bruised by the mental pummeling. That was twenty years ago. You'd think she'd let it go by now, but not Ms. Mullens. She *lives* for hating me.

We were on page ten of the *New York Times*, when the homicide call came in. Ms. Mullens insists we read the newspaper from cover to cover every day.

Even the obituaries?

Even the obituaries.

At first I'd refused. I wanted to get my news from the internet. My resistance didn't last long once Ms. Mullens discovered she could give me gas by triggering certain spots in my brain. Gas coming from a human can be eye-watering. Imagine what it's like when your diet consists of fresh and rotting corpses. No amount of Febreze can combat the odor.

The phone rang again. I looked at the number and debated whether to ignore the call. It was my day off. I'd planned to finish reading the paper, then hit the cemetery later for a quick bite. I glanced back at the article. The headline read "Billionaire Lawrence Koffman Makes Miraculous Recovery Thanks to New Swiss Treatment." I scowled and shut the paper, then retrieved my voice mail.

I wasn't done reading that article, Ms. Mullens's disembodied voice said.

"You can finish it later. Time to go to work."

2

I had no idea when I walked into the room that I'd be staring at a severed ghoul's hand. Sure, the ghoul could've left it behind. It was always possible. But no ghoul worth his salt willingly abandoned a perfectly viable limb, which meant we were looking for a dead ghoul.

Ghoul-on-ghoul violence wasn't unheard of. It happened on occasion, especially with the fresher turns, but if that was the case here, why leave the hand behind? There was another possibility. We could be dealing with the other kind of ghoul killing—the for-profit kind. Either someone was in the black-market body-part business or we had a Harvester on our hands. Those two things weren't mutually exclusive. People who can see through a ghoul's human disguise often become Harvesters.

There seems to be something with the genes. When you have the correct ABAAGGT arrangement to spot a ghoul—it's like smelling asparagus in urine, or so I'm told—you also have the arrangement that makes you a complete whack-job sociopath asshole that has no compunction in using that ghoul's body for your own bullshit needs.

Everybody knows the story: young man meets gorgeous girl at a bar. She takes an unlikely interest in the

butt ugly fellow. Buys him a drink. Invites him back to her hotel. Another drink. Next morning, he wakes up in a bath of ice. A sign on the mirror saying "Call 911" and a big scar where one of his kidneys used to be.

Yeah, it actually happens. But *you* only hear about it when it's a mistake—if the guy was anorexic or a heroin user and the Harvester thought he was one of us. They only take one because our kidneys grow back and a good farmer always leaves something behind to harvest next year.

Harvesting has always occurred. Someone figured out that transplanting a ghoul organ into an uninfected person gave the human another twenty years of life—and a very healthy appetite.

True, it tends to lead to a sickly, pallid look. You know when you see some super-rich Wall Street financier and he's looked the same since the '70s, just a little more . . . *moist*? Trust me: it isn't from rich food.

Ghouls tend to view being harvested as a minor inconvenience. That would change if the news spread that Harvesters had started hulling ghouls, raiding their bodies for every salvageable part, leaving only the skin husk behind.

Humans have bogeymen. Ghouls have Harvesters.

3

I scanned the crime scene again, doing my best to ignore the vomit of color. From the outside, the three-

story, red-brick row house had looked like all the others on the quiet Upper West Side block until you stepped inside.

The purple shag-carpet-covered living room had faux-wood paneling and furniture that could only have been found from Dumpster diving. The carpet had squished beneath my booty-covered shoes as I followed the sound of voices coming from a nearby room. Turned out to be the kitchen or what was left of it.

The kitchen was one of those 1970s olive-green nightmares with orange accents and a yellow Formica table thrown in to insult the senses. I blinked as my eyes tried to adjust to the contrasting colors. The table had been smashed down the center. Chairs were strewn about the room in various stages of dismemberment. The green doors to the cupboards were hanging from twisted hinges as if someone had tried to rip them off and failed. Glasses and plates littered the area, leaving no discernable trail through the debris.

I hadn't noticed the hand on the white linoleum floor at first. The explosion of color had blocked it from view. Gray and slightly shriveled with dark blue veins that ran from wrist to knuckle, the limb's long fingers appeared to be in working order.

My mouth watered as I looked at the hand and wondered what the forensic guys would do with it once they were done examining it. They'd assume the limb came from a corpse. And they'd be right . . . now, since ghouls don't survive with outer parts missing for long.

But it hadn't been a "dead" corpse when the limb came off. I could tell by the scent. Ghouls have better olfactory senses than a bloodhound.

I stared longingly at the limb. Could always use an extra hand. Never knew when one might need replacing or when hunger would circumvent my better judgment. My fingers twitched as I fought the urge to pick the limb up and shove it into my pocket.

Detective Cory Harris saved me from acting on the impulse when he walked into the room. He hunched down and touched the hand with a gloved finger. A paper clip of a man, Cory finished examining the hand, then looked at me. "What are you doing here, Max? I thought it was your day off."

I shrugged. It had been my day off, and I hadn't asked for overtime. With all the budget cuts, we barely got paid for the hours we put in. I didn't know why I'd been assigned to this case. "Captain called me. Told me to take point."

Cory's gray eyes narrowed, pinching his face into an angry exclamation point. Blond hair frisked his pointy ears but never reached his neck. His oversized brown suit sat forlornly on his narrow shoulders, making him always appear as if he were playing dress up in his father's clothes. He was too cheap to get a custom job or maybe he was just self-conscious about his lanky body. I never asked which it was. Didn't really care. He'd disliked me from the get-go. And I was okay with that. It's not like I'd taken this job to make friends.

The only reason you have this job is because of me, Ms. Mullens said. *Without me, you'd be living in some run-down cemetery, digging for scraps.*

"Shut it," I said.

"Excuse me?" Cory asked.

"Nothing." I waved my hand to dismiss the comment. "Where's the body?"

"It's up here," he said. "But I have to warn you, it's been here awhile. A month at least, if the level of decomp is any indication. You're never going to believe where we found it." His voice rose with excitement as he led me up the stairs to the first bedroom on the right.

A bed sans frame had been shoved against the far wall away from the lone window in the room. Rumpled clothes lay on the floor and in overflowing baskets, but none hung in the closet. A massive grandfather clock had been wedged into the corner. The forensic team stood around it, along with a few uniforms that had first arrived on scene after the neighbors complained about the smell. The uniforms couldn't seem to control their snickering. I pushed past Cory and the men in blue to take a closer look.

Someone had folded the body in half and shoved it into the clock. The pendulum had somehow skewered the man's right eye in the process. My gaze landed on the victim's face and I froze. The forensic guys thought the body had been here for a month.

I knew better.

I was talking to it four nights ago.

4

Benny was why I kept a photo of a boa constrictor in my wallet.

Benny Frost, or Benny the Bean, had been a useful informant and a pretty crafty ghoul. He was a native New Yorker whose point of pride was that he never stepped foot off the island. He kept his ear to the ground and was always good for a tip, especially when a trail ran cold. Had a bizarre bat-shit fear of snakes. Never seen anything like it, but his extreme phobia occasionally came in handy when he was feeling less than cooperative. Benny would crawl up a wall if you even mentioned a snake, and the photo would send him into a panic attack. Miss Mullens found this highly amusing. It was one of the few things we agreed on.

Benny had been harvested a few times—which was unusual, but he'd taken the personal invasions in stride. It had helped that the parts had grown back. That was the big difference between being harvested and being hulled. One you could recover from; the other got you escorted out in a body bag.

The coroner finally arrived. "Detective Goodman," he said, acknowledging me before doing a quick visual exam on Benny. He ordered the body removed from the clock.

I watched Benny's chest deflate as they laid him flat. "What's missing?"

The coroner glanced at me. "Can't be sure, but it

looks like every organ. I'll know more once I get him back to the morgue. We'll figure out the cause of death then."

I rather think removing all his innards and folding him in half might have a teensy bit to do with it, Miss Mullens added.

I ignored her. I didn't like the idea that a Harvester had suddenly turned greedy. I couldn't afford to have more dead ghouls turn up. Eventually someone would notice a pattern and order an investigation into the deaths. How do you explain ghoulism to an organization that didn't know that ghouls existed?

Benny and I weren't what anyone would call friends, but I did like the guy. He had a way of getting under your skin and he was always good for a laugh. I had no idea how he'd ended up inside the clock or in this home, for that matter. As far as I knew, Benny was homeless. And this wasn't exactly the kind of neighborhood that courted squatters.

I turned to Cory. "Do you know who owns this place?"

He shook his head. "We're trying to find out now. How do you know it's not the victim?"

I watched the coroner zip up the body bag. "Because he's one of my informants—was one of my informants."

Cory's gaze sharpened. "Was he working with you on anything specific?"

"No." Whatever had happened to Benny had noth-

ing to do with my caseload. How had the Harvester found him? And why not properly dispose of the body? Discarding it like month-old rubbish was bound to draw unwanted attention. The clues were few—

Maybe for you, Miss Mullens said. *Some of us have already formed a theory. A rather good one, if I do say so myself. I wouldn't expect someone whose brain requires pictures with captions to understand. Tell me, along with regenerating your organs, does being a ghoul thicken your skull?*

Closing my eyes, I counted to ten slowly, then asked, "What's your theory?"

Cory blinked. "I don't have one yet. Let's see what the coroner gets off the body first."

I clamped my jaw shut and nodded. I couldn't exactly tell him I'd been talking to a dead octogenarian.

5

You really don't remember, do you?

"Remember what?" I said, as I navigated my car through midafternoon traffic. Ms. Mullens and I had been playing this guessing game since I left the crime scene. Foot patrol had canvassed the neighborhood, but no one reported hearing anything. Unusual for the neighborhood, but not for New York. I wasn't surprised. Harvesters were quick, efficient, and silent.

She sighed. *The article in the paper.*

"What article?" I laid my hand on the horn as a taxi cut me off.

Ms. Mullens huffed. *Now you're being purposely obtuse.*

"Listen, old lady, I don't even know what that means." I couldn't see her shake her head, but I felt it inside my cranium. "Knock it off. You're making me dizzy." She shook harder and faster, giving me internal whiplash. I pulled the car over. I barely got out the door before I puked. A knuckle bone shot out of my mouth and bounced off the curb before landing near the sewage drain. Gasping, I stumbled out of the car and kicked the finger the rest of the way in. People on the sidewalk ignored me and kept walking.

I win! Ms. Mullens shouted.

I wiped my mouth with the back of my sleeve. The last thing I needed was to have my dinner clinging to my face. A ghoul's digestive system wasn't built to expel food. The mouth worked as an intake-only valve, which made throwing up painful. "You happy now?"

6

I climbed back in the car and waited. Ms. Mullens couldn't go long without talking. It wasn't in her nature. My patience paid off.

Fine, she said. *I'll give you a hint. He made a miraculous recovery.*

"You think Lawrence Koffman is involved in Benny's death. The billionaire? Why?" I asked. It seemed unlikely that someone like Benny would ever come in

contact with Koffman. They didn't exactly run in the same circles.

It's logical, really. A couple of months ago we read that he was terminally ill. Now suddenly he's better. You said so yourself that a Harvester was involved. A billion dollars can buy a lot of body parts.

I looked up the phone number for Koffman Funds and managed to bullshit my way up to the assistant of his assistant's assistant, but no further. It was enough. My phone rang thirty minutes later. Surprisingly, it was Koffman himself, launching immediately into that offensive that rich assholes specialize in, threatening to sue the city and get me fired if I didn't stop harassing him. Innocent people don't act that way. His behavior was especially telling since I hadn't mentioned why I'd phoned. I waited for him to finish, then quietly said, "We need to talk about Benny Frost."

His rant stopped immediately. Silence reigned for a few moments, then he calmly gave me his address. The place turned out to be a luxury high-rise in a must-have zip code. Koffman's penthouse was located on the seventieth floor. The elevator opened straight into his home.

Past a pat-down from a couple of Brioni-suited goons, Koffman was waiting as I stepped into the white marble foyer. "Make it quick." He glanced at his Rolex. "You have fifteen minutes."

"You look good for a man who was terminally ill a couple of months ago," I said. "Death wears you well."

He smirked, and I knew it was true. I could see the damp skin, the cracks that never quite heal. "Get to the point, Detective."

"How did you find Benny Frost?"

Koffman walked over to his minibar and poured himself a scotch. He didn't offer me one. Instead, he took a big swig of the amber liquid, staring at me over the rim of the crystal glass. "Homeland Security is one of our biggest customers," he said. "We provide sniffer machines at bus terminals, train stations, ferries, and at airports. All it takes is an extra calibration to get the machine to detect decaying flesh, along with explosives residue. Names, addresses, and occupations are collected and stored for later use. It's really quite simple."

My heart slammed into my ribs. He knew what I was and where I lived. They could've harvested me at any time.

Ms. Mullens gasped, shocked into silence for once in her life. I wouldn't be dying alone if I got hulled.

Fear quickly turned to anger at his arrogance.

He caught the change in my expression and laughed. "At first, we thought there were only a few hundred of you, but it turned out that you number in the thousands. With so many, there's really no need to be quite so circumspect."

That was news to me. I didn't think there were that many of us, but I don't get out much. "What did you take from Benny?"

Koffman grinned. "I needed its heart, its liver, kid-

neys, lungs." He paused. "Oh, and a spleen, whatever that is."

How positively delightful, Ms. Mullens said. *He used all those organs from the same ghoul. Greedy and clueless. The combination doesn't get any better than that.*

It was my turn to smile.

Koffman's grin slowly faded as he noted the change in my demeanor. "No one will believe I had anything to do with this crime. You know it and I know it. Ghouls don't exist, remember?"

I nodded in agreement. Everything he'd said was absolutely true. "I have no plans to arrest you," I said.

Koffman's eyes narrowed.

"But I have a question," I said, reaching into my pocket for my wallet. "How do you feel about snakes?"

He blinked in confusion. "Snakes? What in the hell do snakes have to do with Benny Frost?"

I stepped forward and showed him.

It truly is an interesting sight when someone suddenly discovers they have an insane fear of snakes and actually takes a running leap off their seventieth-floor balcony.

Presumptuous Beast Throws Sumptuous Feast

MIKE BARON

"The great white hunter," Count B'orloff sneered as his chauffeur-driven Hispano-Suiza soaked up gully-whumpers that would have cracked a caisson. "Buys the biggest estate in town, declares himself the sine qua non, the ne plus ultra, the cat's pajamas, and invites the thread-bare gentry to sup at his table."

The Countess laid her long ivory hand on his leathered sleeve. "Please let's not work ourselves into a lather, dear. Herr O'Malley brings much-needed work to the province. And no one liked watching that house fall into desuetude."

"The sheer unbridled ignorance of the man," Count

B'orloff continued as if his wife had not spoken. "To add insult to injury, he invites us at the height of the full moon. The man calls himself a nature expert. How could he be unaware of the demmed werewolf, or is this some sort of juvenile test? For all his accomplishments, this O'Malley fellow comes across as remarkably insecure."

"Dear," the Countess continued, fitting a Turkish cigarette to her ivory holder, "please let's not psychoanalyze the man based on a dinner invitation. Let us give him the benefit of the doubt. He may turn out to be delightful company."

"He's Irish," the count said with disgust, as if that alone explained everything. "Not even your proper Englishman who goes to Rhodesia and finds diamonds. No. He makes his living taking upper-class English twits into the brush where they corral some hapless beast and beat it to death with sticks."

"I'm sure that's not the case," the Countess averred, tiring of the Count's attitude. "Oh, look!" she cried with girlish enthusiasm. "The Vieblers are here! And that's Count Epicstein's Bentley, is it not?"

The Hispano-Suiza pulled up beneath the marble portico of an immense wedding cake of a house, lit windows overlooking the brick turnaround, their arched shape giving them an expression of surprise. Six or seven expensive automobiles, including a Mercedes 500SK and a Bugatti Royale, were parked on the expansive lawn. A liveried pug-ugly held the car door

for them, ushering them toward the entrance where a toady in a liver-colored waistcoat made notations on a clipboard.

"Count and Countess B'orloff," the toady intoned. "So good of you to come. Please proceed to the main salon where bwana is waiting to greet you."

"Did he say 'bwana?'" the Count whispered. The Countess rolled her eyes.

Countess on his arm, Count B'orloff sashayed to the balustrade overlooking the main salon, where Lord Patrick O'Malley vigorously pumped hands and flashed his too-white teeth. A tall, thin, dark man, Count B'orloff was aware of the effect he had on those who were not familiar with him, in his jet-black suit and black satin cape lined with red. Some bumpkins mistook him for a vampire. Countess D'angela was similarly cadavered in a form-fitting black taffeta gown that flared at the calves, her deep décolletage decorated with a strand of black pearls. Her silken jet hair hung in a waterfall straight down the back of her gown.

Lord O'Malley was exactly the type of fellow Count B'orloff despised: mesomorphic, ruddy-cheeked, cheerful, and gregarious. Those teeth! Like massed Hun shields turned toward the sun! That mustache! It belonged on a Texas Longhorn! A coterie of eager debutantes hovered at the hunter's perimeter.

The toady appeared at the Count's left elbow. "Count and Countess B'orloff!"

O'Malley stepped forward to grasp the Count's

delicate hand in both his ham-sized fists, pumping the Count's arm as if trying to shake birds off a clothesline. The Great White Hunter wore tweed pants with jodhpurs stuffed into leather cavalry boots, a tweed jacket with leather patches on the elbows and collar, and an open shirt of high-quality muslin the Count recognized from his last trip to Savile Row. A half inch of fresh bandage peeked from O'Malley's right sleeve.

"Very pleased you could come, Count!" O'Malley enthused through his teeth.

"Don't be silly, old chap," the Count said. "Wouldn't miss it for the world. Welcome to the neighborhood. I hear you're quite the hunter."

"Man is at his best when he hunts," the bumpkin brayed.

"And you, my dear . . ." O'Malley seized D'angela's hand. The Count feared their host might rip it off. "You are a vision of continental sophistication and loveliness."

The Countess blushed at the man's brash charm. "Tell us about your latest escapade."

"I can't do that, madame," O'Malley said, twirling his mustache. "It would ruin the surprise! But I can tell you last year at this time I was in the American West hunting mountain lions in the Rockies."

Count B'orloff sniffed. "Where might that be?"

"In Colorado, in the American West. A chain of mountains that dwarfs the Carpathians. Only Switzerland has anything similar."

"What's a mountain lion?"

"Also known as the American puma! A fearsome beast that weighs up to two hundred pounds. Took me two shots to bring him down. As a young man I vowed to cull every possible trophy from the wild. I have hunted snow leopard in the Himalayas, jaguars in the Amazon, rhinoceroses in Africa. By the time I killed my American puma, I had pretty much written the big-game book."

"And the reason you honor our miserable burg," the Count said, smiling ironically, "is that you heard of our supernatural predators."

"Precisely," O'Malley burst with satisfaction.

Other guests displaced the B'orloffs on the receiving line. The Count snagged glasses of champagne and spotted Manfred Viebler, who had the estate next to his own. B'orloff went over to where Manfred stood by the groaning board, eating deviled ham on a cracker.

"Manfred, old boy! What do you make of this, eh?"

Manfred looked up, his gaze encompassing the silent circle of trophies occupying most of the wall space. Lions from the veldt, a tiger from India, various members of the deer family (with and without antlers), a stuffed bobcat, several eagles, a snow leopard, a thylacine and a moose.

"Fellow seems determined to kill one of anything, wouldn't you say? In any case, it was unconscionable for him to hold his event on this night of all nights with that cursed beast on the loose."

"Then why are you here, old boy?"

Manfred shrugged unhappily. B'orloff knew full well Viebler had married a Viennese actress less than half his age. "Bella wanted to come. When I tried to explain the situation, she sneered at me. Love, eh? What we do for love."

"Nevertheless, you took precautions," B'orloff said.

Manfred nodded solemnly and patted his waist-coat. "My man Delmer is an expert shot with the .450 Martini-Henry. Had to sacrifice a lovely tea service left to me by my great-aunt, but such is the price we pay for living in these times. If all else fails, I've got my father's dagger."

"Good God," the Count exclaimed.

"What is it, dear?" the Countess said.

"What if the fellow killed it? That might be the very reason he came. Having exhausted the fauna of Africa, he's after our werewolf!"

"Is that a bad thing?" Manfred said. "The creature kills someone every time there's a full moon."

"I'm not defending the creature," B'orloff said. "But consider . . . those of us representing the diminishing aristocracy, hoarding inherited fortunes, we do not welcome the world's scrutiny. Fear has been our friend lo these many years. Fear keeps the outside world at bay. Even the King's Exchequer fears to tread, and that helps keep taxes low."

Manfred stroked his chin. "Well, when you put it that way . . . it's degrading property values. Are you suggesting we stop trying to kill it?"

B'orloff glanced all around to make sure he wasn't being overheard. The Countess gripped his upper arm. "Don't start, dear."

The Count lowered his voice to Manfred's ear. "I'll go further. We should consider giving it what it wants. The gaols are full of gypsy trash. Feed the beast a gypsy or two. We kill two gamecocks with one shot: assuaging its hunger, and sending a message to the gypsy tribes that they are not welcome here."

Manfred stroked his prickly chin. His eyes went round. They narrowed to gun slits. "You don't suppose . . ." he said.

"What?" the Count prodded.

"The great white hunter." Manfred nodded to their host, chatting up a huge bald-headed man in a naval uniform with gold epaulets. "You're absolutely right, Count. That's why he's here."

"How presumptuous. Taking it upon himself to deprive our community of a creature that certainly has more claim to this land than he does."

"He wouldn't dare," Manfred said.

The Count prodded Manfred with an elbow. "He's wearing jodhpurs. Of course he'd dare."

Manfred shuddered with revulsion. "Oh, dear," he said.

The Count peered down. "Problem?"

"The menu," Manfred gestured.

"Well, he promised a surprise. And we mustn't let him down. Wouldn't want the fellow to think we

were *chicken,* wouldja?" The Count winked. "Are you chicken or aintcha?!"

Manfred inhaled deeply through funneled nostrils. "I'm hungry enough to eat a werewolf."

As if on command, the majordomo in the liverish suit tapped a silver spoon against leaded crystal from the entrance to the dining room. "My lords and ladies, dinner is served."

The guests filed into the elegant, walnut-paneled dining room with a cut-glass chandelier and a splendid boar's head mounted over the immense fireplace. All the guests sat at an enormous dining table on which O'Malley had deposited place cards.

The Count and Countess B'orloff found themselves seated to their host's left and one seat down at the enormous walnut table handmade in Carpathia. An intricate carving at least six feet long depicted plumed royals on horseback pursuing a wolf through the forest. A pack of hounds nipped at the wolf's heels. Manfred Viebler and his girl bride Bella were seated to the left of Countess B'orloff.

Waiters in black slacks and white shirt circulated, depositing greens in front of every guest. The Countess regarded her salad with enthusiasm. "Look, Udo. Where on earth do you think he found arugula? He must have had it brought in from Italy."

For several minutes there was only the susurrus of muted conversation and the chewing of greens. Their host stared at his own dish, never touching it. He raised

a crystal chalice of merlot and a silver spoon. TING!
he rang the chalice. TING!

As waiters whisked away dishes with the speed and
alacrity of pickpockets, all eyes turned expectantly to
their host.

"Dear friends," the lord of the manor rumbled, "and
friends I hope you will be, I thank you for welcoming
me into your community. Yours is one of the oldest
bastions of civilization in Eastern Europe and I am
fully cognizant of your rich and tragic tradition as well
as your reticence to welcome outsiders. Most of you
know me as a big-game hunter and leader of expedi-
tions to the Dark Continent. But I also consider myself
a biologist, and in fact hold a degree in that discipline
from Christ Church college in Oxford. Toward that
end, I have sought to catalog the world's most diverse
biological predators, from the fearsome cape buffalo to
the lion of the veldt. You have seen my thylacine and
my dire wolf."

Their host paused, deeply ruminative, as the wait-
ers again swarmed the table setting down great bone
china dishes upon which sat thick slices of a savory red
meat. At the far end of the table, a lesser duke surrepti-
tiously took knife to platter before his wife snatched it
from his hand.

"In any case, it was my intention to serve up the
very beast that has terrorized the countryside for lo
these many years." Their host set his misshapen knuck-
les on the table and looked down. "I had already sent

the invitations when I set out last night to make good on my vow. Unfortunately, I failed."

There was a collective gasp from the table.

"The creature left its mark on me. On your plates is a wild boar I bagged this morning served in a cranberry sauce. Please—enjoy."

There was a smattering of applause from the far end of the table, then an outpouring of clapping and exhortations. "Bravo!" "Well said!" "You tried!"

Viebler leaned across D'angela to hiss, "No prayer."

"Indeed." The Count sniffed, cutting into the red meat before him. The Countess dug him in the ribs and nodded. Their host sat staring at a loaded fork as if he'd never seen such a thing.

The Count set down his knife and fork.

"I say, O'Malley," he said in a concerned baritone.

There was no reaction.

"Bwana!" the Count barked.

Their host looked up, bewildered, then broke into a smile. "What can I do for you, old man?"

"Are you all right? You look a little pale."

O'Malley smiled, mustache twitching. "Never better! Bit past my usual bedtime. Early to rise, early to bed, et cetera."

The Count looked at the slip of bandage poking out from O'Malley's sleeve. "The beast marked you, eh?"

O'Malley could not stop himself from staring at the Countess's elegant throat. "Eh? That's right, a mere scratch. Not like I was bit or anything."

O'Malley's brow lunged forth and sprouted hair like a woolly mammoth. His snout elongated with a painful popping sound, scimitar canines descending from his upper jaw.

"Oh, hell!" the Count exclaimed. "The bloody fool got himself nicked!"

The Countess laid her ivory fingers on the Count's sleeve. "The district really can't support two were-wolves, dear."

The Count rose and urged the Countess back with his arm. All around O'Malley the dinner guests rose and edged away from the table.

"Delmar!" Manfred bellowed, drawing his silver dagger. "Fetch the Martini-Henry!"

Bad German

EDWARD BRYANT

Enos Harkman, perhaps the greatest psychic detective of the twentieth century, finally stumbled into the twenty-first century a decade or two late by obtaining a BlackBerry. In truth, he didn't buy it so much as accept it ungraciously as an All Souls' gift from his trusted assistant Torg. Torg had used the BlackBerry himself for a few years before replacing it with a highly modified iPhone that, so far as Harkman could tell, monitored the contents of the refrigerator, ordered new stocks, gave the delivery boy directions for finding the house, cooked supper, and sorted the scraps into various categories for recycling. For all Harkman knew, the iPhone could process the scraps into biofuels, sub-prime mortgages, or ectoplasm.

Torg didn't so much as snicker when Harkman fumbled helplessly with the BlackBerry's keyboard—a

grace note the detective appreciated deeply. Harkman felt that offering the dusky giant a position of executive responsibility—as Harkman's assistant—had been one of the bravest things he had ever done. Not only was Torg eighteen inches taller and a hundred pounds heavier—all of it corded muscle—but Harkman had to admit Torg was smarter. Torg bore his burdens with modesty and a sense of ungodly psychic competence. Harkman hoped his assistant would never develop the sense of ambition that would trigger him to form a competing consultancy. Or worse, simply stuffing Harkman's body into a fifty-gallon steel drum and dropping him into a bayou.

"Sir," Torg said, dropping five spatulate fingers lightly on Harkman's shoulder. "Sir!" He added a tone of urgency now. "I believe we have a client. I asked him to take a seat in your study."

Harkman jerked fully awake and, for a moment, looked around the brightly lit kitchen. "Of course." He pulled himself erect and followed Torg toward the stairs.

The second-floor study was a calm, measured room of dark hardwood and exotic art. As Harkman entered, he saw the presumed client was a gentleman of middle years dressed in a linen suit of some quality. The man rose to meet his hosts.

"Mr. Harkman? I'm Samuel Turner. I'm delighted you could see me at such short notice."

"It's my pleasure, sir," Harkman said, taking the

leather padded chair behind his desk. "May I ask how you come to be here?"

"A friend of a friend," said Turner. He twisted the brim of the linen hat in his lap. "I despaired of figuring out what horror was afflicting my new home with only my own resources and those of my wife to draw upon. I began complaining to all my friends. One on the golf course was apparently familiar with your work. After an alligator snatched and swallowed my ball in the sixth hole water trap, he attempted to cheer me by offering a referral to you."

"Ah," said Harkman. "I am flattered. So tell me, Mr. Turner, what is the nature of your horrific affliction?"

The visitor was silent for a few moments. Then he said, "My wife and I recently purchased our dream home in the Garden District. It's an old residence on the Rue Atelier. Like the French Quarter, it is one of the higher points in the city. It allows us to have the rare cellar. The house is not so old as some, mind you, but is still well over a century. I am told its predecessor burned to the ground in the 1880s. At any rate, Marianne—my wife—and I looked forward to growing old gracefully in this place once I gave up my practice and retired."

"You're a doctor?" said Harkman.

"A surgeon. I'm with Mercy Central in Chicago. I still commute each week for certain procedures. Marianne and I have always loved the romance of the deep South."

"It's a sentiment I can well understand," said Harkman. "But what about the horror you've encountered?"

Turner released his tortured hat and steepled his fingers. "We've been in the house only a month. From the beginning there were strange noises late at night. Primarily from the cellar. Bestial noises."

"Perhaps, oh, rats?" said Harkman.

The surgeon shook his head. "Louder. I've heard rats in medical school. More of a shrieking. At first, when I investigated, they ceased upon my entering with a light. The cellar dates back to the time of the previous dwelling. We've planned to use it for storage and for wine."

"Of course," said Harkman encouragingly.

"This past Friday . . ." Turner's voice trailed off momentarily. "This past Friday, I followed the noises into the deeper end of the cellar. There was snuffling, snorting, and, as I mentioned a minute ago, shrieking. I asked my wife to wait upstairs. She seemed not unwilling to comply. Then I took a light and my nine-millimeter Glock and adjourned below. The darkness seemed, well, *darker* than it should. My light barely affected it. The noises became more horrid. Then I became disoriented. I suddenly thought I was surrounded by humanlike figures that capered and screamed. Panicking, I fired my pistol, to no apparent effect. I could see nothing in the muzzle blast. The screaming continued and I fell to my knees." The surgeon stopped in apparent distress.

Torg adroitly filled in the embarrassing gap. "May I bring you gentlemen some coffee?"

"Yes," said Harkman.

"Extra cream and sugar, please," said Turner.

By the time Torg returned with the tray, the distressed Turner had regained his composure. "Let me quickly finish," he said. "While on my knees in the darkness, I sensed movement all around me. Then it hit me."

"Yes?" said Harkman. Torg shot him a warning glance.

"No," said Turner, "I mean it really *hit* me. Dollops of something disgusting, soft and hot, horribly redolent of a summer privy. In a moment I was briefly encased in what I can describe only as a fecal cocoon. Then . . . it melted away and was gone. The scent remained, but my light came up and showed I was alone in the brick cellar. Shadows of cardboard boxes danced, but that was all. The phantoms were gone." Turner expelled a long breath. "You see why I need help?"

Harkman set his cup back in its saucer with a decisive click. "I must see your cellar myself," he said.

"Soon?" said Turner with a tone almost of childish hope.

"Tonight."

The Turner residence was indeed an impressive edifice, a neat construction of brick and frame, framed by

oak and bougainvilleas, and rising two storeys from the shaded street. Torg found space to park the van in front of the home and Harkman supervised as his assistant unloaded the cases of sophisticated equipment.

"We've pretty much got it all," said Harkman to Turner and his lovely wife waiting in the front hall. "There's audio and video, all with high-gain detector capability. There are EMF detection units and electro-voice phase filters. We have electroplasmometers—"

"*Ecto*plasmometers," Torg corrected him gently.

"Whatever," Harkman said with a touch of asperity. "We have all that we'll need."

Turner made a round of introductions and Marianne extended a soft hand with a firm grip. "Gentlemen, thank you for agreeing to visit. My husband has been a bit beside himself."

Harkman thought Turner looked a mite put out by his wife's remark. "It has been unhelpful to my sleep." Turner gestured to the house behind him. "Where does all this gear go?"

"Various locations around your home," said Torg, "but most of it is, of course, destined for the cellar."

"Let me help." Turner grabbed for an aluminum-encased oscillograph. Torg snatched it up ahead of him.

"No need, sir. I can handle it." With some mildly proffered help from Harkman, Torg wrestled four cases toward the indicated hallway. "This way?"

"All the way down," said Turner.

Wooden stairs became brick steps, and those

turned to carved stone. The overhead lights yellowed and flickered as the four descended. "Only a bit more," said Turner. Torg showed his teeth in a broad grin. He was not even panting.

"Here we are," said Marianne Turner. The bottommost end of the cellar stretched into the shadowed distance, damp stone floor broken by the occasional moldy carton.

"This way," said Samuel Turner. "I'll show you exactly where—"

Enos Harkman tripped on something and tumbled forward into the suddenly complete darkness. He landed on knees and hands and rolled across the tightly fitted blocks. He cried out and realized there was no echo, the oppressive atmosphere wrapping him in a silence akin to the grave.

"Torg!" he called, but there was no reply. "Dr. Turner!" Nothing. He came to rest with his breath knocked out, but little else apparently amiss. Harkman lay quiet for the moment, refilling his lungs with air. Then he fumbled his way to his knees, ineffectually slapping his pockets in search of a flashlight. Nothing; no torch, no matches.

He stared into the black, eyes straining. Was there some sort of ambient illumination? Yes! He was sure of it. In front of him, a spectral glow began to form. In the glow, a line of humanoid forms silently regarded him.

"I am not your enemy," Harkman rasped out. "Speak with me."

One of the figures raised an arm—and shrieked. Harkman recoiled. The scream, inhumanly edged, coiled around him. The sound embodied pain and anger, an agony that suggested suffering beyond all human measure. Another scream joined the first; then other cries rose up. They wove a sudden symphony of blades and hooks, rusted needles and rent flesh tearing asunder. Harkman wanted to squeeze his eyes shut; more, he wished to plug his ears. Instead, all he could do was gawk as the figures gestured at him, pointing and crying out.

Then the spectral chorus line took a nasty turn. The figure that had originally gestured drew its arm back and flung something directly at Harkman. The psychic detective felt a dollop of something soft and hot splatter against his face. Some of the missile splashed into his lips, smearing against his clenched teeth. The texture was viscous and grainy, almost fibrous. The smell was horrendous, exactly as Samuel Turner had described it.

Other arms rose and lashed forward. More material projected from dark figures smeared against his face and chest, arms and abdomen. Harkman felt nauseated, attempting to spit out what already had penetrated his lips. He bowed forward, then flailed his arms, attempting to rise to his feet.

His nostrils and his throat were clogged with spec-

tral material. He could not breathe. Harkman felt the helpless state of unconsciousness approaching, the inexorable doom of drowning. He tried not to inhale.

The barrage of gelatinous missiles continued until he was upright. Then the clangorous cries abruptly ceased. The bombardment ended. His claustrophobic end via foul suffocation withdrew. Harkman stared into a darkness that abruptly changed its texture.

It was only basement *night* again. There were no accusing figures.

There was only the cellar.

"—I saw them," said Samuel Turner's tense voice.

"Sir?" said Torg, voice concerned. "Are you all right?"

Harkman beat frantically at his clothing, stopped suddenly as he registered no clinging foulness. He was clean again, but the memory of the odor lingered. He looked around at his companions.

"Upstairs!" he cried. "We are through here. For now. Let us adjourn upstairs. I require a whiskey."

"And the equipment?" said Torg.

"Bring it all," Harkman answered. "You should have a whiskey too."

On the succession of steps upward, Harkman said to no one in particular, "You saw nothing? Heard nothing?"

"You convulsed and fell to the floor, Mr. Harkman,"

said Marianne Turner. "Needless to say, we were concerned."

Samuel Turner nodded in agreement.

Torg shook his head. "I could sense you were confronting the spirit world. But that was all. I saw and heard nothing."

They reached the first floor of the Turner home. Looking ahead to his future needs, Harkman said to Mrs. Turner who was busying herself at the bar in the living room, "Please pour me a second whiskey while you're at it."

"A good bourbon," said the surgeon.

"Only the best," Harkman agreed.

The four sat around the table with their drinks, the Turners on the overstuffed love seat, Harkman and Torg in leather wingback chairs.

After finishing his first whiskey, Harkman said, "I am developing a theory, but it is going to require some research. If I work all night tonight, I just may have something to tell you tomorrow evening." He blinked and addressed Samuel Turner, "Do you have an idea of who lived in this house before you?"

"Not really," said the surgeon. "The realty woman said it had been unoccupied for more than a dozen years before we made an offer. Apparently our predecessor died here in the house. The Realtor said he was a single man of some years who kept to himself. The neighbors said he had something of a Teutonic accent and referred to himself as a visitor from the South."

"That's a good start," said Harkman. He looked thoughtful and turned to Torg. "My man, I am going to require some help now that I am beginning to draw upon the apparently boundless resources of the Interweb."

Marianne Turner politely covered her slight smile with pale fingers.

Oblivious, Harkman said to Torg, "I think tonight will be a most excellent night for you to teach me how to gooble."

"Perhaps you will be satisfied with simply googling, sir."

"Whatever." Harkman sat back and picked up his second whiskey with a sigh.

The research had gone well, and Harkman had even managed a few hours of sleep in the early morning. Torg and he joined the Turners in their handsomely appointed library the following evening at seven. As well as their hosts, whiskeys were waiting.

"I have learned much from the magical, um, Internet," said Harkman. "It is a fantastical tool I'm sure I will utilize much in the future. For one thing, I believe I know who the mysterious person who lived in your home prior to the two of you was."

The Turners looked intrigued. "Please tell," said Marianne.

"He was a doctor, a German fellow whose experi-

ence dated back to the Second World War. As it happens, he gained some notoriety when he cooperated with the Nazi SS in a variety of Eastern European concentration camps."

The surgeon started to open his mouth.

"No." Harkman shook his head. "This was not the infamous Herr Doctor Mengele, though he might be considered something of a disciple. Your dweller here fortunately did not experiment upon Jews and Romany, Catholics and the retarded, parents and children. He restricted himself to animal testing with the ambition of someday adding the strength and durability of the beast to the physique of human soldiers. He didn't get far, but he did torment and use up a considerable supply of test primates."

"Ah," said Torg. "Monkeys."

"Indeed," Harkman said. "Many indeed. Our good doctor escaped the allies at the end of the war and found a new home in Argentina. It was from there he migrated to the Crescent City after a time."

"'The visitor from the south,'" quoted Marianne Turner.

Harkman nodded. "Indeed," he said again. "Not only did he take up residence here, but he began using the deeper cellar for his unholy research. No one can say how many primates perished in what you doubtless suspected might once have been slave quarters. I believe much blood must have been mopped up by the previous doctor."

Samuel Turner looked a bit queasy.

Harkman fixed the surgeon with a keen stare. "Did you, sir, experiment on primates in medical school?"

"I did."

"As did I," said Harkman, "in my graduate school days."

Samuel Turner appeared uncertain about how to interpret this.

"You've seen apes at the zoo," said Harkman. "You know how they express displeasure. I believe that is what is happening in your cellar. You may require several rites of exorcism. The spirits of the departed test subjects are not completely moved on. They retain a genuine anger and desire to express their feelings. They hated the departed bad German doctor with an abiding passion. They're not so happy with you or me either."

"You mean—" said Samuel Turner

"Yes," said Harkman triumphantly, "*polterscheists.*"

Torg rolled his eyes in the direction of the ceiling.

Marianne Turner cast her glance at the floor.

Enos Harkman looked rightly proud of himself.

The Halloween War

BRIAN J. HATCHER

I pulled into the Hunt Valley Marriott's parking lot a little after one p.m., lucking into a parking spot near the front entrance. I grabbed my overnight bag and headed inside. One of the smokers sitting on a bench near the front entrance called out, "Great costume!" He meant it. Walking around in broad daylight is something I could get used to.

A family of three waited by the front desk. Dad checked in while Little Daughter swung at the end of Mom's arm. She looked at me and smiled. "Mommy!"

Mom smiled and nodded. "He sure is tall, isn't he, honey?" she said.

Dad received the key card for their room from the front desk clerk. His eyes widened when he saw me.

You can never tell how an adult will see you. "The convention?" he asked.

I nodded. Holding the Conclave here, during the same weekend as a horror convention, allowed us to blend in with the crowd. "You?"

"We're only here for the night. We head to DC in the morning. Forgive me for staring, but you're a professional, aren't you?"

"In a manner of speaking," I said

"Frankenstein, right?"

"What gave me away?"

"Don't get me wrong. Your makeup is really creative. You didn't go for the obvious. It's just that, when I was a kid I was a big reader. Still am. TV and movies never interested me as much as a good book. Believe it or not, my first experience with the Monster was right out of the pages of Shelley's book. I was eight years old the first time I read *The Modern Prometheus*. Must have read it a dozen times since. And it's weird, but I swear you look just the way I pictured him as a kid. Exactly like him."

"I take that as high praise. Thank you."

"You're welcome. We're going to head up to our room before the craziness starts. Enjoy your convention."

"And you have a safe trip," I said.

"Bye-bye, Frankenstein," Little Daughter said, and I waved at her. They headed down the hallway to the elevators.

I wondered what I'd looked like to that man. It didn't matter. I looked exactly the way he wanted me to. That is, after all, what I'm supposed to do.

I checked in and planned to head up to my room to rest. Some of the convention attendees congregated in the hotel bar, and I spotted Dewey in the center of the bustling crowd, people scrambling to get their picture taken with him. Dewey basked in the attention. Not that long ago, he was the avatar of a nearly forgotten serial killer in a truly forgettable 80's slasher movie. In *Library of Blood*, disgraced librarian Dewey Decker stalks and kills a group of teenagers who, as kids, failed to return books to the library. Pure camp. But Hollywood, in the grip of remake fever, took a chance on a remake of *Library of Blood* and wound up with a surprise hit on their hands. Dewey was a star again, bigger than ever. It's why he'd been chosen to represent the True Monsters at this year's Conclave. How quickly things change. Not even a year ago, had Dewey walked into that bar, he would have been invisible. Literally.

Dewey stepped away from his adoring public and parked himself in front of the bar. At his left arm sat a girl in a purple corset that hardly covered her breasts and a pouffed black lace skirt that hardly covered her butt. To Dewey's right, a stocky biker guy started chatting him up. Biker Boy wore a *Phantasm* T-shirt and horror movie patches on his jacket. I wasn't sure if that was supposed to be a costume. I pushed my way

through the crowd until I got close enough to hear them talking.

"So, Dewey," asked Biker Boy, "what do you like better? The original or the remake?"

Dewey finished his pint of Blue Moon. He fished the orange slice out of the glass and bit into the rind. "Why choose?"

"Yeah, well, I think I can guess. You're dressed up like the new guy."

"They were both effin' brilliant," Dewey said.

"Hey, you want another Moon?"

"You, sir, are a gentleman and a scholar." Judging by the empty glasses, Biker Boy had been buying for a while.

Dewey patted the girl on the thigh. "How you doin', hon?"

"Still half a beer left."

"How'm I supposed to take advantage of you if you don't hurry up and get wasted?"

"Ask," she said. She gave him a look. You know the one.

I wasn't trying to cock block Dewey, honest. It just happened to be the moment I decided to butt it. "I see you made it," I said.

"Hey, Frank," Dewey said. "Pull yourself up a chair."

Biker Boy freaked when he saw me. "Dude! You look like someone shoved you through a plate-glass window. Awesome! You and Dewey got the costume contest on lockdown."

At least I could tell how Biker Boy saw me. "It's not about winning contests," I said. "It's all about the love."

"I hear ya, brother. Must have taken you forever to do those scars."

"Not as long as you'd think," I said. "Dewey, step out with me for a minute."

Dewey slid off the bar stool. The girl wrapped her arms around him. "You're coming back, right?"

"Soon as I'm done," Dewey said, "I'm booking right back here. Maybe later we'll go someplace private and you let me check *you* out."

She giggled when he said that. Swear to God.

Conventiongoers packed the lobby, so Dewey and I went outside to talk.

"Unbelievable," I said.

"Hey, there's nothing wrong with a little innocent flirting. And guilty flirting, that can be fun, too."

"Whatever," I said. "Have you seen Dracula?"

"You can forget about him. Minute he got here, he and Vlad Tepes hightailed it to An Poitin Stil. Irish pub down the road."

"They're probably deep in shepherd's pie and Guinness by now."

"You going after him?" Dewey asked.

"No point." Dracula and Vlad had crossed enemy lines and become friends. Can't blame them for ditching the Conclave. Funny thing is, if we'd just put the two of them alone in a room, they'd come up with a fair and amiable agreement that would benefit both

sides. No fighting, no need for the annual Conclave. Of course, fair and amiable was something neither side wanted.

"What do we do?" Dewey asked.

"Guess it's just you and me."

"So Dracula gets to skip out?"

"When you have his seniority," I said, "we'll see what you get away with. I have more seniority than Dracula and I still go."

"Yeah," Dewey said, "but you love it."

"We have a duty."

"Yeah, well, I better get back before my bar stool or my Goth chick gets cold," Dewey said. "I have an evening of watching you and Rasputin browbeat each other all night long to look forward to. If I'm going to get through that, I'll need to get good and drunk."

"Rasputin's not coming."

"Am I the only one who can't catch a break? Who's negotiating for the Real Monsters?"

"They won't say. Thinks it gives them some kind of edge, but it's not like they'll change their playbook."

"Or that we'll change ours. The Conclave's just a pointless circle jerk. The True Monsters lay down the law, and the Real Monsters rattle sabers. Everyone complains about shit that no one has any control over. Then we all whip out our dicks. Anyone's grow since last year? No? Okay, see you next year."

"The Conclave holds the Real Monsters in check.

You realize what would happen if they held influence over the Darker Places? Ever hear of the Dark Ages?"

"That was a million years ago. We got it back, and nothing's changed since. This year'll be just like the others. Boring as hell."

"Trust me," I said, "the last thing you want is the Conclave to get interesting."

I walked Dewey back to the bar. I made him promise, twice, that he'd be on time for the Conclave. I figured I'd have to go looking for him anyway. He cozied up to his chippy, and I went to my room.

The hot shower felt wonderful. I stepped out of the tub and wrapped a towel around my waist. Steam fogged the large mirror, but I know what I look like, at least when others aren't looking. People forget that in the book I'm self-taught, well read, and rather intelligent. But still, I'm an avatar. I'm whatever anyone needs me to be.

Dewey was right, though. I do enjoy the Conclave. It gives me intellectual stimulation I don't get anywhere else. But I also understand what's at stake.

I set the alarm clock for 10:45 p.m. and called the front desk for a wakeup call, just to be sure. That would give me enough time to dress and track Dewey down before midnight. I stretched out on the bed and went over my strategy for the Conclave as I drifted off to sleep. I didn't expect any surprises, except for the one.

Who would represent the Real Monsters at the Conclave? What were they planning?

• • •

Dewey waited for me in the conference room, leaning back in a chair at the head of the table. "You're late."

I set my briefcase on the table. "The conference doesn't start for another ten minutes."

"I meant, late for you. Admit it. You were looking for me in the bar."

"I thought, on the slim chance your lady friend hung around, you might have gotten detained."

"Slim chance? Hardly. I left her sleeping in my room."

"You're kidding."

"What can I say? Horror con girls are the best. First they want to prove they're creepier than you are, then they want to prove they're kinkier."

"You can stop right there."

"First thing she asks me when we get to the room is, did my library have any good books on tying knots?"

"Can we stop talking about this now? Please?"

Dewey couldn't stop smiling. "I love horror conventions."

"As do I," said Elizabeth Bathory as she walked in. "Boys here are such easy prey."

Elizabeth looked as if she had just stepped out of a tub of steaming virgin blood. Sticky rivulets trickled down her indiscreet flesh. Her bare feet stained the floor where she walked. Her velvet robe, trimmed in ermine, provided little modesty and her ludicrously

ample breasts threatened to fling it open at any moment.

Elizabeth snaked an arm around Dewey's shoulders. "But I grow tired of boys." Her voice was unadulterated Garbo. "Perhaps you'll show me what a True Monster can do."

"Yeah, that's what you said last time," Dewey said. "Emphasis on *said*."

Elizabeth flashed a poisoned smirk. "Ah, but this year, I may feel a little more generous."

The Real Monsters had Dewey's number, and sent Elizabeth to distract him. I wanted Dewey distracted as well, so, thanks guys. Although an avatar, she was also a Real Monster. The image she projected was not how anyone wished to see her but how she wished to be seen. The reasons for this made the Real Monsters both pitiable and dangerous.

"I guess Vlad Tepes won't be joining us," I said to Elizabeth.

"His love of Irish stew, I will never understand."

"So, who are we waiting on?"

Elizabeth's smile dripped honey and venom. "No one. Here comes our negotiator."

With a thousand guesses, I would've never picked Osama bin Laden. But there he was. The avatar of Osama bin Laden to be more accurate, with over a decade of hatred and fear to play off. I think I would have preferred the real one.

Elizabeth and Dewey sat down. Bin Laden walked

up to me. For a moment I thought he wanted to shake hands. "Before we begin," he said, "I have something to say."

"Okay."

"We've a long evening ahead of us, so I want you to understand, as they say, where I'm coming from. I don't like you. I loathe all so-called True Monsters. I loathe what you are. I loathe what you stand for. Most important, I loathe the damage you cause. Since you can no longer inspire fear, you instead choose comedy. You have become jesters and fools and make light of the darkness. That makes you dangerous, because you steal from Humanity what it desperately needs most."

"And what's that?" I asked.

"Fear. Fear of government and police, fear of each other, fear of their own mortality. Fear makes Man noble. Without it, they would annihilate themselves. One day they will, unless I stop you. And I will. I shall drive your influence from the Darker Places until not even a memory of you remains. I just thought you should know that."

"All right, then," I said, then took my place at the table.

"What did he say?" Dewey asked.

"I really like this guy," I said. "He's gonna make my job so much easier."

Bin Laden sat next to Elizabeth on the other side of the conference table. Elizabeth not so subtly let her robe fall open. Unimpressed, I opened my briefcase

and pulled out a few file folders. "I assume everyone's seen this year's movie grosses."

"Do I look like a movie producer?" bin Laden asked.

"I'm sorry?"

"Movies grosses?"

"You know why we're here, right?" I asked. "The Real Monsters have complained about the amount of media representation they've received since the Conclave started. Keeps us arguing for hours."

"You think I care about such foolishness? I'm sure it amused you to waste Rasputin's time with such pointless debate. But I am not Rasputin, and you will not play the prattler with me."

"Fine," I said, "if you have something else you'd rather discuss, be my guest."

"It surprises me," bin Laden said, "that the Conclave has been around so long, and yet one topic has never been discussed."

"Which is?" I asked.

"Halloween, of course."

"There's a reason for that," I said. "And if you don't know, I'd suggest you find out before you get in over your head."

"But I do know. The True Monsters control Halloween, and we have no say in its celebration. You use Halloween to mock us. People dress up like you, or us, to make light of fear. I will not allow this to continue."

"What do you propose?" I asked.

"I will accept nothing less," said bin Laden, "than full control over Halloween."

"Are you nuts?" Dewey asked. Elizabeth giggled.

"You're sure there's nothing else you wish to discuss?" I asked.

"There is nothing else worth discussing."

I slid my folders back into the briefcase. "When do you want your answer?"

"I will not allow this Conclave to conclude until this has been settled."

"Very well," I said. "The answer is no. And thus, it seems, this year's Conclave has concluded." I closed my briefcase and rose from the table. "Finished in two minutes. I'm sure we've broken some kind of record."

Dewey scooted away from the table. "And the bar's still open."

"I'll go with you," I said. "I'll even buy the first round."

"Let's go before you change your mind."

"Excuse me," said bin Laden, not rising from his chair. "Where do you think you're going? Did you not hear what I said? The Conclave isn't over, not while the issue of Halloween is still on the table."

"The hell did you say?" Dewey asked.

"I heard him," said Elizabeth. "Didn't you?"

"See, that's the thing," I said. "Halloween isn't on the table. It's damned well off the table, and that's where it'll stay."

"Afraid?" asked bin Laden. "You should be. With-

out Halloween, the True Monsters are nothing. Less than nothing. Can you imagine, do you dare imagine, what would happen if Halloween were no longer yours?"

"I guess we'll never know," I said.

"Pardon me." Bin Laden pulled a cell phone from his robes. He had it on vibrate and it buzzed until he answered it. "Yes? Ah, good. Can you have someone bring them to the conference room? Thank you." Bin Laden hung up the phone. "Mr. Higginbotham will be here in a few minutes. I've petitioned the Holiday Committee to assume authority over Halloween. They agreed to hear my petition and make a summary judgment. You may want to stay for this."

"Are you insane?" I asked.

"All these Conclaves, and never once have you pressed your advantage. You have contented yourself to maintain a balance of authority. A move as bold as this never once occurred to you. That is the power of fear. The moment you stopped being an instrument of fear and fell under its shadow, you were mine from the moment I chose to destroy you."

"Benji," Dewey said, "you just made the biggest damned mistake of your life."

"Shut up, Dewey," I said. "I have to think."

"Come on. We're not going to lose Halloween. It's the second biggest holiday in the United States, thanks to us."

"Then why is the Holiday Committee here?"

Mr. Higginbotham entered the room with a small mob of accountants, corporate lawyers, and other sundry administrative personnel. They covered the entire table with ledgers, files, charts, and record books. More chairs were brought in. Everyone sat except for the four of us; there were no places left.

I saw a look of absolute dread on Dewey's face. It was well justified.

Bin Laden and Elizabeth met Mr. Higginbotham at the head of the table.

"Thank you for taking the time to see us," bin Laden said.

"If there is anything I can do for you," Elizabeth said, "please, let me know." She was, of course, leaning over the table.

"You seem to be missing some of your clothes," Mr. Higginbotham said.

"Oh my, but you're right. What should I do?"

"Find them."

"My dear," bin Laden said, "let me handle this, please." Elizabeth pouted off.

"Mr. Higginbotham," I said, "I apologize that you came all this way to contend with an issue that shouldn't be an issue in the first place. However, I'm not sure I'm qualified to speak for the True Monsters in a matter of this importance and humbly request forbearance until such time as it can be determined who should represent the True Monsters in this matter."

"The True Monsters believed him a proper repre-

sentative for our Conclave," bin Laden said. "However, if he considers himself unqualified to attend, he should certainly leave."

"This meeting has been called as a courtesy," said Mr. Higginbotham. "We are prepared to resolve this issue without hearing from either side. If you do not wish to participate, the True Monsters can still appeal our decision at a later date via the regular channels. The choice is yours."

"Then I shall speak for the True Monsters," I said.

"Proceed," said Mr. Higginbotham.

"I must profess a measure of surprise at these proceedings. Never would I have imagined the True Monsters' dedication and service to Halloween would come into question. Halloween has thrived under our guidance. Its observance bleed-through is second only to Christmas. The entire month of October belongs to Halloween. It is a holiday beloved by young and old alike, because of our diligence."

"Then you would say you're satisfied with Halloween?" asked Mr. Higginbotham.

I saw the trap set in those words, a trap bin Laden hoped I would spring. I weighed my answer carefully. "Whatever more the Holiday Commission would wish us to do, we would, gladly."

"And that," bin Laden said, "is my point. True, Halloween is highly regarded and enjoys the privileges of other holidays, except for one: it is not nationally observed. Perhaps Mr. Frankenstein feels a day off

from work or school is of little consequence, or perhaps he is sincere when he says the True Monsters were mindless of their duties. However, it is obvious that if they had the ability to make Halloween an observed holiday, they would certainly have done so by now."

"If Mr. bin Laden wishes to imply the Real Monsters could serve Halloween better," I said, "I assure you this is not the case. Halloween would lose everything it has gained. One need only look at their attempt at an unauthorized holiday in Detroit to see what they would do with Halloween."

"It was never proven we had anything to do with Devil's Night," said bin Laden.

"I suggest you limit your remarks to facts," Mr. Higginbotham said, "and refrain from speculation."

"Thank you," said bin Laden. "Mr. Frankenstein could undoubtedly keep you here all evening with speculations on what we might do with Halloween. I need no speculation to show exactly what the True Monsters will do. They mean to keep the status quo. Mr. Frankenstein has threatened as much, this very evening. I do not deny the growth Halloween has experienced, but the True Monsters have brought Halloween as far as they can. It is time for new leadership to take Halloween to new heights."

"Thank you, gentlemen," Mr. Higginbotham said. "Please step outside, and we will let you know our decision shortly."

In the hallway, I could barely contain my rage. "Everything you said in that room was a lie! You don't give a damn about Halloween. You think turning it into a night of terror will do anything but destroy it? There won't be anything left of Halloween, and it will be your fault."

"And you're still naïve enough to think that matters," bin Laden said. "Halloween may thrive as a night of blood, or it may fade away. Either way, we win. But the credit for destroying Halloween is yours. I thank you. For being exactly what I needed you to be."

Only then did I realize. Bin Laden saw me as a coward, craving safety, always running from confrontation as if villagers carrying torches hounded my steps. And I was that coward, for him. Because I'm nothing but a goddamned avatar.

The deliberations were short. Mr. Higginbotham's staff exited the conference room. Bin Laden and I went in while Elizabeth and Dewey stayed out in the hallway.

Mr. Higginbotham motioned for us to sit. We sat at opposite sides of the table.

"A change in a holiday's administration is not something we take lightly," Mr. Higginbotham said. "We would do this only for the best interest of the holiday. Although Halloween has grown much since its beginning, we have not seen much improvement since the 1970s, and there has been a noticeable decline in trick-or-treating. The fact that Halloween has failed

to gain observed status has not escaped our notice. However, Halloween's overall growth cannot be overlooked. Therefore, it is the decision of the Holiday Commission to give the True Monsters a period not to exceed two years to obtain nationally observed status for Halloween. If, after two years, they are unable to do this, the Real Monsters will assume administrative authority for a period not to exceed fifty years, after which time their progress will be reviewed by the Commission." Mr. Higginbotham rose to leave. "My suggestion, Mr. Frankenstein, is that you use your time wisely."

After Mr. Higginbotham left, bin Laden got up from the table. "Not as expedient a victory as I would have hoped, but patience is, as they say, a virtue. Next year's Conclave will certainly be interesting." Bin Laden went to leave, but he stopped at the door and faced me. "We're going to be watching you. I just thought you should know that." Then, he was gone.

After a few moments, Dewey wandered in. "So, what happened?"

"We have two years. If no one gets the day off for Halloween by then, we've lost Halloween to the Real Monsters."

"I don't believe it. What do we do now?"

"What can we do? We either find a way to pull it off or somehow convince the Commission to change its mind." I slid out of my chair. "I'm heading up to my room to crash. I'm in no mood for barhopping tonight,

but I promised you booze, so you can put them on my room tab."

"Why couldn't you have offered when I felt like drinking? Damn. 2012 is gonna be a hell of a year."

"More than that, Dewey. It might very well be the end of the world."

Oh, the Ho-Ho Horror

Joel A. Sutherland

(For Alex and Murphy, for inspiring this story.)

How any parent can say they love Christmas with a straight face is beyond me.

Ginny and I host an annual Christmas party for thirty to forty of our closest casual acquaintances and strangers. Neighbors I hardly know, co-workers I can't stand, distant relations and in-laws I hold a special dislike for. Idle chitchat and an endless loop of Christmas tunes compete for my disdain, while people's dirty kids run their dirty shoes over my Persian rug and paw their dirty hands over my fifty-eight-inch flat screen. Someone inevitably gets drunk from two measly glasses of spiked eggnog and talks too close to my face with gar-

lic breath before running off to vomit in the bathroom, no doubt leaving some bile on the tiles behind the toilet. Sort of like a special little present for me to find later. What would Christmas be without special little presents?

God, I hate our annual Christmas parties.

Although, we can't call them Christmas parties anymore, can we?

No, that would offend *someone* out there, so Ginny buys the invitations that say "Holiday Party" or "Festive Gathering" or, failing that, buys blank cards and writes "End of the Year Party," as if that will hide the religious undertones of the event, despite the fact that she alternates writing each letter in red and green ink. It drives me banana sandwich.

And that's just the parties. There's plenty else about Chistm—the holidays—that makes me want to bury myself under a mound of overdue January bills. Shopping mall carols. Crowds. Battles to buy the year's overpriced must-have toy. Subarctic temperatures. Shoveling driveways. Dorky sweaters. *It's a Wonderful Life* repeats. Crippling debt. Traveling nonstop to visit the in-laws. The in-laws, in general. Lining up for my kid to sit on fake Santa laps. The psychotic reindeer that's eyeing my fingers—as if they were a pile of carrot sticks left outside a child's home for it to eat on Christmas Eve—as I'm chained to the wall of a dank basement, unable to defend my outer extremities.

But I'm getting ahead of myself.

Back to the Holiday Party.

I couldn't breathe. The house was oppressively stuffy thanks to all the people I wanted nothing to do with. When Ginny started passing out Christmas crackers (something else to add to my list of holiday pet peeves: those flimsy multicolored paper crowns and the people who wear them) I grabbed my coat and my keys (which were weighted down with a Swiss Army knife key chain—last year's Christmas present from my wife, thank you very much), then stepped outside.

I inhaled deeply and exhaled with a sigh, watching my breath stream from my mouth and nostrils in a misty cloud. The night was frigid but calm, lazy snowflakes drifting to the ground. Up and down the road the streetlights shed light for no one. It was too cold and too late for anyone to be outside. I smiled. I was alone.

"Whatcha doin'?"

"Jesus fuck!" I yelled, jumping and spinning around like a ballerina on speed. It was my boy, and by the look on his face, "Jesus fuck" was not a regular part of his vocabulary. "Gregory. I didn't hear you come out."

"I saw you grab your coat. Sorry."

"It's okay," I said. Although the temperature was approaching -20ºC, I began to wish I had left my coat inside. "What do you want?"

He shrugged his shoulders and mumbled something unintelligible.

"I was thinking of taking a walk. You should head back in. You don't want to catch a cold and have to spend the rest of the party in bed."

On second thought, that didn't sound like a terrible idea.

"Don't wanna," he said. "Wanna go with you."

"All right, then," I said with a sigh. The kid was incorrigible. "Grab your coat, earmuffs, and mitts and let's go."

He stared at me and smiled.

"Quickly now," I added, "before someone catches wind of our planned escape and alerts the guards."

His smile contorted into a panicked grimace.

"There aren't actually any guards. Go."

His smile returned as he bolted inside and returned a moment later with his winter gear bundled in his arms. Snow crunched loudly underfoot as we walked, Gregory slipping into his puffy purple coat (his mother's doing, not mine), rainbow-patterned mittens and earmuffs in the likeness of Pikachu.

"You look good."

"Thanks," he said. No sense of sarcasm. Sure, my boy was a little weird, but walking with him sure as hell beat staying at the party. As we walked side by side, I felt an odd sensation and part of me wanted to stop to give the boy a hug. I gave him a manly pat on the shoulder instead.

Little did I know that this once dreadful, now peaceful night would end with my current predica-

ment, held hostage and staring down Rudolph the Red-Tempered Reindeer.

Still, even if I did, I probably wouldn't have gone back to the party.

"Grandma, *Shrek the Halls,* and fruitcake."

We had detoured out of our neighborhood, crossed a country road and were walking along a twisty wooded path behind the local hockey arena. How long had the boy been nattering on for? I had zoned out ten minutes before and had no idea what he was talking about. "Huh?"

"Dad!" His voice was thick with exasperation. "Those are my three favorite things about Christmas. Now it's your turn."

Ah, yes. He was obviously referring to our once yearly trip to Montreal to visit my mother in between Christmas and New Year's; he had watched that *Shrek* special every day in December since we'd bought the DVD for him a couple of years back; and the boy can pack away fruitcake with the best of them.

What a weird kid.

I'm so goddamned sick of that DVD and fruitcake is disgusting, but we probably should try and visit his grandmother more often. If I survive the night, that is.

"Dad! Your three favorites!"

"Hm? Oh, right. Um . . ." I scanned the forest around me. "Snow, and . . ." His earmuffs caught

my eye. "Pokemon winter apparel, and . . ." Up ahead around a bend I spotted a pine tree farm. "Christmas trees."

As soon as I said that last one I regretted it.

"Me, too!" He slowed his pace as he gazed at the trees that rolled up and down over the snowy hills like an ocean of green and white waves, frozen in time. "Dad, are we going to have a Christmas tree this year?"

"Look, son," I began but trailed off. Something in the way he was looking up at me, so full of optimism, hope, and, yes, Christmas spirit, made me start to choke up. That weird feeling of wanting to hug him washed through my body again—the last thing I wanted to do at that moment was slap him with the cold, hard truth.

How does one look their kid in the eye and say, "Sorry, we can't afford a tree this year because Daddy's former boss is an asshole who laid off one of his most loyal employees three weeks before Christmas. But, hey, at least our family room won't look so weird—I can't afford presents this year either, and wouldn't that have been dumb to have a tree with no presents under it?"

Damn, I wasn't always this cynical. Especially around Christmas.

I used to love the decorations, the carolers. The hot chocolate after a cold night's tobogganing. Taking Gregory to the Santa Claus parade and oohing and aahing at the procession of lame floats. Hell, I even dressed up as the big guy himself one year and paid

surprise visits to my nephews and nieces on Christmas Eve. Scared the bejesus out of little Laura—she's been terrified of fake Santas ever since—but man, those were good times.

And there I was, out in the middle of a field, trudging through the snow, avoiding my own freaking Christmas party, pissed and bitter and unable to give my boy a simple goddamn tree for Christmas. Surrounded by tall, silent pines. No one else in sight.

Something had to give.

I reached into my coat pocket and pulled out my key chain. The red Swiss Army knife glinted in the moonlight, as rosy as Santa's cheeks.

"Yeah, kiddo," I said, feeling the Christmas spirit seep back into my soul. "We're going to have a Christmas tree this year."

It had seemed like a good plan at the time—use the saw on my Swiss Army knife to "liberate" a pine tree from the frozen ground and "borrow" it for the season—but I quickly realized that it was actually a sucky plan. Maybe the suckiest plan ever conceived. But I didn't care. I was getting my family a tree for Christmas.

Still, as my biceps began to seize up from the strain of using a two-inch saw to cut through a thick tree trunk and the newly formed blisters on my palms popped, freeing clear liquid and blood to trickle down

my forearms, I began to wish I had a more appropriate tool to complete the task at hand.

I had sent the boy home with a message for his mother. "Tell her I'll be home soon," I said, "and tell her I'm bringing the cheer." If I could have seen my own face, I'm sure it would have looked wickedly demented, but the boy just smiled, giggled, and turned and ran. A good kid.

I began to huff and puff as my tiny saw passed the halfway point. Sweat stung my eyes and dripped from my nose and chin. The scent of pine burned my nostrils. My blood began to flow more freely from my palms, splattering the needle-covered snow. It painted a beautifully festive picture on the ground, red, white and green. I laughed at the thought, ignored the searing pain, and quickened my pace.

Soon I was near the end of the trunk. I pocketed my bloody knife, grabbed ahold of the treetop, and yanked. Wood cracked and an owl took flight from the concealment of a nearby tree, the powerful flapping of its wings fading away as it went. The tree fell to the ground with a crash and then the night grew eerily quiet. I paused and scanned the hills around me, ready for someone to come charging out of one of the rows of planted trees, alerted by the racket I had caused.

Nothing happened.

My head pounded with a thief's high. It felt like my blood was coursing through my veins with renewed vigor. Confident that I had pulled off a successful crime

yet eager to hightail it back home, I grabbed the trunk of the tree and began to flee.

It was hard work, dragging the tree with its dense branches through the snow. So hard that I had only made it five feet when I saw a giant red sleigh crest the hill in front of me. A single reindeer, foaming at the mouth and eyes ablaze, pulled it. The animal was larger than the reindeers at petting zoos, more like a small moose, and it gnashed its teeth when it spotted me. A figure stood up in the sleigh. Portly, bearded, and dressed head to toe in red velvet, there was no mistaking who it was. But the look of pure fury etched in his face was all wrong.

Santa Claus pointed at me and bellowed, "Who dares to steal one of my trees?" His deep voice seemed to shake the snow from the branches all around us.

All I could think in response was, *Oh, I didn't know I was stealing from Santa*, but instead of saying anything I simply pissed eggnog-scented urine down my left leg.

Okay, so the reindeer wasn't actually the size of a small moose, it wasn't foaming at the mouth and its eyes weren't ablaze. Those were embellishments of my overactive imagination and the panicked adrenaline that had consumed me in the heat of the moment. It did gnash its teeth, though. A lot. I would learn that was Rudolph's trademark move.

It's not the real Rudolph, of course, nor is Santa the

real Mr. Claus. Do I need to mention that those are make-believe characters? Actually, under my present circumstance, it feels oddly necessary.

"I'm not the real Santa," Santa said as he tied my wrists together with a strap of red leather covered in tiny gold bells. I stood rooted to the ground and let him have his way with me. What can I say? Even though I knew he wasn't really one of the most powerful men in the world, I had a deep-seated and powerful reverence for the suit. "The name's Randall Jenks. I own this tree"—he hefted it up into his sleigh—"and all the others. This is my farm."

Regardless of his introduction, I knew I wouldn't be able to think of him as anything but Santa. He grabbed my bound wrists, looped a length of rope through the binding and tied it to the back of his sleigh.

"And you've gotta pay for trying to steal from me."

Rudolph gnashed his teeth and Santa hopped nimbly into his ride. With a crack of his whip, Rudolph took off at a gallop, and we—Santa seated comfortably, I dragged along the ground rather uncomfortably— were whisked away to Santa's farmhouse.

Which brings us up to speed.

Santa's basement is a particularly nasty place. Think of the abodes of Buffalo Bill and the Teenage Mutant Ninja Turtles and you get the idea. I rattle the chains holding my arms above my head to the old stone wall

behind me. I discover the wall is crumbling and the chains aren't too securely attached to it, but that wasn't my purpose. I rattled the chains involuntarily—my whole body is shaking thanks to the ride here and the "I want to eat your fingers" look in Rudolph's eye. The reindeer clomps slowly toward me and, you guessed it, gnashes his teeth.

Why did I have to steal a tree from a deranged psychopath? Why did my boss have to lay me off only twenty-one days before Christmas? Why is this farmer masquerading as Old St. Nick?

"You're probably wondering why I'm dressed as Santa," Santa says, "and why I have a sleigh and a reindeer."

"No," I lie. I don't want to give him the satisfaction.

"Sure you are. Who wouldn't be?" He steps so close I can smell a hint of nutmeg and cinnamon on his breath, and I catch myself wondering if he isn't really who he claims he isn't. "Three years ago business was in the crapper. People weren't buying real trees anymore. Artificial trees could be purchased on the cheap at any discount department store and people were becoming so damned eco-conscious. Thank you Walmart. Thank you Al Gore."

Rudolph's gaze isn't flinching from my hands. I curl my fingers into fists reflexively—not so much an act of aggression as an attempt to hide my much loved and needed digits.

Santa steps back and begins pacing the base-

ment, looking at me only occasionally. "The world was changing. I was forced into confronting the truth that if I wanted to eat"—Rudolph's tongue wets his hairy lips—"I'd have to change with it."

"So you bought yourself a Santa suit," I say.

"Very good! I bought myself a Santa suit. And a sleigh. And let us not forget the reindeer. His name is Harvey, by the way."

But I know he'll always be Rudolph to me.

"I hoped that kids would drag their parents to my farm to meet Santa, and while here, their folks would buy a tree. Christmas is, after all, for the kids."

For the first time since I sent him home I think of Gregory, and I'm glad he left when he did. Like Santa said, Christmas is for the kids, and I'd hate for my boy to have to see me kill the big guy in red. That might put a damper on the holiday for him for, gosh, a couple of years at least.

But that's the only way I can foresee this night ending. Either I die, or Santa dies.

"And it worked! Families came in droves. They fed Harvey, they took pictures of little 'uns in the sleigh, and they all wanted a piece of me. Santa sells." He pauses, and both his smile and the twinkle in his eye fade. "But I still didn't sell enough. Tree sales only rose marginally. Most people came for the free family fun and left without opening their wallets and purses. Cheapos." From his right pocket Santa pulls a knife. It gleams in the light of the basement's solitary bulb,

dangling from a cord overhead. "And to make matters worse, I began to notice fresh stumps in my fields each and every morning." From his left pocket he pulls an oversized candy cane. Somehow I find this more menacing than the knife. "Poor sales, the cost of all the razzle-dazzle, and stolen stock. It all adds up to guaranteed bankruptcy. So I decided to take action. If I'm going down, at least I'm taking one thieving son of a bitch with me. And wouldn't you know, you're the first thieving son of a bitch I've caught." With a sound like metal scraping bone, he shaves a piece of candy cane from the tip. It plummets to the ground completely unlike a gentle snowflake, and I feel my heart plummet with it.

He's whittling a dagger.

A sick, twisted, delicious dagger.

"You know," he says, his hands busily carving his cane of death, "it costs a lot of money to feed Harvey. He's got a voracious appetite. Carrots only tease him. What he really craves is meat. You got any on you?"

Behind Santa—oh, sweet Jesus—behind Santa I see a pair of small feet appear down the stairs. It's hard to see in the dark, but the puffy purple coat, rainbow mitts, and Pikachu earmuffs can only belong to one person.

The boy.

His eyes widen and his mouth forms an O as he sees me chained to the wall. Or maybe he's just excited to see Santa Claus. Either or.

At least Santa and Rudolph haven't heard him. Yet. The boy ain't the quiet type.

Santa touches his finger to the tip of the candy cane. "Ooh, sharp," he says.

And then he does it. Gregory jumps up and down and yells, "Santa Claus! It's really you!"

Santa turns.

Rudolph turns.

Santa says, "Who the fuck?"

The boy's expression turns from glee to shock.

Rudolph crouches, as if he's about to charge.

I kick my feet off the ground and land on the back of Rudolph's neck, squeezing my legs on both sides.

Rudolph charges. At my boy. The hairy, stinky son of a whore.

I hold on with my legs and all my might. We move forward. My arms are pulled back behind me. The chains strain in the wall.

And then they break free.

Rudolph rockets forward with me straddling him like a horse.

Santa grabs hold of the boy.

"Gregory! Down!" I yell. I'm afraid that if I yell "Duck!" he'd look around for water fowl.

He ducks.

Santa turns to face me as Rudolph and I near him. I swing my arms wildly past his face. The chains, still attached to my wrists, hurtle through the air.

The poor bastard doesn't even have time to blink.

Skin tears, blood sprays, teeth shatter, an eyeball dislodges and the big man crumples in a heap. But before he collapses he tosses the candy cane in the air.

I catch it.

In one swift motion I plunge the dagger into Rudolph's neck. The beast bellows a pained gurgle, gnashes his teeth one final time, and collapses even harder than Santa did. I'm thrown forward and hit the ground with a thud. I tuck my shoulder and roll but the impact hurts like hell. I come to a stop on my back and look up, dazed as all get-out.

The boy steps into my line of vision and looks down at me. His expression is hard to read.

What have I done? I've caved Santa Claus's face in with a chain. I've plunged a candy cane into Rudolph's neck. I've messed up my son for life.

Plus, I've ruined Christmas.

Gregory opens his mouth and says, "Hi, Dad."

I'm too shocked to answer.

"You okay?" he adds.

I remain silent.

"Sorry I came back." He kneels down beside me and wipes some reindeer blood from my brow with the back of his purple sleeve. "I went home to tell Mom you'd be back soon with the cheer, but she was already asleep. Everyone had left. I waited up for you but got scared. I didn't know what had happened. I had to come find you."

What a good boy. What a good effin' boy.

The pain coursing through my body seems to dissipate a little. I sit up and wrap him up in my arms, squeezing him to my chest. Gregory squeezes me back.

"You saved my life," I say, not yet ready to let him go.

"Dad, we killed Santa Claus," he whispers in my ear. He doesn't sound too upset about it.

"Nah, just some farmer named . . ." What the hell was his name? "Just some farmer."

"Oh. Okay, then."

And just like that, he's fine. He's stronger than I've ever given him credit for.

We stand together and I drape an arm over his shoulder. He's taller than I realized. Guess it's time I started paying more attention.

"Is it wrong to kill a man?" he asks.

"Not in self-defense."

"Is it wrong to take a dead man's tree?"

I reach into my pocket, pull out my wallet, and toss a bill onto dead Santa's ample belly.

"Not if you pay for it." That was my last twenty. I have no idea how we'll get through the holidays. But what the heck, it's Christmas.

Hoping for a miracle, I say to the boy, "Let's go home and decorate our tree."

The Unfortunate Persistence of Harold Francis Beamish

AARON POLSON

On their way to drunkenness, a pair of seventeen-year-old boys swayed across the Wellman River Bridge in a rusty Ford F-150 moments before hitting the dead man. Bobby, pale and thin as a twist of plain paper, slugged back the last swallow of beer, crumpled the can with his left hand, and tossed it out the window, aiming for the railing. But the can flew wide, winked in a flicker of moonlight, and vanished into the darkness below.

"Whoo-hooo!" he howled out the window. Heavy metal pounded from the truck's speakers, cranked too

loud despite a loose wire and buzz in the dash. Bobby thumped his liberated hand on the side of the door to the beat. "That's some badass guitar playin', D."

"Yeah, but your damn speaker's blown and you're likely to put a dent in your door like that," Darren mocked. The linebacker took a sip from his own can, rubbed the stiffness in his knee with the other hand, looked up at the bend of dark roadway ahead, and dropped the beer. "Jesus, stop!" His hands locked against the dashboard as cold foam leaked onto the rubber mats at his feet.

Bobby sent the brake into the floor with his right foot, the tires locked in a howl, and both boys tumbled forward. The body hit with a thump, a dull metallic sound muffled by flesh and clothing. Gears whined in protest as Bobby thrust the truck's shifter into park. His beer-addled brain had received the impulse a split second too late.

"Shit."

Tiny insects swam through the Ford's headlight beams. The engine puttered at idle, shaking the seat and rattling the empty can at Darren's feet. Neither boy moved for a long minute, but then Bobby lowered his forehead and rested it against the steering wheel.

"Had to be a deer," he muttered.

"Like hell." Darren lifted a finger and pointed to the windshield. "I saw his face, Bobby. All white and big as a frying pan. He looked right at me."

Bobby's door groaned as he pushed it open. His

feet struck the rough asphalt with a dull crunch, and he staggered a few meandering steps toward the front of the truck. The vehicle waited, growling on its haunches.

"Hey, I can't get out," Darren called.

"Climb out my side. The lock's busted, remember?"

Darren grunted as he scooted across the bench seat. A moment later, they stood side by side on the blacktop, staring down at a lumpy body, a man, one arm cocked above his head, the other twisted under his back. The moon reflected in the man's face, painting it a shade of silver gray like a pile of raw clay. Countless crickets and bullfrogs joined the engine's chorus.

"Definitely dead, Bobby."

"Aw, hell!" Bobby's fist pounded into the fender of his truck. He yelped and proceeded to stuff the scraped and bleeding knuckles into his mouth. Darren approached the corpse slowly, knelt, and put a hand on his jacket.

"Soaked, too."

"Bud?" Bobby mumbled with his hand in his mouth.

"Whassat?"

"Is it blood?" Bobby asked again, rubbing his sore hand against his pants.

"No." Darren leaned a little closer, sniffed, and scowled. "River water. He's as cold as a fish."

Bobby drew back one foot and kicked the fender. "Goddammit, I killed a man," he complained, hopping backward with throbbing toes.

"Don't think so."

"What?" Bobby stopped hopping.

Darren's hand hovered over the dead man's face, trembling slightly at a nasty gash in the side of the head. "He's been dead awhile. Real cold." He rose to full height and dried his palm on his shirttail. A chill breeze whispered through the trees on either side. Darren squinted into the stretch of road behind the truck as Bobby paced a circuit between the taillights and driver's door. "How was a dead man—"

"What the hell are we going to do?" Bobby interrupted Darren's thought process. "I'm drunk, D. I killed a man and I'm drunk . . ."

"Shhhh. Quit blubberin'. You didn't kill anybody, but we can't call the cops with both of us drunk." Darren cocked his head to one side, listening. "Someone's comin'." He moved to the body and poked his hands under the arms from behind. "Hurry up and grab his feet."

Bobby stared for an instant, enough time for his dulled senses to take over. "Let's leave him—"

"Too late. Now, come on. In the truck." Darren's face flushed with serious intent, and his eyes caught sight of a brown wallet on the pavement. He hesitated.

Bobby started to whine. "But . . . we could just leave—"

"But nothin'. Never mind leaving him. Who's gonna believe he was already dead?"

Bobby tugged at his mess of dark hair. "Why do you keep saying that shit about him bein' dead before?"

"Just help me, all right?"

They hoisted the corpse toward the back of the truck. Cold, fetid water soaked into their clothes, through Bobby's untucked flannel shirt and Darren's hooded sweatshirt. They heaved the body over the side and rolled it onto the bed. It landed with a dull thud and tiny crack as the skull bounced against sheet metal.

"Poor bastard," Bobby said.

"Ain't gonna hurt him anymore." Darren climbed into the driver's seat. "Get in, dammit!" Headlights crested the hill behind them on the other side of the bridge. Bobby yanked the passenger door open and tumbled inside. With a pop and a groan, the truck slid into gear, and they rolled away.

"Thought you said that door was busted."

Bobby looked up, his face pale and green against the dashboard lights. "Just from the inside."

The taillights overtook them, and a black sports car whizzed past, fading into a pair of red taillights before slipping around a curve. The truck slowed, and Darren cranked the wheel toward the right shoulder.

"What're you doing?" Bobby's eyes swelled as he white-knuckled the door handle.

"Heading back to the river, you dumb bastard."

"River?"

"We gotta stash the stiff." Darren nodded over his shoulder. "Smelled like the river, so I figure we might as well plant him back in there."

A break in the trees over the river broke open the

midnight sky as the truck bounced across the narrow bridge. Darren twisted his hands on the steering wheel, looking for the pull off that led to a few fishing plots near the bridge. Bobby continued to mumble under his breath.

"Quit your yammerin', would you?"

"You didn't kill the guy, D." Bobby tucked his lips together in a pout.

Darren shook his head. "No. But you didn't touch his cold-as-a-dead-carp skin. I'm sure he was already dead . . . had a scar on his head, like a bullet wound."

"Bullshit . . . Where's the blood?"

"Dunno." Darren's eyes ballooned as he shook his head.

Bobby shifted in his seat and peered, pale-faced, at the body in the back. Arms and legs flopped like a carnival ride with loose bolts. The boys tossed in their seats while the truck navigated a few assorted dips in the rutted dirt road. A splash of cold mud sprayed across the passenger window. The truck rattled to a stop, and Darren clicked off the lights.

"Leave 'em on, okay?" Bobby pleaded.

"What?"

"It's so damn dark."

Darren punched Bobby in the arm. "Chickenshit, you want to broadcast to the rest of the world we're dumping a hobo into the river?"

"Please, man?"

Darren shrugged. "Let's get this done."

Bobby pulled at his lower lip between two fingers as Darren hopped from the cab. The crickets and bull-frogs had taken a break. The headlights glinted against broken beer bottles, and the river lapped against the muddy banks, snaking around the bend back toward town in one direction, vanishing beneath the bridge in the other. Darren glanced at the flickering surface of the water and back toward the truck bed. A shadow shifted, and a damp chill brushed against his neck.

"Come on, you wuss," Darren chided Bobby as he forced his own reluctant legs to move. He lowered the tailgate and tugged the body out by the ankles. The foot jerked; Darren's hands fell open, and he reeled backward.

"What?"

"The fucking thing moved." Darren's eyes narrowed. "I thought it moved."

"Couldn't have, right?"

Darren shook his head. "Right. It's . . . it's just late."

Their boots shuffled in dirt and crunched glass fragments as they slid the corpse from the tailgate and hauled it to the edge of the river. Both strained to see under the glare of Bobby's halogens, and they swung the body three times to gain momentum, releasing at the apex of the third arc so the body flopped over the edge and landed with a plash and spray of murky water, a perfect belly flop. It bobbed, turned over, and stopped.

"No . . ."

"Oh, shit."

The dead man, highlighted by the truck's high beams, hooked one arm on a length of driftwood, and bobbed at the surface of the water. Shadows danced and played on the dead man's face, appearing as though he smirked at the boys.

"I figured he'd float," Bobby said.

Darren glared at him. "Why didn't you say somethin'?" He slid down the bank, landing on a few smooth stones at the edge of the water.

"Hey! What're you doing?"

Darren waded into the waist-high water, shivering as the cold muck soaked through his jeans and settled around his legs and testicles. "Setting our friend free." With his hands at his sides, Darren wobbled through the current toward the corpse.

"Darren?" Bobby flinched.

"What now?"

Bobby waved to the bridge. "I hear a car."

A few feet away from the body, Darren paused, listening. His ears filled with splashes, his bones chilled from the rush of frigid water, his stomach tight and knotted.

"I don't hear anything—"

Darren froze. The flash of headlights cut the words from his mouth.

Bobby ran for the river, tumbled headlong, and crashed into the cold water. "Get that damn stiff outta here." In slow motion, he staggered past Dar-

ren, toward the dead man, but, just as he reached out, the body rolled over, slipped from the grasp of the tree limb, and began rolling downriver.

"D-did you see that?"

Darren's eyes locked onto the headlights as they slowed in the middle of the bridge. His face flashed to the bank, Bobby's truck, and the high beams. "We're in deep shit."

"The stiff moved. Swear to God, man."

"Get down, you dumbass." With tremendous effort, Darren pulled his lethargic feet from the mud, grabbed Bobby's arm, and dragged him to his knees. Both boys were up to their necks in the cold water, both their hearts pounding in their chests as the headlights swung around the dirt road at the end of the bridge and pulled into place next to Bobby's truck. The riverbed echoed with two slamming doors followed by muttering too distant for either to make out.

"D—who are they?" Bobby whispered.

"Don't know. Maybe the guys that . . ." Darren held his finger to his head like a gun.

Dark silhouettes shuffled across two sets of headlights. Two large bodies gathered in front of Bobby's truck, blotting the light. One shape raised an arm and brought it down quickly. Glass shattered, and one headlamp went dead.

"Mothermmph—"

Darren clamped a wet and fishy hand across Bobby's mouth.

Crack. The other lamp sputtered. Black shadows against a dark sky swelled at the edge of the river.

"Duck," Darren whispered and dragged his friend with him, making an underwater tackle on the smaller boy. Bobby struggled, kicking and clawing, but Darren was stronger, and held him under as long as he could. When they surfaced, sputtering, they heard doors slam, and the other set of headlights wheeled away back toward the road.

"Sons of bitches . . ." Bobby panted. "D—they . . . smashed my lights."

"Lucky they didn't smash us."

"The—" Bobby stopped abruptly, his eyes ballooned, and he thrashed out of the water. Scrambling on the muddy bank, he slipped twice, caught his footing, and scampered toward the truck. Darren followed, steadily mounted the embankment, and shook as much water from his clothing as he could.

"What's your problem, Bobby?"

Bobby's face went white under the sliver of moon, pale and bloodless. "G—grabbed—my leg."

"What?"

"Somethin' yanked my leg. Pulled on me just now." Bobby slouched against the driver's side fender of the truck. "That dead son of a bitch."

Darren's fingers ran through his hair, chasing out as much muck and filth as possible. Nature fell in with its chorus again, a rhythm of crickets and frogs punctuated by a distant hoot of a barn owl. Coupled with

his soaked clothes, the raptor's call broke a shiver over
Darren's back like a half-rotten two-by-four.

"Bullshit."

"You said he kicked you earlier, right?"

Darren tugged at the waistband of his sweats.
"Imagined it. That guy was done. Dead. Finished.
Cold. He had that bullet wound."

"No blood, though."

"Right . . ."

"So how'd he get outta the river and down the
road?" Bobby frowned. "Let's just go, okay?" He tugged
his door open.

"Can't."

"What?"

"Tires slashed. At least the front two." Darren
walked over and kicked the rubber with a dull thud.
He slumped to his haunches and looked under Bobby's
open door toward the rear. "Got those, too."

"D?"

Darren tugged at his hair again. "What Bobby?"

"You leave this note in here?"

"What note?"

Bobby's fingers trembled as he held up a slip of
paper with dark scribbles on it, scribbles that spelled
out: *Looks like you'll have to walk into town. Have fun
with Harry, boys. He's all yours now.* His other hand
held up a brown wallet.

"Not mine."

Bobby dropped the note and flipped open the

wallet. "Belongs to a fella named Harold Francis Beamish."

"Lemme see that." Darren took the wallet, feeling the smooth leather and stitching. "It's cold . . . like it was wet. I think I saw it on the road earlier, back where you . . ."

"Hit the stiff?" Bobby slammed his truck door. "This is nuttier than your aunt Lucy, D. What do you think they mean, 'have fun with Harry?'"

Darren tossed the wallet back on the truck's hood. "We've gotta get back to town."

About a hundred yards away, a rustling noise echoed under the bridge. Bobby's wide eyes flicked between the wallet and Darren. His mouth opened.

"It's Harold Francis Beamish . . . he's a goddamned zombie."

"Bullshit." Darren said it, but felt the bile rise in his throat, pumped by the maniacal assault of his heart.

"I'm not sticking around . . . either Beamish gets us or his buddies." Bobby backed away slowly, turned, and ran, sprinting into the darkness toward the road.

Rustle.

A shape shambled closer. The moon cut across a pale face. Darren lowered his head and dug his heels into the dirt like a wind sprint in football practice, taking a right angle away from the stumbling form near the bridge. His chest burned, and his stinking, water-soaked clothes dragged against him, but he made the main road and beat his feet against the asphalt across

the bridge. His left knee, the knee with reconstructed ligaments from a vicious chop-block last season, howled, and his gait slowed to a crooked, limping jog. Bobby was only a few dozen yards ahead, leaning on his knees. He doubled over and retched onto the pavement.

"We . . . follow . . . the road . . . into town," Bobby panted. He wiped his mouth against his flannel-sleeve.

Darren nodded, but his eyes caught the tire marks on the shoulder. "This is where we hit him."

"What?"

"Harold whatshisname."

Darren saw the headlights in Bobby's eyes. A car, behind them. He lowered his shoulder into his friend and lunged, sending both of them into the ditch in a crumpled mass. Brittle grass and twigs scratched and gouged at their exposed skin, and Bobby sat up with a jagged line across his cheek.

"What the hell did you do—"

"Shhhh," Darren pressed a finger against his lips. A vehicle, invisible to the boys in the high grass, zipped by, its tires buzzing against asphalt. They lay in the grass for a moment, both listening. The night had grown colder, and puffs of breath came in little clouds.

"I wanna go home, man," Bobby whined.

"I know . . . I know." Darren rubbed his sore knee and suddenly snapped his head to one side.

"What?"

"Listen," Darren whispered.

The sound was faint: a scraping of feet against the road, as though someone dragged two wet and stiff legs across the asphalt, a slow but persistent shuffle in their direction.

"D . . . I think I peed myself."

"It's river water."

"No . . . it's warm."

"God, you're useless." Darren shook his head, pushed himself off the ground, and limped toward the road.

"W-where you going?"

Darren glanced back at Bobby with a trace of a smile working on his lips. "That last car sorta gave me an idea . . . I'm going to make sure ol' Harold stays right in the middle of the blacktop until another moron comes zipping over the bridge. Then, wham"— he slapped a fist into the opposite palm—"Harold's their problem, and we can get your sorry ass some clean clothes."

Dick and Larry

D. L. SNELL

"Looks like a guillotine," Dick observed as he and Larry approached the trapdoor in the woods.

"It's a trap," Larry replied.

"What kind of trap?"

"Did you bring the containment unit?"

"It's called a Nikon, Larry." The camera hung around Dick's neck. "This thing's got more megapixels than your brain."

"Did you bring the ectoplasmic injector?"

Dick raised an eyebrow. "The *turkey baster* is in your proton pack, Rick Moranis." He rhymed the surname with a planet, the one with the o-ring. "Now, *what kind of trap?*"

Situated along the Collings Mountain Trail, the cell consisted of two-by-twelve planks and telephone poles, preserved in creosote but weathered and grow-

ing lichen nonetheless. The trapdoor, mounted on vertical tracks, hovered above the entrance.

Larry supposed Dick was right: the door *did* look like a guillotine. Although he didn't know how big a guillotine was, exactly. Definitely bigger than a zillion.

Larry crouched and examined the ground. He walked on his haunches to spots of interest, sniffing fir scales and dirt.

Dick rolled his eye. "What are you doing, Larry?"

"Looking for droppings." He tasted a stick.

"I don't see any droppings."

"Yeah, you've only got one eye."

"And it sees just fine, thank you very much. If you can't tell me what this place is, you're *walking* out of here."

Larry found something pearly on the ground and picked it up.

"It's just a sequin," Dick said.

Larry put it in a specimen baggy anyway.

He went to step into the cell, but the trapdoor cast a shadow over him; it was definitely bigger than a zillion—and he couldn't even count that high.

He shuddered and sneaked under the door as quickly as possible.

In the cell, something had busted the floorboards. Something big. Larry's nose detected only old wood and pee. Not the smells he'd expected.

Outside, Dick fingered his digital camera. "I can't take pictures of this cage, Larry. I don't think *The Cur-*

rent Courier publishes juvenile carvings of pot leaves and the scatological pranks of apes. What're you doing in there anyway?"

"Well," Larry said, retrieving a Tupperware container from his proton pack, courtesy of JanSport. "I took out the bolt that the Forest Service used to deinstall the trapdoor back in the late, uh . . . Middle Ages. Now I'm just laying the bait."

"Bait?" Dick asked as Larry opened the Tupperware and scooped up its invisible contents. "Looks like *air*."

"*You* look like air," Larry said as he hung the bait on a hook in the ceiling; the hook was cabled to a cotter pin in the trapdoor, so if something pulled the bait, the gate would drop and lock. Larry understood it perfectly.

"If it's not air, then what is it?"

"Ghost turkey."

Dick rolled his eye. "I should have written about Table Rock."

"No, this'll make you a journalist, bro—cross my heart."

"That's exactly what you said when we hunted down the infamous Bandage Man of Cannon Beach."

"He was real, wasn't he?"

"It was Halloween. You punched the kid in the neck."

"Yeah, well . . . I went as Chuck Norris; what'd you expect?" Larry took out the ectoplasmic injector and

basted the bait. "Anyway, this is better, hope to die, stick a needle in my . . ."

Dick narrowed his eye.

"Um . . ."

"So what kind of monster eats ghost turkey, Larry?"

"Only one that I know of."

"Which one?"

"Bigfoot's ghost."

"Great!" Dick threw his hands in the air. "So I not only need to believe in Bigfoot, but in ghosts as well?"

"And ghost turkeys," Larry added.

"You know what, Larry?" Dick tapped his foot in the dirt. "You can hitch a ride home with El Chupacabra, comprendo?"

He started to walk away.

Larry glanced at the guillotine. "Hey!" he called, lunging out of the cell. "Wait!"

Dick turned his head, and Larry struggled to find something to say. "What happened to you? You used to love this kind of stuff."

"Yeah, Larry, it was all fun and games . . . until someone poked out my eye."

Larry blushed. "It was . . . possessed."

"It's called a nervous tic, Larry. And for chrissake, did you *have* to use Father McKy's crucifix?"

"You can always hike up the mountain for your article," Larry said, changing the subject. "Take pictures of the Applegay Lake."

"It's the Apple*gate*, Larry." Dick tapped his foot again

and shook his head. "You can spend the night here if you want; I'll pick you up in the morning." He started to walk away.

So Larry said, "I'm telling Mom."

Dick sighed. After a very long silence, he turned around and crossed his arms. "Just tell me one thing, Larry: have you put any thought *at all* into how a wooden cell is supposed to hold a ghost? Can't they just walk through walls?"

Larry smiled. "Abba cadaver, bro." He began to cast containment spells on the trap.

"You hear that?" Larry asked. He wore a brown beard of s'mores and graham-cracker crumbs.

Dick, with his keen eye, glanced into the darkness beyond the campfire; they had pitched their tents next to the collapsed miner's cabin, where the trappers once awaited Bigfoot.

"I don't hear anything," said Dick. "Except your heavy breathing."

"No," Larry replied, trying to hear over the creek and the pounding of his heart. "The howling: it's . . . a mating call."

"Wait—ghosts *mate*?"

"Duh. Where do you think ghost babies come from?"

Dick glanced around again, acting worried. "Well, then, let's put out the fire—it'll scare off Bigfoot!"

"Ghosts aren't a'scared of fires, Dick."

"Yeah. Unless they're *ghost* fires."

Larry stirred the coals with a branch. "Good point . . ." He peered into the silent darkness, his face more and more crestfallen with every uneventful minute.

He licked the chocolate around his lips, and a sudden memory brightened his eyes.

"Hey, want to hear a ghost story?"

Dick shrugged.

"I heard the trappers actually caught Bigfoot and never told anyone once. They gave him, like . . . a whole *barrel* of whiskey. I think they had their own still or something.

"So they got all piss-drunk playing quarters with Bigfoot, and . . . remember those bumper stickers back then about the spotted owls getting endangered?"

"Yeah, I remember," Dick said. " 'Save a logger: wipe your ass with a spotted owl.' "

"Yeah—that's it! Turns out Bigfoot had one of those bumper stickers on his pickup truck; he was a big-time logger. So he got all drunk that night and . . . did what the bumper sticker said with his ass. What he didn't know was that the trappers were owl conservationists. So they shot Bigfoot—in the foot."

"Mmm. Shoot the only Bigfoot in existence to save a stupid owl. Perfect sense."

"Well, it was Bigfoot's fault," Larry said, crossing his arms. "Big oaf stepped in his own poop and died of gonorrhea."

"And yet no one ever donated his remains to a museum. Interesting."

"Well, no, Dick, *they shot Bigfoot.* They'd go to *jail.*"

"Actually, Larry, we don't have that law. Not in Oregon. Lil Pantry would probably sport pictures of the kill right there next to the lotto winner and the catch of the day. But kill a spotted owl and . . ." Dick shook his hands and went "Ooooo" like a ghost, then laughed at his own joke.

"You know," Larry said, "you're not smarter than I am. You think you are, but you're not."

"Yeah? Prove it."

At first Larry couldn't. Then he said, "I took all those special classes in school and you didn't, so *there.*"

"Hmm, forgot. You're Momma's special little boy."

"We don't have the Bigfoot law right *now*, Dick, you're right. But back then, yes. I read all about it in *The Local Inquirer.*" After a second Larry added, "What makes it so hard for you to believe anyway?"

Dick stared at him for a while with his one eye; he only needed one, he was such a good aim. Finally he opened his mouth to say something. Bigfoot howled instead.

Dick startled.

Larry did, too, but in an instant a smile stretched across his s'mores-covered face. "Come on, we need to . . . The trap!" He grabbed his proton pack and unzipped the pouch.

Dick tried to settle in his chair. "Probably just a

coyote, Larry. They can sound like that—like they're screaming."

"Have you seen my EMP recorder?" Larry asked, rummaging through his bag.

"Your what?"

"My EMP rec—my electronic voice phenomenal, uh . . . my press-record thingy! For ghost words!"

"You left it in the car."

Larry growled and flung Scooby Snacks out of his pack, trying to stop the tears from boiling over. It was okay; he didn't need the recorder. He dropped the bag. "Let's just—Where's the flashlight?"

"I've got it," Dick said.

"And your camera?"

"You mean containment unit? It's right here." The Nikon hung around his neck.

"Well, come on!" Larry started running up the trail toward the trap, emitting a high-pitched "Eeeeee!"

Dick stood and folded his chair. "I'm not going anywhere, Larry. And neither are you. We're going home."

Larry stopped, and his jaw dropped. At first he didn't understand his brother's reaction. His mother had always said understanding people wasn't his strong suit. But *this* he finally understood.

"You're just a'scared," he said.

Dick barked, "I am not."

."Are too. You're a'scared of me. Always have been."

"Wait . . . afraid *of* you?"

Larry crossed his arms.

"Look," Dick said, "I'm pretty sure this isn't what Dad meant when he said to humor you and play along. I've been doing that my entire life, Larry, and I'm sick of it. So pack your things and let's—"

"No. You can't make me."

"Larry . . ."

"How about you just tell Mom why you let me chase after Bigfoot's ghost all by myself."

Before Dick could stop him, Larry dashed up the trail.

"Damn it, Larry—get back here!"

No more than thirty feet, darkness fell black and complete. Larry stumbled forward over roots and ferns, crying hot tears and gritting his teeth. That Dick!

Suddenly he ran into something solid and hairy. It clawed at his face, and he shrieked.

"Larry?!" A flashlight beam followed him, illuminating just far enough for Larry to see the trail.

The thing that had scratched his face loomed over him: just a mossy old tree.

Larry scrambled onward to the trap, then ran out of Dick's light and hid behind a Douglas fir.

"I can see you," Dick said.

Larry tried not to move.

"You're squatting in poison oak."

"*You* are."

"That's enough, Larry. We're going home."

"Shhh—you'll scare the ghost away!"

"Goddamn it, Larry, there is no such thing as Bigfoot's ghost!"

Larry picked at some leaves that were brushing against his crotch—until he remembered that Dick had called them *poison oak*. Larry liked oaks, but he wasn't sure about poison.

Dick stepped closer and shook the light at him. "You really want to know why I don't believe in this stuff, Larry? You really want to know?"

Larry said nothing and picked at the leaves.

"Remember Dad's African ghost knives?"

"Yeah, of course. They kill ghosts."

Dick chuffed. "'But not just African ones,'" he said, quoting their father. "You know I googled those knives for an article, Larry?"

"The one you wrote for Wikip—"

"Doesn't matter where I published it; sometimes you write just for the love. Point is, there's no such thing as African ghost knives. Dad *lied*."

Larry's mouth hung open. "This isn't like . . . that joke you played on me, where you said Dad really isn't on vacation forever?"

Dick shined the light in Larry's eyes, and Larry quickly dried his tears.

"Yeah, Larry." Dick moved the light back down. "I'm just joking you. Sorry."

Larry let out a deep breath, and Dick probed the darkness with his light; the Bigfoot trap cast a giant shadow.

"Look, Larry, there is no ghost. Let's just—"

In the woods, something moaned.

Dick stiffened. "What's—?"

"*Shhh!*" Larry scanned the darkness for ghost orbs. Didn't see any. And when he heard the branch snap, he knew they weren't dealing with a ghost.

He jumped to his feet and yelled, "Go!"

Larry ran into Dick. Their limbs entangled. Dick's eye got poked.

"Ow! I can't . . . I can't see!"

In the woods, the monster crashed through bushes. Dick staggered toward the trap, and Larry clung to his legs.

"Let— Get up!"

"Dick!"

"I said get up, I can't— My eye!"

"I'm trying to! I—"

Right behind them, something moaned. Melodically. With too much tremolo. Larry smelled something horrible and rotten.

Just inside the trap, Dick's legs slipped out of his grip, leaving Larry on his back right below the guillotine.

The monster lunged, and Dick yanked the bait.

The trapdoor fell.

Larry felt a moment of pain, and then a bright light blinded him. He floated through total darkness like a ghostly turkey feather, until he settled beside his brother in the cell. Dick was screaming Larry's name and was staring down at the ground.

I'm right here, Larry said, but Dick didn't seem to hear him. So Larry looked down, too.

The flashlight, which had fallen to the floor, angled its beam across the busted old planks. Larry's head lay just inside the trap, staring at the ceiling with s'mores still on its face. The rest of his body lay outside. The trapdoor divided the two.

Grumbling, the monster went for Larry's corpse. There was a ripping sound. Darkness shrouded the beast, whatever it was.

"You leave him alone!" Dick cried. "You leave my brother alone—"

Your camera! Larry said, grabbing Dick's muscle.

Dick glanced around, suddenly much whiter; he looked like he'd seen a ghost.

Get it on camera! Larry said, shaking him.

Slowly, Dick nodded. He lifted the viewfinder to his eye and snapped a shot.

Outside, the monster groaned and hit the gate, as if trying to bat away the camera flash. Dick kept snapping photos, faster and faster. Sequins on the monster's jumpsuit sparkled.

The beast tried to cover its eyes and beat at the door all at the same time, but finally it gave up and loped into the woods, running into a few trees as it went.

Dick didn't stop clicking until the camera was full.

Larry patted him on the back, told him everything would be okay, he didn't have to be a'scared of him anymore; everything would be okay, he felt fine.

Dick shriveled.

Dick wept.

After the accident, the Forest Service had removed the trapdoor from the Bigfoot cage, which now remained dark and empty. Dick, standing just outside, powered on his brother's EVP recorder to pick up any supernatural sound.

"Larry . . . if you're still in there . . ." He held up a copy of *The Current Courier*. "Got my name on the front page, Larry. Dick Schingle, right above the fold. And I got the pictures in there, too. Bona fide photographic evidence, first of its kind."

Voices sounded somewhere in the woods. Dick glanced in their direction and cleared his throat.

"I can't, uh . . . I can't lift your containment spells, Larry. You wrote them in Elvish. With crayon. The comic-book guy told me it's not even a known dialect of Elvish, so . . . you're stuck.

"I also want you to know . . . I was never afraid of you, Larry. Not *of* you. I wanted you to know that."

The voices in the woods drew closer, and Dick's head beaded with sweat.

"This is ridiculous," he said as he pulled out his father's African ghost knives.

He set down the EVP recorder. "Tell Dad I . . . tell him . . . hell, just tell him Mom says hi."

With that, Dick lunged into the trap and stabbed

the air with the mystical knives, hoping to feel some-thing—anything at all—when he stabbed his brother's soul.

"Are you nuts?" someone said behind him.

Dick nearly jumped out of his skin.

Two kids stood outside, gaping at him.

"What're you doing here?" Dick asked, lowering the knives.

"Snipe hunting," the stupid one said with great conviction. "What are *you* doing here?"

Dick thrust the paper at them. "My brother died here. Don't you boys read the news?"

They squinted at the article and the photograph, which had been taken at night from inside the cell. "Is that . . . ?" the dumb one began.

Dick nodded as he picked up the EVP recorder and shut it off. "First picture ever proven authentic."

"So he *is* alive," the smart kid replied, studying the picture of a snarling Elvis.

"No," Dick said, "the King is dead. Well . . . undead. It was his zombie that killed Larry. Still had the jump-suit. And the hair."

"Hey, I found a mistake," the dumb one said, pointing to the caption below the photograph. "Who's Pelvis Resley?"

Dick's face filled with hot blood. "*You're* a mistake."

In their first sign of intelligence, the kids glanced nervously at the knives.

Dick shook his head and forced a smile. "Keep the

paper, boys. It's signed. Might be worth something someday."

He started downhill away from the trap, but stopped halfway down and rewound Larry's EVP recorder. He pressed play and heard himself talking: "Tell Dad I . . . tell him . . . hell, just tell him Mom says hi." Then he heard his ghost knives slicing the air.

Dick turned up the volume and cocked his ear toward the white noise. After a second he heard Larry screaming, *Stop, stop—you almost got my eye!*

At the Bigfoot trap, one of the kids laughed. The smartass was taking a dump in the cell and was tearing Dick's newspaper into strips of bathroom tissue. The dumbass was screaming at him to stop, stop littering— he was a conservationist!

Dick smiled and continued down the trail. He'd leave the kid's droppings in there for a while. Larry deserved it for dodging the ghost knives—sometimes he could be a real dick.

Son of . . . a Bitch!

Sam W. Anderson

"C'mon, Joe, give me a steak already."

The cheapskate pretends not to hear me and focuses on his grill. If he thinks I'm going to shut up for some hamburger, he best think again—but that'd probably tax his puny brain. Of all the possible people here in this great big city, I get stuck with Joe as the only one who can understand me. He's just a lousy postal worker, sworn enemy of any self-respecting creature. A butcher, now that would have been nice.

"I said, give me a fucking steak."

"You know, I'm shocked to hear dogs have such foul mouths. Especially a golden retriever. You seem so nice."

"Fuck you." I lift my leg on the chain-link fence

SAM W. ANDERSON • 259

separating our yards. "Have you listened to us bark, Joe? Do we sound like we're singing ballads and lullabies? Pretty much everything we say is yelling because you're too self-absorbed to listen."

I shouldn't be so hard on the guy, but it's too damn hot to care. I can't remember a summer this miserable, and all I have is this warm water full of dead ants and grass clippings. I'd rip out somebody's throat for some of that cold stuff in the big bowl in the bathroom. Damn, that's some tasty water.

Joe stands on his small patio and flips the meat. Definitely hamburger. He looks even more pathetic than usual with his cutoff shorts and pasty legs. He bobs his head to the beat of music blaring from his house—some rap song about big butts. Humans are weird.

I'm ready to walk away when I spy Cat at the pet door. I hate Cat. Damn thing gives me the creeps with its slitted eyes and nine lives. That's simply not natural. I turn back—hamburger's plenty fine, anyway.

"You thought about our earlier talk?" I ask. He tosses a patty over the fence, and I catch it. In two bites, it's gone. Fuck, I love hamburger! I remember this every time.

"How could I not?" he says. "A guy hears the neighbor's dog talking at him, it kind of stays fresh in the mind." Joe smiles, like he's said something of value.

Looking at his goofy grin, I almost feel sorry for the putz. He's dumpy and quiet, and I've never seen

any of the good-smelling ones come to his house. His hair is like a Brillo pad. I've chewed up one before—they break apart and get stuck in your teeth. Taste like shit, too. Was in no way worth the beating I got.

"Are you going to do it?"

"C'mon, Max, be serious."

"Joe, you're talking to a dog, and I'm the one that's supposed to be serious?" Of course, I'm talking to this pea brain, so . . .

As he bites into his hamburger, ketchup squeezes out down the front of his undersized T-shirt. It looks like blood across the goofy guy with huge ears printed on the shirt's front above the words "Ross for Boss." It also looks delicious.

"Sorry, Max." Another bite, and more ketchup escapes. I salivate. I smell another patty on the grill and hope it's got my name on it. "I don't believe any of this," he says, still chewing. "I ain't going to do it."

I'm almost relieved. The whole idea seems retarded, anyway, but I can't let it go without trying one more time. Cat's right here watching, and I'd never hear the end of it. In my nicest bark I say, "Come here, Joe."

"You're not going to pee on my shoes again? These are brand-new L.A. Gear."

"Nah, that's only funny the first time." But, damn, is it funny. "I just want to talk. You know—canine to man."

From two blocks over, I hear Ginger barking at me to "leave that poor guy alone." If she hadn't had gotten

fixed two months ago, I may have listened to her. That schnauzer snatch holds no power over me anymore.

Joe ambles closer, the scent of ketchup and hamburger grease grows stronger. He crouches by the fence, and sweat pours off him. "Okay, what do you want, Max?"

"I thought you said you don't believe any of this shit."

"Yeah . . . and?"

"Then why'd you come over here? You must think I'm talking to you, right?"

Joe stands. As he searches for a philosophical argument to counter, I lift my leg and piss on his shoes.

"Goddamnit!"

"I was wrong. That's funny every time."

"I ain't giving you no more beef."

I think he probably will once I put on my cute, I'm-so-innocent face. That's as close to a sure thing as Ginger used to be.

"Listen, Joe, and listen good. The Demon says you're The Chosen One. He won't let you rest until you do his bidding." I'm really selling the goods here—my tail is wagging so hard you'd guess I'd found a stash of hambones. I think smoke comes out of his ears as he mulls over my words. "He's watching you," I say. "He sees you when you're sleeping. He knows when you're awake."

"What? Is he the Santa Claus demon?" Joe laughs at that one.

"What the fuck is a Santa Claus?"

"Never mind." He wipes his shoe in the dead grass and nearly falls.

"The Demon told me this morning that today is the day. He knows you have a gun, so use it already."

"You talked to him today, huh?" A smug look crosses Joe's face. "Well, then, what did he say I was doing last night?"

Joe thinks he has me, but I know from a pretty reliable source what Joe does on Tuesday nights. "He said you were watching a *Maude* rerun." I don't much get the box with the people inside—much less what a rerun may be—but that Maude bitch, her voice raises my hackles. "And he said you were jerking off to the one they call Carrol."

Since the blood rushes from Joe's face, I know my source is right. "Don't be so embarrassed, man. We all do it. Maybe not as much as you, but—"

"Shut up."

"I prefer a good blanket, all wadded up. That's an afternoon well-spent right there."

"Shut up!"

"Or a pillow. Especially if Steve's pissed me off that day, I like to leave a nice surprise for him at bedtime." And that *is* something worth the beating—pardon the pun.

I've hit a nerve. Sulking, Joe strides toward his house in his stained L.A. Gear.

"Oh, c'mon, Joe. Give me a break." He reaches for the sliding-glass door. "I'm sorry, okay?"

"Screw you, Max." I think up a ton of jerking-off jokes when he says this, but decide I've pushed far enough. "Your whole idea is stupid," he says. "I'm not going to talk to you anymore."

"Wait!" Thoughts bombard my mind—Ginger in heat, the patty still sizzling on the grill (fuck, I love hamburger!), Ginger in heat, Cat peering at me through the pet door (I hate Cat). I need to focus; I can't let him go. And it just slips out: "The Demon, he's here."

That stops Joe. Cat steps through the door, his hind legs still inside the house. Ginger's yapping notches up to supernag. Joe turns and takes a couple of tentative steps back toward the fence. He squints, searching my yard as if he can see The Demon.

"Where?"

Shit, I've stepped in it now. And I'm concerned with what to tell Joe, too. With no idea what to say next, "Can't you feel him?" seems as good as anything.

"All I feel are wet feet and a sunburn coming on."

For a moment, time stops. I'm losing him. Cat's stare burrows a hole in the back of my head. I can't think clearly. I wish Cat would just leave and take his damn slitted eyes and damn nine lives. I'm suddenly afraid and I shiver.

"Oh my God, Max—you all right?"

I can't answer. I just quake more.

Joe runs to the fence, looking like a baby human first learning to walk. I worry he might tumble with

every stride he takes. "It's The Demon, ain't it? He's possessed you."

Bingo! (Fuck, what a stupid name.) What else to do? On instinct, I flip on my back and flop about the grass. Howling adds a nice touch.

"Jesus, Max." Joe's voice has ratcheted an octave. His excitement adds to mine.

"Help me! The Demon, he's upon me." Benji or Lassie, they ain't got shit on me. Rin Tin Tin, eat your heart out.

The adrenaline surges as the performance continues. I spring to my feet. From the corner of my eye, my tail taunts me. I'm too excited to stop myself, and I whirl after it. Faster and faster I spin, nipping, but never quite reaching it. Then, when I'm about to quit out of exhaustion—ta-daa! I catch it. For the first time ever, I catch it.

Now what?

I shake my head, trying to yank the damn thing free, and growl in my you-just-try-to-take-that-food-from-me tone. Chomp! It may not be the smartest thing, but I'm in a frenzy, damnit. I yowl and lose hold of my tail. I come to a stop with my front paws spread wide and my head bowed. The panting comes so fast, I'm woozy.

From behind, I hear Cat enter the house. I wonder if felines can laugh, because if so, I'm sure he is. But they probably can't—their asses are wound too tight.

"Are you The Demon?" Joe asks.

"Who wants to know?" The voice is my deepest bark, and even I must admit, it's kind of intimidating.

"It is I—The Chosen One." The melodrama in Joe's delivery makes it hard for me not to break character. "What do they call you?"

My mind's a blank. "Um . . . Ginger. Yeah, bow to me—I am Ginger."

The barking from two blocks down reaches a frenetic pace. Here, I thought I favored the salty language, but the real Ginger is teaching me a thing or two. *Don't bring me into this!* she barks. As mad at me as she sounds, I guess it doesn't matter anymore that she's fixed.

"Where's Max?" Joe asks. "Is he in there?"

"Tonight. You must act tonight, or I'll return tomorrow to impose my wrath." I snarl, exposing as many of the pearly whites as possible. It looks like Joe's committed an assault on his cutoffs. "Two women, am I clear?"

"Yes, Ginger." He bows his head. It looks so silly, my tail wags despite myself. He raises his head and steps backward. When he reaches the patio, he stumbles.

"And give me that hamburger." He reaches for the spatula. "Tomorrow you better have steak for Max. Rib eye."

Joe tosses the patty like a girl throws a ball. As I devour it—fuck, I love hamburger!—he runs inside his house. The sliding-glass door locks.

• • •

Cat jumps on me, waking me from my evening nap. Since this whole thing started, he's been waking me at the same time every day—right before the thing they call the news comes on the box with people inside. I don't like the news. All it does is make everybody angry.

"Nice touch yesterday with the Maude reference," Cat says. "I told you that would come in handy."

I turn my back. I can't stand looking at those eyes.

"I hope for your sake he followed through."

The music for the six o'clock news begins. Then, as if by magic, a guy with what looks like plastic hair appears in the box with people in it. I don't trust those people. I can't smell them.

"Our lead story for tonight: Two women were shot in the early morning hours in the Park Hill neighborhood." My heart jumps. No way could it be Joe. I try calming myself. It's the city, for fuck's sake—there are shootings every day. "According to witnesses, a man approached the women on the street. He removed a handgun from a paper bag, fired three shots, and walked away."

"He did it," Cat says. The joy in his meow is disgusting. "That worthless human showed some backbone and did it. Used the bag like I instructed and everything."

"The first victim, twenty-two-year-old Laura Bonita, died at the scene. The other victim's name

hasn't been released, but police say her injuries are not fatal."

"Goddamnit!" Claws rip across my back. I spin on Cat, ready to pounce. He glares at me. I cower at the malice in his eyes. Those damn eyes and damn nine lives. I've tried killing him before, but he just won't die. He's evil, I say, evil.

"He has to do better next time, Max."

"No. No way. I'm not doing this for you anymore."

But I look in Cat's eyes and know this is just the beginning.

Her Lucky Day

ALLISON BRENNAN

Vi stared at the man lying naked on the floor and knew
she'd screwed up big-time. What was his name? *Jus-
tin*. Justin no-last-name because either he didn't tell
her or she forgot. When you screwed a different man
for money every night, who the hell cared about their
names?

*Just pay me in cash, baby, and I'll call you whatever
you want.*

But Justin wasn't breathing and she feared he was
dead, and nothing about dead was good. Especially
when the dead body was sprawled on the plush white
carpet of a five-star hotel room in Century City under
the name of Jaysen Enterprises, a company she did
business with on a regular basis at a thousand a pop.

She'd only been having fun with the bastard. He
wanted kink; she gave him kink. He didn't care about

her; he only came to satisfy his own cravings. So what if she wanted a little fun at his expense? He was a jerk, he'd *bruised* her flawless skin. No one put marks on her, thank you very much; she'd had enough of that shit from her bitch of a mother.

All she did was drop a little pill in his scotch and take some pictures for her retirement fund. Heidi Fleiss had *nothing* on Vi.

Her real name was Stephanie Violet Browning, but she worked under Vi Brown. She'd forgotten what it was like to be Stephanie. It was the name her mother used to scream at her before slapping her around. But Mommy Dearest was dead. (Was it wrong to celebrate her mother's death? She still popped a bottle of champagne on the anniversary of Candace Browning's accident with a tall building. It wasn't like she'd pushed her or anything, the woman was drunk.)

Stephanie was the name her teachers used when they sent her to the office for whatever stupid rule she'd broken that day. And it was the name the high school vice principal used when he offered her the ultimatum that indirectly changed her life: get down on her knees and suck his dick or be expelled.

She chose expulsion.

So it was perhaps ironic that ten years later, at the age of twenty-five—old for a call girl—she was working the streets. Or, rather, the executive boardrooms and corporate five-star hotel suites that rose high above the streetwalkers who got their meager hundred

on a good night getting down on their knees and giving head to a half dozen drunk pricks.

Vi hooked in style. And she would not let the dead Justin No-Last-Name ruin her life.

She didn't panic. She'd never panicked a day in her life, even when she was seventeen and one of her johns nearly strangled her while he screwed her. The damage to her throat had been permanent, and now she could only speak in a low voice that she'd trained to sound sultry and seductive. Vi didn't hate men, even after that no-name john—who'd only gotten *ten years* for attempted murder. Ten years for nearly killing her so he could get off. Vi hoped some big burly felon choked *him* all the way while getting off.

Vi looked around the plush room. She couldn't exactly toss his body off the balcony. She was strong, but she couldn't lift the big guy. And she knew enough about cops that they'd probably be able to figure out that he'd been dead before he went splat.

Leave him here. Walk out. That was a plan. She dressed quickly, pulling the slinky shimmering blue dress over her head. Sexy, but not slutty. She could be seen in nightclubs and not have the bouncer toss her for solicitation.

She slid on her spike shoes and hesitated. There was the matter of her prints in the hotel room—which sucked because she was in the damn system—and probably a hundred security cameras that recorded their ascent to the fourteenth floor. She could bribe the

night manager, but that only went so far—she doubted murder would be on the hotel staff bribe list. Vi'd been arrested twice, no more than a couple hours in the pen, but that was enough time, *thank you very much*. She wasn't going to do ten to twenty for involuntary manslaughter. And what if some high-and-mighty hypocritical judge decided to go all moral on her and push for more time?

There were her pictures—insurance—but that was her retirement money. She didn't want to use them to stay out of jail. And she needed time to set up blackmail, time which she didn't have now with the dead prick on the floor. She mentally went through her clients—there was a prosecutor in there and a defense lawyer. Maybe she could call one of them, show him the photos, tell him to help her or his life was over as he knew it.

In the time it took for her to put it all together, the cops would find the body, pull her prints, see her pic, and she'd be in lockup in twenty-four hours. She could run, but for how long? She had money, but not enough to keep under deep cover. She didn't have an alternate identity to walk into right this minute.

Well, shit.

The door opened and Vi jumped up, heart pounding, certain it was hotel security or the cops. Instinct had her glancing around for an escape route, but common sense told her there was nothing she could do. She backed into a table and knocked over a vase. It landed with a soft thud on the plush carpet.

A woman entered. Not just a *woman,* but the most gorgeous woman Vi had ever seen. Vi didn't swing that way—unless her clients paid her enough—but *if* she were going to go lesbo she'd do it with this chick. Golden hair—not blond, not brown, but *gold.* Sultry blue eyes—big and almond shaped and they just sucked you in; you couldn't look away. This woman knew makeup like nobody's business. Her perfect face—her *flawless* skin—had been carved by a god. Vi was hot, but this woman was steaming.

Vi had never seen her before in her life. She should tell her to get the hell out of her room, but she suddenly couldn't say anything.

"Hello, Stephanie," the woman said.

A chill ran down Vi's spine. "I don't know you."

"I know *you.*"

The stranger walked over—*glided* over—to dead Justin.

"You're not a cop."

The woman laughed and smiled down at Justin's body almost like she was about to seduce him. Vi took another step backward, thoroughly confused and feeling trapped. "It seems like you have a little problem here."

Vi attempted a feeble lie, knowing as she said it that it was stupid. "I found him like this. I—"

She laughed again. "Oh, Stephanie. I *know* what happened. You can't lie to me, but it's sweet that you tried."

"Don't call me Stephanie!"

"'Vi' is so . . . *common*. But I'm willing to compromise, since we'll be friends for a long time. Violet is nice."

Friends? This woman was on crack. Vi just wanted to get out of this room and disappear. "Who are you? How do you know me?"

"We don't have much time. He's nearly dead."

Vi did a double take and stared at Justin. She shook her head. "He's pushing up the daisies. Gone. No pulse."

"His heart is slowing down, but still pumping blood through his body. He has three minutes, twenty-eight seconds—or so—left. You have two choices."

Vi opened her mouth to ask how the *hell* she knew all that, but didn't.

The woman said, "You can call an ambulance. They won't arrive in time, and honestly, there's no saving him. Even if they did resuscitate him, he'd never recover. If *you* had tried to resuscitate him ten minutes ago when he first collapsed, he might have had a shot. But you panicked."

I don't panic.

But maybe she had. Just for a minute. His collapse had stunned her.

"You'll have to talk to the police, probably tell them you don't know what happened, he just had a heart attack or something, right? You'll be arrested for solicitation, probably would have gotten off, but when they

find the drugs in his glass and his bloodstream, they'll look at you hard for murder, too. Might be able to plea to a lesser charge, but you'll be in jail for years. By the time you get out, you'll be too old to do your job. And those pictures you've been saving for a rainy day? No one will care about them in twenty years."

The woman could read her mind. That was the only explanation for how she knew what she knew. Or maybe it was a set-up. Blackmail. The bitch had a camera in the room, had seen her spike Justin's drink.

"What's my other choice?" Vi didn't trust the woman. She didn't trust anyone.

"I'll take care of everything."

Now it was Vi's turn to laugh, but her low, scratchy chuckle sounded more scared than humored. "Right. *You'll* take care of the whole thing. How much?"

The woman laughed again. "I don't care about *money*." She wiggled her fingers in disgust. "That's my brother who's greedy."

"Then what do you want? Nothing's for free."

The woman was dead serious. "You're absolutely right. Nothing is for free. I will take care of this thing," she waved her hand dismissively over the dying man, "and in exchange, I get your body."

Vi blinked several times. "You want to screw?" Okay, to keep her out of prison she'd do whatever this woman wanted her to do. It wasn't going to kill her. But why? Why was she helping her? She didn't have to commit a felony to get laid. Vi was certain that there

were plenty of bi hookers who'd happily give this chick everything she wanted without murder in the mix.

The woman laughed again, amused. The back and forth from high humor to seriousness disturbed Vi more than anything they'd discussed. She was chilled to her bones, an icy cold that wasn't going away.

"Violet, what I propose is far better than *screwing*. I will give you such power over men that they will pay you anything to have sex. They will drain their bank accounts. They will sign over their houses. They will get on their knees and beg for you."

Vi wondered if this golden-haired woman was moving in on Rachelle's territory. Rach would be pissed off, but Vi liked the woman's style. Well, she would have liked it except that she was pretty certain that this gorgeous, bizarre lady would—and could—slit her throat without hesitation.

But did Vi really have a choice? Did she really think she could walk away or take her chances with the criminal justice system? Just the *thought* of being behind bars terrified her. A day she could live with. Years . . . her chest tightened as panic, full panic, hit her.

"You have less than a minute. If he dies, I can't help you. The second his heart stops pumping, I'm powerless."

Vi didn't know how the woman was going to save him, or save her, but she had nothing to lose.

"All right," Vi said. "If you can clean up this mess, then I'm yours. Tell me what your name is."

"You won't be able to pronounce it," she said. "But you can call me Violet."

Before the statement sunk in, the woman dissolved right in front of Vi. She turned to . . . smoke. Dark, foul-smelling gaseous smoke that made Vi gag. She stepped back, one, two steps, tripped over a chair, and kept going until her back was up against the wall. This was *not* happening. She was hallucinating. Justin had drugged her. Ha ha, joke's on her. She was tripping on LSD. That was it. None of this was happening; it was just a big scary figment of her imagination.

The stinky smoke wrapped itself around Justin's dying body and disappeared. Whoosh. Gone.

Justin sat up and smiled at her. "Hello, Stephanie."

Vi wished she could faint. Just drop to the floor and forget everything. Wake up tomorrow in her own bed and believe that this was a nightmare. Bad trip, this one. Yes, sir, bad trip. Go away. Wake up. Do *something*.

She breathed deeply, the smell still making her gag, but she needed to clear her head.

I'm losing my mind.

Oh, that cleared it all right. Everything in the room sharpened focus. The messed-up bed. The glasses they used. The bright lights of the City of Angels mocked her through the windows, twinkling in laughter, the joke's on you, baby.

And Justin stood there and leered at her.

He'd been dead, dammit! Now he wasn't. What was a dead guy who walked? A zombie? There was no

fucking thing as zombies. Right? That was Hollywood and freaky sick writers who thought up that stuff. Not real.

Vi would check herself into rehab if she like *drank* or took drugs or anything. That was it, she'd shoot herself up with heroin and pretend she was strung out and check herself into a nice facility with padded white walls.

"I don't like this vessel," Justin said. It was Justin's voice, but not his tone. "Do what I say and I'll solve your problem."

Vi could only nod. What else could she do? Justin was dead. Now he was alive. She was going insane.

"Get your things."

Vi grabbed her purse and then her jacket.

"Wh-what about the cameras?" Vi asked. She couldn't believe she was talking to Justin as if he was the golden-haired woman. That wasn't possible.

And Justin rising from the near-dead was?

"I've already taken care of the cameras."

Vi felt like she was in a trance. This just *couldn't* be happening. Isn't that what everyone thought when faced with the impossible? She never used drugs, but she was certain this was how she'd feel if she did. Unreal. Disconnected from her body.

Justin took her hand. It was cold. Vi looked into his face, still unbelieving. His eyes were the same blue as the golden-haired woman who turned to gas as Vi watched.

Had his eyes been blue before? Maybe . . . but not like this. Not this electric blue.

On the way out of the room, Justin took the glass she'd spiked and put it in Vi's oversized leather purse.

"Where are we going?" Vi asked, her voice deeper and more unnatural than usual.

"To get rid of the body."

Vi realized then that she'd gotten in way over her head, but she followed. She didn't really have a choice.

They left the hotel and walked along Wilshire Boulevard. Justin was talking.

"It feels so good to breathe real air." He breathed deeply in and out, smiled. "I almost feel alive."

Almost?

Justin squeezed her hand, leaned over, and said cheerily, "We're going to have so much fun together! I'll let you watch the whole time, you'll get a kick out of it. Really. I've been *bored* for so long."

"For how long?" Vi asked before she realized how stupid the question sounded.

Justin laughed. "Since I was banished. But I'm free now, and everything is as it should be."

They walked together, hand in hand, like lovers. Vi caught their reflection, distorted, in a blackened office window.

Justin practically *glowed*. But he was no angel.

Vi didn't know how long they walked, but they ended up at a reservoir. Miles from the hotel, but Vi

didn't feel tired or sore even in her shoes. Numb was more like it.

"Perfect," Justin said. He smiled at Vi and kissed her full on, his cold tongue probing hers. He tasted like meat that had turned green. Vi grimaced and turned away.

He reached into her purse and took out her switchblade. She'd almost forgotten it was there—she honestly hadn't been thinking about protecting herself from a dead man—but now Vi started to shake.

Justin was playing games with her. He'd faked his unconsciousness, hired the woman, drugged her so she saw the gas or used some Hollywood special effects in the hotel. He was now punishing her because she tried to drug him. He knew about the pictures she'd taken, and now he was going to blackmail her. Hell, he could take them and blackmail all the important people she'd screwed. It was just a scam, only this time she was the victim.

Life was so not fair.

She turned to run, but he grabbed her, his grip firm. Her wrist cracked and she yelped in pain.

The switchblade opened in a flash and she felt the tip of the knife pierce her stomach. She couldn't fight back, stunned, the pain like a drug, freezing her. The steel sliced through her hard abs, ripping them open, and Justin pushed the edge of the blade up, up, up to her sternum. The only thing she could think of in that moment was that Justin was a modern day Jack the Ripper, cutting open prostitutes.

I'm going to die.

Justin pulled the knife out. "I'll be right back," he said. "You have at least five minutes before you bleed out."

She fell to her knees, her hands on her stomach. She felt her intestines in her palm. In the dim street-light, her blood glistened, nearly black as it seeped through her fingers and dripped onto the pathway. She wanted to run, but couldn't. Her legs didn't move. She couldn't rise from her knees, but kept sinking lower until her head hit the ground. She was *bleeding to death*. There was no one to save her, no one at the reservoir in the middle of the night. She couldn't scream if she wanted to.

"Help. Me." She clutched her stomach.

"You're fine," Justin said as he ran away from her. Ran toward the flood control channel. Without any thought of the barbed wire that was supposed to pre-vent people from doing exactly what he was doing, he grabbed it, pushed it down, and leapt over. Into the water.

What was he doing?

Why did she care? She was *dying*.

Vi rolled over to her back so her face didn't touch the dirty cement. Great, what did she care how she died? She looked up at the stars, her vision blurring. "This is punishment, right?" she whispered.

She was so cold, but sweating. How could she sweat when she was this cold?

Vi supposed this was justice. She'd been playing it fast and loose for years, living well, doing what she damn well pleased. And maybe she did help her drunk mother with her accident. And maybe she did enjoy drugging her johns to make them do things they'd never do without the right encouragement. And maybe she'd already started blackmailing some of them, the ones who'd pissed her off.

She'd been had. She deserved it. But damn if she was going to apologize for it.

She closed her eyes, numb. She didn't feel anything, she was so cold. She'd just . . . go. It was over.

Violet . . .

Vi opened her eyes. The golden-haired woman stood above her. Where was Justin? Right, he'd jumped in the flood control channel. The woman—she made him do it.

"You—stabbed me." Vi swallowed with difficulty.

"Insurance, sweetheart. Now you need me. Because if you do anything to get rid of me, you'll die. But as long as I'm with you, you'll live. Until I get bored again. But you'll help me so that doesn't happen, right?"

Vi couldn't think. The woman turned to gas and wrapped herself around Vi. So warm. So very warm.

Suddenly her heart pounded uncontrollably. Her blood heated, raced, her brain was about to explode. She grabbed her head and screamed, but no sound came out.

Slowly, her heart returned to normal. Her head no

longer ached. She was still hot—too hot—and feared she was sick.

You're not sick, sweetheart, it's just me.

Vi rose from the ground, looked at her torn, bloody dress. But her stomach—her intestines were back where they belonged. There was no mark from the knife. She'd believe it was a hallucination, except for the blood.

Let's get you cleaned up and then we'll have some fun.

And Vi knew that she'd better ensure that the golden-haired woman had fun, or she'd be dead.

"So when you said you wanted my body, you meant it . . . um, literally."

Of course.

"And what happened to Justin?" Did she really want to know?

He drowned. Fifty-fifty chance the police will think suicide . . . or an accident. He did have drugs in his system, after all. No more questions. Questions aren't fun.

"What do you think is fun?"

Getting what I want when I want it. I'm a lot like you that way. Which is why I picked you. Aren't you lucky?

Lucky. Right. She'd avoided arrest for Justin's death, in exchange for her life. An exchange . . . why did she feel she got the bad end of this deal?

"Because," Violet said out loud, her voice sounding normal, like it used to before the guy strangled her, "with your body comes your soul. You people never think of that, which really helps keep me in nice bodies.

Look, I'm not going to get bored if you keep it exciting. Let's change and hit up a club I've heard about. Then we'll *really* have fun."

Vi started walking. She didn't have a choice.

No, you don't, not if you don't want to bleed to death all over the street. But cheer up, sweetheart, you haven't seen anything yet.

A Wing and a Prayer

Sharyn McCrumb

"There is a precedent for it, you know," said the dean. "And think of the money we'll save."

Henry Garner was still staring at the bare desk and empty chair in Dr. Lamplough's former office, vacant since the old man's not-unexpected death near the end of the fall term. Above the smell of institutional furniture polish and ammonia, he thought he could still detect a faint whiff of the elderly professor's beloved peppermints and the spectral fumes of stale office coffee. Martin Lamplough had been with the university nearly as long as grade inflation. His name was still painted on the frosted glass of the office door, above the words "Folklore Department—Chairman."

"Money that we do not in fact have," said the dean,

jingling the keys. "The recent state budget cuts have made it impossible to fill the position, anyhow—unless someone would like to take on the job without an increase in salary?" He stopped, peering hopefully at Henry.

"No, I quite see your point," said Henry hastily, backing out of the empty office. "We are all teaching the maximum load as it is, because, of course, Dr. Lamplough's classes had to be parceled out around the department. So nobody really has time to assume the duties of department head. All those reports to fill out, the record keeping, the faculty senate . . ." He almost succeeded in repressing a shudder.

"There you are, then. It's really the best solution. I'm sure you'll agree. After all, it is a very small department. Just the six of you. Well, five now. I like to think of this appointment not as a fiscal necessity, but as a memorial to dear old Lamplough. After all, he was a scholar of Native American folklore, first and foremost. And who knows, it might get us a bit of publicity, which is always useful."

Yes, thought Henry, nodding glumly. *If your idea of publicity was derision.* Still the only way to deter the dean from taking this step would be to assume the bureaucratic duties himself in addition to his already ludicrous workload, and that was not to be thought of.

"So you'll share our decision with the rest of the faculty, Dr. Garner? Good man." The dean wandered away, a budgetary Jack the Ripper, in search of fresh victims.

• • •

Thus it was that at the afternoon department meeting the following afternoon, Henry Garner faced his colleagues and made the announcement, trying to be, if not enthusiastic about the plan, at least carefully neutral. In a faltering economy, it did one's career no good to oppose the administration.

"He's mad," said Alvin Hillenberg (Norse studies and Tolkien). "He ought to be locked up. We should hold a press conference and expose him."

"Er—the dean is already holding his own press conference," said Henry. "And he's right. There is a precedent. I looked it up. In 2008, the Sardar Bhagat Singh School of Business in India appointed the monkey god Hanuman to their faculty. Office and everything."

Jeremy Cole, the Graeco-Roman mythology specialist, said: "I suppose he works for peanuts."

Dr. Acharya smiled, her dark eyes sparkling. "No. That would be Ganesh. Of course, the appointment is purely ceremonial. For luck, I suppose."

"Because they can't afford to pay anybody," said Henry. "And as I understand it, the actual work will be done by Mrs. Ingram and the office staff. Not that much of a change from Dr. Lamplough's final years, really. But I suppose the administration felt that, *nominally*, we ought to have a chairman, and so they appointed one."

"And didn't let us vote," said Dr. Hillenberg. "Typical."

"Well, Alvin, who would you have suggested?" asked Dr. Acharya, tapping him playfully on the arm. "Some hairy linebacker of a Norse deity? Thor?"

"Well, definitely not one with an elephant face or six hands, Apoorva. I can certainly picture that image in the college brochures!"

Henry cleared his throat, and—probably coincidentally—the bickering subsided. "Because Martin Lamplough's specialty was Native American folklore, the administration thought that it would be fitting to choose a deity from somewhere in that pantheon. And I believe in these days of political correctness there were other considerations, too. To choose a male deity would leave them open to charges of sexism; a hunter god would offend the animal rights people; they didn't want anyone who was associated with violence."

"That leaves Tinkerbell," snapped Professor O'Meara (Celtic Studies).

"That's funny," said Dr. Hillenberg. Like many people who lacked a sense of humor, he was making a diagnosis rather than actually appreciating the jest. "Oh, I do hate changes, especially in the middle of term. I almost wish Old Lamplough hadn't died. Well, not that—oh, you know what I mean!"

Henry summoned a wan smile. "In the event—and not that it matters, I suppose—they went with the Raven, revered by Pacific Northwest tribes.

Apparently he goes by many names, none of which are easy to spell, so the dean found a photo of the Raven totem online, and he has asked one of the art majors to copy it onto the office door."

Dr. Acharya nodded slowly. "So . . . our new department head is . . . the Raven? The god Shani travels astride such a bird."

"It's not a bad choice," Professor O'Meara conceded. "In Celtic mythology there is the war goddess Morrigan, who took the form of a raven, and, of course, there are the ravens of Bran."

"And in Norse myths we have Huginn and Muninn," said Dr. Hillenberg. "Odin's ravens."

"Quite a multicultural choice," murmured Henry. "How about you, Cole?"

"Nothing special in Greek or Roman lore that I can recall, but I suppose a bird would be as good a department chair as anything. What about you, Henry?"

Henry Garner sighed. "Well, I do fairy tales, you know, and general mythology. Oral histories, urban legends, and so on. Ravens are always turning up, but then so are frogs and cats and everything else you can think of. I am taking over Dr. Lamplough's Native American mythology class, though, so I expect I'll be learning as I go."

And that was that, really. The university saved thousands of dollars that it did not, in any case, have to spend, and the Folklore department got a new chairman, who was only slightly less vague and out of touch

than the previous one had been. A senior art student, whose specialty was anime, graciously consented to stretch a point and copy the red and black Inuit raven totem on the office door: a stylized rendering of the raven spirit, executed in slashing lines and an inlay of intricate patterns, which, when you stood back and looked at it, formed the approximate shape of a bird. It bore no resemblance to any corvid that had ever lived, but somehow the lines managed to convey an expression of fierce intelligence.

"Very—er—picturesque," said Henry, who was called upon to pronounce the work satisfactory.

The young man in acrylic motley rubbed at his nose with the tip of a paintbrush. "Thanks, dude. You got a tissue? I splotched the paint a little on the beak and had to scrape it off the glass with a razor blade. Nicked my finger. But, hey, the paint's red there, so it doesn't show."

Averting his eyes from the sight of the boy's bleeding index finger, Henry fished a crumpled handkerchief out of the pocket of his jacket and handed it over. "Keep it with our thanks, young man. You've done a fine job."

Mrs. Ingram, the department secretary, received the news about the new department head with her usual impassive stare. Her attitude conveyed the impression that, after twenty years of employment at the university,

nothing would surprise her, except possibly mature and responsible behavior on the part of the faculty members. Henry had informed her of the decision even before he convened the department meeting, because he felt that telling her would be the greater ordeal. Not that she would express an opinion, of course, but there emanated from her waves of tacit disapproval, suggesting that their folly and absurdity had finally exceeded even her expectations of reprehensible behavior.

"I'm not feeding no birds," she said when Henry had wound his way through a torturous explanation.

"No, Mrs. Ingram, of course not. The raven, you see, is symbolic. There won't be any actual bird in the office. It's only a gesture—you know, a mythical creature chosen to head the Folklore department. The dean seemed to think it was quite clever."

"He would," muttered Mrs. Ingram. She sighed. "Well, I suppose it won't make much of a change from the poor soul who had the job last. Might as well have been in a birdcage, that one. So I'll just carry on as usual, shall I?"

"Absolutely," Henry assured her.

Things went smoothly for the first week or so, but then Dr. Acharya cornered Henry in the hallway after her morning class, her dark eyes blazing with scholarly indignation. "There are thirty-two people in my class, Henry. You can see the roster for yourself here. I thought we had agreed that we would take no more than twenty-two students in a class."

"Well, Apoorva, my dear, I suppose you're a popular instructor," said Henry, trying to extricate himself with flattery. It did not work.

"Thirty-two students, Henry!" She shook the roster sheet inches from his nose. "This is a university, not a fast-food restaurant! I have written out a formal protest—"

"But I am not the department head," Henry reminded her. "I suppose you could go to the dean, but of course, he'd want to know if you had gone through the proper channels." Henry nodded at the door across the hall, with the red and black raven totem on the frosted glass.

Dr. Acharya stared. "You are seriously suggesting that I take it up with *him*?"

"Well, you know, for form's sake," said Henry, glancing at his watch as he edged away. "I have a class."

"You're all mad!" she called after him, shaking her papers like a battle standard. Then as Henry's retreating form disappeared around the corner, she shrugged and shoved the papers under the department head's door.

Without admitting even to himself that he was doing so, Henry managed to avoid Dr. Acharya for the rest of the week. He hated confrontations, and it seemed to him particularly unfair that he should be subjected to them on account of a situation that was in no way his

fault or under his control. When he saw her again in the hall on Monday morning, she smiled and waved at him, so he ventured an inquiry.

"Er—did you get your class situation resolved?"

Her smiled broadened. "It resolved itself, Henry. All ten of my excess students took sick within the last two days. Apparently, they are in no serious danger, but they will all be out for the rest of the term."

Henry blinked. "Distressing news, of course," he said. "Very sad for them, but I am glad that you got your wish. Er—exactly what illness did your superfluous students come down with?"

They both glanced at the image of the raven on the closed door. Dr. Acharya hesitated for a moment, and lowered her voice to a whisper, "Avian flu."

The strange coincidence of the reduced class size made such a remarkable story that, without really intending to, Dr. Acharya had told everyone in the department about her good fortune within two days of its occurrence. Everyone laughed and congratulated her on her class reduction, and one or two of them made feeble jests about the new chairman being more efficient than most of his flesh and blood predecessors.

Purely on a whim, and perhaps because he had not entirely recovered from his morning hangover, Professor O'Meara slid his own hastily scribbled note under the chairman's locked door. He had been ambling

unsteadily down the hall, reluctantly bound for his eight a.m. class on Irish Folklore, when he happened to catch sight of the painted raven, leering at him from the frosted glass. He glared back at it for a few seconds, and then he whipped out his grading Sharpie from the outer compartment of his computer bag and scratched a brief note on the back of a junk mail envelope he found in his overcoat pocket.

I don't want to teach an eight o'clock class.

It made him feel better, anyhow, he told himself, squinting through his headache, as he wobbled away down the hall to the classroom.

Two days later, it snowed fifteen inches.

In deference to the off-campus students, and, of course, to the professors and campus workers, the chancellor cancelled morning classes. In a memo to the faculty, he said that while he could not condone any more class cancellations, he did recommend, in view of the icy road conditions, that professors endeavor to reschedule their early morning classes. Chris O'Meara sent an email to that effect to the students on his class roll, and discovered that every one of them had a two p.m. time slot free. At the next class meeting they voted unanimously to meet at that hour for the remainder of the term.

This time there was no pretense of discretion. O'Meara told his colleagues and anyone at the bar

who would listen about the marvelous new department head and the wonders he had wrought. He even affixed a little bag of sunflower seeds to the doorknob of the Raven's office. The next morning the sunflower seeds were scattered across the hall, and in his office mailbox, Dr. O'Meara found a photocopied Internet article on the dietary habits of *corvus corax*. Mrs. Ingram disavowed all knowledge of the memo.

"But they eat grains and berries," O'Meara insisted. "In addition to carrion. It says so right here."

Mrs. Ingram shrugged and went back to her word processing. "Apparently, this one doesn't."

Young Jeremy Cole, who hated to be left out of anything convivial, made a great show of writing up his request on departmental stationery, and collecting a little crowd of admirers in the hallway to watch him submit it. He even made a little ceremony of reading it aloud first. "Dear Chairman Raven," he intoned. "I, Professor Jeremy Cole, instructor in the Department of Folklore, respectfully request that I be given a new Mercedes-Benz, and this week's winning state lottery ticket worth seven million dollars. I shall be ever so grateful for your kind assistance in this matter." He acknowledged the scattered applause with a mock bow and slid the paper under the door with a flourish.

Nobody really expected anything to happen regarding Cole's flippant petition, and nothing

ever did. "After all," Dr. O'Meara was heard to say, "department heads are not responsible for matters in our personal lives." The Raven was judged to be entirely within his rights to ignore Cole's frivolous requests, as any other department head would have done. Cole tried again later, with a less public but equally silly request, but since no one reported any sightings of Angelina Jolie anywhere near the campus, or indeed in the entire state, this effort, too, was deemed a failure.

There was a postscript to this incident, which did not become fodder for the faculty gossip mill. A few days after Jeremy's second facetious attempt to petition the department head, he was working late in his office, and he chanced to go to the supply closet to refill his stapler. There on the floor of the closet was a sprung mousetrap, its tiny victim still warm but quite dead. On impulse Jeremy abandoned his stapler, carefully lifted the mousetrap, and set it down outside the Raven's door.

He admitted all this privately to Henry a week later. "It was just an impulse," he said. "I suppose I was curious."

Henry nodded sympathetically. "And did anything happen?"

"Well, when I came in the next morning, the trap was gone. That could have been the cleaning crew, I suppose. I didn't like to ask. But then yesterday I got a phone call from someone in Hollywood. Someone

famous. They're planning a picture set in ancient Rome, and the star had a technical question for a mythology expert."

Henry stared. When he could trust himself to speak, he said, "Jeremy, do you mean to tell me that Angelina—"

"No. No. Russell Crowe."

Henry, whose office was across the hall from the Raven, now kept his door open most of the time. He found himself keeping an eye on that portal, half expecting to see someone—or something—go in or out, but nothing ever did. He did sometimes get the feeling that the painted eyes of the Raven were watching him, but he dismissed this as a fancy born of his own uneasiness. When his colleagues laughed and bragged about the marvelous Raven and drew up silly wish lists, he did not join in the merriment. Henry was not amused. His mild dismay had progressed from misgivings to alarm.

In his spare time he began to read all the reference material that he could find on ravens, both ornithological information and mythology.

He learned that corvids have the largest brain size among birds, that they can speak and amass vocabularies of hundreds of words, and that they had been observed making simple tools: wire devices to enable them to retrieve bits of meat from inside a narrow pipe. Their preferred food was carrion, although they were

known to hunt and kill upon occasion, and they could eat insects, seeds, and berries if nothing more palatable was available. Interesting, but not really germane to the creature behind the closed door.

Henry turned his attention to folklore. In Pacific Northwest cultures, the Raven was the trickster god, the counterpart of the coyote or of Loki in Norse mythology. That was worrying. For trickster beings, benevolence is purely a whim, and their mood could change for no reason at all. In European myths, because of their fondness for carrion, ravens are linked to war and death, as well as to prophecy.

He wasn't sure what he was looking for exactly, but he did think that the more information he could accumulate, the better he would feel about the situation. If anyone had asked him about it, Henry would have insisted that the granted wishes were simply coincidences, but some undomesticated portion of his mind, the part that was only in ascendance at three a.m., told him that sooner or later somebody was going to ask for the wrong thing.

The weeks went by without incident until midterm exams. One evening Henry, who had just posted midterm grades, was on his way back from the library, where he had checked out more books on ornithology. In the parking lot he was confronted by a hulking student from his nine o'clock class (Introduction to World

Myths). The young man, who was built like a thumb, was wearing a letterman's jacket over a football jersey. He blocked Henry's path, clenching and unclenching his fists, while his breath made little clouds in the frosty November air. *Like a dragon,* thought Henry, wondering where the campus cops were when you needed them.

"You gave me an F, man!"

Henry found student confrontations distasteful, but he was inured to them by now, and he never allowed himself to be swayed by threats or pleas for mercy. "I didn't give you anything," he said calmly. "You earned the grade you received."

The young man thrust his face close to Henry's, and in a cloud of beer fumes, he roared, "You can't flunk me! Do you know who I am?"

"Darris Bradshaw, I believe," said Henry, mentally ticking off names on his roll sheet.

"The starting quarterback, that's who! Averaging nineteen points per game, that's who!" Henry might have been more sympathetic if Mr. Bradshaw's research paper had not seemed so familiar to him. He could not prove it, but he suspected that, with minor changes, this paper had been handed down through the ranks of the Athletic department, copied over the years by various unknown scribes, like an academic Book of Kells. He was not impressed with this student's honesty, with his intellect, or with his class attendance record.

"And I took your stupid fairy tale course for an easy

A, because if I get less than a 2.0 the coach will bench me."

"That is unfortunate," said Henry, attempting to edge past him. "But the grades have been sent to the registrar. It is out of my hands."

"Yeah? Well, who's your boss?"

Inadvertently, Henry glanced up at the dark stone building that housed the Folklore department. In one window there was light. "I suppose you could take it up with the department head," he said, pointing toward the glowing window.

Darris Bradshaw took a step back, scowling upward. "So this department head—he's your boss? If he says you have to change my grade, then you'd do it?"

"I believe I would," said Henry softly.

"Well, okay, then." He stepped aside to let Henry pass. "I'll go see him now. And he'd better listen to reason, or else."

Henry put his hand on the student's arm. "Are you sure you won't reconsider? It isn't the end of the world, you know."

Bradshaw scowled and pulled away. "No. It's worse. It's the end of my football career. But I'll get that grade changed if it's the last thing I ever do."

Henry glanced over his shoulder, watching for a moment as Darris Bradshaw lurched toward the folklore building, and then he hurried to his car and drove away without looking back.

Darris Bradshaw did not turn up for class the next

day. His disappearance made the front page of the local paper's sports section and headlines in the campus newspaper, but despite all the publicity and the anguished sound bites from the coaching staff, who saw their winning season go down the drain, the promising but academically hopeless young athlete was not seen again.

For the next few days people complained about a bad smell on the floor where the folklore department was located. "Drains," said the maintenance man. Henry went out and bought a case of air fresheners.

The rest of the term passed uneventfully. Henry heard no more tales of his colleagues making requests of the department head, but he carefully refrained from bringing up the Raven in faculty meetings or even in casual conversation. The copy machine never seemed to be out of order anymore; they finally got the new phone system they had been requesting for months; and, unless it was his imagination, there seemed to be fewer spelling errors in the students' written work. Still, things do occasionally go well from time to time, even at a state university. Maybe that's all it was.

One sunny spring afternoon when Henry was in his office, grading essays to the soothing sounds of Grieg, the door burst open and the dean bustled in, the ill wind in an otherwise balmy afternoon.

"Ah, Dr. Garner! How are you this fine day? Spring in the air!"

"Why should I?" murmured Henry, still intent on the essay.

"No, I meant—well, never mind. I came to have a word with you, if you can spare me a few moments."

Henry looked up, wondering what would happen if he said no. But that, he decided, would only prolong the encounter, so he laid down his pen and arranged his features into an expression of polite attention. "Yes, Dean?"

The man couldn't come to the point immediately, of course. Settling himself in the guest chair, he embarked upon three minutes of weather-related chitchat (Henry got the impression that the dean actually rehearsed these conversational gambits, and perhaps even timed them). But finally, daunted by Henry's brief, noncommittal responses, the dean said, "I just wanted a word with you about administrative matters. We are contemplating changes."

Henry felt a nerve in his cheek begin to twitch. "Oh? What changes?"

"Well, you know, this business of having an imaginary creature as a department head was a charming bit of whimsy—although it did not generate as much publicity as we might have hoped. Still, it was a fiscal necessity, but over the long term, you know, it won't do. It simply won't do."

"The arrangement seems to be working well enough," said Henry carefully.

The dean steepled his fingers and endeavored

to look sympathetic. "Still, we feel that it is time to resolve the situation with a more permanent solution."

Henry's silence was like a wall, but the dean heaved his bulk over it and reached the point at last. "In view of the reduced size of the Folklore department and its lack of a chairman, we—that is, the provost—has decided that the best solution would be to merge this department with Anthropology. Thus, their department head, Professor Simpkins, would oversee both faculties."

"Willard Simpkins is not in control of his *own* faculties," said Henry before he could stop himself.

The dean chose to take this remark as a witticism. "Always so clever, Henry. Such a quick thinker." He hoisted himself out of the chair. "Such a pleasure to see you, as ever. But I must run along now. Must be doing. I can rely on you to inform your colleagues of the administration's decision, can't I?"

After a moment's pause, Henry nodded. "But who's going to tell—er, the present department head?"

The dean's laughter echoed down the hall as he left. "Such a wit!"

"So there you have it," said Henry.

In the conference room, his four colleagues were regarding him with varying degrees of consternation.

"Merge with Anthropology!" said Hillenberg. "You cannot be serious. Their idea of research is to collect anecdotes from waitresses."

"Not the Earth Shoe People." Jeremy Cole shuddered. "The jargon! We'd need a translator to attend department meetings."

"Never mind the meetings!" wailed Apoorva Acharya. "They'll try to make us attend their beans and rice suppers in support of Guatemala. Or Guantanamo. Or one of those G-spots."

"We can't let them do this," said O'Meara. "My blood pressure won't stand it. We must fight this."

"I think we must," said Henry Garner. He handed each of them a blank sheet of department stationery.

Half an hour later, the faculty of the university folklore department had adjourned to the hallway, where they stood in silence before the painted image of the Tlingit deity. Then one by one they slipped their memos under the department head's door.

Barewolf

DANIEL PYLE

As the Case-thing padded through the woods, his paws
sank into the moist earth all the way to his dewclaws.
Shallow pools of mud filled the bottoms of the prints
he'd left behind. Many prints. He'd been hunting all
night. He walked under a dead pine and saw the moon
in the empty space above. Not full, but close enough.
He resisted the urge to call to it.

His stomach growled. Saliva dripped from his jag-
ged fangs, and he licked his muzzle with his long, black
tongue.

Less than a mile to the north, a man-snack moved
from inside a den to outside. The Case-thing stopped
and sniffed. His nostrils flared, and he lifted his snout
higher. The saliva in his mouth stopped dripping and
started pouring.

He licked his muzzle again and ran.

. . .

He stopped in the bushes just shy of the man-snack, poked his head between two bunches of leaves, and flared his nostrils. His stomach growled again, but he doubted the man-snack could hear. Men-snacks usually only responded to the growls that came from the Case-thing's throat.

The man-snack walked across a wooden platform and stepped into a box filled with hot water. He wore no clothing. His dangling parts slapped against his thighs as he moved. The Case-thing could smell the dangling parts. They smelled very chewable.

Once inside the water-filled box, the man-snack leaned back and closed his eyes.

A woman-snack exited the den through a sliding glass wall. She was also exposed. Her hairless teats bounced a little but didn't sway. The Case-thing could smell plastic inside, beneath the real meat.

She carried two containers filled with liquid that smelled both sweet and salty. It wasn't the same liquid that filled the box. He wondered why they needed anything but water.

The woman-snack brought the containers into the water box and handed one to the man-snack. He said something to her in a language the Case-thing could almost remember, and she laughed. She moved around the box and sat beside the man-snack. She was in heat.

As was the man-snack, of course. Men-snacks were always in heat.

The wooden platform stood a whole jump above the ground. The Case-thing eased between the bushes and slunk toward the snacks.

The woman-snack laughed again, and then the two snacks were sharing saliva. They were both sweating now, and not just from the hot water. Even through the water, the Case-thing could smell the blood rushing into the man-snack's dangly bit.

When the Case-thing came close enough to the platform, he put all his weight on his back paws and sprang into the air. His saliva trailed from the sides of his muzzle and streamed back across his head. He cleared the railing on the side of the platform and landed paws first on the wooden planks.

The snacks separated and screamed. Their screams were pathetic things: quiet, weak, gurgly.

The Case-thing's snarl echoed off the house to the side, the platform below, and the snacks ahead. The man-snack emptied his bladder as the blood moved from his dangly bit to his thumping heart. The Case-thing listened to the woman-snack's heart, which was also scrambling like a trapped animal. She held on to her urine, and he reminded himself to drain her before he snacked. There was nothing worse than a mouthful of pee.

He sprang onto the edge of the water box. The woman-snack tried climbing out over the opposite

side, but the man-snack didn't move at all. He stared at the Case-thing. His wide eyes looked delicious.

The Case-thing swiped at the woman-snack's neck, severed her spinal cord with his scythelike claws, and nearly took off her head. She slumped over the side of the water box, her smooth hindquarters pointing up at the sky, one arm caught beneath her body, the other swinging through the arc of blood jetting from her neck.

After he'd turned to the man-snack, the Case-thing licked his lips. He leaned forward, sniffed the snack's face, opened his mouth wide, and with a single, lightning-quick chomp, bit off the top of the snack's head.

Bone and hair and brain dribbled out of his mouth and fell into the water as he chewed. The man-snack's body drooped to the side and splashed into the water, which had gone from clear to pink to red. The Case-thing crunched bone, swallowed throatfuls of half-chewed remains. He stuck his snout in the water and bit into the man-snack's arm. He pulled the rest of the snack out of the water and dragged it out onto the wooden platform. The snack dripped water, dripped blood. The Case-thing buried his mouth in the snack's guts and scarfed up chunk after chunk of his innards. He smelled the woman-snack's flowing blood slow to a steady drip and growled satisfactorily as he sucked up a long string of intestines.

In his frenzy, he almost didn't smell the approach-

ing she-thing. She was halfway to the platform before he looked up from his snack and sniffed at her. She was wet and muddy, of course, but also starving. He could smell the drool in her mouth, hear her gurgling belly.

She jumped onto the platform near the water box and lowered her head submissively. The Case-thing chewed for a moment and watched her. He took one more bite of the man-snack's guts and then backed away from the kill.

The she-thing raised her head and stared. He dipped his head toward the carcass and took another step back.

Have some.

Never lowering her eyes from his, the she-thing took a hesitant step forward. When she seemed to be sure he wouldn't attack her, she rushed toward the fresh meat and pulled out a muzzleful.

He watched her eat. Her fur was lighter than his own. A blond coat that looked brown and might have been downy fine if it hadn't been thick with mud. Her long, wide muzzle sported dozens of teeth that gnashed and clicked as she fed. She was a little scrawny, but still well-muscled. Her tail wagged as she dipped her head back into the flesh crater the two of them had made.

A few swallows later, she looked up at him and dipped her own head toward the meat. He guessed she'd staved off the worst of her hunger and went to join her. Together, they picked the body clean and then dragged the she-snack from the hot water. They fin-

ished half of the second snack before the she-thing accidentally chewed into one of the plastic nonteats and hacked little bits of it back onto the platform.

When neither of them could eat another bite, the she-thing lowered her head in a kind of bow.

Thank you.

She wasn't in heat yet, but she was close. Close enough.

The Case-thing moved in and licked a streamer of blood from the she-thing's muzzle. She returned the gesture, and the two of them bathed each other for a long while. When his blood had completely filled his own dangly bit, he rubbed his head under hers and began to move along her side. He would circle around to her rear and take her from behind. He could smell the hormones coursing through her body—telling him to do it, to do it hard—as well as his own thick musk.

Except he never got around to her tail end. Halfway there, she growled and pulled away from him. Her hormone smell disappeared. He looked at her, saw that she was looking at his back. She took another step away and wheezed at him. Hyenalike.

The she-thing's laughter infuriated him. He crouched and growled at her. Spittle and blood sprayed from his mouth as he bared his teeth.

Instead of getting into a defensive stance, the she-thing wheezed again and jumped off the platform.

The Case-thing considered giving chase, hunting her down and ripping the laughter from the bitch's

throat, but in the end he stayed with his kill and let her go.

He knew what had driven the she-thing away. He'd first noticed it two or three cycles ago. It had started as a thin patch, but was now a hairless swatch of back skin that no doubt shone in the near-full moon.

His bald spot.

The doctor was an old man with thick glasses and a stooped gait. When he came shuffling into the room, he had his nose buried in a chart and squinted his eyes like a kid trying to see Mars through a pair of toy binoculars.

"Mr.—" He blinked at the chart. "Oswald."

"It's Case," said Case. "Jerry Case."

The doctor squinted harder and Case was afraid the old geezer was going to burst a blood vessel or something.

"Uh . . . are you going to be doing my procedure?"

"Oh, yes," the doctor said. "I perform all the intricate surgeries here." He looked up at Case, smiled, and winked a too-large, magnified eye.

Case was glad to see that at least the doc's sense of humor hadn't totally shriveled up with the rest of him.

"I'm Dr. Abrams." The old guy offered the five liver-spotted digits at the end of his arm and Case shook carefully, afraid that if he squeezed too hard, the wrinkled fingers might turn to dust in his hand.

"Jerry Case," he said in case the doc had already forgotten.

The doctor pulled a stool from the other side of the room to a spot just beside the table on which Case was sitting and plopped down on top of it. He closed the file and held it on his lap. "So," he said. "You need some more hair?"

Case nodded.

The doctor brought a hand up to the side of his mouth and whispered, "Pubes?"

"Wha—" Case floundered. "What? No . . . I . . . no. Gross." He wrinkled his nose and scooted away from the old man.

"Some guys like a hairy thatch," Abrams said. "You wouldn't be the first." He squinted up at Case's head. "Anyway, you can't want it on your head. I know I don't exactly have a pilot's vision, but I can see well enough to know that you've got a full 'do up there. The hairline might be receding just a smidge, but nothing a man your age needs to worry about."

The doctor's own hair was a wispy spider's web draped across his gleaming scalp.

"I don't need it for my head." Although he doubted the doctor could really see him even from just those few feet away, he lowered his gaze. "I—" He cleared his throat and tried again. "I need it for my back."

He looked up in time to see the old man cock his head and furrow his brow. "Your what?"

"I have this spot—"

"Your back?"

Case nodded, realized the man probably only saw a swaying blur, and said, "Yes."

Abrams wheezed, brought a fist to his mouth, coughed into it, and then wheezed again.

Case had a brief recollection of a female werewolf hyena-laughing at him. He gritted his teeth.

"I'm sorry, son," the doctor said when his bout of coughing ended. "We don't do that sort of thing here."

Case asked him why not.

"Why would we?"

"Because," Case said. "I need a transplant, and you're a hair transplant specialist. What do you care where I put it?"

The old man wheezed again but managed to get hold of himself a little more quickly this time. "We're in business to help people, Mr. Case, not make side-show freaks."

Case glared at him.

The old man coughed again, and Case imagined him hacking up one of his internal organs. The thought sent a hunger pang through his stomach, which rumbled almost immediately. Case licked his lips. They'd started to thin already. He felt his nose recede into his growing snout. His teeth stretched into wicked fangs, his ears flapped against the sides of his head, and his body began to rip its way through his clothes.

When the doctor realized what was happening, Case was no longer Case. He was the Case-thing.

The doctor screamed, but it was too late. For him, and for everyone else in the building.

Walmart's rug selection was pretty sparse. Case wondered if maybe he should have gone to Target instead. While he browsed, a woman strolled into the aisle steering a wobbly cart with one hand and pushing the loose strands of hair out of her face with the other. A drooling toddler sat in the front of the cart, slobbering all over the handlebar and the woman's fingers. A pile of food large enough to gag a whale filled the cart's main compartment. The woman pawed through a couple of nasty-looking rugs that appeared to have been barfed upon—maybe to hide stains so you didn't have to clean it as often. She passed on those particular monstrosities (from the dusty looks of the things, she wasn't the only one who had) and wheeled her cart closer to where Case stood.

"Not much to choose from, is there?" she asked when she noticed him.

Case shook his head. He squatted and pulled out a thick, brown, two-by-three-foot number. The rug certainly wouldn't have looked good anywhere outside a shrine to the '70s, but the fibers were thick, silky, lustrous.

"What do you think of this one?" He held it up for the woman's inspection.

She said nothing, but the eyebrows she arched

spoke whole diatribes. *Your call*, the brows said. *It's your rug, but we wouldn't put that thing in our house. Hell, we wouldn't use it to wipe our shit. If eyebrows could shit.*

"That bad?"

She shrugged. "It's definitely not my style, but maybe it will go with your décor."

Case's décor was the last thing on his mind. "Yeah," he said after studying the rug for another few moments. "Maybe it will."

He thanked the woman, tucked the rug under his arm, and went off in search of some superglue.

In his shoebox of an apartment, Case used a pair of heavy-duty scissors to cut the rug to size. He stripped out of his clothes, kneeled on the floor beside the reshaped rug, and spread the entire 16-oz bottle of superglue ("SUPER DUPER-SIZED SUPER-GLUE" the label proclaimed) on the rug's underside. He sat down at the end of the rug and did a reverse sit-up until his back pressed against the film of sticky glue. When he was all the way down, he wriggled a little from side to side, back and forth.

He lay there for almost half an hour, giving the glue time to set, letting the rug meld with his body until the two of them were one and the same. When he stood up, he went immediately to the bathroom for a look in the medicine cabinet mirror.

The rug didn't match his hair exactly—it was a few

shades darker—but that was all right. That was perfect. When he became the Case-thing, he tended to get dirty. With mud. With blood. His normal chestnut-colored follicles became darker brown, almost black. Every once in a while he'd find clumps of the stuff strewn about his apartment after a hunt. Shed? Torn out? He could never quite remember, but he guessed more than a few of those clumps had come from the space between his shoulder blades and his ass.

He reached over his shoulder and gave the rug a tug. He was able to shift it around a little, but only as much as the skin beneath would allow. It was stuck fast. He smiled and headed for the front door.

The only way to know for sure was to give it a little test run.

The Case-thing burst out of the snack-den's front doors and skittered to a stop on the cool concrete path. He breathed in the world around him, smelled dozens of snacks in the den behind, several more in the open, concrete-floored area ahead. There were no other things around—not yet—but once he'd spilled some blood, they'd come running. In a populated area like this, there'd be a whole pack.

He smelled a young woman-snack taking bagged food out of the back of her rolling metal box. It wasn't the woman-snack his snack-self had met earlier, the snack he only vaguely remembered, the snack he'd

barely been able to smell and hadn't thought of as a snack at all. Not at the time. This was a new smell. A younger smell. And this snack had no child-snack in tow.

The Case-thing padded between two more of the rolling boxes and found the woman-snack with arms full of plastic bags, trying unsuccessfully to kick shut the hatch to her metal box. He growled at her and she spun toward him. The muscles in one hand loosened and the bagged food crashed to the concrete below. The other hand squeezed. He could smell the muscles working. He licked his muzzle.

As the woman-snack screamed, her bladder let go and the front of her pants were suddenly ripe with the stench of urine. The Case-thing tried to unsmell the piss and, of course, couldn't.

The snack tried to run but slipped in her own spilled food and fell to her haunches. He was on her in a single bound. He tore a chunk from the side of her throat and flung the hunk of meat aside, trying to distribute the smell of the kill as widely as possible. Not that it would matter. If there were any things within five miles, they'd smell the carnage.

While he waited on the others, the Case-thing chose a few of the choicest bits of meat—the teats, the rump, the dangly-bit holder—and wolfed them down. There were other snacks nearby, all hiding. He saw one man-snack in a metal box a few jumps away. The snack stared through the box's glass side, eyes wide and full

of tears. Even through the metal and glass, the Case-thing could smell the snack's fear.

The first thing to arrive was another he-thing. The Case-thing growled at the new, smaller thing and the small-thing backed away, also growling but very low in his throat, unassertive. The Case-thing had always been the alpha, and he promised himself that he would remain so despite his scanty pelt.

The small-thing looked at the man-snack in the metal box and took a step toward him. The Case-thing lowered his head.

You have my permission.

The small-thing leapt onto the hood of the metal box, rammed his face through the glass, and tore the snack out in less than a second. The man-snack screamed once before the small-thing ripped out his throat. The small-thing swallowed the meat after only a few perfunctory chews.

When the first she-thing arrived, she looked first at the small-thing and then at the Case-thing. The Case-thing gestured toward the woman-snack. He and the she-thing went through the ritual: share the kill, pick it clean, bathe each other.

When she approached his back, the Case-thing tensed. She rubbed her head against him, pulled away momentarily, rubbed against him again, and then pulled away for good.

She backed off.

The Case-thing waited.

She wheezed.

His growl started as a soft gurgle in his throat and escalated into an earthquakelike rumble that seemed to shake the whole world.

The she-thing began to revert back to her snack self. Her muzzle shortened, her teeth shrank, her hair retreated into her skin. Her large, glowing eyes paled. She stopped changing halfway through. Just enough, he guessed, to regain control of her vocal chords.

She said two words the Case-thing could almost understand. He let the words replay over and over in his mind. When he finally realized what she'd said, the earthquake of a howl became a nuclear bomb of a howl. He leapt at her before she could change back and gutted her on the spot. As her intestines spilled out across her half-formed body, the Case-thing stepped back to watch her die.

Nice rug, were the words she'd said.

Other things had come. A pack of them, as he'd guessed. The small one on the hood of the metal box took a final bite of his snack and then hopped down to the concrete.

Some of the things were wheezing at him. He turned to face them one at a time, growling.

What are you looking at?

The things turned from him and padded away. He was still bigger than them, still stronger. They wouldn't test his temper.

When they were gone, and when the she-thing had breathed her last breath, the Case-thing clawed at the fur on his back. The fur that wasn't fur. He jerked his head over his shoulder and chewed at the stuff. When he had dug away all the fake fur, chomped down through the hide to the raw meat beneath, he stopped and panted.

He looked up at the sky, saw the now-full moon, and wailed at it.

"It's quite common," the psychiatrist said, "for men to feel a sense of inadequacy when they begin to lose their hair."

Case listened to her from the armchair on the other side of the small room.

"But I have to ask: do you think you might be blowing things slightly out of proportion? After all, you have very nice hair. Many men would kill for hair like yours."

Case laughed.

"May I ask what you find so amusing?"

He shook his head. "Never mind. And anyway, it's not the hair on my head that I'm worried about."

"Not—" She looked at him for a moment before glancing down at his crotch. "Ahh."

Case crossed his legs and said, "No. Jesus. What's wrong with everyone?"

She looked him in the eyes again. She smiled but

didn't laugh. When her eyes flicked down to check her watch, Case felt his face begin to morph.

"—time is almost up," the woman was saying.

"Yours is anyway," the Case-thing said and leapt from the chair.

American Banshee

ERIC JAMES STONE

Filiméala finished her keening as "Dapper" Donny O'Grady, head of the O'Grady mob, breathed his last. Leaning over his bed, she planted a kiss on his age-mottled forehead. She was glad he had died peacefully at home rather than in a rain of bullets, like too many of the extended family.

"Right, then, we're done with that infernal screeching," said Harry. "Time for you to be on your way."

Filiméala sat up straight and fixed her gaze on Harry. Even at thirty-five, he still had the air of an impatient six-year-old. She had never been sure whether his nickname "Hair-Trigger" was the result of his impatience or the cause of it. "Show some respect, lad," she said. "Your father has just passed on. I have sung his soul—"

"Right, right," Harry said. "My father, may he rest, et cetera. But I'm head of the family now, and there are going to be some changes, starting with you."

"Me?" Filiméala could not keep the startlement from her voice. She had been with the family O'Grady for over five hundred years, even following some of them to America during the Great Famine—though her spirit still yearned sometimes for the hills of the Old Country. The last major change in her life had been over sixty years ago, when Dapper Donny's father had convinced her to keen the deaths of all members of the O'Grady mob, even if they were not family by blood. What could Harry want of her?

"Yes, you. My father was one for the old ways, but this is the twenty-first century. We don't need a banshee shrieking about, frightening the neighbors, whenever someone's going to die."

"Bean Sídhe," Filiméala corrected. "The B is—"

"That's exactly what I'm talking about. We're in America, so speak American. But that's not the point. The point is, you're a symbol of the past."

"Your father and grandfather—"

"Are dead. And all you could do was wail about it. Now, if you could actually warn us someone was going to die in time for us to prevent it . . ." He cocked an eyebrow at her.

She shook her head. Harry had never been the brightest fish in the barrel. "That's just foolishness, lad.

If you prevented a man from dying, I would not feel the call to sing his death now, would I?"

Grabbing her by the left wrist, Harry said, "I am head of the family now. You will show me respect."

She nodded.

He twisted her arm behind her back. "They say if you capture a banshee, she must tell you the name of who is going to die. You must have been giving my father that information, which could still be useful, even if the death can't be prevented."

"Rubbish," Filiméala said. "If it's obvious who will die, like your father on his deathbed, then I know, just the same as anyone else. But usually I keen the death without knowing whose it is. Who told you such nonsense?"

"I read it on Wikipedia," Harry said, his voice defensive.

She didn't use the computer in her room for much more than emailing some of her sister *Bean Sídhe* back in the Old Country, who were constantly forwarding her chain letters and YouTube clips. The Internet did not seem worthy of trust to her, because she did not understand the magic behind it. Humans were different—willing to rely on magic beyond their mortal comprehension. "I believe I know my own powers better than Wikipedia."

"Whatever." Harry released her arm and waved dismissively. "If you can't make yourself useful, then I see no reason not to replace you."

"Replace me?" Her voice rose to a squeak, and she struggled to lower its pitch and speak in a reasonable tone. "I have served your family faithfully all these centuries, and now you want to bring in another *Bean Sídhe* to take my place? I promise you, she can tell you no more than I."

"Not another banshee," he said. He pulled his cell phone out of his pocket. "The head of one of the Haitian gangs owed me a favor. One of his men voo-dooed an app for my iPhone that will warn me when an O'Grady is going to die, but since I can set it to play any mp3 I want as the warning, it's more discreet—and a whole lot easier on the ears." He grinned at her. "You, my dear, are obsolete."

Filiméala pulled her gray cloak tight around herself. "If you have no need of me, then I will retire to my room."

"I don't think you understand yet," said Harry. "Get out of my house and don't come back."

Filiméala found it hard to breathe, like she had been kicked in the stomach by a stubborn mule. "Where shall I go? What shall I do?"

"This is America, the land of opportunity," Harry said with a sharky grin. "I'm sure you'll find something."

Dapper Donny's widow, Meara, slipped some paper into Filiméala's palm as a couple of Harry's strongmen

escorted her to the sidewalk outside the walls of the mansion.

Filiméala had not been outside the walls in decades. She resisted the urge to throw herself against the gates and beg to be allowed back in. She straightened her shoulders and walked away. She would not give Harry the satisfaction of seeing her devastated.

Éire. Back to Éire. That was where she would go, back to the emerald hills of the Old Country, where she would forget all about the family O'Grady and her brief hundred and sixty years in America.

But not by ship this time. With a small shudder she remembered the journey by steamship, all the passengers crowded together in a space hardly big enough to contain them.

No, she would take one of the aeroplanes of which Donny had often spoken. How grand it must be to sail above the clouds, free as a nightingale on the breeze. She would merely have to ignore the fact that she did not understand the magic that held aeroplanes up in the air. Perhaps it was the same magic that had prevented a steamship made of iron from sinking like a stone in the ocean.

But first she must get to the airport. She looked at the papers Meara had given her: several hundred-dollar bills. She hoped it would be enough.

After some frantic waving on her part, an orange-colored taxicab pulled over and she got in.

"Where to?" asked the driver.

"The airport, please," Filiméala said, faking confidence.

"Which one?"

"Em . . . One with aeroplanes that go to Éire—Ireland?"

"You want JFK?"

She wasn't sure what that meant, but across the years, Donny had spoken about an American president named JFK, and if she recalled correctly he had been of good Irish stock. Maybe it was a sign she was on the right path.

"Take me to JFK," she said.

After a terrifying ride filled with unexpected jolts, random noises, and a great deal of cursing in a tongue unknown to Filiméala, the driver pulled to a stop and said, "You probably want Aer Lingus. That's this terminal."

She gave him one of her hundred-dollar bills, and he drove away very happily.

It took a quarter of an hour for Filiméala to get to the front of the Aer Lingus line.

"What is your final destination?" asked a pert lass behind the counter.

"I just want to go back to Éire," Filiméala said.

The lass's brow furrowed. "You don't have a ticket?"

"No." Filiméala dropped the rest of the money Meara had given her on the counter. "Is that enough?"

After counting the money, the lass typed at her keyboard. "You're in luck. There's a seat available on

our five forty-five flight to Dublin for seven hundred forty dollars. Will that do?"

"Yes." Filiméala sighed with relief. Everything would be better once she got back to Éire.

"I'll just need to see your passport," the lass said.

"Em . . . my what?"

"Your passport."

"I don't have one. Can I buy one here?"

The lass got a strange look on her face and excused herself to go talk to an older man.

After several frustrating conversations during which Filiméala was forced to explain over and over to each new person that she came to America years ago without a passport and that all she wanted to do was go back to Éire, they put her in a room to wait for someone from the Irish consulate.

She had a feeling the explanation that she had come across the Atlantic one hundred and sixty years ago was not going to go over well. They would never let her go back to Éire.

A television on the wall cycled through news stories. She let the babble fade into the background as she wallowed in her misery, until she heard a familiar song. She looked up to see on the screen something she had seen on YouTube: a middle-aged woman singing before an audience that went wild with applause. She began to listen to what the newsman was saying.

"While in the past their show has focused on singers under thirty, the producers of *American Idol* have

announced that they would also like to find the American equivalent of Susan Boyle, the forty-eight-year-old Scottish singer who became an overnight Internet sensation. So for all you older singers out there, maybe this is your opportunity to make it big. The open auditions start tomorrow at Giants Stadium."

Harry had told her this was the land of opportunity. Maybe it was time to stop feeling sorry for herself and start making a new life for herself. If a Scotswoman could become a star, why not an Irishwoman—and one of the *Bean Sídhe*, no less?

Just as she stood up to walk out, the call of death hit her. Somewhere, five members of the O'Grady mob were about to die.

Harry had dismissed her from her service to the family—there was nothing to bind her to the O'Gradys any longer.

But the call was too strong. Dapper Donny had never been one for mob wars, so she hadn't sung for more than two deaths at once in decades. Filiméala tried to resist, but her knees buckled. The keening tore at her throat until finally she stopped resisting and let her voice burst forth.

The television screen shattered.

A uniformed man opened the door. "What are you—"

She directed her keening at him, and he grabbed his ears.

Filiméala walked past him and out of the airport

terminal. She no longer needed an aeroplane. Her life had a purpose now: to become an American Idol.

Filiméala could not count how many people were in line to get into Giants Stadium, but surely it was thousands. Some of them even had tents. A lad with a clipboard handed her a sheet of paper with a series of questions to fill out, including date of birth. Filiméala first decided to make her age forty-eight to match this Susan Boyle, then after eyeing the youth of the other contestants, changed it to thirty. She gradually shifted her appearance to be more youthful, turning her silver hair to golden blond and smoothing the wrinkles of her skin. The persona of an old woman had served her well in a culture that valued age, but that time seemed long gone. America valued youth and beauty, and she needed to be more American if she wanted to be an American Idol.

Just to be safe, she de-aged herself down to twenty-five, then twenty.

"Whoa!" said the lad behind her in line. "What happened to the old lady?"

"Em," Filiméala said, "my grandmother held my place in line until I could get here. You won't tell anyone?" And she gave him a wink.

"Secret's safe with me," he said. "I'm Kip."

"Filiméala," she said. The name would have to be thrown out with her age, she realized with regret. "Call me Fi." And she wrote Fi O'Grady on the form.

After several hours, she and Kip, along with two other aspirants, were ushered into one of several large tents being used for auditions. A gray-haired man sat behind a folding table.

"Okay, let's hear what you've got," the man said.

Filiméala sang, her voice converting the silly required pop number into a powerful ballad filled with longing and hope. She continued to sing past the specified twenty seconds, filling the tent with her song. As she let the final notes drift away, the man wiped tears from his eyes.

"Wow," he said. "I can't wait to see what Simon—"

Filiméala was so caught up in the moment that the call of death caught her completely off guard. The lament for twelve O'Gradys burst forth from her mouth, and everyone in the tent grabbed their ears to seal out the sound, then fled.

Something within her had changed. Filiméala's keening had never been so powerful before. It was as if she had tapped a new source of power—and unfortunately, she was not used to handling it. Before she could get it under control, the fabric of the tent was torn to shreds, which whirled around her in a tornado of cloth.

Amid the screaming, panicked chaos of thousands of aspiring singers, Filiméala walked out of the stadium.

She would never be an American Idol. But perhaps it was time to show Harry just how useless a *Bean Sídhe* was.

• • •

Harry sat behind the mahogany desk in what had been Dapper Donny's study. He didn't look up from the papers he was reading when his men escorted Filiméala in.

She sat in a maroon leather chair and waited.

Without looking up, he said, "Your message said you had found a way to be useful?"

"Yes." She spoke meekly, like a penitent child.

He looked up, then started as he took in her new appearance. "Like the new look. Maybe I can find a use for you as something other than a banshee."

Filiméala felt the call of death, and a moment later tinny music began to play in Harry's pocket. He pulled out his iPhone and stared at it.

Suppressing the desire to keen, she leaned forward. "Does the voodoo in your phone tell you the name of who is going to die?"

"No."

"I can tell you," she said, her voice a rough whisper as she held back the song.

He snorted. "You said before that you couldn't."

"Things are different now. I think after all these years in America, my *Bean Sídhe* power is tapping the strength of America, rather than Éire."

"Right, then," he said. "Is it one of the O'Malley boys? I sent them to deal with some Italian trouble-makers."

"'Tis neither of the O'Malley boys," she said. "The name of the one who will die is Harold Standish O'Grady."

His eyes widened as Filiméala unleashed her full voice. He leaped from his chair and clapped his hands to his ears while screaming an inaudible order to his guards. The force of the song slammed him back against the oak-paneled wall and pinned him there.

The flesh of his face rippled, then piece after piece tore away. The bones of his skull fractured, then refractured again and again until they were ground to powder, held in place only by the standing waves of sound produced by Filiméala's keening.

She stopped, and the remains of Harry "Hair-Trigger" O'Grady collapsed into a wet heap on the floor.

Filiméala became aware that the guards had their guns pointed at her. They were repeatedly pulling the triggers, resulting in ineffective clicks since they had run out of bullets. Metallic dust lay on the floor a few feet in front of them, remnants of the bullets shattered by her song.

"Now, now, lads," she said. "I have nothing against you. And if you behave yourselves, it will be a good many years before I sing for your deaths."

They stopped pulling their triggers but continued staring wide-eyed at her.

She walked around the desk and poked at Harry's corpse with her toe. "It seems the O'Grady mob lacks a

head, and somebody needs to stop the mob war the late Mr. O'Grady began." In a whisper, she added, "You're the one who told me this was the land of opportunity."

Filiméala sat down in what had been Harry's chair and swiveled to face her guards. "Tell the rest of the clan that I'm in charge now."

"What should we call you, ma'am?" one of them asked.

"Filiméala O'Grady," she said. The continuity of the surname was important. But she also needed a nickname, so she added, "The American Banshee."

The Epicurean

AMY STERLING CASIL

By summer's end, Vanpirs had grown somnolent, not leaving his flat for days before the *Schlachtfest* was to begin in the *Alter Markt*. He sat at a small yellow table by the iron hearth, reading a French tourist guide about the preparation of Pomeranian *Tollatschen*, a dish rich with pig's blood, bacon drippings, and raisins.

For the *Schlachtfest*, Stralsunders gathered in hundreds, the women in their dirndls and men in old-fashioned suits, gobbling pig knuckle, *leberwurst*, *knockwurst*, dozens of waxy, greasy boiled potatoes, and of course, *blutwurst*.

It was the smell that brought Vanpirs to loiter near the *Schlachtfest* in an alley paved with thirteenth-century stones. Standing quietly in his close-fitted black jacket, Vanpirs looked only slightly different from the Stralsunder men. One would only have noticed that

his hair was darker and straighter than most, and his face was more chalk than pink. Few Stralsunders could maintain such a trim profile after years of *Schlachtfest*s and, following that orgy of pig meat, Oktoberfest *bier*, drunk in competitive German quantity.

Vanpirs spied three Deutsche maidens leaving the *Alter Markt*, holding each other by the elbows, laughing.

"*Ja, das Tollatschen! Zu viel!*" said one of the women.

"*Weit zu viel!*" said the one in the middle.

Even Vanpirs's suspect German told him that they had eaten a great deal of Pomeranian *Tollatschen*, the bloody dish he'd been reading about. His nose told him they had washed it down with *weissbier*.

After a brief exchange of pleasantries, two of the women stood mesmerized as he fed on the first of them that reached his waiting arms. Ah, the rich sweet-sour flavor of *Tollatschen*, full to bursting with pig blood, bacon fat, and plump raisins. The late summer beer was also not bad, Vanpirs thought.

At the end, Vanpirs was as full as the women had been, and he staggered from the alley.

"Ho! You've had a bit much!" called some town revelers.

"Indeed I have," Vanpirs called back. "*Pommerische Tollat!*"

They laughed. "*Ja! Pommerische Tollat!*"

It was not until Vanpirs had nearly reached his flat when he felt the most curious sensation. His limbs

were heavy and would not move as he wished. He tried to leap up the steps as was his usual habit, but instead, he found himself lying on his back, staring at a torn veil of clouds wisping across the rising Baltic moon.

He lay there for some time, slowly moving his fingers and toes but nothing more, until at last his elderly neighbor Herr Kahler arrived.

Herr Kahler, a stooped and balding man who limped around Stralsund in a black leather jacket studded with *Polizei* and ABBA patches, leaned over Vanpirs and said, "Eh, what? You've had too much *bier*, young fellow."

"No," said Vanpirs.

"Moderation in all things, I say!" He poked Vanpirs with his cane.

In any other circumstance, Vanpirs would have fed immediately on the old gent. But Vanpirs's limbs would not respond.

"Please, Herr Kahler," he whispered. "Help me."

"Bah!" Herr Kahler said. "I cannot. My health card authorizes me to lift no more than two kilos."

"Please, lend me an arm," said Vanpirs. He thought he saw the faintest glimmer of the morning sun rising over Stralsund's ancient spires.

Herr Kahler turned and saw the flicker of light as well. He bent slowly, and held out his arm.

"You will forgive me, Herr Vanpirs," Herr Kahler said. "It is unwise to come too close to a gentleman of your persuasion."

Vanpirs grabbed Herr Kahler's arm. Slowly, he managed to lift himself to a kneeling position.

"Your condition seems most unusual," Herr Kahler said. "I would urge you to consult Herr Glücklich, the *Apothek*, at your earliest convenience."

Legs trembling, Vanpirs managed to stand. *"Ja,"* he said. *"Danke."*

"Now get inside. For myself, I plan to fix a cup of hot tea. I should think by the time the water boils, the sun will have risen over the cathedral." With a brief nod, Herr Kahler indicated the spire of Stralsund's oldest structure.

"Danke," Vanpirs said, inching toward the door of his flat.

"You'll have no trouble seeing Herr Glücklich tomorrow evening. He keeps late hours." Herr Kahler smiled, and for such an old gentleman, he had remarkably strong white teeth.

"He's in Lindenstrasse?"

"Ja," Herr Kahler said. "Please be kind enough to let me know what he says. I shall be taking a brief trip tomorrow, but I'll be curious to find out your prognosis after that."

Vanpirs looked up at the clouds sweeping across the moon. To the casual eye, it would have seemed a full moon, but Vanpirs saw that it was waxing gibbous. He suddenly understood the true nature of his neighbor, wondering how he had not noticed before.

"Herr Kahler," Vanpirs asked, "why is it that you seem so enfeebled?"

"Ah," Herr Kahler said without turning. "Some of us know how to thrive in the present day."

Vanpirs, wondering whether Herr Kahler had meant his hideous jacket or aged appearance was the secret to successful lycanthropy, entered his flat just as the sun began to rise and fell to the floor in a heap.

The shop of Herr Glücklich the Apothek looked like an ordinary pharmacy to Vanpirs, but he entered anyway, as he felt so wretched that he would have snorted packets of Dr. Oetker's dried custard if it could have improved his condition.

To the young, pimply man behind the pharmacist's counter he said, *"Wo ist Herr Glücklich?"*

"I can help you," the young man replied.

Vanpirs reached across the counter and grabbed the young man's jacket. "Herr Glücklich," he growled.

"Oh, ja!" replied the young man, and he craned his pocked neck, calling, *"Herr Apothek!"*

A tidy man of about fifty emerged, straightening his glasses.

"Danke, Herman," he said. "Go and clean the *klo."*

After two or three rabbitlike blinks, Herman scrambled away and disappeared to the rear of the shop.

"I come on the recommendation of Herr Kahler," Vanpirs said.

"You've been attending the *Schlachtfest?"* Herr Glücklich asked.

"*Ja,*" Vanpirs said.

"And you did as all others do, I suppose," the Apothek said. He busied himself with arranging a display of ribbed condoms on his counter.

"I don't feel I did anything out of the ordinary," Vanpirs said. "But as I went home, I found myself unable to climb the steps to my own flat."

The Apothek looked sharply at him, and Vanpirs said, "I needn't tell you how unusual *that* is for a man of my . . ."

"Proclivities? Hmmn," said Herr Glücklich in a businesslike tone. "Roll up your sleeve."

Vanpirs undid his cuff and complied with the Apothek's request.

"Press the flesh with your fingers," he said. "Just so." He lifted the loose sleeve of his pharmacist's jacket and pressed his own forearm with two fingers.

Vanpirs frowned but pushed his left forefinger into his wax-pale arm.

"Now take the finger away," Herr Glücklich instructed.

Vanpirs removed his finger. A neat dent remained in his flesh.

"How long has this been going on?" asked Herr Glücklich.

"I don't know," Vanpirs said, staring at the dent.

"It is the curse of our modern age," the Apothek concluded.

"I don't—" Vanpirs thought he knew all imaginable curses and this was not one of them.

"You should be aware that I am a senior authority in my field," Herr Glücklich said.

"That is very good," Vanpirs said, staring at the dent and feeling faint.

"Gentlemen such as you are not immune to the complaints suffered by the general population."

"But I am immortal," said Vanpirs.

"We are all dependent upon our environment, Herr—"

"Vanpirs."

"Herr Vanpirs," the Apothek repeated, not unkindly. "This is why I asked about the *Schlachtfest*, although I was quite certain that you had attended, merely by examining your color." He leaned across the counter and took Vanpirs's dented arm, holding it up and turning it this way and that.

"So," said the Apothek. "Here you clearly see an abnormality. And I will tell you its source."

"Please," Vanpirs said. What would cause such a dent! In his perfect flesh!

"Cholesterol," the Apothek concluded.

"What?" cried Vanpirs.

Ja," Herr Glücklich said. "Although your metabolism would seem flawless, maintaining you through dozens of ordinary lifetimes, even it is no match for today's high-fat diet."

"But I do not eat . . . food," Vanpirs said. "This is impossible."

"Most possible. It is the fat-rich blood of those you

are feeding on. Cholesterol deposits itself directly in the altered cells that comprise your flesh. This is a buildup of many years, Herr Vanpirs. Today, with the number of people out there with fatty blood, it's becoming increasingly common among those of your *persuasion*."

"Fat, in my flesh?" Vanpirs asked, stunned. He had not loosened his belt in three hundred years.

"Ja," said Herr Glücklich. "There is only one cure. You must change your diet. I would recommend oat bran under other circumstances."

"How can I—"

"Herr Vanpirs," the Apothek interrupted. "My advice is to eat more simply. Frequent athletic events and health resorts. Perhaps consider enrolling in a commune of environmental enthusiasts."

"Vegans?" Vanpirs said. "That's—disgusting. Can you not give me a—pill? A shot?"

Herr Glücklich shook his head. "This has taken years to develop. It will take years of correct eating to rectify."

"Ridiculous," said Vanpirs. "I can't understand why Herr Kahler sent me."

"Herr Kahler is also afflicted by our changing times. He has developed a sensitivity to modern chemical products. I've advised him to switch to biodegradable infant laundry soap, among many other changes."

"A werewolf using baby soap?" Vanpirs said, laughing. As he buttoned his cuff, Vanpirs noticed with satisfaction that the dent was entirely gone. Perhaps he

should feed upon the Apothek. That would teach the smug fellow.

"I thought you could help me," Vanpirs said. "But this is absurd. I suppose that I've come in contact with some sort of holy water perfume."

Herr Glücklich shook his head. "In that case, your lips would have blistered," he said.

Vanpirs felt his lips. "It was something like that. I'm certain of it."

"Tell me, then," Herr Glücklich said. "Do you particularly enjoy feeding on those who've finished a tasty meal?"

"Of course," said Vanpirs. "Do you think I'd prefer some pimpled youth eating nothing but fried chicken?"

"Ah," Herr Glücklich said, holding out a business card. "Of course not. Let me give you my card."

"I do not need more absurd advice," Vanpirs said, throwing the card down on the counter. "Or a diet."

Herr Glücklich appeared nervous for the first time since the discussion began. He cleared his throat, tapped his fingers lightly on the counter, and said, "You are playing with fire in this matter. Quite literally. This fatty material is most combustible. And unlike your victims, your body is not comprised of seventy percent water, which does not burn. Surely you've heard that the percentage of water in the bodies of the obese may decrease to less than fifty percent. In that case, I would not recommend those individuals stay in the sun on a hot day!"

Vanpirs looked down at his completely flat stomach, then back at the Apothek. "You're mad," he said. "I've never been fat—"

"It is the concentrated fat collected in your flesh and not your external size or weight that is of such great risk," the Apothek said. "Why else do you suppose the old films such as *Nosferatu* encouraged the myth that vampires burned to a crisp upon exposure to daylight? When too close to little boys with magnifying glasses, some have!"

"Rubbish," Vanpirs snapped. Then he smiled, most unpleasantly.

The Apothek's voice quavered only a bit as he said, "I should let you know that I am myself a strict vegetarian, and I had a dish of anise bulbs and garlic this morning, as I do every day."

Vanpirs's nose had told him so, and this was the reason he now left without even the tiniest drink of the Apothek's blood.

Idiocy, Vanpirs thought as he strode home. Risk of fire, burning like some fat, roasting pig? He was as fit and slim as he'd ever been—why, he'd never even gotten a sunburn and one day stayed out for hours on the beach at Cannes, attracting juicy young women with his slender, perfect physique. He stopped for a moment in an alley behind an oyster shop, waiting for a brief, moist snack. It turned into a bit more than a snack; after leaving the two overfed university students piled neatly beside the restaurant's trash can, he went home,

feeling very much improved, and fell into a dreamless slumber.

Exchange rates being what they were, Vanpirs decided within a day of his interview with the Apothek that he would join the great numbers of his fellow Europeans in traveling to the West.

He discovered a travel website that specialized in his particular interest: epicurean tours. He copied down one of their itineraries and made arrangements privately for accommodations at each venue.

For sentimental reasons, he planned first to visit the Seymour Hamburger Festival. He had spent many pleasant years in Hamburg ensconced in a thirteenth-century flat near the Deutsches Schauspielhaus. The American hamburger fest took place in a small Wisconsin town that was the home of "Hamburger Charlie," the reputed inventor of the ubiquitous American sandwich. It was also the home of Charlie's assistant, Emil Wurm, a man whose name Vanpirs found familiar, indeed, reminiscent of one of his former familiars.

It was difficult for Vanpirs to accommodate to American lodging, but he learned quickly that certain hotels had blackout curtains, as well as the meaning and purpose of the "Do Not Disturb" sign to be hung for the maid. Vanpirs soon learned that if he reversed the sign at the proper moment, he might pick up an

extra meal, though disposing of the maid's body was always a concern.

As the hamburger festival began, Vanpirs was disappointed to see so many "commercial" meals offered. But the evening hamburger cookoff held much promise. Vanpirs noticed the festival mascots entering and exiting a small building. This turned out to be a retreat for the costumed hamburger bride and groom. The burger costumes were bulky, and the teenaged mascots eagerly took breaks, where they could remove their foam prisons and drink cold cola and eat ice cream. The pair were also served quarters of the contest hamburgers—which were quite gourmet and up to Vanpirs's discriminating standards.

The bride and groom were biting into the last of the contest burgers when the winner was announced—a Southwestern-themed sandwich, with pepper-jack cheese, black bean and corn relish, and ancho chiles. As the excitement outside built, Vanpirs slipped into the tent and experienced the full flavor of the festival's offerings.

He hadn't thought he would care for American ice cream, but to his surprise, it was decadently rich and delightful. And the combinations of flavors on the medium-rare, flame-cooked burgers were irreplaceable. The toppings, particularly cheese, whet his appetite for more. Thus inspired, he moved on to the next festival, one dedicated to cheese, conveniently located in the nearby Wisconsin village of Little Chute.

Vanpirs waited for the festival to begin, amusing himself by watching small, pink children riding the tiki-themed hotel waterslide as well as playing his "Do Not Disturb" sign game with well-fed Wisconsin hotel maids.

After a few days Vanpirs was perusing the local newspaper in the hotel lobby when he heard guests talking about a reporter from the Green Bay newspaper. She was at that moment interviewing people in the hotel lounge, asking about "maid disappearances."

To amuse himself, Vanpirs found the reporter in the bar sipping a Cosmopolitan. He sidled next to her, identifying himself as a Romanian food critic. After pleasantries, he told her that Europeans were constantly amazed at the violence that seemed so common in America.

"No one ever disappears in Romania," he told her and agreed to let her take his picture.

She seemed delighted to snap photo after photo of him, and Vanpirs was pleased to see his comments appear on the Internet within hours, although there was a small note to the effect that the pictures had not come out properly, perhaps due to a lack of sufficient light in the hotel lounge.

Vanpirs's exuberant feeding that evening led to a four-state search for the "Festival Cheese Killer." Soon after her coverage of the triple-homicide of the festival's first, second, and third-place winners, the Green Bay newspaper reporter obtained both a paperback

book deal and an offer for a reality show. The story was especially touching, considering that each victim had achieved a lifelong dream of winning a cheese-off trophy and ribbon, yet before they could fully savor their winnings, each had lost her life by unexplained exsanguination.

Leaving Little Chute, Vanpirs traveled to Eau Claire, Michigan, for the annual Cherry Festival, which encompassed patriotic fervor as well as a cornucopia of sweets. Vanpirs monitored the evening's Sit-N-Spit contest with great humor.

Perhaps because he had been so profligate at the cheese festival, Vanpirs held back at the Cherry Festival, only feeding on the elderly former mayor and his twin brother. The next day it seemed clear to everyone that the duo had succumbed after tying too many cherry stems into knots with their tongues during the day—a family talent—and by gobbling a five-pound cherry pie that evening.

As he left Eau Claire, Vanpirs struck on the idea of purchasing a motor home, which afforded him reliable daytime privacy and darkness, and which also opened up the entire landscape of great American food festivals.

In the coming weeks in his Coachmen Epic, Vanpirs attended International Pancake Day in Liberal, Kansas, the Oakhurst Chocolate Festival in northern California, and the Star of Texas Barbeque *and* Pig Out at the Park. These last two featured pork product competitions, much like the Pomeranian *Schlachtfest*.

By the following spring, Vanpirs had sampled regional specialties across America. A dim awareness in the criminal justice system had begun to flicker, however, because the FBI had begun to track the "food festival killer," and Vanpirs had chuckled to see mention of the pattern of killings on MSNBC.

Vanpirs left Texas for Florida in early March. His destination was Orlando, although he was quite certain that the food at the Disney resorts was dreadful. He had no intention of visiting those locations: he was headed straight for the Pillsbury Bake-Off.

The quintessential American food event took place in a massive convention hall in which no natural light ever entered, thus qualifying it as a culinary paradise for Vanpirs. Acres of blissfully cool, sun-free indoor real estate was packed with food displays, demonstration booths, and in the contest hall, one hundred identical cooking stations for the contestants.

Less appealing was the fact that the Pillsbury Bake-Off, as a commercial event, had been overtaken by contemporary ideas of "healthy eating." After several low-fat chicken and tofu demonstrations and a teeth-gritting low-sodium, high-fiber, fat-free blended horror of Lovecraftian proportions, Vanpirs wandered into the contest hall to watch the intricate preparations for the Bake-Off. This was simple, for he carried a digital camera and a slightly altered set of press credentials

that identified him as a critic for the glossy European publication *Epicurean*.

His urges to feed ebbed and flowed, but he willed himself to wait for the contest dishes to be prepared and tasted, telling himself that victory would be his following the announcement of the one-million-dollars winner that evening.

As the long day wore on, Vanpirs's head felt light and strange. Perhaps, he thought, it was the great number of warm bodies in the convention center overwhelming him. He rested for a moment by the red, white, and blue balloon arch through which the hundred Bake-Off contestants would run on their way to their identical cooking stations. After a moment Vanpirs found himself sharing space with the Pillsbury Doughboy.

"Do you like hamburgers?" Vanpirs asked in an effort to make light conversation.

"No, man," the Doughboy said. "I'm vegan."

"Ah," Vanpirs said, which explained the repulsive, weedlike odor of the Doughboy's sweat.

Vanpirs watched the contestants enter to great fanfare, greeted by the Doughboy. He took photos, and toured the kitchens of those who were preparing main dishes; American desserts were simply too sweet for his European palate.

A cherubic brunette with flashing eyes preparing a chicken casserole was absolutely divine. Vanpirs watched, smiling, as she chopped ginger, then garlic,

then spooned an entire can of cream of celery soup into a bowl and began to mix. He wanted to lick her neck.

Vanpirs leaned ever closer to her tempting, moist neck when he was overcome by a strange, keening wail that filled the convention hall, pulsing and threatening to burst his eardrums.

"I smell smoke!" he heard.

"We're all going to die!" someone else shrieked.

Terrible, brilliant lights flashed. Vanpirs grimaced and lowered his head.

The brunette had dropped her spoon and was speaking to him.

In misery, Vanpirs uncovered his ears.

"Sir, your leg is smoking," she said.

Vanpirs looked down. Twin streams of smoke were curling up from the cuff of his carefully pressed Euro jeans.

"How can this be?" he asked.

"There are a lot of ovens on around here. It wouldn't be hard to—"

"That man is on fire!" screamed a blond woman, pointing at him.

All at once every contestant save the kindly brunette threw down their utensils. A nearby judge went down, shrieking, as Bake-Off cooks, friends, relatives, and sundry hangers-on stampeded toward the balloon arch.

They enveloped the Doughboy. Vanpirs caught glimpses of his collapsed white form as the crowd parted, then coalesced in waves.

"Come on," said the brunette. "Let me help you."

Vanpirs nearly fell against her as she took his arm. Gratitude and terror mixed in equal parts in Vanpirs, along with the insistent desire to bite the woman, even as she tried to help.

"There is no . . . help for me," he gasped, remembering the Apothek's warning. He should change his diet—it was the endless fat, the grease, the oily blood of all those he'd tasted for so many— Why hadn't he listened?

Most of the crowd had headed toward the arch, while there was another exit sign flashing only yards from it, and she led him toward it.

"I—I have to rest," he said. Perhaps the fire would go out. And how had it started? There were over one hundred stoves in the hall and all of them turned to high heat. Had it been a spark from a stray gas lighter? A fiery crackling of burned cake from a contestant's humiliating failure? It could have been any of these, for Vanpirs's body had long since been comprised of more highly flammable cholesterol than long-dead bone and sinew.

Vanpirs' helpmate bit her lower lip as he sat heavily in a chair by the exit.

"It's getting worse," she said. She began patting at his leg with the hem of her apron, which produced nothing but an even more concentrated jet of smoke curling from the cuff of his jeans.

She lifted the cuff to see the source of the smoke and blinked.

"Oh, my," she said.

"What is it?" Vanpirs asked in alarm.

"Why, I can see—" she said. She found herself unable to tell him that she'd seen a rapidly darkening bone, roasting and crackling along with a big patch of oily flesh, just like a barbecued beef rib on the grill. She bit her lower lip and said, "Oh, gosh. I think I should get some help."

Vanpirs's head was spinning with the need to bite, and he almost did not notice the small silver cross hanging around her neck. "Please do," he said in a small voice as he pulled quickly away.

"You stay right here," she said, wagging her finger as if he were a naughty child. "I'll be back."

She needn't have warned him, for neither of Vanpirs's legs would move any longer. It was exactly as it had happened in Stralsund, only ever so much worse. He noticed with terror that smoke had now begun to rise from his other ankle.

He rolled up one of his sleeves and watched the skin darkening, even crinkling here and there. Before his eyes, it burst into flame.

"No!" he cried.

But it was, of course, too late for Vanpirs. The flames were already inside of him. And though he could not feel pain, he could feel the flames feeding, as flames will do upon finding a great deal of combustible material such as concentrated human cholesterol, all in one place.

• • •

The Orlando firefighters were reluctant to immediately enter the building, so it was therefore several hours later when, out of direct reach of the facility's sprinklers, a pair of waxy white feet clad in expensive French leather loafers were found resting beneath a chair near the exit. Upon the seat of the chair was a pile of greasy black ash, in the midst of which was discovered an odd set of dentition containing a matched pair of long ivory teeth.

The Ghoul Next Door

NANCY KILPATRICK

He's a ghoul all right, but he ain't the only freak in *this* neighborhood. That's a fact. Take my word for it.

There's hairy old Jack down the block, for instance. Raise the dander on anybody's neck, though come to think of it I ain't seen hide *nor* hair of him lately. And the Laveaus at the corner? Bunch of deadbeats, if you ask me. Him and the wife cement themselves to the front porch all night long every summer, guzzling some concoction she brews, staring off into space. How they manage the payments on their "crypt" as they call it, that's the question. Lucinda Varney next door—face of an angel and that's where the connection to heaven ends. Don't get me wrong. I love that girl dearly, as if she was my own daughter—if I had a daughter, which I

don't—and I was her natural mother, but I've watched her suck in more than one fellow, wearing skirts up around her . . . But I guess you wanna hear about the ghoul.

He come to our neighborhood last year, 'round the time the lake swallowed up the Francis girl. Let me see . . . It was Halloween, All Saints', some of them 'round here call it.

The ghoul—his name's Henry, just so we all know who we're talking about—didn't bring much, only a heavy-looking, flesh-colored backpack. No suitcases, boxes of pots and pans. You know, no household things. 'Course, it's only a room he's got, at Liz Nedrob's. Lets the one at the back. Not much bigger than a broom closet, but he was alone, far as I could tell, though I'm just a wrinkly, so what do I know.

Anyway, this young fella moves in on my other side and that's the last anybody sees of him till Thanksgiving, the day everybody stuffs themselves on bird flesh and lives to regret it.

I wouldn't do it, and I'm one of the worst old fools you're likely to meet. But I'm no tofu or whatever eater, so let's get that straight.

I sit here most days and well into the night so I get a pretty accurate picture of the comings and goings—passes the time. Not that I'm a busybody, mind you. It's just that I'm retired now—acted in the silent films, I did, and even a couple of early talkies, though they cut out most of my lines. I don't get around much any-

more so there's plenty of hours to stare out the window. Though I couldn't care less how people live their lives. Between them and their maker. 'Course, that's how I first seen him eating raw flesh. The ghoul, that is.

It was after midnight and one of them bitter nights when what they call the wind chill factor puts you well into the deep freeze. Naturally there was nobody outdoors, man nor beast. I was watchin' a bit of television—them housewives that are so desperate, they're right on the money, ain't they?—when I glanced out the window like you do. Well, it was dark and lonely out there, wind bashing trees, a touch o' snow tornado-swirling like'n it'd drag you down to hell given half a chance. I was surprised to see old man Jack's big furry wolf dog—also named Jack; don't that beat all?—taking a stroll across the street. While one o' my old rivals gnashed her teeth in a Polident commercial, I watched Jack head for the alley beside my house, probably following the scent of some foxy bitch.

Out o' the corner of my eye I see something movin', a shade within range of the streetlight. The hound's at the mouth o' the black alley between me and Liz's when he stops dead in his tracks. Tail goes rigid. Ears and lips pull back. He lifts his muzzle then turns it this way and that, like he's sniffing the air and catches a whiff of somethin' he ain't sure he likes.

A gust comes outta nowhere and whips branches every which way and knocks over a garbage can. But that old wolf-dog stands rooted to the spot like he's

froze. Suddenly his fur springs straight up from his body. I can't hear him but I can see he's howlin' like he's seen a ghost. Before I know what's got him spooked, some dark shadow snakes outta the night and snatches Jack up.

Well, I couldn't believe my eyes, which have deteriorated real bad, I'll grant you, but they still do the job. I watched awhile, but there was nothing more to see. 'Course, I thought I imagined the whole thing. I was about to turn back and switch the channel in case they were showing one of my old black-and-whites when a car tears up the street. For a split second the beam of one headlight catches a pale thin face and a crazy red eye just where Jack was standin'. It was him, all right. Henry. Likely having hisself a feast of dog flesh.

Now that's sickenin', I'll grant you, but the things I've seen in my time. And the young people of late. Bloodless wonders, shrouded head to toe in black cowhide, pasty faced, looking like they'd swallowed a gallon of embalming fluid for breakfast. . . .

Well, I won't go on. Let's just say there's plenty of stories if you wanna hear 'em.

Anyways, the second time I seen the ghoul at his trade was just after Christmas. Come to think of it, maybe he only gets hungry on bona fide holidays. Pigs out like the rest of the human race.

This time there was snow on the ground, oh, six inches or so. You know how bright it looks around Christmas? The holiday lights plus the white cover-

ing everything? A little like daytime so things is pretty clear.

What I'm getting at is, if I had my doubts, now I was sure.

Sure as I am that there's a condo of sorts waiting down at the cemetery with my name chiseled on the mailbox.

He come out of Liz's wearing a brown fur coat and scarf up around his face, so he stood out real nice against the crystal snow. I watched him hunch his shoulders against the cold, then head on down the street. All of a sudden he stops. I look to where he's staring across the road. It's the Laveaus' youngest.

All bundled in a new peppermint-striped snowsuit, cute as that youngster can be, building a snow-something in front o' the house.

I can't for the life of me remember if it's a boy or girl.

They give the kid one of them names so's you're never sure. Pat, it was, now that I think on it. Anyway, when I look back at Henry to see what he's up to, he's nowhere to be seen. Naturally this makes me uneasy. Mary Laveau's flat-featured face appears at her window, checking on the little one, then she's gone. Suddenly, from out of nowhere, the tyke turns its head, then starts toddling toward the burned-out garage next to the Laveaus'. Well, I was fit to be tied. I waited a bit but when the kid didn't come out I got on the horn to Mary. Damn line was busy and I know she's got

call-waitin'. People talk too much on the phone, that's what's wrong with the world today.

Anyway, before I could get through to her, I checked the street again. I was at a bad angle but it looked to me like a fat candy cane jutting out from the charred doorway. I took a gander through my field glasses and, sure enough. But by then Mary's on the sidewalk, searching all over hell and gone for her young 'un. Never seen that woman so animated. Wasn't long before she spotted the snowsuit.

The police came. An ambulance. Wasn't enough left to cart off to the morgue, I'll tell you. All the neighbors were out there giving statements. I would've told what I knew but nobody asked. They never do. And every time I tried the Laveaus', the damn phone was busy or the answering message machine thing came on, and I ain't about to talk into one of them squawking monsters. I didn't feel right, but I was start-ing to wonder just what I did see, and I figured the cops knew what they were doing. It was up to them to finger the ghoul. At least, that's how I explained it to myself back then.

Well, time passed, as it does, and everything died down so much it just kinda faded, if you know what I mean. I didn't see Henry so I didn't know if they'd caught him or he'd moved on or what. Until tonight. Valentine's Day. Right on schedule.

Just after sunset, as per usual, saucy Lucinda comes flying down her front steps, all painted up for a night

on the town. I swear that girl lives in another world. She grins up at the moon, which is full and clear, then starts down the walk, but she don't get two steps, though, when I see young Henry appear from between the hawthorn hedges. It's like he's been stalking her. Biding his time.

Now Lucinda's a pretty thing, tiny, a bit too thin, but she takes after her folks. And modern, you might say. Of the "me instead of you" generation. I was good friends with her mom and dad before they were killed one morning by some maniac. Streets aren't safe, I tell you. Anyway, she inherited a pile and she's independent in other ways, too, but they made me a godmother of sorts and I promised the Varneys years ago if anything happened to them, I'd keep an eye on their girl. I was already feeling a bit guilty about Mary's offspring, so naturally when I spot Henry I start to worry.

Before Lucinda gets a chance to say or do anything he walks right up to her, bold as brass, takes her by the arm like they'd knowed each other a lifetime, and leads her back into the house.

Now Lucinda ain't the brightest female. She not only don't put up a fuss, she licks her lips and practically yanks Henry up the steps. They disappear inside lickety-split.

I'm no prude. I was young once. I remember what it's like to be hungry. But that Varney girl, she's starving. Had to have been to go with Henry.

Well, I consider what to do. I try phonin' Lucinda.

Her voice on her blasted voice mail sounds like some disembodied spirit. There ain't but one thing left and that's to pick myself up and get on over there.

Moving's not as easy at it once was for me. The old joints squeak a bit. Ticker's winding down. Took me a while to drag myself down my steps and up hers. I knock. Nobody answers. I let myself in.

Haven't been here since old Varney invited me over one night to admire his collection. Photographs, it was. Ancient tombstones, mausoleums of the past, cemeteries in general. He was an oddball, all right. Anyway, looks like a century since anybody's bothered cleaning, judging by the cobwebs. Lucinda doesn't take the care with her home that she does with her appearance, that's clear.

I hear a sound in the basement and figure that's where he's got her. No use hollering, that'd just scare him off. I head on down the twenty-five cellar steps—counted each one. Took my mind off the agony.

The cellar's windowless, dingy concrete, with a big oil furnace stationed in the middle and shadows clinging to all the corners. It's in the same musty state as the rest of the house. I spot a door and hear a thump behind it. Might as well open it. I come this far and wouldn't want to waste my energy.

Well, I'll be damned. If it ain't Lucinda and Henry, curled up together on an old cot, tight as triffids. She's got those pearly whites sunk into his neck and he's gnawing away happily on her inner thigh.

"Lucinda!" I growl, in the deep tone I was famous for in my movies. I thought they'd both hit the ceiling.

She blinks a couple times, recognizes me. If looks could kill. To her credit, she thinks the better of expressing that and instead gets embarrassed. She opens her mouth but before there's a chance of anything coming out I tell her, "Get on upstairs. I wanna talk to this fella. Go on, now!"

Like I say, Lucinda's long on looks and short on brains, but she's got enough sense to disappear.

Henry stares up at me, half defiant, half terrified, about to bolt or attack. "Calm down, son," I say. "We gotta talk."

That doesn't put him at ease any. My bones are tired from all that climbing so I sit myself on the edge of the bed. The kid scuttles away like I'm some human-sized insect. "Now look here," I begin. "I been watchin' you."

His eyes get big. The thought never occurred to him.

"Saw you the night old Jack disappeared. And the Laveau kid. And now with Lucinda."

He seems kinda haunted by bad memories but stands up for himself. "I wasn't gonna hurt her."

"And I wasn't born yesterday. I seen what you were doin'."

His mouth twists into that petulant look kids get that makes the rest of us wanna swat 'em. "She's no angel," he says. True, but a right poor defense, in my books.

"Lucinda may not be innocent, but she's one of us and you ain't."

Well, saying that hurts him and that makes me feel guilty. After all, I guess in my heart of hearts I don't believe he's all that different. Only, you know, a bit ghoulish. "Son, you just can't move into a tight-knit community like this and upload—is that what you kids say?—your peculiar ways on everybody. The neighbors won't stand for it. We got our rules, like everybody else, and when folks choose to live together they gotta cooperate and learn to get along. You can't go preying on your neighbors. It just ain't done."

Well, that appears to be a new thought to him. He considers it and nods a bit. I figure I'm getting through.

"Now you and Lucinda," I say. "What're your intentions there?"

The kid shifts a bit but thinks it over before answering. "I love her," he blurts. "A lot. We have things in common."

Yeah, I think, me and Frankenstein got things in common, too. Both of us could use a face-lift.

"We're getting married."

Well, this is news. "When'd you two decide that?"

"Tonight. Lucinda wants you at the wedding. After all, you're like a mother to her."

I grunt. Truth is, it'd solve quite a few problems. The kid will have to grow up, take responsibility. Learn to fit into the community. They'll live next door so I can keep an eye on things. And if there's one female

capable of settling somebody like him down, it's prob-ably Lucinda. Whether or not he can settle *her* down's another matter.

Maybe I'm getting mushy in my dotage but the idea of a wedding seems right. He's a ghoul, a young ghoul to be sure and, yes, he'd made a few mistakes, but haven't we all.

We've never had a flesh eater living among us and it'll take some getting used to, no doubt about that. Hell, when *I* first moved here it caused quite a stir. But the more I think about it, the more I realize he'll fit right in, once everybody gets over their fear of the unknown.

Well, the wedding's set for the night of Mother's Day, as kind of a thank-you to me. You know the way kids in love think—if I'd turned Henry in right off, they wouldn't've met. Or, as Lucinda put it, "Mummy, we owe it all to you."

Daycare of the Damned

NINA KIRIKI HOFFMAN

You sign one stupid contract in blood when you're sixteen, and the rest of your life goes down the crapper.

My Demonic Despot didn't give a damn that I was legally a minor. And I was so dumb I didn't even get much for my soul.

I did the sign-your-name-in-blood thing at a party I went to, to impress girls I didn't even like. That bitch Angela put *my* contract on some special paper she got out of a locked drawer in her dad's desk. Everybody else pretended to prick their fingers and signed contracts on regular copy paper with fake blood from little capsules supplied by Angela. I was the only one stupid enough to actually use my own blood.

And what did I get for my soul?

No, not eternal youth and beauty. Not fame and a recording career or stardom.

I just wanted people to like me.

The joke was on the other girls at the party. They invited me there to humiliate me for daring to try to be their friend, and they all ended up liking me and wanting me to like them. They were so, so sorry about the mean little trick they played.

Heh.

A couple years later, His Deep Darkness offered to renegotiate. I could get my soul back for just two little favors.

I was going to take him up on it.

I paused on the spotless white marble doorstep and checked my uniform—corduroy overalls striped in pink and white over a white blouse, and white shoes, all of which I expected would be stained by the end of my first day at Exceptional Daycare. "For Special Children," the sign out front said. I had checked their website. They were very exclusive, and there was a waiting list to get in.

I was relieved I'd landed this job. My Scary Spitemeister wanted child sacrifices, and he was really picky. He didn't like children with blemishes, and they had to be well-nourished and well-loved. He wanted a matched set—boy and girl, but not related to each other. He preferred that they have similar coloring, for balance, he said.

I pressed the recessed doorbell of the stylish, heavy

door. A tall, thin woman in a full-length blue dress opened the door and stared at me a moment before allowing herself a small smile. She had severe, white-streaked brown hair wound around her head in a braid coronet and pale crystal eyes. She was a stranger to me, nothing like the very friendly woman who had interviewed me for the job. She looked chilly. Plus, she was a head and a half taller than me. Shortness is another of my genetic lottery losses, though I'm not quite short enough to qualify as a dwarf.

"Come in, Magda," said the woman. "You're right on time. We appreciate that here at Exceptional."

I bobbed my head, not sure what the best response was.

"I'm Mrs. Richter, the supervisor. Did Alice explain what your duties will be?" asked the woman.

Alice had conducted my job interview. She gave me some weird tests I didn't understand, then handed me a load of paperwork, including a very involved and confusing contract. My second contract. I tried to read it more carefully than I had my first. It said once I signed it, I would work there no matter what kind of challenges the children presented. I couldn't quit for six months, the contract said, under severe penalties.

I had to wonder.

My Evil Overlord told me to sign it, though, and because I was trying to win back my soul without losing my gift, I did.

"Yes, ma'am," I said. "Alice said I'd be working with

the younger kids. I'm supposed to keep them from hurting themselves or others, supply midmorning and midafternoon snacks, clean up as necessary, and generally just watch to make sure things are fair and no one's left out."

"Did she explain the special challenges we face here at Exceptional?"

"No, ma'am," I said. My heart sank. Special challenges implied less-than-perfect children. Maybe I'd read "Exceptional" wrong.

Mrs. Richter cocked her head, stared toward the ceiling. "Hmm. She must have had a reason. Perhaps she—" Mrs. Richter frowned. She studied me, then nodded. "We'll just see how you do," she said. "If you can't work with the little kids, I'll assign you elsewhere. Please follow me."

She led me deeper into the building. The hallways were carpeted with hushy plush, so our footsteps got swallowed and we glided like ghosts. The doors we passed looked thick, with steel-reinforced bottom halves and narrow windows of heavy glass toward the top, high enough that Mrs. Richter could look in. I couldn't see anything in the rooms beyond patches of ceiling. There were no sounds anywhere, which wasn't what I expected from a daycare center.

I glanced up at a window in a door as we passed and saw a flash that looked like lightning dazzle across the ceiling.

Mrs. Richter had been facing that direction, too.

She shook her head and led me to the end of the hall. She opened the last door on the left. "We'll start you with the specials," she said. "Elly, this is our new assistant, Magda. She'll be helping you out today."

"Oh, good," said Elly. She was wearing pink-and-white-striped overalls, like me. She was a large woman, with a lot of red-gold hair, most of it messy already. Her front was streaked with colors, but I couldn't tell if they were from paint, food, or the unspeakable Other.

"Alice did her intake and didn't explain about our special students," Mrs. Richter said. "Magda, this is Elly. Good luck." She shoved me into the room and closed the door behind me. The snick of the lock startled me.

Uh-oh.

The room was pretty big. There was a broad expanse of carpeted space covered with scattered toys and tiny furniture. A wall of cubbies lurked on the left, some with things in them, some empty. The narrow windows in three walls were all higher than my head, and the glass had wire net in it. None of them looked like they opened. An upright piano stood against the right wall, with a big basket of semimusical instruments (flutes, thumb pianos, maracas, and bongos) on the floor beside it.

A large table to the left held art supplies. Five kids sat around it, their legs dangling from tall chairs, and all of them hunched over, with big paper in front of them. They wielded fat brushes loaded with poster paint.

They were perfect. Three boys, two girls, all blemish free, rosy cheeked, and happy. One of the girls was a nice shade of cocoa, with tight reddish-brown curls, and the other was a peach-skinned blonde with green eyes and ringlets. One of the boys was blond as well, and another had black hair and blue eyes. The third boy had olive skin and a shock of red hair. They were all gorgeous.

Not a clear matched set, but maybe the two blonds—

"Let me introduce you to our Specials," Elly said. Her voice was warm and reassuring, though she looked pretty frazzled for so early in the morning. "This is Ian." Elly tapped the black-haired kid on the shoulder. He looked up at me, and his blue eyes narrowed.

"Hi, Ian. I'm Magda."

"You're stained," he said and returned to his painting. It was black and red and showed a horned figure holding a pitchfork in one hand and a spear in the other.

I glanced down at my uniform. Nope, no stains yet. Maybe the kid was mental.

"This is Jezra." Elly tapped the red-headed kid. He cocked his head and stared at me with amber eyes. A dusting of freckles flecked his nose. If I were choosing a kid for myself, he was the one I'd choose; he didn't look like any other kid, but he was beautiful. My Dark Master liked stereotypes, so he wouldn't like Jezra. That made me happy.

The little boy smiled at me. He looked impish.

"You're interesting," he said. He had loaded up on green poster paint and seemed to be painting trees, though they looked more like blobs. Maybe they were green apples.

"Thanks," I said. "You're interesting, too."

"This is Fanny," said Elly, patting the blond girl on the head.

Fanny glared up at Elly. Elly snatched her hand back and covered her suddenly blazing cheeks with both hands. "Sorry, Fan. Sorry. I forgot. No touching." Tears tumbled from Elly's eyes. "Magda, no touching Fanny. She doesn't like it."

"Okay," I said.

"This is Dwyn," Elly said, more subdued, indicating the blond boy. Her eyes softened. A smile lifted her cheeks. She looked like a proud mother.

Dwyn laid down his brush (he was painting a picture of a big red heart) and stared at me. He stood up on his chair and leaned toward me. His gaze was hypnotic. I'd been thinking Jezra was my favorite, but I could feel something twisting in my chest, an impulse to love and worship this little cherub. Then there was a snick in me somewhere, a kind of snapping like a stretched rubber band being released, and the impulse vanished. I leaned a little toward Dwyn to see if *my* spell would work on *him*.

Dwyn smiled. "You're funny," he said.

"And this is Keshia," said Elly, gesturing toward the brown girl.

Keshia looked at me, as most of the others had, evaluating. "You're connected," she said. "To what?"

"Um," I said. I had the feeling I was in trouble. These kids were special, all right. Maybe special the same way I was. Maybe beyond my ability to snatch.

Dilemma. Two horns. Maybe more.

Magda in a pinch again.

So what else was new.

Keshia pouted. "Answer me," she said.

Fanny poked me with her brush, which was loaded with orange paint and left a big streak down the front of my overalls. One self-prophecy fulfilled. "Answer," she said.

"What was the question again?" I asked. I glanced at Elly, wondering if she was as strange as these kids were.

She looked defeated. And totally, dreadfully, unrelentingly normal.

"What are you connected to?" asked Ian. "What stains you?"

"Oh, uh," I said, "a bad bargain."

"With who?" asked Dwyn.

"I dare not speak his name," I said. "And anyway, I can't pronounce it."

"Did he send you here?" asked Jezra.

"Yeah," I said.

"You supposed to do anything?" asked Fanny.

"Yeah."

"Involving us?"

"Not you specifically," I said. "But yeah."

"Woohoo! We caught one!" Jezra laughed, his delight infectious. The other kids all grinned. I smiled, then laughed. I couldn't help it. Which made me suspect something about Jezra's power. Even Elly giggled.

"Oh, boy!" said Ian. "You're a bad guy! We totally get to experiment on you!"

"I, uh—"

Elly was smiling.

"What are *you* grinning about?" I asked her, trying to mask my panic.

"It's so much easier when I don't have to protect the assistant from the children," she said. She waved at the kids. "Carry on, children. Enjoy."

"Oh, boy," Ian said again.

Fanny held up her hand. "I get first dibs," she said. "Jezra got the last one and wrecked her in a week, and Ian got the one before—"

"And I haven't had one in forever," said Keshia.

"You guys never let me have one," Dwyn said.

"Because you never do anything interesting with them," Ian said. "We already know what you can do. It's boring seeing it over and over."

"I haven't had one in forever," Keshia repeated. "I think it's my turn this time, Fanny."

"How about we both work on her?" Fanny said.

"Okay," said Keshia. "What's your next thing to try?"

"I got this new ability about a week ago. I used it on

the maid at home, and she fooshed and stopped working. Mom got mad at me. She had to call the mage doctor to fix the maid, and then the maid quit. Mom has trouble getting staff who stay. She said I can't use power at home anymore."

"What if you wreck her? I get to go first," Keshia said.

Fanny looked grumpy. "Oh, all right. No fair sending her someplace we can't get her back from."

"We can tie a rope around her."

"Oh," said Ian, "like that worked so well the last time."

"I didn't know those tiger-shark things were waiting on the other side to bite through it," Keshia said.

"All we got back were little pieces of that guy," said Jezra. "No more visits to worlds like that."

"Send her to Gwylla," Ian said. "See if she can get us more of that mack fruit."

"Forget that!" yelled Fanny. "It turned me blue."

"You don't have to eat it," said Ian.

"Wait a sec." I had thought my plans were nefarious, but these kids were on a whole other level. I felt like the floor had risen up to close around my ankles. "What happens if they hurt me?" I asked Elly.

"We have excellent medical benefits at Exceptional," said Elly. "If we can't fix you, we'll find care for you. It was in your contract."

Dwyn said, "I already tried my talent on her, and it didn't work. I claim rights. I haven't had anyone to use in a long time, and she's different from the others."

"You already tried?" Ian yelled. "That's cheating!"

Jezra said, "Did you hear what he said? I've never heard of Dwyn's talent not working on anybody but us. Magda, don't you just loooove Dwyn?"

"I could love him if he'd let me give him to my Malevolent Master."

"Wow," said Jezra. "Maybe we should find out more about you before we—"

"No fair," said Fanny, pouting. "I want to—"

Keshia came to me. "Sit down, Magda," she said. She grabbed my hand.

A hot jolt ran through me. My muscles tightened; then I relaxed and heaved a sigh. My power worked best with physical contact.

Keshia froze, then thawed. She stared up at me, tilted her head, and smiled the kind of smile a catalog kid smiles when she's wearing a very cute outfit and knows it. "Will you play with me?" she asked, and she suddenly sounded like a little kid instead of a calculating midget.

"Sure, honey," I said. I'd practiced my Like on the kids I babysat for in the old neighborhood, until His Infernal Majesty started making interested noises. I didn't want to snatch kids I knew.

Now that my Like had engaged, Keshia wouldn't think of doing anything evil to me. I said, "What do you want to do? We could read, or—looks like there are a lot of cool toys here."

She kept hold of my hand and looked at the wall of cubbyholes. She shook her head. "You pick."

"Hey!" yelled Ian. "What just happened?"

"Interesting," said Dwyn. "Sorta like mine."

Elly straightened and stared at me, her eyes widening. She lifted a hand and flashed some finger symbols at me, but I didn't know any sign language, so I just shrugged. Maybe she was casting a spell?

Keshia tugged on my hand, still smiling. "Mags?" she said.

If the kids weren't impervious to my power, I'd better touch them quickly, before they got any warier than they already were. "How about some more art?" I asked. I settled Keshia on her chair and brushed Jezra's hand with the back of mine. The jolt heated me again, and I smiled at him. He smiled back, then frowned, then smiled.

I moved around the table and gripped Fanny's and Ian's shoulders, though Ian tried to duck.

"Don't you touch me, intruder!" Fanny yelled.

My jolt hit, twice. Fanny struggled against it, her face twisted in fury. She pointed at me. An orange glow surrounded her hand, then concentrated at her fingertip. She shook her hand toward me, but at the last second she pointed away. A sizzling bolt of orange fire shot up into the ceiling and left a smoking, ember-edged hole a foot across.

"Gosh," she said. "What was I thinking?" She hugged me around the waist.

Ian's face unfrowned for the first time since I'd entered the room. He looked confused. His hand

plucked at my overalls. "Mags," he said, and he, too, sounded like a little kid.

I exchanged glances with Dwyn. He dropped to the floor from his high chair and backed away from me.

"Not gonna let you touch me," he said. "How long does it last?"

I smiled at him. "For always." As far as I knew.

"Damn," he said. "You're the most dangerous one we've ever had."

"Why don't you let me touch you now? I'll catch up to you sooner or later. Your power bounces off me."

"The power I tried first does, anyway," he said, "but I have others. Did you make the other kids stupid?"

"Shut up," Keshia said.

"You're the stupid one if you think we're going to let you get away with that, Dwyn-Dull," Fanny said.

"Who you calling stupid?" Ian said. He kept his grip on my pocket, but with his other hand, he flicked fingers at Dwyn. Dark feathers shot from his fingertips and splattered over Dwyn, who choked and dropped to the floor, spasming. Ian nudged me with his fist. "Get him, Mags."

"Traitor!" Dwyn managed to say between coughing fits.

I knelt beside Dwyn, with Fanny and Ian still clinging to me, and Keshia and Jezra close behind. I reached toward Dwyn's face. He tried to roll away. Jezra put his foot on Dwyn's stomach, holding him down.

The black feathers melted. Dwyn stopped coughing. He stared up into my eyes. "Now that you've done whatever you did to the others, will you give us to your Master?"

"I don't know," I said. I'd never used my Like on anybody with powers of their own before. The kids had gone mushy on me, but I wasn't sure my power could overcome their survival instincts. If I did the summoning here, and Mr. Ugly showed up—

Anyway, I was having doubts about the whole thing. I'd done dumb things before, and I wanted to learn to think through consequences better. It occurred to me that if I actually gave kids to His Awesome Awfulness, my soul wouldn't be in very good shape when I got it back.

"No," I said. My dream of getting out of my first contract melted like snow in summer sun. Colors dimmed.

It wasn't like I knew what to do with my soul when I had it.

Dwyn sighed and stopped squirming under Jezra's foot. I touched his cheek. My jolt didn't come. We stared at each other. He smiled a half smile. "We're too alike," he said.

"Have to work it the way normal people do," I said.

"Okay."

Though if Dwyn had other powers—I just had the one. . . .

Oh, well. "Let him up, please, Jezra, and thanks for your help," I said.

"Anytime," said Jezra. He took his foot off Dwyn's stomach.

Dwyn sat up, then leaned over and kissed me on the cheek. My heart twisted; I felt again the overwhelming urge to adore and worship him.

It passed.

Fanny smacked Dwyn. "Quit it," she said.

"Yeah, yeah. Just had to check."

Elly sighed and put a smile on her face. "Well, now that that's all sorted out, shall we get back to work, children?" Her grin was eerie and extra wide.

"Is that what you want, Mags?" Fanny asked.

"Sure," I said. We all headed over to the table. The children climbed back into their chairs, picked up their brushes, and got back to work.

I edged around the table to Elly. She held up a hand, palm toward me. "Don't touch me," she muttered.

I shrugged. My Like could work without touch. It just took longer.

"Are all the kids at Exceptional like these?" I asked.

"No," she said. "Some are worse. Some are normal. Well, special in a different way."

"Huh." I wondered what powers, exactly, my kids had. It would be worth finding out.

I couldn't give these kids to His Mighty Maliciousness, but maybe, just maybe, I could give His Mighty Maliciousness to the kids.

Season Tickets

DEREK CLENDENING

Drew couldn't believe that some schlemiel would actually fall for it! He'd pulled a few fast ones in his day, but this was one for the ages. Maybe it wasn't the most honest move he'd ever made, but it was for a good cause.

Since his parents had booted him out of their basement, he'd been forced to find his own apartment, which meant that he now had expenses to cover and he had to count his pennies. He was only twenty-eight and knew people older than him who still dwelled in their parents' basements, extra rooms, and attics. At least he was employed and took out the garbage once in a while. Why couldn't he stick around a few more years?

But he'd gotten over it. Well, almost. Each time he ate a frozen dinner, or had to scrub his own under-

pants, he couldn't help but feel bitter. Still, he'd weathered self-dependence without giving up too many of his favorite things. The apartment had tapped out most of his paychecks, but he'd learned how to stretch the remains. But, when Dave, the ticket agent from the Buffalo Bills, had called to ask why he hadn't renewed the season's tickets that he'd owned since he was eighteen, he couldn't answer. Worse still, he couldn't afford them.

He'd tried to talk himself out of buying the tickets. First, he told himself that the cash wasn't there. Next, he reminded himself that the owner hadn't fired the head coach in spite of the highway billboard that had been erected to demand it (and to which he had contributed financially). But no amount of self-convincing worked. Drew was hooked and needed help. But next year. He could go and seek help next year.

And so he ventured onto eBay for the first time. But what to sell? He didn't have diddly-squat kicking around the apartment, unless he could hock the expired bottle of mustard in his fridge. He needed to scrape together something that someone would actually want to buy, but it seemed impossible. His only valuable possession was his collection of Bills memorabilia, and that was out of the question.

And then he offered to sell his soul.

But who would want to buy my *soul?* he thought. *I'm just Drew Wilson from Buffalo, New York. I'm a Walmart associate without any prospects for promotion, and if you*

need a tailgating buddy, you could do a lot worse. But why would someone want my *soul?*

He put it up for sale anyway, wrote a description (clean, shiny, and in mint condition! Motivated seller!), affixed an outrageous price, and awaited an interested buyer. Before long he had a hit, and he popped up in his chair to stare at the screen. Mister Lawrence Adams sounded as determined to buy as Drew was to sell. All that was left was to make sure that no strings were attached. When he found none, he clapped his hands together, rubbed his palms, and accepted his offer.

But he would sign nothing over until he was sure that Mister Lawrence Adams wasn't shitting him. *Show me the money!* Drew thought. He wouldn't sell his soul with nothing to show for it.

For a moment he did wonder why this Adams dude wanted his soul so badly. *What's he going to do with it?* But the prospect of ticket money wiped all that out.

So, once the money appeared in his account, he decided that he should send Mister Lawrence Adams something tangible. He composed an email to say that he, Drew Wilson, did solemnly sign his soul over to him for an amount of three thousand dollars. That sounded official enough. He fired the email off and decided that he needn't hold his laughter in.

And then it dawned on him: with that kind of dough, he needn't renew the same old shitty upper corner seats where he'd toiled for years. He could have the best seats in the house! He phoned up Dave, the ticket

agent, and upgraded his account to lower bowl seating, smack dab on the fifty-yard line.

Of course, he knew that some poorer fans would be jealous of his new seats. His best Bills-backing bud Frank would be pissed when he learned that he'd been jilted in the upper corner. But Drew decided to phone him up and explain just how kickass his new tickets were. Friends had to understand.

"Ten years and you're just gonna up and leave me for better seats?" Frank said.

Drew heard the jealous *Put yourself in my shoes. If you could have tickets to die for, wouldn't you take 'em?*, whiny tone in his own voice already.

"Come on, dude," Drew said.

"I don't get this. Yesterday you couldn't even afford to renew the seats you had and now you've got the fifty-yard line. What did you do? Sell your left nut to science?"

"Oh, that's for me to know and for you to worry about, ha ha ha ha!"

Drew couldn't tell his friend the truth, not Frank, who devoured Sylvia Browne and obsessed over the occult. Besides, he had come across an idea and meant to stick by it. Maybe his personality would be auctioned off next. Or his wit and charm. To him, the free enterprise system allowed a man to sell off whatever the hell he wanted.

"Dude, really, I can make it up to you," Drew said. "We'll still tailgate together, so the first box of steaks and case of beer is on me. Sound good?"

"Least you can do now that you're friggin' rollin' in it."

"'Kay then, bud. See you bright and early Sunday morning."

He clicked the phone off, kicked back in his chair, and laced his fingers behind his head. This was going to be one hell of a season.

Bars of sunlight peeked through his blinds the next morning and Drew covered his eyes. Morning wasn't his friend, but then it seemed like there were so few times a day that he wanted to be up and hopping. Not unless it was Sunday and he was going to a Bills game. Then he had the stamina of a champion. He decided to drag himself out of bed and crawl into work, otherwise his three grand wouldn't stretch very far.

When he pulled the covers off of his naked body, he saw that his skin had turned a shade of light green, from head to toe. And he felt slippery to the touch. His stomach was still ivory white, which made him wonder if he would grow gills next and turn into a fish man.

He leaped out of bed, struggled to catch up with his breathing, but he couldn't calm himself. How the hell had this happened overnight? He'd only sold his soul, not traded cash for a gypsy curse!

In the bathroom mirror, he saw that his face had changed for the worst. Dark lines circled his blood-shot eyes, and his cheeks had sunk. His once muscular

arms now sagged below the armpits and his tongue had turned black.

When he checked below his beltline, he saw that his dick and balls had shriveled up like raisins. He threw his hands over his face and tried not to cry. He'd had enough bad luck with the ladies before he'd sold his soul, and it would be worse now that his twig and berries had gone to seed.

But he refused to believe that this was the result of selling his soul. No, he'd come down with something rotten, something vile, but not something that he couldn't fix. He'd get some rest, or go to the doctor, but he wouldn't live with this forever.

Deep breaths. Nice and slow. In and out. He decided that if he closed his eyes and opened them, it would all go away. The Drew Wilson that he knew and loved would be back to normal.

So he closed his eyes.

And when he opened them to see that he still looked like a zombie, Drew knew that he was in serious trouble. There was no way in hell he could go out looking like this. And he sure couldn't go to work either.

When he phoned in sick to Walmart, he didn't know what to tell them. He'd been so consumed by the changes that he hadn't bothered to try and sound sick.

He could only imagine what they would've said had he told them that he'd sold his soul

Who the hell would want to buy your soul? he imag-

ined Bonnie, his supervisor, asking, and then maybe laughing.

But that wasn't foremost on his mind. How the hell would he get rid of this? Surely he couldn't just mosey down to the emergency room and ask the doc to give him two of whatever and call him in the morning.

Frank would know what to do. All that reading had to have armed him with some information on this, even if he didn't want to admit that it was because he'd sold his soul to Mr. Larry Adams. But if it meant swallowing his pride to make this go away, he would do it.

When Drew skipped up to Frank's apartment, he pictured his reaction, and pulled his trench coat over his face. He'd said nothing of his condition when they'd spoken on the phone. He'd only said that he was desperate for help. The years he'd spent teasing Frank for being a grade-A kook he now regretted and he prayed that Frank would know some weird-ass magical cure for him. This was not like a scraped knee, a broken toe, or the clap. Normal medicine meant nothing, he thought.

When the door swung open, Frank nearly barreled over with laughter. Drew stuck his hand on his hips, forced air out his nostrils, and waited for Frank to pull himself together. At this point, his reaction seemed more vapid than anything.

Frank held on to the door, sighed, and calmed himself. "Sold your soul, didn't you? Silly bastard."

"Yeah, yeah," Drew said, "dumbass thing to do, I know."

"But who'd want to buy *your* soul? I mean, seriously. Well, unless you want to backtrack in life then maybe I can—"

"Would you shut up and help me already?"

He motioned Drew inside the apartment.

"Wait," Drew said. "You can tell that just from looking at me?"

"'Course! Classic zombieism from selling your soul. You're nice and empty and hollow inside without it, I can see that. Symptoms are usually the same, but everyone has their nuances. Don't take long for it to kick in."

"So, you're telling me people do shit like this? I mean, exchange their soul for something, then have some bodily change?"

"More common than you think, my good man." He slapped Drew's shoulder. "Happens all the time, just never hear about it. Why would someone admit they're turning into a zombie?"

A *real* zombie? Drew patted himself then knocked on his temple. His brains hadn't eluded him and he hadn't felt the voracious appetite for human flesh. How he could be a genuine zombie was beyond him.

But what the hell was he thinking? That was all assuming that this stuff was for real. But why else would someone buy his soul? Still, he understood that Frank's advice was his only chance.

"All right, so I've turned into the walking undead," Drew said. "No soul, no brain, no nothing. But if that's true, you've got to know how to get me out of it."

Frank grinned. "Maybe."

"Maybe? What the hell do you mean *maybe*?"

"Why should I help you? After all, you just ditched me in the upper corner for seats on the fifty-yard line. Could've been charitable, too, but you and your big bucks couldn't be bothered to take me with you."

Drew almost dropped to his knees. "Come on, man, I've gotta get out of this. I'll do anything. Seriously."

"Okay, I'll take 'er easy on you, dude. One price sounds right to me."

"What price?"

"How 'bout you turn over those juicy season tickets?" Frank yawned and stretched. "Then we'll talk."

And if that wasn't the sweetest plum. If he had to give up the very seats that landed him in this mess, the cure hardly seemed worth it. Before he decided to sooner be a zombie, he convinced himself to be cured at any cost.

"'Kay, whatever you want." Drew wiped his forehead. "Once the ticket book comes in the mail, I'll turn it over to you. Promise."

Frank paused and slanted his eyebrows. "I'm gonna hold you to that. All right, so you've sold your soul and you're practically a zombie. Remember who you sold your soul to?"

Larry Adams was his name and Drew figured that

he'd remember the name until his dying hour . . . or until he became a total zombie.

"Yeah, so what do I do?" Drew asked. "Hunt the bastard down and steal it back from him?"

Frank slapped Drew upside the head. Drew curled up and nursed the stinging spot.

"No, you dumbass," Frank said, "you can't steal a soul, even if it used to be yours. It's all buy, sell, and trade in this racket. No exceptions."

"So I go to the guy and tell him I need my soul back so I don't turn into a goddamned zombie?"

"Hope to God he's got a heart, number one. But don't expect him to sell it back to you at face value, no matter who he is. Any customer wants to make a profit on his investment on resale."

"What in God's name are you talking about?" Drew asked.

"This dude could be a soul broker, for all you know. And if he is, he might've sold it to someone else by now."

"A soul broker . . . now I've heard 'em all."

"Don't make fun." Frank sat up straight. "If he still has your soul, he might charge you a lot more than he paid for it."

"So what else is there to it?"

Might as well buy something worthless and sell it for ten times more, Drew thought.

"Nothing, man. Just hope to God this guy is in a giving mood."

"Wait." Drew stood up and pointed at Frank. "I just forked over my season tickets to hear something that simple? You're a fucking crook!"

"Take it or leave it, dude. You wouldn't be anywhere without the info. Besides, I'm not the one who's gonna be feeding on human flesh to live before long."

Drew sent one email after another to Mr. Lawrence Adams, telling him that they needed to talk, and that it was urgent. Hell, he'd practically begged for an audience with him. He'd left his phone number in every email and waited by the phone. If this dude really bought, sold, and traded souls, surely he knew that would happen to him, Drew thought. Worse still, he probably didn't give a rat's pitoot.

Finally, the phone rang, and Drew scrambled to answer it.

"Hello?"

A cracked-sounding voice asked, "You Drew Wilson?"

"Yeah."

"Lemme guess what this is about. Want your soul back, huh?"

"Gee, how could you guess?"

"They always think they're smart as shit when they sell it, but they always come crawling back within days. Hell of a racket for me, though."

"Okay, okay, dumbass decision and I'm paying for

it like crazy. Would you just spare me the petty bullshit and sell me my soul back?"

"Can't do that, boss."

Drew made a fist then let his fingers uncurl. "Why the hell not?"

"Already sold it to someone else. Like I said, good market if you can break in, and souls sell fast . . . guess you know all about that, though."

Drew fought the urge to say, *Listen, you son of a bitch, just get me my soul back or, so help me God, I'll reach through that phone and pop you one!*

"Mr. Adams, listen. I'm desperate. Isn't there any chance you can help me get my soul back?"

Adams paused. "Always a chance there, boss. Money talks and bullshit walks, though. If you've got enough of the dough-ray-me, the dude I sold it to might be willing to hear you out. Remember, I said *might*."

If he'd had a nickel to spare, Drew knew that he wouldn't have sold his soul in the first place, but he hoped to God that he could bluff this guy.

"Okay," Drew said, "tell me what to do."

"Hookay, all right, normally I wouldn't break customer confidentiality for anything but, hey, I've come to have a soft spot for losers like you. The dude who bought your soul was a guy named Daniel Remington."

Adams gave him Remington's email address but he refused to disclose his phone number. That was fine by Drew, as his shaky hand would hardly allow him to jot

down the email address. Drew then hung up on Mr. Larry Adams without so much as a thank-you, a good-bye, or a kiss my ass.

Before he fired the email off to Remington, Drew decided to go for broke and be honest. His final draft made very clear the fact that he had no money to buy his soul back, but that he would gladly be his best friend, his bodyguard, or do the dirty work if he wanted someone killed if he would just have mercy. He clicked send and hoped to God that this Remington dude had a heart.

An hour later, an email from Daniel Remington appeared in his in-box and Drew nearly knocked his laptop over in his rush to open it. The seconds the email needed to load felt like an eternity. But instead of a regular email, he saw the Miami Dolphins logo load, inch by inch. Its little eye taunted him, as it did two Sundays every year.

Below it, he found a message that read: HAVE ANOTHER GREAT SEASON IN BUFFALO, SUCKER!!!!!!! DOLPHINS RULE!!!!!!!!!!!!!!!!!!!!!

The Close Shave

MIKE RESNICK AND LEZLI ROBYN

It's two thirty in the morning, and The Close Shave is starting to fill up. Which figures. After all, how many places can you go for a trim and a shave in the middle of the night?

Basil is in the chair now. I knew him back before he changed, when he went to bed after the eleven o'clock news like normal people, when he howled at a pretty girl it was because all the guys did. But that was, oh, maybe five years ago—before that mangy-looking dog bit him.

Otis is reading the newspaper. I knew him back in the old days, too. I can remember when he'd pick up a paper to see if the Geldings had finally drafted a linebacker, or if Can't Miss was running the next day, or if the Pharoahs' cheerleaders had been arrested for indecent exposure again—important stuff like that.

These days—well, these nights—all he reads are the obituaries.

Morton just comes to hang out. I mean, there isn't a hair on his whole body, or any skin either, now that I think of it. He's just bone as far as the eye can see. Looks kind of like a refugee from Halloween. He never bothers anyone—I think he's just lonely—and to be honest the main reason I let him sit there is the hope that sooner or later he'll buy a can of pop from the machine I keep in the corner and I'll see where it goes once it passes through his . . . let me see, *lips* is the wrong word, and he hasn't got any gums either. Through his teeth, I guess.

Harold comes by once a week, maybe a little more often, usually for a shave. While he's here he always asks for a shampoo. I keep telling him that I don't shampoo snakes, and although he claims they're perfectly harmless, that they *like* soap and water, the one time I sat him in the chair and leaned him back and got ready to shampoo some of the slime off the snakes, one of them gave me a great big reptilian smile, and it had teeth—*sharp* teeth—and from that day to this I don't give shampoos to male medusas (or female medusas either, though none has asked yet).

"Take a little off the top, Sam," says Basil.

"Right," I say, brushing it out a bit to make it easier to cut.

"And the sides."

"Got it," I say.

"And the chin."

"That's a shave," I say. "It'll be an extra five-spot."

"I thought we were friends, Sam," he says in a hurt tone.

"I am your friend all day long," I respond. "But when I open up The Close Shave at ten o'clock at night, I am your barber for the next eight hours, and never the twain shall meet."

"Okay, trim the mustache and beard," says Basil with a shrug. "And maybe the neck and the forearms and the backs of the hands."

I just stare at him.

"All right, just a trim and a shave."

I lay out my equipment, because Basil's hair isn't like most people's (which figures; it's been a long time since anyone mistook Basil for a people) when suddenly he lets out a howl that damned near shatters my front window.

"Come on, Basil," I say. "How can I have cut you? I haven't even started working on you yet."

This is followed by another, more plaintive howl.

"Basil, what the hell is it?"

He points through the window to Hepzibah McCoy's second-floor apartment across the street.

"She's getting undressed and she forgot to pull her shade down again!" says Basil, emitting a third howl.

"You're a werewolf," I say. "Can't you just wolf whistle?"

"Oh, the litters I could have with her!" says Basil.

"Maybe she doesn't like the hairy type," offers Morton, who is all bone and as unhairy as a billiard ball (and less colorful as well). Otis keeps telling him that he should wear pants, but I cannot imagine why, and neither can Morton. Besides, I figure his waistline comes in at a quick three inches. Do you know how hard it is to find a belt that size?

"You guys are so normal," says Harold in bored tones. "A girl with gazongas like that, if she's still on the loose and living alone, maybe she wants something a little unusual."

Three high-pitched voices say "Absolutely!" "For sure!" and "You betcha!" and I look around to see who is talking, but I don't spot anyone.

"Who said that?" I demand.

"Me and my two pals," says one of the purple snakes that is growing out of Harold's head. "Wanna make something of it?"

"Harold," I say, "your hair is talking to me."

"It talks to me all the time, mate," he says with a shrug as his mild Australian accent comes through. Then he adds, "Except when I comb it. Then it just screams bloody murder."

Well, his hair starts arguing amongst itself about which of them Hepzibah McCoy would most love to run her fingers through, and I pick up my scissors and go to work on Basil, and everything is going along nicely when suddenly he turns his head.

"She has gone into the bathroom for her shower!" he announces to the room at large. And a second later he makes another announcement, which is *"Ouch!"*

"I am sorry, Basil," I say, "but I am not *very* sorry, because you are an adult and you know better than to make sudden movements when someone is working your mane over with a scissors. I will get a styptic pencil, or a bandage, or some concrete mortar, and you will be good as new in just a minute."

Otis has been sniffing the air, and now he is staring hypnotically at the drop of blood on Basil's neck, and his pupils are dilated and his hands start shaking and suddenly there is a little bit of drool on his chin.

"Blood!" he whispers.

"Control yourself Otis," I say sharply.

"Blood!" he repeats.

"You don't know who he's eaten lately, or what diseases they might have been carrying," I say. "Just lean back and relax."

"Blood!" he hisses, standing up abruptly.

"Otis," I say, "this is as boring and one-sided a conversation as I have had in quite some time. Now you sit there and behave yourself or I'm going to get really annoyed with you—and don't you dare turn into a bat! Do you know how hard it is to shave you when you're hanging upside down from the ceiling?"

Otis starts pouting, feigns disinterest, and again buries his nose in the late edition's obituary column. I return to taming Basil's mane, but then the bell on

my door rings and so I turn, expecting to greet another of my regulars. Instead, the unexpected walks in: a human.

"Hello," I say. "Welcome to The Close Shave."

"Good evening," he says.

Morton fidgets, creaking slightly, while Basil growls softly under his breath.

"Do you need a trim?" I ask, not knowing what else to say—it has been years since a human required my services, especially at this time of night.

"No," he says. "I am looking for a medusa."

Harold looks up in surprise, his hair slithering around in excitement.

Then the man says the unthinkable—at least to me. "I want to die," he states. "I heard that I could find you here. I require your assistance."

"Why?" asks Morton gently.

"Death is overrated," intones Otis morbidly. "Do you know how much harder it is to keep these teeth from decaying since I became undead?" he continues, displaying his fangs to Morton, who is still looking (can I say looking? What with him having no eyes and all) at the man in the doorway.

"Be quiet, Otis," I say. I turn to the newcomer. "Why do you want to die?"

"Because life is not worth living," he answers in a voice top heavy with self-pity.

Otis licks his lips somewhat seductively. "Well, if *that's* the way you feel about it . . ."

"Otis," I say, "how many times have I told you: you don't bite the customers."

"But he *wants* me to," says Otis, almost keeping the whine out of his voice.

"No," says the man. "I've tried that, and it didn't work. Apparently vampires can't drink my blood."

"I view that as a personal challenge," replies Otis.

"They can't drink mine either," pipes in Morton, always wanting to fit in.

Basil, no longer growling, speaks up. "Morton, you don't *have* any blood."

"We're getting off topic," Harold states suddenly. "The crux of the matter is, I'm a pacifist." He shrugs. "I won't kill anyone—with or without their permission."

"Why didn't you tell me that before?" I complain, thinking of all those times I'd refused the money to wash his slimy hair for fear of hungry little teeth.

"I like to see you squirm," he says, grinning as his hair slithers around him like a halo.

Well, the man has stayed quiet throughout this entire little exchange, but now he clears his throat. "You misunderstood me. I don't expect *you* to kill me. I just want your permission to let one of your snake compan-ions bite me." He sighs heavily. "Maybe *that* will work."

"Pick me!" "No, choose me!" "What about me?" is the chorus that instantly responds to his request as little snake heads jump up and down in childish enthusiasm.

"Oh, in that case, be my guest," says Harold with another shrug. "I'm not responsible for their moral

choices. I'm from Australia, so my snakes are amongst the most poisonous in the world, however"—he raises a hand, immediately stilling the writhing snakes—"I suggest you ask Cecil. He's got the biggest fangs."

The other snakes sigh and sink back down to float around Harold's head in dejection as the man walks over and raises his wrist to Cecil. A dainty little head reaches out and sinks its teeth into the man—

—and a few seconds later the head pulls back, its slimy body wracked by sobs.

"He hurt me!" squeals Cecil. "He broke my fangs!"

"Is there such a thing as a dentist for snakes?" asks Otis, looking up from his newspaper to watch Harold trying to console his hair.

Out of the corner of my eye I see the man sink into one of my barber chairs, despair written all over his face. "I can't even die properly," he laments.

"Why do you want to die at all?" asks Basil.

"I'm tired," says the man.

"That seems a little severe," says Basil. "Whenever I'm tired I take a nap."

"I have been tired for two thousand years," says the man.

Everybody allows that two thousand years is a long time to be tired, and even fifteen hundred is no picnic if push comes to shove.

"Have you got a name?" I ask.

He kind of half smiles and half snorts. "I've had one hundred thirty-four of them."

"I knew a Juan Domingo Pedro Jesus Riccardo Jose Felipe Sanchez," I say. "He could grow a beard while he was signing his name. But I never met anyone with one hundred thirty-four names."

"I haven't had them all at once," he explains. "I meant that I've had one hundred thirty-four over the centuries."

"Who *are* you?" I ask.

"I'm the guy who should have kept his mouth shut on Golgotha," he says.

"Golgotha?" asks Morton. "Isn't that out by Des Moines?"

"No," says Basil. "I think it's on the California coast, just south of San Jose."

Cecil slithers down to the vicinity of Harold's ear. "You want to tell them, or should I?"

"Golgotha is where Jesus was crucified," says Harold. He stares at the man. "Only one person who was there should still be around. Gentlemen, say hello to the Wandering Jew."

"Really?" asks Morton.

The man nods his head.

"No wonder you're tired," continues Morton. "That's a *lot* of wandering." He stares at the man. "So do we call you Wandering or Jew?"

"I change my name to fit in with my surroundings," he answers. "This is twenty-first-century New York. Call me Goldberg."

"Okay, Goldberg," says Basil, starting to look a

shade more human as the moon goes behind a cloud. "So you want to kill yourself. Tell us about it."

"It's not as easy as you would think," says Goldberg, frowning.

"Telling us?"

"Killing myself."

"Sure it is," says Basil. "A silver bullet to the heart will do it every time."

Goldberg shakes his head. "Not mine. It's been tried."

"Don't listen to him," interjects Otis. "What does a dumb animal know, meaning no offense. If you want to die, get someone to drive a wooden stake through your heart."

Goldberg looks even more unhappy. "It doesn't work."

"All right, then," says Otis. "Go out to the beach in a thong at high noon."

"I don't burn," says Goldberg miserably. "Or react to poison." He looks at Cecil. "Or get sick. Or get cut. No matter how creative I get, I just can't die."

"How creative *do* you get?" asks Morton.

"King Arthur tried to stab me with Excalibur once," begins Goldberg. "He couldn't pierce my skin. Robespierre sentenced me to the guillotine; the blade broke on my neck. Tamerlaine spurred his favorite horse and tried to run me down; the horse bounced off and was never the same again." Goldberg shakes his head sadly. "So I figure if one man can't bring me eternal peace,

maybe a bunch can. I show up, ready to be sliced to ribbons, at Rosebud River—and Custer makes his last stand at the Little Big Horn fifteen miles upstream that same afternoon. I intercept a message that the D-Day invasion is set for Pas-de-Calais, and I'm there with the Nazi army ready to be blown sky-high—and it turns out that the message was *supposed* to be intercepted, and the invasion takes place at Normandy." He sighed deeply. "It's been like that for centuries."

"I still say just take a long nap," says Basil. "Whenever I'm bored that's what I do."

"Have *you* been bored for centuries?" asks Goldberg.

"Ten minutes is usually my limit," admits Basil.

"Maybe you should travel the world and see the sights," suggests Harold.

"I've been traveling the world for two thousand years," answers Goldberg. "I'm the Wandering Jew, remember?"

"You must have seen some fascinating things," offers Morton. "Notre Dame, the Taj Mahal, the Forbidden City . . ."

Goldberg shrugged. "Common. Pedestrian."

"Oh?" says Harold. "What *has* impressed you?"

Goldberg thinks for a minute. "There was a town hall in the mountains of Tibet. Held about eighty people. Very pretty." He frowns. "Destroyed in a landslide in, let me see, 582 AD—or was it 583?"

"Still, if you've been wandering for a couple of

thousand years, give or take, you must have seen a lot of things," allows Morton. "What was the most interesting sight you ever saw?"

Goldberg gets a faraway look on his face, but he doesn't answer.

We stare at him for a minute, and then Basil says, "You go into catatonic trances a lot, do you?"

"I was just remembering," says Goldberg.

"The most interesting sight?"

"The most beautiful."

"What was it?"

"She wasn't an *it*," says Goldberg. "At least I don't think so."

"*She?*" repeats Basil. "This just became a lot more interesting."

"It's tragic," replies Goldberg, a tear trickling down his cheek. "She's the real reason I want to kill myself."

"That's funny," says Basil. "I almost never want to kill myself when I see a beautiful woman. I just want to kill all the guys in the vicinity." He turns to Otis. "How about you?"

"I can't kill myself," answers Otis. "I'm *already* dead."

"We're getting away from the subject here," says Harold.

"What *was* the subject?" asks Otis.

"The most beautiful woman Goldberg ever saw."

"That's right," says Otis. He turns to Goldberg. "So tell us about her."

"She was the most beautiful, the sexiest, the most exquisite creature in the history of the human race," says Goldberg, and everyone perks up when he uses the word "creature." "And I should know. I've been here for enough of its history."

"I'm sure glad you don't speak in superlatives," I say.

"She was absolute perfection," continues Goldberg.

"You say 'was' and not 'is,'" notes Basil.

"Well, he did meet her centuries ago," chimes in Harold.

"Millennia," Goldberg corrects him.

"How did she die?" asks Otis, who has a professional fascination with such things.

"I don't know if she *is* dead," says Goldberg.

"Not a lot of women make it past their two thousandth birthday," I say.

"She is not a lot of women," says Goldberg. "She is the most perfect woman who ever lived, with a face that could launch twice as many ships as Helen's, and a body that would be the envy of every Playmate."

"A woman that perfect should be pretty famous by now," suggests Basil.

"The two don't necessarily go together," said Goldberg. "The Mona Lisa was a frump. No one ever heard of her good-looking kid sister."

"So has this perfect female got a name?"

"Of course she does," says Goldberg.

"You gonna tell us, or do we have to guess?" I say.

"Her name is Salome."

"Like, as danced before the king?" asks Harold.

Goldberg nods his head.

"I've always wanted to see the Dance of the Seven Veils," says Basil. "How was it?"

"Heavenly!" sighs Goldberg. "And it was the Dance of the Five Veils. They cleaned it up for the history books."

"I don't recall reading anything about Salome after the dance," continues Basil. "Maybe she died back then."

Goldberg shakes his head. "I saw her again in Rome, and then Athens, but I never got close enough to talk to her."

"Then why haven't we heard about her, if she's all that sexy and beautiful, and a good dancer to boot?"

"You have," says Goldberg. "H. Rider Haggard wrote her up as Ayesha, Edgar Rice Burroughs disguised her as La of Opar, Kurt Weill put her in a musical as Venus, John Cleland named her Fanny Hill and described her perfectly. . . . She has appeared many times, thinly disguised, down through the ages."

"And just as thinly dressed," notes Harold.

"I saw her briefly, from afar, in Persia in the fifth century," continues Goldberg. "Then I spotted her in Mecca in the eleventh century, Greece in the twelfth, India in the fourteenth, China in the sixteenth, but I could never get close enough to speak to her. Since then I've seen her in Tahiti, Kenya, England, Russia, Brazil, New Zealand, and Passaic, New Jersey."

"Well, it does explain your wandering," says Morton.

"I can't go on. Two thousand years, and I still haven't gotten close enough to meet her or touch her. It's been one hundred seven years since I last saw her just across the river in Jersey, the perfect woman—and a capricious Fate hasn't let me get within fifty feet of her in two millennia. She's lost to me, and I want to end it all." Another tear rolls down his cheek as Cecil and the other snakes watch in fascination. "If I can't kill myself, maybe I'll just destroy the world."

"*Can* you?" I ask.

"You think blowing up the world is the sole province of jihadists?" he shoots back. "Every mad scientist and rejected suitor wants to at one time or another."

"With the whole world to wander, what are you doing here in New York?" I ask. "Are you following some lead?"

"No," he answers miserably.

"Then why?" I persist.

"Your delis make the best blintzes and knishes," says Goldberg.

"Makes sense," Basil chimes in. "If you're going to be miserable, at least be well-fed and miserable."

"He should let the *yenta* I married cook for him," I say. "That'll take ten years off of anyone's life."

"Yeah, marriage is a death sentence for any man," agrees Harold, grinning.

"A death sentence just isn't what it used to be in the good old days," notes Otis.

Just as he says it, a bearded old man who knows a little something about death sentences enters the shop, dressed in a black robe and carrying a sickle. "That's hardly *my* fault," he says. "I keep taking them. It's *you* who keeps bringing them back."

"Who are you?" asks Basil.

"The sickle doesn't give it away?" says the old man.

"You're the Grim Reaper?" continues Basil.

The old man nods.

"That's a hell of a moniker to be stuck with," offers Harold.

"I enjoy my work," he says, "but even *I* don't think I'd care to be known as the Jolly Reaper."

"You're really *him*?" asks Goldberg, who's been staring at him since he entered the shop.

"I'm really *him*," answers the Grim Reaper. "Sam will vouch for me. I often come here on my break. It's the one place in town where I can avoid temptation. I'll be leaving in a few minutes."

"Take me with you!" shouts Goldberg.

"Don't be silly," says the Grim Reaper. "You're off-limits to me, you know that."

"Can't you try?"

"If I get any closer to you than I am right now, I get a migraine like you wouldn't believe, plus an attack of nausea. You've been cursed, pal."

"Maybe it's worn off," suggests Goldberg hopefully. "When's the last time you tried to take me?"

"Sumatra, 1749 AD," answers the Grim Reaper.

"Took me a whole week to recover, and it was close to a century before I could eat blowfish again."

"Won't you try once more?" says Goldberg. "Please?"

"It's not going to work."

"Please?" repeats Goldberg more desperately.

The Grim Reaper shrugs. "What the hell." He begins approaching Goldberg. Then, suddenly, he grabs his stomach. "I'm gonna be sick! Sam, where's your bathroom?"

I point to the back room, and he makes a beeline toward it.

"Some Grim Reaper!" snorts Otis.

"You heard him," I say. "Goldberg is cursed."

"My wife isn't," complains Otis. "She's uncursed *and* undead."

"Then why do you always complain about her?" asks Basil.

"Because she's also unforgiving," answers Otis. "I mean, it's not as if I can walk into a restaurant and order a quart of blood. So of course I find nourishment in nubile young women. Their skin is softer, their blood is richer, their screams are more exciting. *And they don't make demands on me.*" A pause, coupled with a frown. "I should never have bitten her that third time . . . but I was so *hungry*. Now I can't get rid of her." He turns to the back room and raises his voice. *"And some people are no damned help at all!"*

"You weren't listening," notes Morton. "He *took* her. *You* took her back."

"Details, details!" mutters Otis.

"If she bothers you that much, kill her again," suggests Basil. "I'll bet if you run a wooden stake through her heart, the Reaper will accept her."

Suddenly Otis's entire demeanor changes. "I'm kind of used to her," he says. "And she tastes so good."

"Well, then?"

"If only she'd stop reading all those idiot vampire romance novels and assuming I'm like that every time I go out, we'd get along fine."

"When's the last time you brought her a present to show you cared?" asks Morton.

"I took her to the dressing room after the hockey game last week and gave her first choice," says Otis. "I got the leftovers. How's *that* for a present?"

"That's nice," says Morton in a voice that sounds less than sincere. "But when's the last time you brought her flowers?"

"She can't eat flowers," replies Otis.

"Neither can the other fifty million women who get them from time to time," says Morton.

"Right, mate," Harold chimes in. "She's more than just an appetite, you know."

Otis looks thoughtful for a moment. "Okay," he says at last. "I'll give it a shot." Then: "Live ones or dead ones?"

Morton sighs. "Talk to some florists. They'll figure it out."

Basil starts howling again. There's no sense ask-

ing why, because the moon is full in the sky and his humanity is buried beneath a wolf's exterior. I look out the shop window, and sure enough there is the incredibly shapely silhouette of Hepzibah McCoy closing her curtains. I find myself sympathizing with Basil; that is one hell of a view to be deprived of.

Everyone but Goldberg is looking mournfully at Hepzibah McCoy's darkened window. Goldberg is gazing intently at my bleach bottles. He senses my curiosity and glances up with a small smile.

"Tried that," he states simply.

"Acid?"

"It just cleanses my insides."

"Jump into any active volcanoes lately?" I ask wryly.

He sighs deeply. "Not since Pompeii."

The subject seems hopeless, so I turn my attention back to Basil's ears. Then I hear the most enticing voice I have ever heard, but it does not sound like it is in an enticing mood.

"What does a girl have to do to get a good night's sleep around here?"

I turn to see the most luscious creature I have ever laid eyes on standing in my doorway. My heart starts pounding. My throat goes dry. My palms start sweating. She is to the average beautiful woman what Shaquille O'Neal is to the average midget. My first thought is that the Church should hire her, because once a man sees her there is no way he cannot believe in God.

Basil starts panting and drooling at the sight of

her, so I cuff him over the head. It is a reflex action, because I am still unable to pull any coherent thoughts together.

Morton hops out of his chair with an enthusiasm I've never seen in him before, and instantly offers it to her. This makes me realize that she might actually be a patron, and that in turn brings me back to the here and now.

"Hello," I hear myself say in a shaky voice. "Welcome to The Close Shave."

She doesn't immediately respond, but instead runs her hands sensuously along the arm of my leather chair before turning back to me, all business. "How hard can it be for you to find a muzzle for your mutt?" she asks, glaring briefly at Basil before turning her hypnotic gaze my way again. "Every time I go near the window he howls . . . and my bed is beside the window." She pouts, and I feel my heart beating in triple time. "It's late," she continues, "and I need my beauty sleep." She puts her hands on her hips to emphasize her comment, but all it does is emphasize her small waist leading up and down to the generous curves that her flimsy dressing gown has slid open to reveal.

"You don't need any beauty sleep, Sheila," states Harold suddenly, with a little too much warmth in his tone. "That I can guarantee."

She throws him a cold glance—at odds with the heat radiating out from her body—and states, "I'm known as Hepzibah, not Sheila."

"Don't get your knickers in a knot, love," says Harold. "Sheila is just an Aussie word for 'girl.'"

"You think *this*"—she opens up her robe—"is the body of a mere girl?"

I'm frozen to the spot, staring. So is Morton, and Basil, and everyone else. Well, everyone except Harold's snakes.

"You're all woman to me!" one yells.

"Let me show you what a night of sleaze and slime can be like!" yells another, as they all squirm excitedly.

Hepzibah smiles, and walks—well, undulates—over to Harold, all her parts moving in thrillingly perfect sync. She reaches out a hand to run her fingers through Harold's hair, causing snake after snake to shudder delicately. "I like excitement," she whispers to them, "and different experiences. Do you think you could . . . *amuse* me?"

"Absolutely!" "You betcha" "In a heartbeat!" say three of them.

"How pathetic," says another.

Hepzibah's hand stills, and there is a dangerous glint in her beautiful eyes. "Who said that?" she asks softly, but with deadly intent.

One defiant snake slithers out in front of the rest. "I did," comes the reply in a distinctly feminine voice. "I'm sick of the vulgar display my brothers make of themselves whenever they see a cute bit of tail." She pokes Hepzibah's hand in disgust. "It's degrading, and embarrassing—and it gives us a bad name."

"Like biting and killing people haven't contributed to that bad reputation," observes Basil wryly, the moon having slid behind an incoming storm cloud.

"It's you!" comes an awestruck voice and we all turn to see who belongs to it—and, believe me, turning away from Hepzibah even for a second takes a major effort of will. And it so happens that the voice belongs to Goldberg, who is staring wide-eyed at her. "After all these years, it's Salome!"

She gives him a good hard look. "I know you," she says. "You're that guy who hooted and hollered louder than anyone when I did my dance."

Goldberg nods his head. He tries to say something, but his voice starts to break.

"Two thousand years and your throat is *still* hoarse from all that screaming?" she says with a smile. "I consider that a high compliment."

"You're as beautiful as ever," he manages to say.

Which is an understatement, because she is even more beautiful now than when she entered the shop, but I decide not to contradict him, and besides my throat is so dry I probably can't get the words out.

Just then the Grim Reaper emerges from the back room.

"Don't be afraid," said Goldberg. "I won't let him touch you."

The Reaper takes one look at her, grabs his stomach, bellows *"You're* here, too? I'm gonna be sick again!" and runs back to the bathroom.

"'Too?'" she repeats, looking at Goldberg with renewed interest. "You're immortal?"

He nods.

"Well," she says, "we have a lot to talk about."

"You'll actually talk to me?" said Goldberg, barely able to contain his excitement.

"Talking's not my long and strong suit," she replies in sultry tones. "But we can *start* by talking."

Basil has to repress another howl. Harold's lady snake looks shocked. Morton tenses, which is harder than you think for a skeleton. Otis merely salivates.

"So do I call you Hepzibah or Salome?" asks Goldberg.

She shrugs, and Basil and Harold almost faint before the last of the shrug fades from view. "Or Eve, or Lilith, or Helen, or . . ."

She goes on and on, and I begin to see that this is not only the most beautiful and exotic creature in the history of this and every other universe, but also a well-named one (or at least a multiple-named one). Not only that, but she's got a real head on her shoulders or she couldn't remember more than half those names.

"It was Salome I fell in love with, so it is Salome I shall call you," says Goldberg. He continues staring at her, his mouth open (which is not always a good idea in New York City, as you never know what might fly into it). "What are you doing here?"

"Telling this wolf to shut up and let me sleep," she answers.

"I mean, in New York. I have been searching for you for two millennia, and this is the closest I've ever gotten."

"Really?" she says. "I'm flattered." Which is wrong, because take my word for it, she isn't anything with the word "flat" in it. "Who are you?" she continues.

"I am a man who has been cursed with wanderlust," answers Goldberg. "A man who has loved you for two thousand years and has forsaken all other women."

"*All* other women?" says Salome, clearly pleased.

"Yes," he says. "Just as I know you have kept yourself pure for me."

"Well, within reason," she says with another shrug.

"I am doomed to wander the world," says Goldberg. "Please tell me I no longer have to do so alone."

"To tell the truth, I *am* getting tired of New York," she says. "Sure, I'll come away with you."

"I'll wait here and count the minutes while you pack your clothes," says Goldberg.

"You've counted enough minutes," says Salome. "Besides, who needs clothes?"

Basil starts whining piteously.

"Then shall we leave right now?" asks Goldberg.

"Why not?" she says, linking her arm in his. "Where shall we go?"

"The Riviera is beautiful this time of year," says Goldberg.

She shakes her head. "I was just there last summer. How about Tahiti?"

"It's not what it was back in Gauguin's time," he answers as they walk slowly toward the door. "How about a fling at the gaming tables in Monaco?"

"Been there, done that," she replies. "Perhaps dinner at Maxim's after we tour the Louvre?"

They are still trying to find a place they haven't both been, or at least aren't tired of, when they walk into the night and out of sight.

"Are they gone?" rasps the Grim Reaper from the back room.

"Yeah, you can come out now," I say.

He comes back into the shop and glares at me. "You got any more surprises for me, an honest hardworking guy who's never done you any harm . . . *yet*," he concludes meaningfully.

"Not that I'm aware of," I say. "You want a trim while you're here?"

He shakes his head and walks to the door. "This has been a very upsetting experience. I've got to go out and find some stale air to breathe."

As he leaves, Harvey the yeti, his shaggy fur dripping ice water, brushes by him on the way in. The Reaper mutters something, and Harvey yells after him, "Yeah? Well, I'm not half as abominable as a guy who takes our starting quarterback three weeks before the playoffs!"

"Hi, Harvey," I say as Basil gets up and the yeti takes his place. "What can I do for you?"

"I've come for a blow-dry," he says in his deep grav-

elly voice. "I've got a hot date with a fire nymph in a couple of hours." He looks around the room. "I've never dated one before. Anyone got any tips?"

A moment later Otis is telling him how to find a fire nymph's jugular, Basil is explaining which cut of her goes best with mashed potatoes and glazed carrots, and Harold's snakes want to know why a fire nymph would prefer a yeti to them.

It's just another night at The Close Shave.

Shaggy Dog Story

STEVE RASNIC TEM

You probably remember that poem from one of those old Lon Chaney Jr. movie classics. The gypsy woman, her face looking like that road map your dad wadded up after one too many wrong turns and shoved into the rear of the glove compartment with last month's missing Beer of the Month Club bill, fetchingly played by the great Maria Ouspenskaya, her eyes as luminous as two cheese crackers on a hot radiator, tells the somewhat put-out Chaney what he can expect every time the moon is full and the Wolfbane blooms.

Not exactly what you want to hear after a homeless man wearing a floral patterned scarf on his head just took a bite out of you, but the threat of six rounds of rabies shots over a four-week period makes for exciting cinema.

The poem invites numerous questions, such as what the hell is wolfbane and can I get some kind of spray for it? And what if the moon is only semibright? Hairy palms and a mullet?

You should hear my Uncle Verge deliver those lines. Slow, sonorous, and full of angst—back in the sixties they got him laid. Now they get him an extra dose of meds at the nursing home.

Uncle Verge's shtick was always family history and legacy. He made that poem sound like some legendary summation of our particular family curse, instead of what the screenwriter threw together when he needed a poetic moment. Verge fed that line to hairless types in a cynical bid for some pity grooming. And he got it, until they got tired of flossing the hair out of their teeth.

Yes, indeed, we're a hairy bunch. The family orders its hair spray by the skid. Family reunions resemble a Civil War reenactment performed by beavers. My father's father used to lose his house keys in his belly hair, along with the remains of three Jehovah's Witnesses who'd knocked on his door before breakfast. And my Aunt Elona, that was one hairy woman. Even her unibrow had a unibrow.

Uncle Verge wasn't the first one in the clan to use the image of the tormented, misunderstood werewolf to his own advantage. You should have heard my mother when I told her I was dating a dog walker from Yonkers.

• • •

See, that's the way it's always been in our family. We act like we're above it all, like the normal rules don't apply to us. Like it's normal to offer a mail carrier as a door prize. But then we're not above pulling that "poor wolfy" crap if we think it's to our advantage, lie on our backs and beg to have our tummies rubbed (or as Uncle Verge used to call it, "stroking the pelt").

It's embarrassing. It's a wonder I'm as normal as I am. Just don't say "fetch" in my presence if you don't want to see me pee myself.

And if a person doesn't look like the rest of the family, if he's not as hairy as a bar of soap in a bearded ladies' spa, well, he's just an embarrassment. He's just the "hairless rat," the "naked coconut," the "depilitated Cossack." My cousins called me all of those names, and in a confusing attempt to belittle me even further, the "Jersey urinal."

Yes, I was born without the family curse, or as my mother so delicately puts it, "an overly generous beard."

I tried to hide it. In grade school I'd shave the family cat, sprinkle the clippings all over myself and tell everybody I had allergies. By the time I was fifteen, when my peers were all jumping into kiddy pools full of mousse and styling gel, I was hanging around barbershops with a vacuum cleaner and a bucket full of contact cement. After a while I decided to go right to the source and became the family's in-house hair styl-

ist, creating the most elaborate pompadours this side
of Paris. (Well, Paris, Texas, at least.) But my mother
recognized that something was wrong. Not once had I
borrowed her industrial Bic Lady Shaver without ask-
ing.

"What will your father say?" That was all she was
worried about.

"He'll say 'Pass me the remote, it's time for *Jeop-
ardy!*'" I replied, whereupon she slapped me across the
face with a carp.

You might think my escape from the family malady
would be a cause for celebration, relief that at least one
of ours wouldn't have to spend his twilight years lug-
ging around five gallon jugs of pet wee cleaner, but not
my family. You'd think I'd deliberately piddled in the
gene pool.

I tried to reason with them. I attempted to appeal
to my father's thrifty side by explaining just how much
I'd be saving in hair accessories and chew toys alone. It
was a waste of time. It's like taking a busload of mon-
keys to a Mahler symphony—they might sit and listen,
but they'd much rather be picking their noses.

My father appeared to consider what I'd just said,
then explained how they'd all been very proud of their
hair, they had lots of it, thank you very much, and they
had no intention of braiding it and trying to pass as a
bunch of goddamned Rastafarians. I thanked him for
his wisdom and shoved a rawhide chew into his mouth.

It's important to understand that although I did not

have the family curse per se, I'd been thoroughly indoc-
trinated in family traditions, interests, and attitudes. I
enjoyed a nice plate of raw meat, for example, with Texas
toast and a modest side salad. I liked chasing things:
cars, people, big shiny balls. I liked crouching naked in
the park and howling at the moon—you meet some of
the most interesting people that way. I was thoroughly
werewolf, sans hair, sans dates on Fridays or any other
night. I wanted to fit in.

So it is a fortunate thing that a clan as old as ours
has developed rituals, procedures for handling just this
sort of occurrence. Although in our family this hirsute
transformation is hereditary, a perhaps more familiar
situation involves some poor clueless innocent such as
a computer programmer or a tax accountant bitten by
a full-fledged member of the Order of the Tooth and
Claw (a kind of werewolf version of the Kiwanis Club).

An essential aspect of this, of course, is that the bite
be survivable, which is far less likely if the werewolf
hasn't yet done his grocery shopping. Youthful passion
can be a factor, which is why the mothers in local towns
often tell their sons to avoid heavy petting if the girl
has more chest hair than they do.

So when a member of our family is born without
the requisite fur suit in his or her repertoire he or she
must endure a bite from a more mature member of the
household. Adolescent members of the family have
referred to this practice, quaintly, as "getting geezer
gobbled."

The desired result is a lycanthrope, the wolf who walks on two legs, when affordable public transportation isn't available. But that "ideal" result doesn't always occur, which highlights a particular misapprehension about our condition which has always bugged me, and which I'm grateful now to have the opportunity to correct.

A common misunderstanding is that we are wolves. We are *not* wolves. Have you ever seen a wolf with dentures (I mean *their own*)? We look like wolves. Sometimes we act like wolves. We are "as if" wolves. The ontological "as if," as in "I may look as if I'm a wolf but I know I am not one. At least I'm pretty sure. What does ontological mean again?" "Wolf" is simply a metaphor, like "gainfully employed."

Think about it this way. Is a starfish a star? I'm not sure it's even a fish. I've never been able to find its mouth—have you? Maybe that's a bad example. How about the lowly foxglove, being neither fox nor glove, and certainly not a fox's glove, which would make it very hard to eat fish, one of its favorites, after tiramisu, but what would really be hard, for anyone, really, would be to eat a starfish, and why would one even want to? I was never very good at biology. My high school biology teacher said my scores barely qualified for sentience.

Of course, I understand such distinctions are of little more than academic interest when one of my relatives is busily retooling your digestive system.

But we're expected to look like wolves. That's a

given. And I didn't even have a five o'clock shadow. Mine had barely made it past one fifteen. So I had to be bitten. "And," my father told me, "you have to pretend to like it. Your Grandpa Jules is going to provide the service. It's an *honor*. He doesn't do this kind of thing much anymore."

Grandpa Jules? I'd always avoided him. He smelled like a cheese shop with a tanning salon in the back.

The day of the ceremony I got up early and started practicing my "transformation face." I knew that a dignified transformation face was probably beyond my reach—I just wanted to avoid looking ridiculous. You can imagine the difficulty. Not to be too indelicate, but the experience of morphing from human into wolf shape is a bit like evacuating your bowels, having an orgasm, regurgitating a week's worth of dinners, and giving birth to a baby all at the same time. It makes for a full evening. If the wrong people witness your transformation your social calendar empties out rather rapidly.

I spent most of the morning in front of the mirror, but I'm afraid the best I achieved was the classic "My groin just exploded!" look.

How do you dress for such an event? And will there be refreshments? You don't want to wear anything too nice, because it's going to be destroyed. Something loose-fitting is most often recommended, but my cousin Vinny likes to wear tight clothes for the occasion—he claims the resulting explosion of material

impresses the ladies. Clothing is a werewolf's number one expense, after breath mints, with a new outfit required every full moon. I finally settled on sweats and an "I'd Rather Be Golfing" T-shirt.

The attendance was somewhat disappointing: my mother, my father, cousin Vinny and Uncle Verge, Aunt Elona, my little brother Lonnie, two old ladies from the bar mitzvah next door complaining they'd run out of cream cheese, and Grandpa Jules, who fell fast asleep as soon as he reached his chair. I wasn't that surprised by all the empty seats, actually—the clan may claim to treat everybody equally whatever their origin, but those of us who have been bitten will always have that stench of the victim about our person and the propensity to dive under furniture when anyone cracks a smile.

The ceremony began with a speech from my father explaining why we were all there, his attempt to reinterpret my follicle deficiency as the beginnings of a noble quest rather effective until he made that strange connection between furry bedroom slippers and codfish. My mother was up next for five minutes of hand-wringing and an elaborate confession involving a bald lingerie salesman consumed during the second month of pregnancy.

Finally Uncle Verge got up to introduce Grandpa Jules. He stood at the front of the hall, both paws firmly

gripping the lectern, leaned forward and looked at each one of us, his eyebrows resplendent and fully unfurled. "Grandpa Jules was a giant among our kind. He was not ashamed of who he was, although from time to time just a little self-awareness might have been nice. But if not for him, none of us would be here today. We could have been in New Jersey instead, with all that humidity! But his like will never be seen again, certainly not his *exact* like, that would be weird, because he never told us he had a twin, or even a brother, which might have been nice, having an uncle to take you to the baseball game, and on to the petting zoo for dinner."

Grandpa Jules sat in the front row grinning ear to ear, literally. Finally Uncle Verge noticed this, obviously realized he'd mistakenly been delivering the man's eulogy, pretended to choke on a hairball, and was dragged from the building.

Grandpa sighed loudly, shook his head, and climbed to his feet. Turning around at the front of the room he motioned me forward. "Come along, Lowell. Let's get this over with."

I had been nervous enough about the ceremony in general, but had tried not to think about the actual biting. I had never been a great fan of teeth, had forsworn zippers in favor of buttons, and avoided pianos whenever possible. Trembling uncontrollably, I came forward, stopped a few feet away, and, in a final desperate attempt to avoid the inevitable, I brushed up my scant bit of hair and imagined myself a giant onion.

Grandpa Jules saw through my clever plan and shuffled forward. Suddenly he was possessed by a violent seizure, began to hack and spit, and after a disconcerting interval of moonwalking, started removing his clothes and folding them neatly on the floor beside him. Stretching out his full four-and-a-half feet of white hairy nakedness he began to strut youthfully in my direction. As one the audience turned their faces away, some melodramatically covering their heads with whatever was available, including skirts, chair cushions, and trash cans.

With each step Grandpa Jules appeared to spasm out a different body part, jaw and ears and elbows, hands and feet elongating and twisting, pulsing and warping. It was all blurry and much too disturbing to focus on, but I swear there was a moment he appeared all haunches, hackles, and hemorrhoids.

At the end he not so much leapt as collapsed at my feet and began to gnaw on my left tennis shoe.

"Grandpa, maybe a little higher," I said.

He twisted his head up furiously, eyeing me with those huge, bloodshot peepers, his mouth full of chewed tennis shoe rubber, Odor Eater insert and Hello Kitty logo. He spat these out and, I noticed, about half his teeth.

This was something new for me. A gaping, wrinkled mess of missing and yellowed teeth and, yes, hairy gums, and flip-flappy coated tongue, clamping onto the fatty part of my calf—if such a ruined mouth

could be said to "clamp"—proceeding to vigorously *massage* its way up my leg.

It's not a favorite memory. To this day I break into severe facial twitching when presented with a plate of succotash.

Some abrasion and scratching did occur, some blood was drawn, but for the most part it tickled, so much so that I became rather hysterical, jumping up and down trying to get Grandpa Jules off my leg.

I've never known whether they were trying to assist him or me, but before I knew what was happening my mother and my father, Lonnie, and a couple of other family members had surrounded us and, grabbing whatever on our bodies seemed grab-able, were tugging and pulling, snarling and yipping, as if somebody had exploded a hamburger bomb at the dog park.

Grandpa, in his nervous excitement, began humping my leg at the same time he was biting it. I have to admit this was a dining experience I personally had never attempted.

Finally someone brought in a garden hose and opened it up on the center of the melee. There ended my ceremony before I even had the chance to announce, "Today, I am a werewolf."

All that occurred years ago and, mercifully, some of the more sordid details have blurred through the mists of time. Uncle Verge and Grandpa Jules are now sharing quality time at a local nursing home, climbing the fences and howling whenever the mood strikes them.

Mother and Father have divorced. He currently lives under a bush in her backyard. I think she still has feelings for him—at least she throws him the better scraps. Lonnie went away to college and now has nothing to do with any of us, insisting that our condition is completely the result of dysfunctional family dynamics.

And I'm a hairdresser in downtown L.A. with a very special clientele. At least now I feel marginally part of the family. Grandpa Jules never actually managed a firm bite that evening—at most some hard-edged gumming resulting in bruises and abrasions. I do go through the change, into something that looks a bit like a crazed Pomeranian. I try to stay out of the public eye during those times—it would be devastating for my business if anyone recognized me. But overall, living as a werewolf these days really isn't that difficult—the hard part is doing it with style.

Eight-Legged Vengeance

JEFF STRAND

I am not typically a vengeful person, despite my "Blood for Blood!" temporary tattoo. But when my girlfriend Erica became my ex-girlfriend Erica the Skank, a bit of revenge was in order.

She claimed that she was cheating on me with my casual acquaintance Dave. However, Dave had an alibi for each weekend in question, and the *Guitar Hero* scores to prove it, so Erica finally broke down and confessed that she hadn't been cheating on me at all—she just didn't want to admit that she was repulsed by the small mole next to my ear. Now, I'm not saying that it's an attractive mole, but give me a break. After six weeks of bliss, we were through.

And so I decided to seek revenge. I didn't want to

kidnap her dog or decapitate her favorite teddy bear or anything like that. I just wanted to do something that was clever and memorable, but not illegal or *too* mean. I invited my friend Dave (a different Dave than my casual acquaintance) over for a couple of beers and a brain-storming session.

"You could burn her house down," Dave suggested.

"No. It can't be anything that would involve the cops."

"Wouldn't they send the fire department instead of the cops?"

"Yeah, but when they discovered that it was arson, they'd involve the cops."

"Bummer." Dave took a swig of beer and swished it around in his mouth. "What about keying her car?"

"Nothing destructive."

"What's wrong with being destructive?"

"Destructive makes it seem like she got to me too much. I don't want to convey rage. I want her to think I'm laughing at her, not punching holes in walls."

"So you're thinking more of a 'nyahh-nyahh' than a 'screw you, hell-bitch'?"

"Exactly."

Dave drank some more beer. "I can work with that. The way I see it, the best alternatives to bloodshed and/or destruction are fear and/or humiliation. Do you agree?"

I nodded. "Fear or humiliation. Yep. Both of those are good."

"Which do you prefer?"

"I'm not sure," I admitted. "Humiliation might be kind of mean."

"Dude, are you seeking revenge or shopping for an engagement ring? You *have* to be mean. That's the whole frickin' point!"

"I know, I know. I just don't want to dump pig's blood on her or anything like that."

"So . . . fear or humiliation?"

"I'm not sure. Let's flip a coin." I reached into my pocket but found it coinless. I reached into my other pocket and found it equally lacking in coinage. "Do you have a coin?"

Dave patted his pockets, then picked up the bottle cap from his beer. "I've got this."

"Okay, if it lands upside down, we'll go with fear. If it lands right side up, we'll go with humiliation."

Dave flipped the bottle cap. It landed on the floor, upside down.

"Humiliation," he announced. "Cool."

"No, that was fear."

"It's upside down."

"I know. That was fear."

"Are you sure?"

"Yes."

"Oh." Dave finished off his bottle of beer. "Fear. Fear, fear, fear. Lots of possibilities in the fear arena. What's she most scared of?"

"Terrorists . . . cancer . . . dying alone . . ."

"What about spiders? Is she scared of spiders?"

"I'm not sure."

"What about a big ol' hairy tarantula?"

"I assume so. We never really talked about it. You think I should mail her a tarantula?"

"Not unless you're a complete *loser*," Dave said. "You've gotta be more inventive than that. Mailing a spider is a level one plan. You have to bring this to level two or three at the very least."

"You're right. What could we do with a tarantula to make it more memorable?"

"Dress it up?"

"Please stop being stupid," I requested.

"My bad."

"We need an inventive delivery method for the tarantula. Maybe a singing telegram or something."

"Do they really do singing telegrams?" Dave asked.

"What are you talking about?"

"I've never actually seen a singing telegram. I thought maybe it was just something they did on TV."

"Are you kidding me?"

"Have *you* ever had a singing telegram?"

"No."

"Then maybe I'm right. Where would you even go to get one?"

"I don't know! Any party store! How can you doubt the existence of singing telegrams? That's the stupidest thing I've ever heard!"

"Sorry," Dave said. "Can I have another beer?"

"Later. Anyway, I don't think we'll find a singing telegram service that will sing a song and then chuck a spider at her. Let's think of a better delivery method."

"It would be cool if we could figure out a way to get it to jump out of a cake, like one of those naked girls."

I sat up straight. "I've got it!"

"What?"

"We could bake a tarantula in a cake!"

"When's her birthday?"

"Not for a few months, but still, there has to be a cake-giving occasion coming up. It's perfect! She gets this nice, beautifully decorated cake delivered to her house. She takes a bite, and something's a bit off. She investigates a little further, and there's a frickin' tarantula baked right into the cake! She freaks out. Vengeance is mine."

Dave rubbed his hands together in malicious glee. "You, sir, are a genius. Albert Einstein never would've thought of that. He would've thought of something about physics or science or something. A spider in a cake. That's brilliant!"

And so our nefarious scheme was hatched. After I gave Dave another beer, we divided up our duties equally: Dave would obtain the tarantula, and I would obtain the cake.

It was a difficult decision. Should I go with chocolate? Vanilla? Angel food cake? Pineapple upside-down cake? After much thought and price comparison, I settled on a yellow cake, since it seemed like it would

show off the tarantula the best. I also bought some yellow frosting and a tube of red goop used for writing words on cakes.

I returned to my apartment and played football on my Xbox until Dave showed up. He had a tarantula in a small plastic aquarium, which he set on my coffee table.

"Cool," I said, tapping the plastic.

"You owe me thirty-five bucks."

"Thirty-five?"

"Twenty-five for the spider, ten for the aquarium."

"Twenty-five bucks for a spider?"

"How much did you think it was gonna be?"

"Free! I thought you'd go to a shelter or something, where they were going to step on it if nobody took it home!"

"It's not a puppy."

"Well, why did you buy the aquarium?"

"It was half price with any pet purchase. I wasn't gonna drive it home on my lap."

I wanted to smack him in the face with an empty beer bottle. "It's not a pet! It's a sacrifice! Why did you get a live one?"

"Where am I gonna get a dead one? You think they have a dead tarantula aisle at Walmart?"

"But . . . twenty-five bucks? It's not even a big one."

"It's average size for the species."

"No, it's not. Tarantulas are huge."

"You're thinking of tarantulas in fifties horror movies," said Dave. "This is a tarantula in real life."

"I didn't think it would be the size of my house, but it should at least be the size of my hand!"

"It's a perfectly good tarantula. Stop being such a whiner."

I held out my hand. "Let me see the receipt."

"I don't have it anymore."

"I'm not paying you back without a receipt."

Dave sighed. "Okay, fine, it was thirty-two, not thirty-five. You're so damn suspicious all the time. Jeez."

"Jerk."

"Cheapskate."

"Drunk."

"Cheapskate."

"Fine." I took out my wallet and dug out a twenty, a five, and five ones. That pretty much wiped out my beer budget for the rest of the month. Who knew vengeance would be so pricey?

"Oh, there was tax, too," said Dave.

"Screw you."

We went into the kitchenette of my studio apartment and I made the cake batter, while Dave provided helpful advice about what I was doing incorrectly, and I provided very specific suggestions about what he could do with his advice. I cursed as some eggshell dropped into the mix.

"Who cares?" Dave asked. "If it's going to have a spider in it, it might as well have some eggshell."

"If she crunches down on a piece of eggshell, she'll quit

eating the cake, then she'll never find the tarantula, and then my devastating revenge will have been that she ate a bit of eggshell." I dug out the shell bit and flicked it at him.

"Ow! Ow! Dammit! You got my eye!" He recoiled and stumbled backward, smacking into the counter.

"I did not."

"Take a look! Take a look! Is it protruding?"

"Move your hand away so I can see."

"I think you poked my iris, dude!"

"Move your hand."

"Oh, crap, I'm gonna be seeing eggshell for the rest of my life!"

"Move your hand." I grabbed his hand and pulled it away from his eye. "I can't see it."

"It's in there!"

"Okay, I see it. It's not jutting out or anything; it's just stuck in the corner."

"Oh, crap . . ."

"It's no big deal. We'll just run some water on it."

"What if the water flushes it up under my eyelid? It could slice my eye all up! Oh, crap . . ."

"Stop being such a baby. It's just a tiny little speck of eggshell in your eye." I took a dishcloth out of the sink, ran it under some cold water, and twisted the corner. "Don't move."

"What are you gonna do?"

"I'm gonna scrub your eye out with a scouring pad. What do you *think* I'm gonna do? I'm going to flick the shell out."

"Be careful."

I poked at the corner of his eye with the cloth. I could no longer see the piece of eggshell.

"It's out."

"Are you sure?"

"Yeah."

"I can still kind of feel it."

"Well, it's not in your eye anymore."

Dave rubbed his eye. "Thanks, dude."

"No problem. Can we go back to making the cake now?"

"Yeah, yeah, sure thing."

I stirred until the batter was completely mixed, then I poured it out into the pan. "When should we add the tarantula?"

"I'd say now."

"How do we kill it?"

"What do you mean?"

"How. Do. We. Kill. It."

"Just bake it."

"We can't just throw a live tarantula into the oven! That's cruel!"

"Dude, it's a bug."

"I don't care. You don't cook things alive like that. It's uncool."

"That's how they boil lobsters. And I think it's how they cook deer."

"Well, it's not gonna happen in my oven."

"Maybe it'll drown in the batter first."

"Shut up." I peered at the spider, which was crawling around on a miniature plastic log. "So what's a quick and humane way to kill it?"

"Stomp on it?"

"Get the hell out of my apartment, dumbass."

"What?" Dave asked. "I wasn't saying that you should stomp it flat and scrape the mess off into the batter. But you could, y'know, stomp on it gently and break its back or something."

"No."

"Cut off its head. It'll still look like a tarantula."

"This would've been a lot easier if you had just brought home a dead one in the first place."

"They don't sell dead tarantulas locally! I already told you that! Maybe we could poison it."

"The cake?"

"The tarantula. To kill it."

I considered that. "I don't think I have any spider poison."

"Do you have any ant poison? That would probably work."

"No. I don't keep a lot of poison in the apartment."

"Do you have any cigarettes? We could blow smoke in there until it chokes to death."

Instead of calling Dave a moron, I gave him a look that said "You're a moron."

"Fine. You're the leader of the Be Humane To Cuddly-Wuddly Spiders movement, *you* decide how to kill it."

"I don't know! I have no idea how to kill a tarantula without squishing it. Screw it. Let's just bake the stupid thing." I turned on the oven.

"We should name him."

"Yeah, sure, let's give a name to the creature that's going to die a horrible, agonizing death because of us. Let's call him Timmy the Tarantula and paint a smiley face on his back."

"We could name him Eight-Legged Vengeance."

"Don't be such a frickin'— Actually, that's pretty cool. Let's go with that." I tapped on the aquarium. "Hello, Eight-Legged Vengeance. How's it going?"

Eight-Legged Vengeance did not respond.

"Maybe we should feed it a mouse as one last meal," Dave suggested.

"Do you have a mouse?"

"No. But I could go get one. I think the pet shop had mice."

I started to give him another "You're a moron" look, but decided that it wasn't worth it. "Let's just put him in the batter and get it over with."

"Sounds good."

I lifted the top off the aquarium. "Okay, reach in there and grab him."

"Yeah, that's gonna happen."

"What, you're scared?"

"It's a tarantula! They're venomous!"

"No, they're not."

"You do it."

I reached inside the aquarium, stopping a few inches away from the arachnid.

"So pick it up," Dave urged.

"I'm going to."

"I hope it doesn't take your hand off."

"I hope it takes your mouth off."

"Pick it up."

"I will."

"Time's a-wastin'."

"Why don't you go home? You've served your purpose."

"No way. I want to see this."

"Well, be quiet."

"Pick it up."

"I am."

"No, you're not. You're being motionless and cowardly."

The tarantula moved toward my hand. I let out a shameful cry and yanked my hand out of the aquarium so fast that I bashed it against the corner. Dave found this to be extremely amusing. I did not.

"Grow up," I told him.

"Oh, God, I wish I'd been taping that! I'd give anything to have been taping that! You looked like such a chickenshit jackass!"

"You suck."

"Reach in there again. It might growl at you this time."

I opened one of the drawers and took out a long

wooden spoon. I poked the spoon into the aquarium and tried to scoop up the tarantula, but it kept scurrying away. "Dammit!

"It probably doesn't like that flavor of cake. You should have bought chocolate."

"I'm just gonna dump it out." I very, very, very quickly reached into the aquarium and removed the plastic log. Then I picked up the aquarium, turned it over, and shook it over the batter. The tarantula didn't fall out.

"He's got some seriously sticky feet," Dave noted.

"Smack the plastic."

Dave knocked on the aquarium. The spider still didn't fall out.

"Shake harder."

I shook harder.

"Maybe you should just pour the cake mix into the aquarium and cook it that way."

"C'mon, keep smacking the plastic. It's just a spider. It can't hang on forever."

"You actually have to admire its resilience."

"I don't have to admire shit! Keep smacking!"

Dave hit the plastic over and over while I kept shaking the aquarium.

"Do you have a squirt gun? We could squirt it off."

"No."

"There was a toy store next to the pet store."

"Keep smacking!"

Finally the spider dropped out of the aquarium and into the batter.

"Thank God," I said. "Open the oven."

Dave opened the oven. I picked up the pan as the tarantula waded through the batter, moving right toward me. I hurriedly slid the pan into the oven and slammed the door shut. We breathed a sigh of relief.

Dave flipped on the oven light. "I want to watch it burn."

"That's messed up."

"How often do you get to watch a tarantula die in an oven? Never. I'm not going to let this opportunity slip by. Oh, crap . . ."

"What?"

"It crawled out of the pan."

I opened the oven. The batter-covered tarantula was on the bottom. "Give me the spoon! Hurry!"

Dave handed me the spoon. I frantically scraped the tarantula off the bottom of the oven and onto the open door. It scurried across the door and onto my kitchenette floor.

"Stomp it! Stomp it!" Dave cried.

"Don't stomp it!"

Dave quickly backed away. "Where is it? Where did it go? Is it on me? Get it off me!"

"It's not on you. It's crawling on the cabinet door."

"Did it get cooked?"

"Not too much. It's still moving. Let's just kill it. I can't have a tarantula running around my apartment."

I swung the wooden spoon but missed the spider. It dropped onto the floor next to my foot. I backed into

the oven door, lost my balance, and fell. I threw out my arms to break my fall, and my hands came down on the hot metal door. I cried out in pain as I landed on my butt.

The tarantula crawled onto my leg. I yelped and tried to shake it off.

"It's eating me!" I shouted. It wasn't actually eating me, but I can be forgiven for exaggerating my situation in my cloud of panic.

Dave crouched over me. "I don't see it!"

"Kill it!"

"But I don't see it!"

"Kill it!"

"There it is!" Dave slammed his foot down, missing the spider but hitting my shin.

"You dick!" I shouted.

"It's too fast!"

"Get something to murder it with!"

Dave glanced around the kitchenette for an effective weapon, then slid a butcher knife out of the wooden holder. I mentally acknowledged that this was not a wise selection, but then the tarantula scurried up my leg and I batted at it in a frenzy.

"Don't move!" said Dave, crouching down. "I'll poke it!"

"Don't poke it!"

"Don't move!"

"If you stab me I'll fuckin' kill you!"

"I'm not gonna stab you! I'm gonna stab the spider!"

"Put the knife down!"

"Trust me!"

"I don't trust you! You're not trustworthy! No knife!"

Dave held the tip of the knife above the tarantula. "I'm gonna poke it! Don't move!"

I froze.

Dave winced and clutched at his eye with his free hand. "Ow! The eggshell is still there!"

The tarantula crawled out from beneath the knife and went underneath my shirt. I flinched so violently that my upper leg slammed up onto the knife tip. I reacted poorly.

"It wasn't my fault!" Dave insisted, still clutching his eye. "I didn't do anything!"

I slapped my palm against my shirt, squishing Eight-Legged Vengeance onto my belly button. Dave pulled the knife out of my leg and stood up.

"Did you get it?" he asked.

I pressed harder until I was positive that my navel was covered with tarantula guts. I yanked my shirt up and wiped the goo off.

"Sorry about the knife," Dave said.

I kicked him in the shin.

He dropped the knife.

It hit my other leg, burying itself about an inch into my flesh. It hurt like hell and I kicked the son of a bitch again, as hard as I could.

He stumbled backward, slipped, spun around in a

failed attempt to regain his balance, and struck the corner of the counter with his face. His eyeball burst upon impact. I wasn't immediately sure if it was the one with the eggshell or not.

Dave silently dropped to the floor, blood and slime oozing from his ruined orb.

"Oh, jeez, I'm so sorry!" I said. "I didn't mean to!"

"That . . . that was . . . that was . . . *ow* . . ."

I yanked the knife out of my leg. "You'll be fine," I promised. "We'll get you to the hospital."

Dave let out what I'm pretty sure was supposed to be a battle cry and dove at me. I instinctively held the knife out in front of me to protect myself (although, in retrospect, my hands would have worked just as well) and an instant later my buddy was skewered through the throat.

He said something. The gargling made it difficult to determine exactly what it was, but the tone was not complimentary.

I pulled the knife out. The huge gout of blood that came out of his neck made it clear that an ambulance would probably not do him a whole lot of good.

So I didn't call one. I held him, crying softly, until he was done bleeding and living.

The apartment manager called and asked if I would please turn my damn television down because it was disturbing my neighbors. I said that I would.

In the middle of the night, I dragged Dave out to my car, drove eighty miles out of town, and buried him

in a shallow grave. I drank a bottle of beer to honor his memory. I drove back home, climbed into bed, remembered that I'd left my fingerprints on the beer bottle, drove the eighty miles back to the grave, retrieved the bottle, and drove back home.

Since Dave had given his life for revenge on Erica, I vowed to complete my plan so that his passing would not be in vain. The next day, I bought a rubber spider from a toy store, baked it into a cake, and decorated it nicely with a "Happy Labor Day" message, even though Labor Day was two weeks away.

That night the news reported that she had choked to death on a rubber spider leg.

Dave would've thought that was kind of funny. So I laughed.

I laughed and laughed and laughed and even kept laughing when the very polite men loaded me into the white van.

Hell, I'm laughing as I type this.

Hee hee hee.

Revenge is fun.

Lucifer's
Daughter

KELLEY ARMSTRONG

Nothing gets my blood pumping like a museum. Millennia of murder and mayhem gathered under one roof. A delicious banquet of guilt-free chaos custom-made for an Expisco half-demon.

I leapt from the car as Karl handed the keys to the valet. Then I saw it.

"No," I whispered. "I'm having a vision, right? A horrible vision."

Karl slid an arm around me. "Actually, I think she's quite beautiful."

We were staring up at a banner announcing tonight's event—the opening of a new exhibition sponsored by my grandmother. She'd said it was a display of World War II memorabilia, in memory of my grandfather. It wasn't.

Smiling down from the banner was a face that horrified me as no vision of death and destruction ever could—my byline and photo under the *True News* masthead.

"The Hope Adams Exhibit of the Inexplicable," Karl read. "Sounds . . . intriguing."

"I can't believe Gran would do this."

"No? Isn't this the same woman who used to take you to churches with brown-skinned icons to prove that God loves you, even if you aren't white? Of course, that was easier than finding horned icons, to prove God loves you even if you are the devil's spawn."

I glared at him. Of course my grandmother—like everyone in my family—had no idea I was a half-demon. But I suspect if she did learn the truth, she'd find a way to convince me *that* was okay, too.

I loved my grandmother. Sure, she could be a bigoted old battle-axe, but it couldn't have been easy when her son—one of Philadelphian high society's most eligible bachelors—announced he planned to marry an exchange student from India. Gran accepted his choice, though, and accepted all of her grandchildren, including the one born after the marriage broke down. She was determined to prove her love, even if it meant sponsoring an exhibition to say, "My granddaughter investigates Bigfoot stories for a supermarket tabloid and, damn it, I'm so proud of her."

Karl's attention had wandered to another sign. This one announced a traveling exhibit featuring the

Amulet of Marduk. I wasn't the only one who liked museums.

"Uh-uh," I said. "You know the rule. No stealing at any event where we are invited guests."

He walked over to the sign.

"Karl . . . We had a deal . . ."

"No, I believe the deal is that I may not steal jewels from *guests* at events to which we are invited."

"Okay, but then taking the amulet would break your deal with Clayton, which says—"

"That I can't steal artifacts of historical significance. The Amulet of Marduk is an Egyptian reproduction. Bling. Very old . . ." He looked at the sign again, and his blue eyes gleamed, the wolf in him spotting prey he liked far more than rabbits. "Very valuable bling."

"No."

"If I'm not breaking the rules . . ."

"Sure you are. Remember the one that says, 'Thou shalt not steal'?"

A faint eye roll at such a bourgeois notion.

"Fine," I said. "I'll go in to the party. You sneak in the back and do your thing, while I hang out with Nelson Graves. Remember Nelson?"

Karl gave a rumbling grunt that sounded suspiciously like a growl.

"Gran says he asked if I was coming tonight and if I was still with you. He said he'd see what he could do about that." I pursed my lips. "It's tempting. He's attractive, under thirty, rich and, best of all, has a job

that's unlikely to land me in a prison visitor's room anytime soon."

He put his hands on my hips. "Start that and you won't get to your party anytime soon."

"I mention another guy, and you feel the need to assert your property rights? A little medieval, don't you think?" I stepped away. "But if that puts you in the mood, think how much better it'll be after a whole evening with Nelson. Provided, of course, that you don't steal anything."

He arched a brow. "Threatening to withhold sex if I misbehave? A little medieval, don't you think?"

Before I could answer, a Town Car pulled up to the curb, my mother in the passenger seat. Karl strode over to open the door. I couldn't see the driver, and tried to remember whether she was coming with the Democratic congressman or the Republican one. I could never tell them apart, and it was so embarrassing when I got it wrong.

As the congressman talked to the valet, my mother pointed to the banner. "For the record, I had no idea she was doing this."

"I know."

"She's just trying to be supportive."

"I know. I just wish she'd find a less"—I looked up at the banner and cringed—"public way to show it."

She hugged me. "I know."

As we climbed the steps, she asked me how my work was going. She never asked about Karl's. I think

she knew he wasn't really in the import-export business. She didn't care. As she'd said even before we were dating, "He's good for you, Hope," and to her, that was all that mattered. For Karl's part, even when she wore her most valuable jewels, that gleam never entered his eyes, which for him was a sign of unparalleled respect.

The congressman—Democrat, Karl mouthed— was waylaid on the steps, and Mom waved for us to go on inside while she joined him.

I stepped through the doors to find myself face-to-face with . . . myself. A giant banner hung from floor to ceiling, just in case anyone had missed the one outside.

"Oh, God," I said. "I don't think I can do this."

"I don't blame you." Karl pointed to a service door. "I do believe that will take us into the rear of the museum, near the display for the amulet. And with those banners all over the building, no one will wonder why you're wandering about."

"Nice try. If—"

The hall went dark. Voices rose in a chant. I heard a scream. Felt a splatter of warm liquid. Licked my lips and tasted blood.

The chanting grew louder, but the screams drowned them out. I strained to see deeper into the vision, hoping to catch a glimpse of whatever was responsible for the delicious chaos washing over me.

The screams faded and I felt Karl's hands rubbing my arms. I blinked and looked around. He'd tugged me into a corner.

"Trouble?" he said.

I shook my head. "Just a vision of past ritual torture or human sacrifice. You know museums. Full of dull, dry hist—"

The hair on my neck rose as a voiceless whisper called to me, promising more sweet chaos . . .

"Hope?"

"Museums," I said, shaking my head, and motioned him into the foyer.

"Ironically appropriate, don't you think?" Karl whispered.

We stood before a display dedicated to human-demon hybrids in myth and popular culture, including Hell Spawn—*True News*'s answer to *Weekly World News*'s Bat Boy.

The whole exhibit was like that—linking my articles to supernatural legends. Fascinating, actually. And, yes, flattering, once I got past the cringe factor.

Tour guides led partygoers through the displays. We were in the first group, with my mother, the congressman, and Gran.

"I wish your father could have been here," Gran said. "He's so proud of you, dear."

"I'm sure he is," Karl murmured. "But it's a long way to travel."

I glowered at him. My *father* might be Lucifer, but my *dad* was still Will Adams. He was on business

in Indonesia and had sent a gift with Gran—a silver armband engraved with mystical symbols. Ugly as hell, but it was his way of showing his support, and a lot more welcome than sponsoring a museum exhibit in my name.

We were discussing the museum renovations when Karl decided it was time to use the restroom. I'd say he felt guilty about those repairs, but Karl never feels guilty. The renovations were his fault. We'd first met here four years ago when I'd tried to stop him from stealing something—surprise, surprise—and nearly got the place burned down running from someone *else* on his tail. Thousand-year-old papyrus scrolls and fire half-demons really don't mix.

Karl hadn't commented on the renovations. Nor had he commented on our return to the scene of our first meeting. I'm sure he remembered—kind of hard to forget—but Karl wasn't the sentimental type. Also, he hadn't made the best first impression. It'd been two years before I'd go out with him, which I'm sure he considers a failure best forgotten, for the sake of his ego.

Gran was pointing out the new plasterwork when the director arrived. "The guest of honor," he said, pumping my hand. "Isn't your exhibit marvelous?"

"It is."

He lowered his voice. "Some board members were opposed to the exhibit, saying it would be pandering to the basest segment of society."

"Understandable. It's—"

"And I said, that's the *point*. Entice them in with the lurid and the ludicrous and maybe they'll get lost on the way to the restrooms and actually see something edifying. In tough times, we all need to do what we can. However distasteful." He nudged me. "You know all about that."

Gran pushed between us. "Actually, my granddaughter likes her work. And I like it, too. Folklore is an important part of any culture and—"

—*a lesson you won't soon forget*, a voice boomed.

I jumped. Mom put a hand against my back. The lights flickered, but no one else seemed to notice. As Gran continued lecturing the director, a tendril of chaos wrapped around me, tugging me deeper into the museum.

Oh, hell, where was Karl? And what was he getting into?

When I said I had to go, Mom tried to stop me, thinking I was upset by the director's comments, but I brushed her off and hurried into the back hall.

No sign of Karl. I closed my eyes and concentrated. I could pick up blips of chaos from the party. Anger. Jealousy. Envy. When I tuned that out, I got a jolt of the real stuff, coming from the jewelry exhibit.

Oh, hell.

I jogged along the dark corridor.

Thrall of Lucifer, heed my words!

I spun, nearly tripping. The hall was empty.

You have rained down chaos and destruction for long enough. May you spend eternity suffering the torment you have visited on so many.

Something wrapped around me, tight as a mummy's bindings. I struggled to get free, shrieked and shouted curses in languages I didn't recognize—

"Hope!"

I snapped out of the vision to find myself on the floor, lying across Karl's lap.

I scrambled to my feet. "You took it, didn't you?"

"What?"

"The Amulet of Marduk. Damn you, Karl, I asked—"

"I didn't take anything."

I grabbed his tuxedo lapel and reached inside the jacket for the hidden pocket.

He caught my hands. "If you want to undress me, there are better places to do it. In fact, I saw a suitably dark—"

"What did you steal?" I asked.

"Nothing. Yes, I was in the room with the amulet. Yes, I have every intention of taking it. But not tonight. I wouldn't do that when—"

Something small and furry scampered past a doorway.

"Rat?" I said.

"No, it smells like—"

Chattering erupted. Then the sound of tiny nails skittering across the floor. The creature darted out of

a dark adjoining room and launched itself at me. The smell of the thing hit me—an awful stink of formaldehyde and badly stored fur. It thumped onto me, claws clutching the front of my dress. A tiny spider monkey face turned up to mine.

A tiny *dead* spider monkey.

Its eyes were beads and half its teeth were missing. At every joint, the fur and skin had ripped open. Sawdust spilled out. Through the openings, I could see bone and the wire that had held the monkey in a pose—until it'd been reanimated and no longer cared to be in that pose.

Karl grabbed the monkey by the scruff of the neck and whipped it away from me. It hit the wall and exploded. Sawdust and fur flew everywhere, including in my mouth. I spat and clawed it out, gagging.

Again, the sounds of tiny, scrabbling nails filled the hallway. I looked up. One arm and one leg were still attached to the monkey's torso as it pulled itself toward me.

Karl strode forward.

"You can't kill a reanimated corpse," I said.

"I can try."

He stomped on it. The arm and leg launched from the torso like rockets.

I winced. "Better hope the SPCA doesn't catch you doing that."

He snorted and kicked the bits into a storage room.

I stared at the tufts of fur and curls of sawdust left

behind on the polished floor. A top-notch necromancer can reanimate long-dead corpses, but what was the chance that one was practicing his craft during a museum charity event? At the same time that Karl was poking around ancient artifacts?

"Show me where you were," I said. "And what you did."

He'd been in the traveling jewelry exhibit, checking out security so he could return another day and steal the amulet. It was still there, though, and he swore he hadn't even touched its glass box. What he *had* handled was a display in an identical case. As a test run, he'd opened it and closed it up again.

"And that's it?" I said.

"I picked up that," he said, pointing to a small, jewel-covered box inside. "The sign says it's bronze with semiprecious stones. It's wrong. The stones aren't valuable, but the box itself is gold. I considered pocketing it but—" He shrugged. "Not while we're invited guests."

"And not when it's an object of historical significance."

He said, "Hmm," which meant that was open to interpretation and he'd interpret it for himself when he came back for the amulet.

I bent to read the plaque. As I did, I saw the pattern on the box he'd picked up—symbols that told me this

was not, as the museum claimed, a fifteenth-century noblewoman's keepsake box. It *was* meant for keeping something, though.

"You opened it?" I said.

"Not intentionally. It seemed sealed, but when I was examining the jewels, the lid popped open. I closed it."

"Not fast enough." I straightened. "It's a soul box for demons. Used by witches and sorcerers powerful enough to bind a—"

Shoes squeaked outside the door.

"I've found you," a breathless voice said.

Nelson strode across the room, gaze fixed on me as if he didn't even see Karl.

"Uh, sorry, we were just looking for the ladies' room. I need to, uh, freshen up." I flashed a smile. "Get looking beautiful."

"Why?" Nelson stopped in front of me. "You are already the most beautiful thing I have ever laid eyes on."

"Umm, thanks . . ."

Behind me, Karl growled.

Nelson dropped to one knee. "I am yours, mistress. I live to serve you. To worship you."

"Guess that demon soul isn't in the monkey anymore," Karl murmured.

"You don't think I'm worthy of worship?" I said. "Maybe—"

Nelson started licking my shins.

Karl turned to me. "You were saying?"

"Never mind. You're going to need to disable him. Just don't—"

Karl grabbed Demon Nelson by the back of his jacket and started swinging him toward the nearest display.

"—do that," I said. "Don't break any displays. And don't break him."

Karl paused, as if considering whether he'd heard me.

Demon Nelson squirmed and shrieked. "Defiler! You are not fit to speak to my master's daughter. You will pay for your—"

Karl dropped him headfirst onto the floor. Then he pinned him under one Italian loafer. I walked closer, staying out of licking distance.

"Who are you?" I asked.

"Nybbas."

He went on, giving his demon equivalent of rank and serial number. He was a demon under Lucifer. He'd gone AWOL a few thousand years ago and had himself a rollicking unauthorized shore leave in ancient Sumer, leaving death and destruction in his wake, until—as I'd seen in my vision—he'd ended up trapped in that box.

Now he was out and very, very grateful. He presumed I was the one who'd set him free. It didn't seem wise to argue.

"I will repay your kindness, mistress," he said, tongue extending, unsuccessfully, toward my shoes. "I

will be your humble slave until my debt is paid, and then you shall tell your lord father how useful I have been, and he will take me back."

I've never met my father. Never wanted to. Again, though, I didn't set him straight.

"That's very sweet," I said. "I'm sure you'd make a wonderful demon slave, but it's the twenty-first century and there are laws against that sort of thing. So how about I just let you go back to Hell, where I'm sure Lucifer will be happy—"

"Nooo!" he howled.

He leaped to his feet, catching Karl off guard, and darted out of his grasp.

"I must prove myself first," he said as he dodged Karl. "If I please you, my master will be pleased."

"Fine, then. Clean my condo for a few days and we'll call it even."

"I must show my respect properly. I will prepare a feast in your honor. A feast of chaos. The sacrifice of a hundred souls—"

"No! No sacrifices. I command—"

"Hope?" a quavering voice called from the hall. "Is that you, dear?"

Nybbas stopped and smiled. "The first offering."

"No!" I said. Then to Karl, "Catch—"

Karl dove at Nybbas and knocked him to the floor. I raced into the hall. Outside the exhibit room, I slowed and tried to look sheepish.

"Hey, Gran," I said. "Caught us doing a little unau-

thorized touring. Karl wanted to see the Amulet of Marduk. He read about it in the paper."

"Is that what he said?"

She smiled as her gaze traveled over my dress and hair, which was in even more disarray than usual. She tried to peer into the room. When I blocked her view, she chuckled.

"Not in a state to be seen, is he?" she said.

"Uh, no, he's just—"

"Karl is a very attractive man, Hope. Very powerful. Very . . . virile." Her eyes shone with something that looked frighteningly close to lust and she tried, again, to peer around me. "It's not easy to keep a man like that happy. It takes a lot of time and effort." That sparkle again as she smiled. "But you seem to be doing a fine job of it. A fine job."

"Er, thanks . . ."

She patted my arm. "I'll cover for you. Just don't be too long."

I returned to the exhibit to find Karl kneeling on the struggling demon.

"She's old," the demon whined. "Let me sacrifice her, so she may do some good in her final days."

"That woman is my grandmother," I said as I walked over.

The demon stopped writhing. "She gave birth to his lordship's chosen vessel?"

It took me a second to figure out that he thought Gran was my mother's mother. Though two weeks in

Nassau had given my grandmother a nice tan, no one was likely to mistake her for Indo-American. But if this demon had racial identification issues, I wasn't setting him straight. Informing him that Gran was actually the mother of the human who'd *shared* his master's vessel didn't seem like a good way to prolong her life.

Nybbas lay still for a moment, then bucked, knocking Karl off. He leaped up and danced back out of Karl's reach.

"This one would make a suitable sacrifice," Nybbas said. "A werewolf is a base creature, unsuited to be consort to a demon princess. Your father would be pleased if I rid you of this embarrassment."

"You want to kill me?" Karl bared his teeth. "You need to come a little closer first."

He grabbed for the demon, who backpedaled, then feinted and dove at Karl, managing to snag his leg and send him crashing to the floor.

"Enough!" I said, jumping between them. "He's not my consort. He's my bodyguard." I turned to Karl. "Stop playing with your prey and catch him. I command it."

Karl arched an eyebrow but charged, foreseeing the demon's feint this time, throwing him down, then pinning him on his stomach again.

Nybbas glanced over his shoulder. "I suppose, as a bodyguard, he is suitable. Sacrifices must be made, though. I will begin with my host."

Karl hesitated and looked down at Nelson's body

beneath him. Then he backed off, just a little. I glowered. He sighed, then leaned on the demon again.

"The princess says you may not sacrifice your host," he said. "Sadly."

Nybbas nodded. "And the princess must be obeyed."

"She must?" I said. "I mean, yes. She must. The princess commands that you are not to kill that host or my bodyguard. In fact, the princess asks that there are to be no sacrifices made on her behalf. She commands you to leave that body and begin your journey home."

"As you wish."

Nelson's eyes glowed yellow, then faded to their normal brown as a warm wind circled us and his body collapsed, motionless, under Karl.

"He's gone," I said.

"Hmm." Karl rose.

"Too easy?" I asked.

"I'd say so."

"Damn."

I grabbed the soul box before we left the exhibit. When I caught up with Karl, he glanced at it and nodded.

"Good idea. It's more valuable than the amulet. Particularly given its purpose. It could fetch a small fortune on the supernatural black market."

"Very funny. I'm borrowing it, then returning it to the exhibit just the way it was before you tampered with it. Demon soul and all." I tried to hand it to him

as we walked down the back hall. "You open it; I'll turn on my chaos detector."

"Open it?"

"That's how the soul got out. Just do whatever you did before. And quickly."

I pressed the box into his hands.

"I think this demon princess business is going to your head," he said.

"Open it."

He took the box and examined it, grumbling that he didn't know how he'd done it the first time so he could hardly be expected to do it again. I concentrated on picking up tendrils of chaos.

I caught a blip of fear. I was homing in on it when a wave of chaos hit. I stumbled back. Karl caught me.

"I think—"

Darkness enveloped me. Voices chanted. A scream drowned them out. The rich coppery smell of blood filled the air. Hot droplets spattered my face. Someone intoned an incantation. The shrieks continued—the screams of a demon about to be cut from his mortal form and shoved into a very tiny box for a very long time.

I yanked free of the vision. Karl was holding me. I was still standing this time, which was always a plus.

"Did you find him?" Karl asked.

I shook my head. "Just another flashback of him being stuffed in that box. Maybe we should split up while you try to open it."

"Or maybe I should just put it back because I can't open it."

"Just keep—"

A shriek cut me off. Karl spun toward the noise. A real scream, then, not a chaos playback. Some days, it was tough to tell.

We took off in the direction of the scream. Everything had gone silent now, but I could feel undercurrents of chaos throbbing through the air. Karl headed straight for them, following voices, I presumed.

We turned the corner. Down the hall, a beefy security guard had a partygoer pinned against the wall. Beside him a red-haired woman bounced, hands clutched by her mouth, doing absolutely nothing to help her date, just whimpering and gibbering.

"We were looking for the ladies' room," she said. "The other one was full. We didn't know this part of the museum was off-limits."

"The guy broke my fucking nose," her date mumbled, trying to talk with his face mashed against the bloodied wall. "This isn't about being outside the party zone. Call nine-one-one before this psycho kills me, Tara."

"You don't need to yell at me, Rick," she whined.

I recognized the voice and the names. Tara Dunlop. During our debutante year we'd approached something like friendship, ending when she caught Rick with me in a back hall a lot like this one. The fact that he'd been pinning *me* to a wall at the time hadn't mat-

tered. I was the little slut who tempted her boyfriend. When I'd had a breakdown as my powers hit, she'd made sure every one of our acquaintances knew why Hope Adams missed her high school prom: because the psych ward didn't grant day passes.

Karl peered down the hall. "Isn't that . . . ?"

"Uh-huh."

I'd told him the story after Tara tried luring *him* into a back room at a New Year's ball.

"Perhaps allowing a sacrifice or two isn't such a bad thing," he said. "Seeing that I can't open the soul box, this might be our only way to get him back to Hell."

"Tempting," I muttered as I began walking toward them. "Very tempting."

"Oh, oh!" Tara chirped. "Someone's coming. It's—" She leaned around the security guard. "Oh."

The guard turned my way. His eyes flashed yellow. "You are early, my princess. The sacrifice is not yet complete."

"Princess?" Tara said.

"Sacrifice?" Rick yelped.

"Is this a friend of yours, Hope?" Tara said. "Figures. Bet you met a lot of them in the loony bin. Is that where you met him, too?" She gestured at Karl. "I heard it was a dating service. Goldiggers-R-Us, for rich girls too crazy to get a real boyfriend."

"Last chance," Karl whispered to me.

"Did someone say sacrifice?" Rick said. "Can we talk about that? Please?"

"There will be no sacrifices," I said, walking over to Nybbas. "I thought I made that clear."

"No, princess. You asked that no sacrifices be made on your behalf. That means you do not wish the deaths to weigh on your conscience. A human failing, but I understand. I will make the sacrifices for you and—"

"And no." I stepped so close I could smell the guard's cheap cologne. "I do *not* want the sacrifices. I command—"

The guard's body collapsed at my feet before I could finish.

"We need to get that box open," I said as we strode down the hall, having left Tara and Rick making a bee-line for the back exit. "Are you sure you don't remember how you did it?"

"Yes, I do. I'm just pretending otherwise to liven up a dull evening."

"Wouldn't put it past you," I said. "But okay. Sorry. We need a backup plan, then. I know Paige and Lucas have a dispossession spell that might work, but we'd need to get them here from Portland. Meanwhile, this bastard has free run of a building filled with potential victims. We need to get everyone out so we can—"

The vision flashed again. I pushed it aside faster now, recovering after only a split-second blackout. When I came to, though, I found myself staring at a red box on the wall.

I glanced over at Karl. He plucked a glove from his pocket, and pulled the fire alarm.

As plans went, it was far from foolproof. For one thing, as the partygoers streamed toward the exits, their chaos washed over me . . . and washed away any chaos being caused by Nybbas himself. Then someone shouted, "Where's the tour group? Has anyone seen them yet?" and I looked over to see the closed doors to the new exhibit.

I yanked on the door. It didn't budge. Karl grabbed it and heaved, tendons in his neck bulging. Then, with a crack, the door flew open and we raced through.

Inside, it was pitch black and silent. Chaos thrummed through the room. Then a whimper, followed by a harsh whisper, someone urging silence.

"I can smell you," a woman's voice sang. "I don't need lights to find dirty, stinking humans."

When the fire alarm sounded, the lights must have had gone off. Now they were trapped as Nybbas hunted them.

"I'll stop him," Karl whispered. "You stay here." He pressed the box into my hands. "Work on this."

"I can't—" I began, but he was gone.

I held the box, fingers running over the jewels. He was right. Opening it had been a fluke the first time, impossible to repeat. All we could do was catch whatever body he'd jumped into and get these people to

safety before he grabbed a new one. With a room filled with fresh bodies to possess, though . . .

Shit.

I turned the box over in my hands, touching the jewels randomly, frantically, as I strained to hear Karl.

"Is that a wolf I smell?" the singsong voice said.

A grunt, then the thud of a body hitting the floor. A woman started to scream. Karl apologized and laughter rang out—in a man's voice now.

"You may be a fast wolf," Nybbas said from his new body. "But you aren't nearly fast enough."

A scream made me jump, and I nearly dropped the box before I realized it was just the vision again. I squeezed my eyes shut and forced it away.

Then a woman shrieked, "Get him off me. Get him off me!" and footsteps thundered across the room. A thump, as Karl grabbed the demon off his new victim. A laugh as the demon jumped bodies. Only this time I recognized that deep chuckle. Recognized it very well.

"Get out of him!" I said. "I commanded you—"

"Not to kill him." Nybbas giggled. "I won't. I promise."

"I command you—"

"I can't hear you!" Nybbas said. "Can't hear anything. I will return to my master and tell him what I have done, and he will be pleased. You can't stop me, princess. I won't let you."

I tried ordering him again, but he just kept getting louder, drowning me out.

The vision threatened again. I pushed it back.

"Now I can smell you even better, humans." Nybbas inhaled deeply. "Better sense of smell. Better night vision. Better hearing." He chortled. "This makes it almost too easy."

I turned the box over. I just had to hold this damned chaos vision at bay long enough to concentrate—

I stopped. Chaos vision. Of Nybbas's incarceration.

"There you are," Nybbas said. "Come here, human. Let me taste—"

An *oomph* and a hiss as whoever Nybbas caught escaped. Then a clatter and a howl of rage as he tripped over something.

I squeezed my eyes shut, wrapped my hands around the box, and cleared my mind. The vision hit with what felt like a left hook to the temple. I hit the floor, and everything went dark.

I heard the demon's screams. Then chanting. Then a man's voice reciting the incantation. I blinked hard, and the vision came clear.

I stood in a temple. At the altar, a bearded man held the soul box aloft. Women in red robes ringed him, chanting. At his feet a bound man struggled.

The sorcerer pressed the jewels on the box. The lid flung open.

One of the women took a knife from her robe, raised it, and stabbed the bound man. Stabbed him over and over while the sorcerer continued the incantation. As the last word left his mouth, the demon was

ripped—still shrieking—from his host, a yellow pulsing light being dragged toward the box. When it disappeared inside, the sorcerer smacked it shut.

I snapped from the vision, but the screams continued. A woman's screams now, her nails scratching the floor as Nybbas dragged her. I quickly hit the jewels in sequence as I recited the incantation.

In the vision, the host had been killed to free the demon, but everything I'd heard about dispossession told me that wasn't necessary. I *prayed* it wasn't necessary.

As I hit the last jewel, the box popped open. I squeezed my eyes shut, and finished the last words.

"No!" Nybbas shrieked. "Mistress, no! I will obey you. I will—"

Yellow light flashed, then a glowing ball streaked toward me. When it disappeared inside the box, I slapped it shut. The box rocked and jumped. Then it went still.

We didn't trust that Nybbas was gone. After escorting everyone out of the exhibit, I assured my mother and grandmother that we were fine. Then, as the fire trucks arrived, we sneaked back inside and canvassed the museum. It was empty. No humans. No demons. Just us, staying two steps ahead of the fire crews.

We replaced the soul box. Keeping it would only alert the museum to the theft. Better to return later with help to seal the box forever.

We were heading for the exit when Karl whisked me into a closet.

"Someone's coming," he whispered.

"I don't hear anything."

He lifted me onto a crate. As he pressed against me, I felt a bulge . . . in his tux jacket. I slid my hands inside the coat.

"You did steal something!" I yanked out a box from the hidden pocket. "Damn you, Karl—"

"Shhh. You don't want us to get caught. Particularly if I did steal something."

"Bastard," I hissed.

I pushed him away. It was a jewelry box, one he must have brought, so if he got caught, he might convince a naïve guard it held only a gift for his girlfriend.

I opened the box and tugged out the contents. A diamond solitaire ring.

"*Not* stolen," he said.

On each side of the diamond, there was an engraved symbol for eternity, matching the charm Karl had bought for me last year. The writing inside matched my charm, too. Three words: *No matter what.*

"Yes, I haven't gotten any more poetic. No more romantic either." He gestured around the closet and made a face. "In my defense, I did try. It seemed perfect—returning to the place we first met. It didn't quite work out the way I planned, though."

I lifted the ring. "So is this . . . ? I mean, is it what it looks like?"

"Ah, sorry. I'm making a mess of this, aren't I? Let's try that again." He put the ring back in the box. "I know this isn't what you want right now. That's fine. I'll wait. But someday, when you're ready . . ." He held out the box. "Will you marry me?"

"You're still asking after tonight? You saw what you'd be getting yourself into, right?"

"Let's see . . . High-society in-laws on one side. The Prince of Darkness on the other. A demon princess for a wife. A lifetime of chaos and general anarchy. Is that what I want?" He met my gaze. "Absolutely."

He lifted the box. Before he could ask again, I took out the ring, looked up at him, and put it on.

About the
Authors

KEVIN J. ANDERSON's first novel, *Resurrection, Inc.*, was nominated for the Stoker Award. Of his hundred or so published novels, a few have been horror, particularly his international bestselling *X-Files* novels, though he is best known for his epic science fiction and fantasy (*Dune* novels with Brian Herbert, his own *Saga of Seven Suns* science fiction epic, and his *Terra Incognita* fantasy trilogy). He and his wife, Rebecca Moesta, have also written the lyrics for and executive produced two rock CDs from ProgRock Records. Anderson is the editor of seven anthologies, including the three bestselling science fiction anthologies of all time. His cats, however, are not particularly impressed.

SAM W. ANDERSON lives in Denver, Colorado, with his wife, two children, a goofy golden retriever

dog, and several skeletons taking up residence in his closet. His fiction has appeared in many venues: online, print magazines, and anthologies. *Postcards from Purgatory*, a collection of his short stories, was released from Sideshow Press in April 2010. Feel free to mock him at his website: www.samscrap.com.

KELLEY ARMSTRONG has been telling stories since before she could write. Her earliest written efforts were disastrous. If asked for a story about girls and dolls, hers would invariably feature undead girls and evil dolls, much to her teachers' dismay. All efforts to make her produce "normal" stories failed. Today, she continues to spin tales of ghosts and demons and werewolves, while safely locked away in her basement writing dungeon. She's the author of the *Women of the Otherworld* paranormal suspense series, *Darkest Powers* young adult urban fantasy trilogy, and Nadia Stafford crime series. She lives in southwestern Ontario with her husband, kids, and far too many pets.

L. A. BANKS, the recipient of the 2008 *Essence* Storyteller of the Year award, has written over forty novels and contributed to twelve novellas in multiple genres under various pseudonyms. She is a graduate of The University of Pennsylvania Wharton undergraduate program with a master's in fine arts from Temple University.

MIKE BARON is the writer of *Nexus, The Badger, The Architect,* and many other comics. He lives in Colorado with his wife and dogs.

ALLISON BRENNAN is a *New York Times* bestselling and award-winning author of fourteen novels and four short stories. Best known for her dark and edgy romantic suspense, her latest Seven Deadly Sins series shifts to the supernatural with the premise, "What if the Seven Deadly Sins were incarnate demons released by witches practicing the dark arts and seeking immortality?" *The San Francisco Examiner* said *Original Sin* is "Seductive, suspenseful and exquisitely written," and the *Providence Sunday Journal* called the series launch "A new genre classic." *Carnal Sin* was a summer 2010 release, and Allison's Lucy Kincaid romantic thriller series begins in early 2011 with *No Way Out.* A California native, Allison and her husband are raising their five kids outside Sacramento. Visit allisonbrennan.com or sevendeadlysinsbooks.com.

EDWARD BRYANT was seduced from science fiction into horror long, long ago while on a long, descending elevator ride with *Dark Forces* editor Kirby McCauley. Since then he's written a considerable procession of short horror stories, including several about the psychic detective who appears in this anthology. Recently Ed was pleased to see Kim Bassinger star in the feature film *While She Was Out,* based on one of his stories.

Inspired by a lifelong love of nature, endless curiosity, and a belief in wonderful things, AMY STERLING CASIL is a 2002 Nebula Award nominee and recipient of other awards and recognition for her short science fiction and fantasy, which has appeared in publications ranging from *The Magazine of Fantasy & Science Fiction* to *Zoetrope*. She is the author of twenty-one nonfiction books, one hundred short stories, primarily science fiction and fantasy, one fiction and poetry collection, and two novels. She lives in Playa del Rey, California, with her daughter, Meredith, and a Jack Russell terrier named Badger. Amy has worked since 2005 as a nonprofit executive for the progressive charitable organization Beyond Shelter in Los Angeles, and she currently teaches writing and composition at Saddleback College, after receiving her MFA from Chapman University in 1999. She is currently the treasurer of the Science Fiction and Fantasy Writers of America.

DEREK CLENDENING lives and works in Fort Erie, Ontario. When he isn't writing or reading, he pursues his deep interest in sports. He is a die-hard fan of the Buffalo Bills (isn't that scary enough?) and the NBA's Toronto Raptors.

DON D'AMMASSA has loved horror fiction since he found a battered copy of *Dracula* at an early age. He is the author of seven novels, 150 short stories, and hundreds of genre related articles and book reviews. He currently

lives in Rhode Island with his wife, Sheila, two cats, and 60,000 books.

HEATHER GRAHAM is the *New York Times* and *USA Today* bestselling author of over a hundred novels including suspense, paranormal, historical, and mainstream Christmas fare. She lives in Miami, Florida, her home, and an easy shot down to the Keys where she can indulge in her passion for diving. Travel, research, and ballroom dancing also help keep her sane; she is the mother of five, and also resides with two dogs, a cat, and an albino skunk. She is CEO of Slush Pile Productions, a recording company and production house for various charity events. Look her up at the originalheathergraham.com, writersforneworleans.com or eheathergraham.com.

BRIAN J. HATCHER is an author and poet from Charleston, West Virginia. His work has appeared in *Weird Tales* magazine, the celebrated *Legends of the Mountain State* series, the poetry anthology *Leonard Cohen, You're Our Man*, and the Stoker award-winning *Writers Workshop of Horror*. Brian is currently editing his first anthology for Woodland Press, entitled *Mountain Magic: Spellbinding Tales of Appalachia*. You can find Brian online at www.brianjhatcher.com.

Over the past twentysome years, NINA KIRIKI HOFFMAN has sold adult and YA novels and more

than 250 short stories. Her works have been finalists for the World Fantasy, Mythopoeic, Sturgeon, Philip K. Dick, and Endeavour awards. Her first novel, *The Thread that Binds the Bones*, won a Stoker award, and her short story "Trophy Wives" won a Nebula Award in 2009. Her novel *Fall of Light* came out from Ace in May 2009. Her middle-school novel *Thresholds* came out from Viking in August 2010. Nina does production work for the *Magazine of Fantasy & Science Fiction*. She also works with teen writers. She lives in Eugene, Oregon, with several cats and many strange toys and imaginary friends. For a list of Nina's publications, check out: ofearna.us/books/hoffman.html.

JANIS IAN has won multiple Grammy Awards since her first nomination at the age of fifteen. Her songs have been recorded by artists as diverse as Joan Baez, Willie Nelson, and Spooky Tooth. Her autobiography, *Society's Child*, was an *O Magazine* summer must-read. She enjoys her day job, but would prefer to write science fiction. Visit her at www.janisian.com.

NANCY KILPATRICK is not known for her humor. This award-winning author of dark fiction puts a rather depressing spin on both life in general and in her work specifically. Still, on occasion she laughs and then, voilà! Out comes a humor piece, like the one in *Blood Lite* and now "The Ghoul Next Door," included in this diabolical sequel you are holding. This disturbing trend

toward amusement shows little sign of abating and can only add a surprising element to her body of work which includes eighteen novels, five collections, over 200 short stories and the ten anthologies she's edited. You can find out more about this demented writer at www.nancykilpatrick.com.

J. A. KONRATH has written a lot of books and short stories. You can visit him at www.JAKonrath.com, or at the local bar. He's probably there right now.

JOHN R. LITTLE won the Bram Stoker Award in 2009 for his book, *Miranda*. His first novel, *The Memory Tree*, was published in 2007, and all five of his books have been very well received. John has a short story collection, *Little Things*, being published in late 2010, and following that are a couple of thrillers he is currently writing. You can see what's up with John's writings at www.johnrlittle.com.

SHARYN McCRUMB is an award-winning Southern writer, best known for her Appalachian "Ballad" novels, including the *New York Times* bestsellers *She Walks These Hills*, *The Rosewood Casket*, *The Ballad of Frankie Silver*, and *The Songcatcher*. Her most recent novels are *The Devil Amongst the Lawyers*, a Ballad novel set in Wise, Virginia, in 1935; and *Faster Pastor*, a comic Southern novel coauthored with NASCAR

driver Adam Edwards. *St. Dale—The Canterbury Tales* in a NASCAR setting—won a 2006 Library of Virginia Award, the AWA Book of the Year Award, and was featured at the National Festival of the Book. In 2008, Sharyn McCrumb was named a "Virginia Woman of History" for Achievement in Literature. Her other honors include: AWA Outstanding Contribution to Appalachian Literature Award, the Chaffin Award for Southern Literature, and the Plattner Award for Short Story. She lives and writes in the Virginia Blue Ridge.

SCOTT NICHOLSON is the author of ten novels, including *Drummer Boy, The Red Church, The Skull Ring*, and *Disintegration*. He has published more than sixty stories, including the collections *Ashes, The First*, and *Flowers*. Nicholson is also creator of the comic series *Dirt* and *Grave Conditions* and has written six screenplays. He lives in the Blue Ridge Mountains of North Carolina, where he works as a journalist and freelance editor. His website is www.hauntedcomputer .com.

MARK ONSPAUGH is a native Californian whose childhood was warped by a whole lot of monster movies, DC Comics, and science fiction. He's a proud member of the HWA and his film, *Kill Katie Malone*, is seeking distribution as he writes this. He's published

some thirty short stories in anthologies like *Footprints*, *The Book of Exodi*, *Dead Bait*, *The World Is Dead*, *Return of the Raven*, *Dead Set*, *The Zombist*, *Triangulation: End of the Rainbow*, *War of the Worlds: Frontlines*, *Timelines*, and *OZ: Shadows of the Emerald City*. His essay on monsters will appear in the slasher compendium *Butcher Knives and Body Counts* from Dark Scribe Press. He's working on a couple of novels and stays out of graveyards after dark. He lives in a well-lit house in Los Osos with his wife, writer/artist Dr. Tobey Crockett and two space-warping cats. Please visit him at his website, www.markonspaugh.com.

AARON POLSON was born on the Ides of March: a good day for him, unlucky for Julius Caesar. He currently lives in Lawrence, Kansas, with his wife, two sons, and a tattooed rabbit. To pay the bills, Aaron attempts to teach high school students the difference between irony and coincidence. His stories have featured magic goldfish, monstrous beetles, and lullabies for baby vampires along with other oddments. You can visit Aaron at www.aaronpolson.com.

DANIEL PYLE lives in Springfield, Missouri, with his wife and two daughters. Despite his certainty that swarms of testosterone-laden boys will someday come buzzing at his door, he has a full head of hair. For now. Read his debut novel, *Dismember*, available now from Wild Child Publishing.

MIKE RESNICK has won five Hugos (and been nominated for thirty-four). According to *Locus*, he is the all-time leading award winner, living or dead, for short fiction. He is the author of 61 novels, over 225 short stories, and two screenplays, and has edited more than forty anthologies. His work has been translated into twenty-five languages.

LEZLI ROBYN is an Australian writer who made her first professional story sale in November 2008, and since then has gone on to make seven more, to American markets such as Clarkesworld, Jim Baen's Universe, *Asimov's*, *Analog*, Hadley Rille Books, DAW, and Tor's 50th Anniversary *Twilight Zone* anthology, alone or in collaboration with Mike Resnick. She has also resold those stories to foreign fiction markets in China, Poland, Russia, Greece, Italy, Czech Republic, Bulgaria, Spain, and Slovakia. She was recently nominated for the Best SF Short Story Aurealis Award for a novelette she wrote with Mike, "Soulmates," as well as having just found out she's made the Campbell Award for best new writer.

JEFF RYAN's *Super Mario: A Biography* will be published by Penguin's Portfolio imprint in 2011, provided the world lasts that long. What if the Mayans forgot to carry the one, and we're really doomed a year or two early? What if the Giant Space Baby (circa 2010, after all) eats us? Jeff lives in New Jersey with his wife and daughters, although Jersey itself may be a wasteland of

filth and despair by the time this sees print. That is, a bigger wasteland of filth and despair.

D. L. SNELL created a game on his website where he's a zombie and you get to shoot him in the head. Snell, along with screenwriter/producer Richard Finney, coauthored "the best damned horror novel" Ray Garton has read in ages, titled *Demon Days*. Snell's website is exit66.net.

LUCIEN SOULBAN (www.luciensoulban.com) is a videogame scriptwriter and novelist living in beautiful Montreal. He was story designer for *Rainbow Six: Vegas*, *Deus Ex 3* and *Farcry 3* as well as having written numerous other scripts like *Warhammer 40K: Dawn of War*, *The Golden Compass*, *Kung-Fu Panda*, *Dawn of Heroes*, and *Kim Possible 3*. He's written five novels including *Dragonlance: Renegade Wizards* and *Warhammer 40K: Desert Raiders*, and contributed to numerous anthologies including *Horrors Beyond 2*, *Butcher Knives and Body Counts*, *Book of All Flesh*, *Dark Faith*, and the HWA's original horror comedy anthology, *Blood Lite*.

Despite taking creative writing classes in the 1980s, ERIC JAMES STONE did not begin seriously writing fiction until 2002. Since then, he has sold over twenty stories to the Writers of the Future, *Analog*, and *Intergalactic Medicine Show*, among other places. Eric lives in Utah, has a website at www.ericjamesstone

.com, and is not in the Federal Witness Protection Program.

JEFF STRAND's novels include *Benjamin's Parasite*, *Pressure*, *Casket for Sale (Only Used Once)*, and *Dweller*. Plus a bunch more. He had a story in the original *Blood Lite* and is pleased to have a second opportunity to ride the coattails of more successful authors. Check out his Gleefully Macabre website at www.jeffstrand.com.

JORDAN SUMMERS is a multipublished author who made the jump from small press to New York by winning writing contests. She's written nine novels and nine novellas in genres ranging from erotic romance to horror. Her latest release, *Crimson* (Tor) completed her Dead World trilogy—a post-apocalyptic twist on Little Red Riding Hood. She also writes urban fantasy and young adult fantasy under the name T. R. Allardice. For information, visit www.jordansummers.com and www.trallardice.com.

JOEL A. SUTHERLAND is a full-time librarian and the Bram Stoker Award–nominated author of *Frozen Blood* (Leisure Books, 2010) and *Be a Writing Superstar!* (Scholastic, 2010), a children's creative writing book. He lives in a small town east of Toronto with his wife, Colleen, their son, Charles, and beloved dog, Murphy, who likes to go for long walks in the woods near the

local Christmas tree farm. Sutherland is currently writing a second horror novel to be published by Leisure in 2011. Visit him online at www.joelasutherland.com.

STEVE RASNIC TEM's latest book is *In Concert* from Centipede Press, a collection of all his short story collaborations with wife, Melanie Tem. Also available is their collaborative ebook *Daughters* (dark fantasy adventure from macabreink.com) and Steve's *Invisible* (a six-CD audio collection from speaking-volumes.com).

CHRISTOPHER WELCH is a happily married freelance writer, reporter, and book reviewer originally from Akron, Ohio. He currently lives in Fort Atkinson, Wisconsin, where he works for the local newspaper and news radio station. He also teaches part time at Madison Area Technical College. He earned a B.A. and an M.A. in English from the University of Akron, with a minor in creative writing. Welch's poetry, fiction, and nonfiction have appeared in various small press and professional publications, including the anthologies *Catopolis*, *Dark Wisdom: The Best of Dark Fiction*, and the first volume of *Blood Lite*. Welch has always thought clowns were cool, especially those driving around in tiny cars.